THE SIREN'S CALL

V, good

"Sean, I am not accustomed to being showered with flattery—no matter how false—so I would appreciate it very much if you would refrain from insisting that I am some sort of legendary siren."

"Siren? Now, I wouldn't call ya a siren, exactly. Those luscious females spent their days callin' men to their deaths. I think I would call you more of a fairy than a siren."

"Oh, for heaven's sake."

"As for what ya said about false flattery"—Sean turned his gaze on her, and Frannie was caught by the gleam shining in their clear blue depths—"my blarney's as good as the next man's, I reckon," he admitted. Then, in a hushed whisper, he added, "But when I look at you girl . . . I'm lucky I can talk and breathe at the same time—never mind tryin' to make up meaningless compliments."

Praise for
FRANNIE AND THE CHARMER

"Ann Carberry has written an emotionally intense and delightful Americana romance that is impossible to put down."

★★★★

Affaire de Coeur

Frannie And The Charmer

Ann Carberry

AVON BOOKS ◆ NEW YORK

FRANNIE AND THE CHARMER is an original publication of Avon Books. This work has never before appeared in book form. This work is a novel. Any similarity to actual persons or events is purely coincidental.

AVON BOOKS
A division of
The Hearst Corporation
1350 Avenue of the Americas
New York, New York 10019

Copyright © 1996 by Maureen Child
Inside cover author photo by Mark Child
Published by arrangement with the author
Library of Congress Catalog Card Number: 95-94626
ISBN: 0-380-77881-5

First Avon Books Printing: January 1996

AVON TRADEMARK REG. U.S. PAT. OFF. AND IN OTHER COUNTRIES, MARCA REGISTRADA, HECHO EN U.S.A.

Printed in the U.S.A.

RA 10 9 8 7 6 5 4 3 2 1

To my father, Ed Carberry, Sr.—
the man who taught me what real blarney is.
Through the years, he's also taught me kindness,
a love of words, and to always trust myself.
Thank you, Daddy—
I love you.

Prologue

San Francisco, 1873

"He's ruined my life!" Mary Frances Donnelly wailed before she slumped against her chairback.

Morning sunlight fought through the layer of clouds and trickled through the bank of windows on the east wall of the family dining room. At that early hour, the saloon below-stairs was empty, as silent as the waterfront street outside.

Mary Frances shook her head, startled by how everything could change so quickly. Only a few moments ago, when she'd hurried into the monthly family meeting, her world was ordered, simple.

No surprises.

Then in seconds, her father, though he was far across the country, had managed to yank Mary Frances's comfortable rug right out from beneath her feet.

And all he'd had to do was send a telegram.

"Let me see that telegram, Frankie," Mary Alice said and snatched the wire from her sister's limp fingers.

1

Mary Frances let it go. She didn't need to see it again. The words printed on that plain yellow paper were burned into her brain. She doubted if she would *ever* forget the shock of reading them. Closing her eyes, she saw her father's message again and again.

MARY FRANCES STOP HAVE SOLD MY SHARE OF HOTEL STOP YOUR NEW PARTNER IS ON THE WAY STOP LOVE TO ALL MY GIRLS STOP DA

Love indeed! she thought miserably.

"When the same thing happened to me," Maggie pointed out a bit too smugly for Frankie's taste, "I seem to remember you saying I was being too 'harsh' with Da."

"This isn't the same thing at all," Frankie countered.

"What's different about it?"

"Well . . ." Mary Frances's gaze slipped away from her oldest sister's. "This is *me!*" she finished sheepishly.

A short laugh shot from Maggie's throat.

"*I* think—" Teresa started.

"No one asked what you think, brat," Mary Alice cut her off and looked at Maggie's husband. "What do *you* think, Cutter?"

This was the first *official* family meeting for Maggie's new husband and partner, though the gambler had known them all for years.

Cutter leaned back in his chair, stuck his long legs out in front of him, and crossed his feet at the ankles. A half grin tipped up one corner of his mouth. "*I* think Kevin Donnelly's been at it again."

"We *know* that, Cutter," his wife snapped. "The question is, what do we do about it?"

"There's nothing you *can* do." Cutter was still the only man who didn't flinch when Maggie's temper was on the rise.

"But there must be *something*," Frankie said, shaking her head in quiet disbelief.

After the mess with Maggie and Cutter, Mary Frances had convinced herself that her father wouldn't meddle again. But she should have known better. Why *shouldn't* he meddle? He hadn't been in town to suffer through the battles between Maggie and Cutter. *His* life hadn't been turned tail over teakettle.

No. Kevin Donnelly merely sent telegrams, manipulating his daughters' lives, then went on, continuing his little "holiday." They weren't even sure where Kevin was. All anyone knew was that he was wandering around the country visiting old friends.

Deliberately she shoved thoughts of her father to the farthest corner of her mind. It wouldn't do the least bit of good to think about him now. As Cutter had pointed out, the deed was done.

The family hotel . . . *her* hotel was now only *half* hers.

Mary Frances's distraught gaze slid from one familiar face to another. Her sisters. As different from herself as strangers would have been, and yet she couldn't imagine life without them.

The Donnelly girls. Or, as their father had

always called them, his "four roses." He'd even named the family businesses after his four very different daughters.

Mary Margaret—Maggie—with her new husband, Cutter, ran the Four Golden Roses. Together they'd built the family saloon into the most popular one on the Coast. Of course, watching the way they behaved toward each other now, no one would guess that just two months or so ago, Maggie had been ready to kill the handsome gambler who'd bought his way into her business.

A small spearhead of envy sliced at Frankie's insides as she saw Cutter slide his hand intimately across Maggie's shoulders. Not that she harbored any untoward feelings for Cutter, of course, but sometimes she couldn't help wishing that she too had someone to love.

But a tiny voice in the back of her mind whispered that this was *not* the time to be thinking of *that*.

Mary Alice sat sprawled in her chair, her gaze still locked on the telegram as if she expected the piece of paper to speak to her. Al's ever-present buckskins looked worn and dirty, giving testament to the fact that she'd ridden all night from the Four Roses mine to be in San Francisco. As usual, Al did nothing the sensible way.

Lastly, Frankie's gaze touched on their youngest sister, Teresa. The only one of the four sisters to miss inheriting red hair and green eyes from their father, Kevin, Teresa was the very image of their mother. But at the moment, not even her night-black hair and sky-blue eyes were enough to detract from the scowl on her face.

As the baby of the family, Terry Ann had been fighting for recognition since the day she was born. And, judging by her expression, Teresa was ready and willing to do battle again today.

However, Frankie was in no mood for her sister's theatrics. She had bigger problems on her mind at the moment.

Al dropped the wire onto the shining tabletop and looked at Mary Frances. "So what're you goin' to do?"

"May *I* see the wire?" Teresa said haughtily.

Al glanced at her, then flipped the paper toward the end of the table. Looking back at Mary Frances, she asked again, "Well? What will you do?"

"I don't know." Frankie shook her head slowly. How in heaven was she supposed to come up with a plan in a matter of minutes?

"She can't very well do *anything*," Maggie said softly, "until the new partner shows up."

"And then?" Frankie asked with desperation in her voice.

"Then," Maggie Donnelly Cutter assured her, "we'll offer to buy him out."

"You offered to buy *me* out too," her husband reminded her while trailing his fingers across the back of her neck. "And I wouldn't be bought."

"True," Maggie said with a smile, "but then *you*, husband, are a very special kind of man."

He nodded, graciously accepting the compliment.

Frankie frowned. She didn't see what their banter was doing to solve her problem, and said so.

Maggie sighed. "Frankie, just because Cutter wouldn't sell, doesn't mean that your new partner won't. *Most* people, I've learned, have a price."

"I hope you're right," Frankie said.

"I am. You'll see."

Maggie sounded so confident, it might have been enough to convince Frankie that all was not lost. If, that is, she hadn't glanced around at the other faces surrounding her.

Unfortunately, the rest of them looked as dubious as she felt.

Cutter's features were suspiciously tight, as if he was deliberately keeping himself from voicing his doubts.

Al, her mouth twisted in a frown, looked skeptical at best.

Teresa shook her head, crossed her arms over her chest, and said, "I don't know about you, Mary Alice. But if Da thinks he can do to me what he's done to Maggie and Frankie— he's got another think comin'."

Chapter 1

Two weeks later

He marched down the center of the road like an ancient king of Ireland.

Horses and wagons careened past him, but he gave them no notice. Riders and drivers alike hurled colorful curses at the tall, dark man, but he ignored them.

His sharp, blue-eyed gaze shot from one building to the next, first one side of the wide street, then the other. Perhaps, he told himself, it would have been easier to take a cab, but he'd come halfway across the country on his own and, by heaven, he could manage the last bloody street as well.

Suddenly he stopped. Booted feet spread wide, both fists on his narrow hips, Sean lifted his chin and studied the prize before him. His gaze fixed on the three-story structure on the south side of the street, Sean Michael Sullivan grinned.

It was perfect. From the top of the gabled roof to the whitewashed front steps, the Four Roses Hotel was everything he'd hoped it would be. Why, there was even a huge empty

lot bordering the right side of the hotel just as
Kevin promised. Lovely.

Good old Kevin.

"Here now!" a voice shouted in a tone too
loud to be ignored.

Sean half turned and looked up into the
deeply lined face of a man perched on the high
seat of a dray wagon. The driver scowled back
at him.

"Mornin'," Sean called.

"Mornin' my Aunt Mabel's ass," the driver
snapped. "You gonna be settin' up camp
there? Or will ya be movin' along sometime
today?"

A hardworking man, Sean told himself, eager to get about his business. Poor soul.

"Well now," Sean said aloud, squinting into
the sun. " 'Tis a fine day and I'm in no hurry."

"Well *I* am," the older man shouted. "Got
folks waitin' on me, so get yourself outa the
way o' my horses!"

Sean glanced at the tired-looking beasts and
shook his head. The man even had his *animals*
working too hard. Didn't he know that each
day was a gift and should be enjoyed as such?
As Calhoun used to say, "Nothing's too important that it can't be put off till tomorrow."
But even as he remembered his late friend's
advice, Sean knew that most people didn't
share that opinion. Ah well, he reminded himself, it wasn't *his* place to tell people how to
live their lives, after all.

It was enough that *he* knew better.

With that thought firmly in mind, Sean
stepped away from the impatient horses and

asked the driver, "Where's the nearest place a man can get a cup of coffee?"

The old man yanked his weatherbeaten hat off and frowned. "Ya don't have the brains to stay out of the street and you're blind to boot!"

Sean dismissed the insult and waited patiently.

After a bit more grumbling, the driver pointed one gnarled finger at a building just opposite them. A hand-painted sign over the door clearly read, "Good Food, Cheap."

"Now will you get the hell outa my way?"

"With thanks." Sean gave the man a theatrical bow, bending at the waist and spreading his left arm wide.

"Durn fool," the driver muttered, just loud enough to be heard, then picked up a short whip from the seat next to him. Swinging it in a wide arc, he brought it down with a snap of his wrist. The whip cracked in the air and the horses took off as if they'd been shot. Sean jumped back as the wagon lumbered past and waved one hand in front of his face to clear away the rising cloud of dust.

He chuckled and shook his head before looking once more at the Four Roses Hotel. At last he'd found it. And now all that was left to do was to meet his new partner.

But first, he thought as his stomach growled a protest, some coffee and a bite to eat. Time enough then to meet Mary Frances Donnelly. Quickly, Sean turned his broad back on the hotel and, after a swift glance at the passing traffic, loped across the street to the restaurant.

* * *

"I am quite sure it is of no consequence," Herbert Featherstone said.

No consequence? Mary Frances silently echoed. How could he say that? Hadn't he been listening to her at all? Did he really think that her fears and worries over the hotel weren't important enough to warrant discussion?

From the corner of her eye, Frankie studied the tall, spare, bespectacled man seated beside her on the circular blue brocade sofa.

Herbert's thin blond hair was parted in the middle and slicked down, hugging his pink scalp. His shoulders were a bit too narrow for his height and seemed to be in a constant slump. The black suit coat and trousers he wore were, as always, in impeccable condition, and his neatly brushed black bowler hat sat perched on his right knee. With one long finger he kept his place in the book from which he'd been reading to her before she'd stopped him.

With a surprising jolt, Frankie realized she hadn't the least notion what book it was.

Herbert glanced at her from behind the safety of his spectacles, then swallowed. His Adam's apple bobbed like a cork in a stream before he spoke again.

"I'm quite sure," he started, but his voice broke and he had to clear his throat before continuing, "your father has done what he thinks best for your future, Mary Frances."

"Yes," she allowed. Perhaps Kevin Donnelly *did* think that his second eldest daughter would benefit from having a new partner in the hotel. But still, she couldn't help feeling a bit betrayed by his high-handed action. He could at least have *warned* her of his intentions. He might have hinted that Maggie was not the only one of his children who would be having her life rearranged.

But then again, that wasn't Kevin's way. All her life she'd known that her father did as he thought best at the time and the devil take the hindmost. More times than she cared to remember, Kevin's impulsive behavior had caused chaos and troubles to fall on his daughters.

And, she thought, Da might at least have given her some idea of *when* this mysterious partner was going to arrive.

Since the telegram had come two weeks ago, she hadn't heard a word and she now felt as though her patience was at an end. Every time the front door opened, her breath caught. Every time there was an unfamiliar step on the boardwalk outside, she jumped. When the mail came, she searched it for some news of the mysterious partner her father was sending.

But there was nothing.

"My dear?" Herbert's voice rose to an uncomfortable pitch before breaking again. "Shall I continue reading?"

Frankie stared up at him dumbly, then shook her head. "I'm sorry, Herbert, but I have a dreadful headache." She should feel guilty about the small lie, but really, she simply couldn't concentrate.

"Then I shall, of course, excuse myself at once."

Frankie hid her sigh of relief. As ever, Herbert was the perfect gentleman. It was one of the qualities she admired most about him.

Growing up in the Donnelly family, she'd had quite enough of unconventional behavior. It was because of her unusual childhood that she had made such an effort to lead an ordinary, calm, *conventional* life.

As she stood and moved to show him out, Frankie began to feel the budding presence of a real headache and wondered absently if it was her punishment for lying.

"If you're unwell, then certainly we can finish this chapter next week."

"Thank you, Herbert." She walked across the lobby to the door and held it open for him.

Sean had sat at the window purposely, so that he could study his new hotel across the street at his leisure. When the door of the hotel swung open, Sean set his fork back down on his nearly empty plate. Now perhaps he would be treated to a peek at his new partner, as well.

A woman stepped into the open doorway and Sean stared at her. Morning sunlight danced off her pale, red-gold hair, and even from a distance, he could see that her fair Irish complexion was as smooth as fresh cream.

Then a tall, skinny man stepped up beside her and made her seem even shorter than she already appeared. Sean's gaze swept over the fellow quickly, then he looked back to the woman he guessed to be Mary Frances Donnelly. The two people looked to be an odd match at best.

The tall and short of it. He smothered a grin, leaned his elbows on the tabletop, and narrowed his gaze thoughtfully.

Kevin hadn't said a word about a suitor. If Mary Frances was being courted, what would that do to their new partnership? Sean snorted and told himself he was being a fool, looking for trouble. Hell. He hadn't even *met* the woman yet. He'd do best by crossing his bridges as he came to them.

As he watched, Mary Frances bent her head and leaned into the man just a bit. Sean frowned. Would she curtsy as well?

Then the skinny man bent down, kissed the top of her forehead, and took off.

Mary Frances stood framed in the doorway for just a moment, and Sean found himself staring at her, watching for her reaction. But she did nothing but step back into the shadows and close the door.

Sean frowned again, lifted his coffee cup, and turned his head slightly to follow the man's progress through the crowd. It wasn't hard to find him; he stood at least a head taller than anyone else.

Not much of a kiss, Sean thought as he took a sip of his coffee. More like a father's kiss for a well-behaved child, than a lover's.

"Can I get you anything else?"

The young waitress's voice roused him from his thoughts, and Sean turned to smile at her.

"No, but thank you, love." He gave his flat, hard abdomen a hearty pat. " 'Tis the best I've had since my own mother set a table."

She gave him a teasing smile, laid his check

on the table, and walked back to the kitchen with a deliberate sway to her hips.

"You've things to do, Sean," he muttered to himself and reluctantly looked away from the saucy waitress. Digging into his pants pocket, he pulled out enough change to cover his bill plus a generous tip, and dropped the coins onto the table.

It was time to meet Mary Frances Donnelly.

"In *my* day, a man knew how to kiss a woman!"

Frankie somehow managed to stifle a groan.

Rose Ryan.

Blast! Frankie thought. She'd forgotten that Rose would be stopping by to drop off the new linen Frankie had ordered from Maggie's suppliers.

"You've been seein' that one for more than a year, haven't ya?"

Frankie slowly turned away from the front door to face the woman who had raised the Donnelly girls after their mother's death. Rose hadn't changed much over the years. Her cheeks were still rosy, her eyes too quick by half, and her tongue still hinged at both ends. Warily, Frankie watched her. Plump arms folded over her abundant bosom, Rose tapped her right foot meaningfully against the polished oak floor.

She was waiting for an answer.

"You know I have, Rose."

"And *that's* all he thinks of ya? After a *year*? A peck on the forehead?" Her full lips twisted slightly. "Are ya sure he *likes* women? Or maybe he's studyin' to be a priest?"

Really, Frankie thought, her head was truly throbbing now, and it would be worse in a matter of minutes. She knew very well that there was no getting away from listening to Rose. No matter what, the older woman would have her say.

Bowing to the inevitable, Frankie told her, "Mr. Featherstone is a gentleman."

"Hmmph! Gentleman, is he?" Rose sniffed, reached up with one hand, and pushed a stray lock of gray hair out of her sharp blue eyes. "Weak sister, if you ask me . . ."

"I didn't ask," Frankie reminded her, but Rose ignored the interruption.

"And it's for damned sure he's no Irishman!"

"No, he's not." And for that, Frankie was grateful. Oh, she was proud of her heritage, and heaven knew she loved her father dearly—in spite of everything. But a woman who wanted peace and quiet in her life had better not try to find it with an Irishman! That was *one* lesson she had learned the hard way.

"What you need, my girl—" Rose started.

Frankie cut her off. "What I need right now, Rose, is a cup of tea." Keeping her voice even, she asked "Would you like one?"

"I wouldn't say no," the other woman grudgingly admitted, "so long as *I* make it. You never could make a decent cuppa."

Frankie's eyes rolled up just before she closed them in a silent prayer of supplication. Then as she started for the kitchen, a knock at the front door stopped her.

"You go and put the kettle on," Rose told her. "I'll take care of this and be in to make the tea in a shake." Marching toward the door, she grumbled, "What kind of fool is it who knocks on a hotel door?"

Grateful for the respite, Frankie was halfway down the hall when the voices at the front door stopped her.

"Ah," a man said, his voice deep and rich with the rolling sound of Ireland. "*You* must be Mary Frances Donnelly! A fine, pretty young lass like yourself *must* be Kevin's daughter!"

Rose's delighted laughter echoed off the walls and drifted down the hall to Frankie. Like the smell of whiskey to a drunk, that laughter drew Frankie closer. With slow, hesitant steps she walked along the hall until she could see the doorway.

As she watched, Rose waved the stranger inside and closed the wide front door.

Then all Mary Frances saw was him. Tall, broad-shouldered, with a head of thick, wavy black hair, the man was wearing a plain white shirt, open at the throat and tucked into a pair of indecently tight black trousers. His knee-high, brown leather boots were scuffed, and the sleeves of his shirt were rolled back to the elbow, displaying strong forearms, darkened from exposure to the sun until his flesh was nearly as brown as his boots.

A small curl of foreboding formed in Frankie's stomach and she swallowed heavily in a futile effort to control it. It didn't mean anything, she told herself. Running a hotel as she did, she welcomed strangers under her roof every day.

But, an inner voice taunted, *how many of those strangers look so . . . at home in your lobby?* And how many of them knew her father? She'd specifically heard him mention Kevin. Unable to look away, she watched the stranger bend down and lift Rose in a bearlike hug.

"Put me down, ya fool!" Rose cried, but the laughter in her voice gave lie to her words. "If ya know Kevin Donnelly, then ya must know good and well that I'm not Mary Frances!" She patted her hair and added, "Though I will say I don't look near the age Kevin does."

"Ah," the man said as he set Rose on her feet again, "then there's *two* young and lovely ladies hidin' out in here, is there?"

Frankie's hands curled into helpless fists at her sides.

"And who is it who's askin'?" Rose demanded with a teasing grin.

The stranger straightened up, smoothed his hair back, then swept Rose a deep bow before saying, "Sean Michael Sullivan, madam. Late of St. Louis by way of places too many to mention—and now . . . San Francisco."

"Well, Sean Michael Sullivan," Rose said with a laugh, "it's a fine name you have for sure. But what would you be wantin' with our Mary Frances?"

Frankie braced herself. Something deep inside her knew exactly why Mr. Sullivan was here, in her hotel. Somehow, she'd known it from the moment she'd heard his voice. She closed her eyes and made one last desperate appeal to the heavens, even though she knew instinctively it was far too late for prayers.

When she heard him speak again, the pent-up air in her chest came out in a rush.

"Kevin Donnelly sent me, love," he said to Rose. "I'm Mary Frances's new partner."

First there was a roaring sound in her ears. Then the sun-bright hallway darkened until she was staring at the front door down a long tunnel of blackness. The images of Rose and Mr. Sullivan wavered unsteadily for what seemed an eternity.

Frankie blinked frantically, trying to clear her vision and at the same time rid herself of the sudden, overwhelming sense of doom that had settled on her. But the tunnel only grew blacker and the roaring in her ears only got louder. Finally then, Frankie surrendered to her feelings, and for the second time in her life, she fainted.

Chapter 2

"Here now," Sean said briskly. "Wake up, darlin'. Wake up, now." He began to pat the inside of her wrists awkwardly and when she still showed no sign of waking up, he spoke again, more loudly this time. "I've been told I'm not much to look at, ya know. But I swear this is the first time a woman's taken one look at me and keeled over!"

Bloody hell! Sean thought and gave a quick look over his shoulder. Where in the devil had the other woman got to? She'd left to get water what seemed hours ago! Was she digging a fresh well?

The young woman, stretched out on the settee beside him, stirred and mumbled something he couldn't quite catch. Immediately Sean's gaze snapped back to her.

This meeting wasn't going at all as he'd planned. For God's sake, the way Kevin Donnelly had told it, Sean had expected Mary Frances to greet him with open arms.

Briefly, Sean sifted through his now shattered plans. He'd imagined it all so clearly, it was hard to believe it hadn't happened.

He was supposed to have been greeted at the door by Mary Frances herself. Then they would have repaired to the sitting room where he would drink tea with her and talk about the hotel. The two of them would get along wonderfully. She would be charmed by his rascally ways and flirtatious nature. And then, after they spent a few days getting to know each other, he would tell her about his *family* and when they would be arriving.

Sean's lips quirked slightly.

It could have been perfect. If Kevin Donnelly hadn't lied to him.

But it was Sean's own fault.

He should've known better than to trust the old bastard.

Hadn't Sean been raised around enough Irishmen to know the difference between blarney and the honest truth? Hell, for that matter, hadn't Sean himself spread more than his fair share of tall tales and Irish exaggeration? A body would think that one liar would be able to spot another.

Hmmph! He rubbed one huge hand across his stubbly jaw and looked down at the unconscious woman.

Not only had Kevin not told him that Mary Frances was the fainting kind, he'd also neglected to mention that she was a pretty little thing.

Pretty! He gave a silent snort at his own paltry word. Mary Frances Donnelly was a sight more than just *pretty*.

Short she was, but from what he could see,

she was nicely rounded in all the right places. Unwittingly, his gaze slipped to the buttons of her shirtwaist as they strained against the fabric with her every breath. Ah, yes. Nicely rounded, indeed. The firm, full flesh of her breasts fairly screamed for a man's hands—*his* hands—to caress them, he thought, barely managing to keep himself from touching her.

Sean shook his head and shifted his gaze to her face. He hadn't seen her eyes wide open yet, of course—but he was willing to bet they were as green as the fields in Ireland. Lord knew, she carried the stamp of Eire on her features. Her strawberry hair fell loose around her shoulders, and her smooth, cream-colored complexion was unblemished but for the sprinkle of golden freckles across her small, straight nose.

Lord, she was a lovely creature! With her fair coloring and her tiny stature, she reminded him of the tales of wood sprites he'd heard in his childhood. Sean smiled at the thought and tried desperately to remember if wood sprites were kind to humans—or if they were tricksters like leprechauns.

Then he snorted at his own foolishness. It made no difference what the nature of the fairies was, Mary Frances Donnelly was a woman. Despite her appearance, she was a living, breathing, red-blooded woman.

And he wanted her.

But even as he admitted that, he realized that it was more than simple lust he was feeling. Much more. The moment he'd seen her slight, crumpled form laid out in the hall, Sean had felt a strange sense of . . . *recognition* shoot through him. It was as if every muscle, nerve, and bone in his body had suddenly come to life after a deep sleep.

Somehow, he *knew* this woman.

He felt it.

His very soul had been waiting for her all his life.

Now if she'd only open her bloody eyes so he could begin charming her, all would be well.

"Here we are, then," a calm voice announced from behind him.

Sean snapped around to face the gray-haired woman. "Where were ya, woman?" he demanded. "Did ya stop to have the water blessed by the Pope himself?"

Rose ignored him and set the tray she carried on the nearest table. A bottle of fine Irish whiskey sat on the red-painted tray. It was flanked by two empty glasses, and off to one side was a smaller glass of water.

Sean sighed. "Lovely idea. A drop of the Irish is just what she needs."

Rose frowned at him. Quickly she poured a healthy measure of amber liquor into the empty glasses and handed one to him before lifting the other. "The whiskey's for us, boyo." she said and downed the liquor in one swift gulp. Winking at him, she added, "Mary Frances wouldn't touch the stuff."

Sean shook his head and watched the older woman as she picked up the glass of water and dipped three fingers into the liquid. "What're ya—" he started to ask, but before he could finish, Rose had sprinkled the water onto Mary Frances's face.

Like a baby at a baptism, the younger woman woke up like a shot, blinking furiously and sputtering just a bit. Then she shook herself and fastened her gaze on him.

Just as he'd thought, he told himself. Eyes as green as Ireland herself. Something deep inside him roared into life as he met his new partner's stare, and for the first time in memory, Sean Sullivan found himself speechless.

A long moment passed when the only sounds in the room were the ticking of the clock and the splash of more whiskey being poured.

Finally, though, Sean pulled in a deep breath, swallowed past the curious knot in his throat, and said softly, "Welcome back." A teasing grin curved one side of his mouth. "We missed ya."

Mary Frances pushed herself into a sitting position and tried not to notice that her left thigh was pressing against the strange man's hip. It wasn't easy, since her flesh seemed to be tingling unreasonably. She brushed away a tearlike droplet of water from her cheek and tried to figure out how she'd come to be lying on the settee in the reading room.

Then all at once, she remembered as everything came rushing back. She had been standing in the hall, watching Rose and a stranger, hearing the stranger introduce himself as her new partner.

Her partner.

Good Lord.

Her gaze swept over his rugged features quickly, thoroughly. High cheekbones, startlingly ice-blue eyes, flesh tanned from too much time spent outdoors, and the muscular build of a man used to hard work. His night-black hair curled over the top of the open-collared shirt, and the dimple in his right cheek deepened the longer she looked at him.

"There now," he said softly, "I'm not all *that* frightening, am I?"

Frightening? No.

Dangerous? Yes.

Deliberately Mary Frances scooted back, swung her feet to the floor, and edged further away from him. It was no mistake. She hadn't imagined it earlier. His soft, singsong speech carried the unmistakable brogue of an Irishman.

"Finished with your faint, have ya?" Rose asked and poured herself yet another whiskey.

"I don't faint."

"That's what I would've said an' all." Rose nodded sagely just before tossing the whiskey down her throat. "Until two weeks ago."

Mary Frances frowned at the woman. It wasn't necessary to relive that small faint at the family meeting. "Isn't Maggie expectin' you back sometime soon?"

"That she is," Rose announced and set her glass down on the tray. "And there's no need to hit me over the head, my girl. I know when to leave." She jerked Sean Sullivan a nod. "Expect you two have some talkin' to do."

Sean stood up and Mary Frances tilted her head back to look up at him. Heavens, he was a tall one. Taller even, she thought, than Cutter.

"Still," Rose said thoughtfully, "before I go, boyo, why don't you just show me the papers you have from Kevin. Not that I don't trust you, mind." She folded her arms across her bosom. "But I'll not be leavin' Mary Frances here alone with ya until I'm sure you are who ya say ya are."

Alone? Mary Frances questioned silently. She was hardly alone. Not with three hotel maids and several guests in residence.

"As wise as she is beautiful," Sean said smoothly before reaching into a pants pocket. He pulled out a neatly folded square of paper, which he handed to Rose.

Rose, never taking her eyes from him, then gave the paper to Mary Frances, whose hand was already outstretched, waiting.

Dutifully, Frankie unfolded the thick sheets. Her gaze moved over the lines of neatly printed information, then reluctantly slipped to the bottom of the page.

With a resigned sigh, she recognized her father's signature alongside Sean Michael Sullivan's.

"It's all right, Rose" she said with another sigh. Then she folded the papers again and gave them back to the man. "Da signed them."

"Well then." The older woman nodded and gave Sean another smile. "I'll be off. Why don't the two of you come over to the Roses tonight for supper, eh? Might as well meet some of the others in this family."

"Mr. Sullivan is probably tired," Mary Frances said quickly, hoping to put off a meeting with her sister and brother-in-law.

"Not a bit of it," the man said arbitrarily.

"We'll expect ya both about seven, then?"

Rose's gaze bored into Mary Frances, and because she couldn't think of another excuse, Mary Frances nodded.

Once the older woman left, silence dropped like an uneasy bargain between them. For some reason, Mary Frances couldn't think of a thing to say. It was ridiculous, she knew. Ever since the telegram from her father had arrived, she'd been talking to anyone who would listen about losing half interest in her hotel. And now that the very usurper was standing in front of her . . . her mind went blank.

Out of the corner of her eye, she watched him.

Seemingly completely at ease, he strolled around the reading room of the Four Roses as though he had every right to be there. Which he did, she thought rationally. But *rational* had nothing to do with what she was feeling.

He stopped suddenly and lifted a small Beleek votive light.

As the stranger held up the fragile china, something in Mary Frances's chest constricted, and her voice when she spoke sounded choked.

"Please. Put that down. Carefully."

He glanced back at her curiously, but did as she asked.

Mary Frances's gaze followed the delicate ornament until it was sitting safely back in its place. Then she looked at him.

It wasn't right.

None of this was right.

He had no business coming into her hotel and making himself at home.

He had no right being so big that he dwarfed the room and its furniture.

He had no right being so at ease when she was a bundle of nerves.

And mostly he had no right being so handsome and affecting her so strangely.

"It's a lovely thing," Sean said, nodding toward the Beleek.

"It was my mother's," Mary Frances told him stiffly. He didn't need to know that the small china votive was all Frankie had of the mother who had died giving birth to her fourth daughter, Teresa Ann. He didn't need to know that no one but *she* touched that fragile piece of her memories.

"Ah," the big man said as he strolled to her side and plopped down next to her. "It's no wonder, then, you're so careful with it." He stretched out his right arm along the rear of the settee, coming uncomfortably close to Frankie's back.

She shifted.

"It's nice that you have somethin' of your mother's to hold on to," he offered. "Me? All I have of mine is this dimple . ... which plagues me something fierce."

She'd already noticed the dimple, thank you very much, she thought. Now, as his smile broadened, that same dimple deepened. Before she could stop herself, Mary Frances asked, "Plague you? What do you mean?"

Clearly delighted with her interest, Sean lifted his eyebrows, and his lake-blue eyes twinkled. "Well now, how can I play the part of a hard, tough man of business when the slightest smile leaves a canyon-deep pit in me cheek?"

He had a point. The rascally charm on his features certainly kept him from seeming the least bit intimidating. On the other hand, she was willing to wager that his charm had helped him far more often than it had hindered.

"I have a feeling that you've used your innocent air to its best advantage," she said quietly.

Sean drew his head back, glanced at her curiously, and grinned. "You're on to me then! But, as you're in business yourself, I'll take no offense at your discoverin' my secret."

She nodded.

"Is there anything else in the place ya want to warn me about touchin'?" He let his interested gaze sweep the room, lingering on every ornament for just a moment.

Mary Frances looked at him. *Me!* she wanted to shout. *Don't touch me!* But that would have been ridiculous. He'd think her crazy, and she wouldn't blame him. Still though, as her gaze slipped to his hand, now resting comfortably on the cushion beside her, a small, unexpected curl of . . . *something* wound its way down her spine.

She tried to shake it off and listen when he started talking again. But it wouldn't go away.

"I mean," he went on, "a man my size

sometimes breaks things without even tryin'." He shrugged, and she saw the muscles in his shoulders shift and roll. "With a little warnin', mayhap I can steer meself clear of danger."

If only he could steer himself out of San Francisco, she thought, everything would be fine.

Something of her feelings must have shown on her features because when Sean spoke again, his booming voice was low and almost comforting.

"We've not got off to a good start, I'll grant ya, Miss Donnelly."

She looked at him and waited for him to finish.

"But . . ." That dimple of his made a brief appearance. "I'm not such a bad fella, and the situation bein' what it is and all . . . don't ya think it's best if we find a way to get along?"

She stared at him for a long moment before silently admitting that he was right. It wouldn't do the least amount of good to antagonize the man right away. After all, there was still a chance that he might be willing to let her buy him out. And the prospect of *that* would be much brighter if she could remain on good terms with him.

"You're right, Mr. Sullivan," Mary Frances said firmly. "Please forgive my faint—but you took me by surprise, I'm afraid." She was instantly rewarded with a smile that sent a shiver through her body. Ignoring that ridiculous sensation, she held out her hand. As her own palm was enveloped by his, she said belatedly, "Welcome to San Francisco."

"That's grand," Sean said and let go of her hand almost immediately.

Their newly established truce was quickly forgotten in the rush of sensation that flooded through him. Idly he rubbed his fingers together. His flesh felt as though it was afire from the inside. The moment he'd touched Mary Frances Donnelly, felt her smooth, silken skin and her fragility, it was as if a lightning bolt had arced between them.

He wouldn't have been the least bit surprised to see that his flesh had been singed on contact. Sean's heartbeat skittered a bit as he realized that his first flash of recognition had been right. There was a link between him and Mary Frances Donnelly.

The strength of that bond made him think that it was an ancient link joining them. The poetry in his Irish soul told him that perhaps this was a centuries-old bond, still strong enough to draw strangers into an alliance that would forge new ties. New promises.

A quick glance at her worried expression assured him that Mary Frances too had felt that jolt of awareness. Then, as her features took on a look of deliberate calm, Sean knew that she wouldn't admit to that feeling if it meant her life.

Well, he told himself, *he* wouldn't remark on it either. Though he'd like nothing better than to draw her into the circle of his arms and feel that lightning blast of strength again, he didn't make a move. No point in scaring the lass into another faint. From the wary expression in her eyes, he could tell she was already feeling cautious of him.

Idly he wondered if *all* men frightened her, or just him in particular.

And if it *was* just him, he assured himself silently, she'd have to get used to him. Because he wasn't going to leave.

Determinedly he jumped to his feet and set the small table in front of the settee to wobbling. As he reached down to steady it, he glanced back at Mary Frances.

"Now that we've met, suppose ya show me around the place a bit?"

She swallowed heavily, sucked in a great gulp of air, and slowly rose like an unwilling spirit on its way to hell. When she was standing in front of him, Sean tried not to notice that the top of her head came only to the middle of his chest. He deliberately ignored how the morning sunshine drifting through the wide windows set her hair aflame. He tried not to inhale her sharp, clean scent and did his best not to notice that her gently rounded curves were heaven-made for a man's arms.

His arms.

God help him . . .

"I—*we*," she corrected, "have a few guests on the second floor, so we'll have to be quiet."

He could see what it had cost her to include him in her statement and wished that he could somehow make this easier on her. But he hadn't the faintest notion how to do that. Instead he settled on doing what he could.

"Like a mouse, I'll be," he promised and nearly broke his promise as soon as he'd made it. The look on her face as she tried to imagine a man his size being as quiet as a mouse was enough to start a booming laugh building in his chest. Forcefully, he choked it back. When he could speak again, he acknowledged, "All right then . . . a *big* mouse."

She glanced at him from the corner of her eye and said quietly, "A big mouse is called a *rat*, isn't it?"

An exaggerated shudder coursed through him. "Brr . . ." he said, and laid one massive palm against his heart as though he were mortally wounded. "You've a quick, cold tongue on ya when ya want to, don't ya, Mary Frances Donnelly?"

She smiled then. Tentatively, slowly, her lips curved, and Sean's breath caught at the transformation. Her features seemed lit from within. One small smile had taken a lovely face and made it beautiful.

He was in terrible trouble.

"Follow me," she said. Then she lifted her skirt slightly as she made for the door and the staircase beyond.

Somehow, he stopped himself from murmuring, *Anywhere.*

For a big man, his tread on the stairs was incredibly light. If she hadn't known better, Mary Frances might have thought he wasn't even behind her. But he was. She knew it. She could feel it.

And, she told herself, she might as well get used to his presence. Unless she could buy him out, he would be living right there. Every day she would see him. Talk to him. She would have to consult with him on decisions concerning the hotel.

She ground her teeth together and told herself to stop thinking about it. At least for now, there was nothing to be done but to take him on a tour of the Four Roses Hotel.

At the top of the landing, she paused, and Sean took a moment to enjoy the surroundings.

Stretching down the length of the hall, a carpet runner in muted shades of green and blue lay in bright contrast to the dark, polished wood floor. The walls were painted in a soft cream color that caught the sunlight streaming in from the window at the end of the corridor. Four small, custom-built bookshelves were lined up against the wall at scattered distances from one another probably so that guests wouldn't have to wander downstairs in search of ready reading material. And on the walls were hung pastoral scenes of the California countryside. The landscapes were breathtaking in their simplicity and color.

Directly beneath the window at the end of the short hall stood a large, hand-painted china vase atop a three-legged table. The massive bouquet of flowers in the vase created a unique blend of scents that drifted toward them on a faint breeze as it slipped beneath the partly opened window.

"Ah," Sean muttered. "Lovely."

"Thank you," she answered, and her shoulders straightened in justifiable pride. "There are six bedrooms on this floor and another four upstairs."

"And how many have got people in them?"

She frowned. Was he already asking about profits? If he was hoping to make a great deal of money out of his new partnership, he was in for a disappointment. But there was time enough for him to find that out.

"Only three right now, and they'll be gone soon."

"Hmmm . . ."

Mary Frances flashed him a look over her shoulder. "The Four Roses is a small hotel, Mr. Sullivan," she started.

"Sean."

She ignored his attempt to get her to use his Christian name. "More of a boardinghouse, really. We can't compete with the larger places like the Occidental and the Grand." She took a quick breath. "*And* we don't attempt to."

"Did ya hear a word of complaint from me, woman?" he asked, his dark eyebrows lifting nearly to his hairline.

"No, but your tone suggested—"

"Pay no mind to my *tone*. If I want to say something"—he winked at her—"rest assured, I'll say it flat out, with no mistakes."

That didn't surprise her. She'd never known an Irishman to hold his tongue. Her own da, if told to be quiet on pain of his life, would *still* be talking when he reached St. Peter's Gate.

Mary Frances sighed, jerked him a nod, then looked straight ahead again. "Three of the rooms on this floor have private baths, and there is a common washroom at the end of the hall that is shared by the others."

"That's grand, that's grand," he muttered. Throwing a quick glance to the ceiling as if he could see through the plaster to the floor above, he asked, "Is upstairs the same, then?"

"Pretty much," she admitted. "Though only two of the upstairs rooms have a private bath."

"Why's that, darlin'?"

She stiffened slightly at the endearment, but then told herself that he didn't mean anything by it. If nothing else, she'd learned early that charming Irishmen tossed out endearments as if they were breadcrumbs to hungry pigeons.

"Improvements, Mr. Sullivan, cost money."

"Sean," he insisted again with a flash of his dimple. "Then the hotel's not makin' enough of a profit to afford to fix things up a bit?"

Profit. Perhaps now was as good a time to tell him as any.

"If you were hoping to strike it rich with this partnership, Mr. Sullivan, I'm sorry to disappoint you. I'm afraid that the Four Roses Hotel is not the big moneymaker that the other family enterprises are. Most times we break even."

"Aye, well." Sean grinned at her. "I didn't expect to find a grand, expensive place, now did I?"

"I don't know what you were expecting."

"Well, then, you'll have to take my word for it. Won't ya?"

All right, she thought. Perhaps he wasn't expecting to make a fortune. But he would know right from the first that she wouldn't sit still for any major changes.

Inhaling sharply, Mary Frances continued in a rush, "We're a small place, as I've said. But this place is also my *home*." Her jaw tightened, and unwittingly, her gaze flew about the familiar neat hallway. "And as for your proposal to *fix* things . . . nothing about the Four Roses needs fixing."

"*Well*." He drawled the word out expectantly. "I wouldn't go so far as to say that."

"Oh really?" Mary Frances took a couple of quick steps, then whirled around to face him. "I'll have you know that this building is in excellent repair."

"Oh, aye. For the most part," he agreed, his gaze slipping from hers to study a small patch of peeling paint that Mary Frances hadn't noticed until that very minute. "Still an' all, nothin's so good that it can't stand tidyin' up a bit."

"*Tidy?*" Her mouth opened and closed quickly as she fought for breath. How *dare* he suggest that her hotel wasn't *tidy*! A slow rumble of temper rolled through her and Mary Frances fought it back. Over the years, she'd nearly mastered the Donnelly temper, and in a relatively short time, Sean Sullivan had shattered her composure far too often. "*Mr.* Sullivan," she started.

"Sean," he patiently reminded her with a nod of his head.

"This establishment is cleaned daily," Mary Frances began, her tone strained. "Every room, whether occupied or not, is given a thorough going over and the sheets on the beds are changed before each new guest arrives."

"I didn't say that the hotel wasn't—"

She cut him off. "There are three maids who work here. Molly, Dolores, and Treasure."

"Treasure?" he repeated.

Mary Frances swept past his interruption determinedly. Her voice rising, she went on. "They all know their jobs and do them well."

"I'm sure they do," he tried to say, "but—"

"It's hardly fair for you to arrive and start making sweeping judgments about the place before you've even *seen* the third floor."

Frankie took a breath. She could feel the hot rush of anger flooding her cheeks and fought to overcome it. The hotel was small, but made up for its lack of space in the warm, friendly atmosphere it offered its guests.

As far as private baths went, Mary Frances hadn't seen any urgency in adding more of them. The hotel had a steady stream of regular patrons, but they'd never been forced to turn anyone away, either. No, as far back as she could remember, the hotel had never been filled to capacity. So it was hardly worthwhile adding private baths to rooms that were seldom occupied.

Truthfully, she thought, the last few weeks had been particularly slow. More and more people seemed to be choosing to stay at one of the bigger, fancier hotels in the city rather than at the Roses. But it didn't matter. The hotel paid for itself . . . barely. And as she'd already told Sean Sullivan, the Four Roses was her home.

And she wouldn't give up her home easily.

Somehow managing to look down at him even while she was tilting her head back to peer up, Mary Frances offered stiffly, "I'll be happy to show you our books, Mr. Sullivan."

"Sean," he reminded her again, then shrugged. "Time enough for that." He reached for her hand, then tucked it into the crook of his elbow. "Let's see the rest, shall we?"

Chapter 3

By the time they'd walked the length of the third-floor hall, Sean was convinced that the hotel was everything he needed and more. Whatever else Kevin Donnelly had stretched the truth about, he hadn't lied about the Four Roses Hotel.

"It's a grand little place, Mary Frances," he said and peeked into another unoccupied room. The entire third floor was empty, and that was all to the good. He'd have to make sure that she didn't go booking any of the rooms. In two or three weeks' time, he'd be needing most of the rooms on the third floor and even perhaps a few on the second.

Ah well, he told himself, time enough to go into all of that.

"I'm so happy you're pleased," Mary Frances said quietly.

He shot her a quick look, his heavy black eyebrows lifting. Sarcasm was something he understood, but he had to admit that usually he didn't hear it delivered so quietly. And so in keeping with a ladylike manner.

"Are all the rooms alike, then?"

"Mainly," she said.

"Mainly?"

She inhaled slowly and Sean forced himself to keep his eyes on her face, not the luscious curves of her bosom.

"There are one or two rooms that are larger, owing to their position in the building."

"Meanin'?"

"For instance, the corner rooms are a bit larger and each of them has a private bath. And a fireplace."

"Up here too?"

"Of course."

"Ah . . ." He rubbed one big hand across his jaw and started down the hall to the door at the end. "Would this be one of those rooms?"

"Yes," she admitted and slowly followed him. "But as it's on the third floor, it also has a sloping ceiling that most people find confining."

Before she'd finished speaking, Sean had flung the door wide and stepped inside.

Mary Frances hurried the rest of the way and entered the room right behind him. "You can't just burst into a room like that, Mr. Sullivan. We might have had a guest in here."

"Sean," he reminded her and continued inspecting the room. "And you said you only had two or three rooms filled at the moment. I figured they would most likely be on the second floor."

She went right on talking, but for the moment, Sean paid no attention. His gaze moved over the large yet cozy room with appreciation. Starched green gingham curtains danced in the ocean air slipping beneath the partly opened window sashes. Sunshine sliced through the shining glass panes and lay in a spill of light across the braided rug alongside the steel-gray iron bed frame. He smiled briefly at the jumble of colors in a pieced-together quilt covering the mattress. An armoire, a small chest of drawers, a writing table and chair, and a small washstand with shaving mirror made up the rest of the room's furnishings. There were even two overstuffed chairs drawn close to a now cold brick hearth.

"Perfect," he mumbled and hadn't realized he'd said it aloud until Mary Frances spoke up.

"Perfect? What exactly do you mean, Mr. Sullivan?"

"Sean." He turned toward her and looked down into those pale green eyes. "What I mean, Mary Frances, is that the room is perfect for *me*."

"For *you*?"

"Oh, aye." Slowly he walked across the wide pine-plank floor and stopped at one of the two dormer windows. He brushed the starched curtains aside and stared down at the street below. "The place suits me fine."

"Well, I can't *tell* you how delighted I am to hear it."

"But I've a feelin' you're goin' to try," Sean teased and glanced at her.

"Mr. Sullivan, you can't possibly mean to live here. In the hotel, I mean."

"And where else would I be hangin' my hat as it were?" He shrugged and raised both hands helplessly. " 'Tis my hotel, isn't it?"

She swallowed heavily and he watched her fingers curl into her palms. "Half of it, certainly."

"Well then."

"Well then what?"

"Well then," he said slowly, patiently, "ya wouldn't expect a man to own a hotel and then pay for a room in someone else's hotel, would ya?"

Good Lord, Mary Frances thought wildly. He means it. He actually means to live in the Four Roses. With *her*! She had to think fast. She had to come up with a reason for refusing him that he would accept. But what?

Grasping at straws . . . *any* straws, she heard herself blurt out, "Mr. Sullivan, *Sean* . . ."

His eyebrows lifted, making the lock of black hair that lay across his forehead look even more charming.

"If you'll only look around you more carefully, you'll see that this room is entirely unsuitable to a man of your . . . *size*."

He grinned at her, and her heartbeat quickened. That crooked smile of his combined with that dimple was a lethal combination. Fortunately Mary Frances had painfully learned not to be swayed by a pretty face.

"The chairs look strong enough to hold me," Sean said. Then in a deep, wicked tone, he added, "And the bed, girleen, appears roomy enough for two."

She cleared her throat and deliberately looked away from the big iron bed. "Be that as it may, perhaps you haven't noticed the ceilings?"

"Hmmm?" He glanced up.

Mary Frances raised her arm and pointed at the heavy beams that sloped down deeply on either end of the room. "A man of your . . . *height* would almost certainly have difficulty avoiding those beams on a daily basis."

Sean smiled again. " 'Tis kind of ya to be concerned, Mary Frances. But I grew up in a room much like this one." He reached up and slapped one of the whitewashed beams. "And I don't mind admittin' that I've bounced me forehead off the ceiling posts more than once in my life. I expect I could survive a few more."

Lord. Mary Frances looked at him and could only hope that her inner panic wasn't etched into her features. One hand still braced on the overhead beam, the other tucked casually into the pocket of his too-tight trousers, he watched her. Taller than most men of her acquaintance, he had broad shoulders that seemed to take up half of the room, and the gleam in his eyes made the air seem too thick to breathe.

Him live *here*? Only two floors above her own room? No. It would never work. She would have to think of *something*. Sean Sullivan was simply too big to ignore. His very presence in the hotel was threatening. Not only to her business and her calm, orderly way of life, but to her peace of mind as well.

He grinned at her, let go of the beam, and walked toward the bed tucked under the eaves.

Struck again by just how soundlessly he moved, Mary Frances told herself that she would never be able to relax in the hotel. He could slip up on her at anytime and catch her completely unawares.

The well-tended iron bed springs hardly groaned when Sean settled himself on the feather mattress. It was his sigh of content-ment that drew her attention.

Shooting him a quick look, she saw that he'd stretched out atop the quilt she'd labored three months to make. His feet crossed at the ankle, Sean propped a pillow behind his back and threw his hands behind his head.

"Ah, Mary Frances," he said, a grin tugging at the corner of his lips, "I think this is goin' to work out fine."

"What?"

"This room, the hotel . . ." The dimple in his cheek deepened. "You and me."

"There is no you and me, Mr. Sullivan."

"Ah well now, that's to be seen, isn't it?"

Her fingers curled into her palms and she hid her helpless fists in the fall of her skirt. Staring into Sean's laughing eyes, Mary Frances silently called down a curse on her wandering father's head.

The noise from the saloon below was a steady hum of muted conversation punctuated with the occasional raucous cheer. Sean frowned and silently compared the party atmosphere below with the stiff, polite air in the family dining room.

Stifling a sigh, he glanced at the shining

floorboards and wished heartily that he was below-stairs with the crowd. From the sounds of them, the customers at the Four Golden Roses Saloon were just the kind of people Sean understood and enjoyed best.

He cast a quick look at Maggie and Cutter. Under other circumstances, he might have been having a fine time with the two of them as well. After all, how rigid could two people be if they owned one of the biggest, most popular saloons in San Francisco?

His gaze swept across Maggie quickly. A pretty woman, no doubt, and one who had learned how to make the most of the beauty God had given her. The woman's rich, red hair was piled atop her head, and small gemstones twinkled at him from pockets of curls. She wore a shamrock-green silk dress that clung to her as tightly as fresh paint on new wood, and her figure was enough to bring any man to his knees.

Except, Sean thought with an inner chuckle, for himself.

It didn't seem to matter that Maggie Donnelly Cutter was by far the most outrageously attractive woman he'd ever seen. Her blatant beauty did nothing for him. Instead, his gaze was continually drawn to Mary Frances.

He glanced at her again and was delighted to find her staring at him too. Sean smiled, and she quickly averted her gaze. But it didn't matter. There was time enough for her to get used to him. Though Lord knew it hadn't taken any time at all for him to know that he wanted to spend the rest of his days looking at *her*.

That pale, soft red hair of hers shimmered in the candlelight, and he couldn't help wishing that he could reach over, pull the pins from her hair, and let the strawberry-gold strands fall where they may. She pulled in a deep, shaky breath, and his gaze was drawn to the bodice of her simple, dove-gray dress. A row of ivory buttons and a tiny white collar closed tightly about her slender throat were the gown's only decorations. Yet Mary Frances's costume was more enticing to Sean than any silk and black lace creation.

Maggie leaned in close to her sister and whispered something that had Mary Frances blushing a most becoming shade of rose. Maggie only smiled, then turned to wink at her husband.

Cutter was undoubtedly aware of Maggie's charms, since the man's gaze almost never left her. His adoration was clearly returned, too. All through dinner, Maggie had been reaching across the table to pat her husband's hand or touch his arm.

Obviously the two of them shared a deep affection. And another time, Sean might have enjoyed their company very much.

However, tonight they were too busy being Mary Frances's family to be very entertaining.

"So," Cutter asked, interrupting Sean's train of thought. "You never did say. How did you come to meet Kevin?"

"Ah, he was a great friend of the man I worked for—Seamus Calhoun." A man, Sean added silently, that he still sorely missed, Lord rest him.

"Calhoun . . ." Maggie tapped her index finger against her chin for a moment.

Sean opened his mouth to explain exactly who his late employer had been, but Maggie shushed him with a wave of her hand.

"It'll come to me," she insisted before turning to her sister. "Why does the name Calhoun sound so familiar?"

Sean looked to Mary Frances and wasn't surprised to see that the closed expression was still stamped on her features. Since she'd given him the tour of the hotel, he'd hardly gotten more than two words at a time from her. Now, maybe she was quiet by nature, but he had a difficult time imagining one of Kevin Donnelly's children as the silent kind.

Besides, she'd managed to fire a few verbal darts at him before she went mute. No, he told himself, it wasn't that she was quiet. It was something more than that.

She didn't want a partner in her hotel and certainly didn't want him living right there under her roof.

"Think, Frankie," Maggie prodded again. "Calhoun . . ."

Frankie? Sean frowned and let his gaze slide back to the woman opposite him. Mary Frances Donnelly didn't look like a Frankie to *him.* She was far too short . . . too *dainty* a thing for such a boyish nickname.

"I don't know, Maggie," Mary Frances said and reached for the teacup just to the right of her hardly touched dinner plate. "I don't remember."

Before Maggie could continue badgering Mary Frances, Sean spoke up.

"You've probably heard your da talkin' about The Magnificent Calhoun."

"That's it!" Maggie slapped her palm down on the dining table, and her crystal wineglass wobbled precariously. Quickly she snatched it and took a hasty sip. Setting it back down again, she looked at her husband and went on, "I don't know why it didn't strike me right away. Da was always tellin' us stories about Calhoun. Don't you remember, Frankie?"

Mary Frances turned her gaze on Sean briefly before shaking her head. "No."

"Oh sure you do. Think back. The Magnificent Calhoun? The most famous magician in County Mayo?"

"Magician?" Cutter asked. He reached into his breast pocket for a long, narrow silver case, then casually flipped the catch and offered Sean one of the slim cigars. After taking one himself, he struck a match and held it out to Sean before lighting his own cigar. Then he blew a long stream of smoke ceilingward and glanced at his wife. "I never heard Kevin mention the man."

"Well." Maggie grinned. "I'm not surprised. All you and Da ever talked about is the saloon and how best to improve business. But when we were girls, he was full of stories about how he and Calhoun had had the run of County Mayo until they sailed together for New York."

"That's right," Mary Frances said, her voice barely audible. "I remember now."

A small smile curved her lips and softened the look in her eyes. She stared at a spot on the wall as if she was looking back into the past. There was a fondness on her features that tugged at Sean's heart and made him glad he was seated behind a table. If he was forced to walk now, he'd embarrass himself for sure. Sean took a long pull at his cigar, hoping the burning smoke in his lungs would prove enough of a distraction to calm his suddenly eager body.

It didn't.

She started talking again, and the hushed, dreamlike tone in her voice was enough to make any man think of candlelight, fresh sheets, and plump pillows.

"Seamus Calhoun, his name was," she said.

"Seamus! That's it, Frankie!" Maggie shook her head and grinned at Cutter. "That would have bothered me all night long."

Sean didn't bother to point out that he'd already told them Calhoun's first name. Obviously Maggie only heard what she wanted to hear.

"Oh, not *all* night, I hope," Cutter shot back, but Sean was paying them no attention at all. Mary Frances was speaking again, and his gaze was drawn inexorably to her.

"Father said that before he came to America, he and Seamus traveled all over the county, putting on shows for the children in the villages."

"Kevin?" Cutter interrupted. "Putting on shows?"

"Well, Calhoun did the entertaining," Maggie threw in. "Da collected the money."

"Ah . . ."

"Father always sounded . . . envious of Seamus," Mary Frances added with a quick glance at Sean. "He said once that Calhoun had magic in his soul. That it was a gift."

"That it was," Sean answered her as though just the two of them were in the room. "But it was a gift he shared easily with everyone who knew him."

"I wonder if that's possible."

"What?" Sean asked. "To have such a gift?"

"No." Mary Frances shook her head gently. "To *share* something that wonderful."

"The gift only becomes more precious when it's shared."

"If you worked for Calhoun," Cutter interrupted, "what exactly did you do?"

Sean's gaze slid to Cutter and away again. Shrugging, he said, "This and that."

"You traveled with a magician and only did this and that?" Cutter studied the glowing tip of his cigar for a long moment before adding, "Surely you can tell us a bit more about yourself."

Sean shifted uncomfortably in his chair. Hell yes, he could. But he wasn't ready to do that just yet. Because once he started talking about life with Calhoun, the rest of his story would come out. And he didn't want Mary Frances knowing anything about his plans for the hotel until the time was right.

He flicked her a quick glance and reassured himself that now was *not* the right time.

"Leave him be, Cutter," Maggie told her

husband. "It's the man's first night in town. Surely you can let him find his feet before knowing everything about him."

"I only wanted to know—"

"You've no need to question the man relentlessly, Cutter," Mary Frances spoke up quietly, but the others turned to stare at her as if she'd shouted. "We know all we need to know for the moment. Father sold Mr. Sullivan his half of the hotel and he's come here to collect his due."

Sean inclined his head in silent thanks. He wasn't sure why she'd spoken up for him. But for now, he'd simply be grateful she had. Of course, she was still calling him *Mr.* Sullivan . . . but he would take care of that.

Maggie's eyebrows lifted and she looked quickly from her sister to the big man at the end of the table and back again. Hmmm, she thought. Something very interesting seemed to be happening there.

She couldn't remember the last time Frankie had looked so flushed . . . so *nervous*. And the big Irishman hadn't taken his eyes off her sister all night.

Maybe, she told herself, just *maybe* Da had done a good thing by sending Frankie this new partner. After all, she had to admit that after her initial reaction to having Cutter foisted on her, everything had worked out handsomely. She tossed a quick glance at her husband and saw that he too was captivated by the change in Frankie. But then Cutter didn't miss much. A gambler *had* to be observant . . . if he expected to be a successful gambler.

Maggie took another sip of her wine and turned her thoughtful gaze on her sister. Perhaps Sean Sullivan would be good for Frankie. Maybe he would bring a little fun into her life. Honestly, for a woman only twenty-four years old, Frankie had the soul of an old spinster.

And privately Maggie had always thought that all Mary Frances really needed was to be kissed. Soundly and regularly. By someone who knew what he was doing. She frowned slightly as Herbert Featherstone's image leaped to mind. Oh, Sean was definitely an improvement over Frankie's usual escort.

She swiveled her head to stare at Sean from beneath lowered lashes. Underneath all that brash Irish charm, Maggie had the feeling Sean was hiding something. Why would a man who supposedly had learned the art of traveling from the king of wanderering magicians want to own half of a tiny hotel in San Francisco?

And why, she asked herself, was he looking at prim, proper Frankie like a starving man looks at a free meal?

As they climbed the steps to the hotel, Mary Frances asked herself again why she'd come to Sean Sullivan's rescue. She should have kept quiet and let Cutter question the man. After all, what did they know about Sullivan beyond the fact that he'd bought his way into her life?

Nothing. Absolutely nothing. But for heaven's sake, if she ever expected to be able to talk the man into selling his share of the hotel back to her, she should at least make an *effort* to keep from alienating him.

A small voice in the back of her mind laughed.

That wasn't the only reason she'd spoken up. For some reason, a part of her had hated seeing Sean so uncomfortable. Clearly he hadn't wanted to talk about himself. And perhaps he had a good reason for that. Perhaps, in his own way, Sean Sullivan was as shy and uncomfortable around people as *she* was.

"Your sister and her husband seem a nice pair," he said, and Mary Frances ignored the ripple of awareness that raced along her spine at the sound of his voice.

"Yes," she said as she reached for the doorknob. "They are."

Sean laid his big hand atop hers, and Mary Frances almost gasped at the contact. His fingers tightened slightly and she felt the doorknob turn beneath their combined effort. A small slice of light from the inner hall lamp fell across them, and Mary Frances looked up at him.

In the soft golden glow, his tanned skin seemed darker and the blue of his eyes reminded her of sapphires she'd seen once in a jeweler's window. His white shirt was open at the throat and his sleeves were rolled up to his elbows. He hadn't changed for dinner, beyond shaving and securing his too long hair back with a leather tie.

When he'd first appeared in the parlor to

escort her to the saloon, Mary Frances had wondered if perhaps he didn't own a jacket and tie. Now, though, she thought that perhaps Sean Sullivan dressed as he did because he knew how well it suited him.

For the life of her, she couldn't imagine the big man's muscular form packed into a confining suit of clothes. He looked as if he was born to the outdoors and the simple clothes of a hardworking man. Something inside her applauded his reluctance to pretend to be something he wasn't.

In her own way, Mary Frances did the same thing.

Since she was a girl, she'd known that she was plain. Too short to be memorable, she was also too . . . *rounded* to be fashionable. Oh, not that she would call herself heavy, by any means. But her figure did tend to be rather *full* in places. And she had decided long ago that putting fine feathers on a sparrow didn't make it a robin. It only made for a silly-looking sparrow.

A small smile curved her lips and she watched a dimple crease his cheek as he answered her smile with one of his own.

"What's this then?" he asked. "A smile?"

She ducked her head but he caught her chin with his fingers and tipped her head up again until she was looking into his eyes. The warmth of his touch seemed to shoot through her body right down to her toes, but Mary Frances told herself it was only because the night air was so chilly.

"Ah now," he said with a shake of his head.

"The smile's gone and I hardly had the chance to enjoy it."

"Really, Mr. Sullivan," Mary Frances managed to say and then moved back a step. "I simply smiled. An act hardly worth noticing, let alone remarking on in such detail."

"I'm not so sure, Mary Frances," he answered, then crossed his arms over his broad chest. Leaning against the doorjamb, he looked down at her. "Your smiles, I'm thinkin', are few and far between."

She edged her way to the open doorway. "Why is that, do you think?"

"I'm sure I don't know what you're talking about." Really, she was sorry now she'd ever had a kind thought for the man. Did he have to create such a scene over a simple smile?

"What I'm talkin' about, Mary Frances Donnelly," he said, then straightened abruptly and took a half step closer to her. Mary Frances scuttled sideways, "is that it's a sin for a beautiful woman to keep her smiles to herself."

She snorted her disbelief and immediately covered her mouth with her hand, embarrassed to have made such an impolite noise.

Sean placed his left palm over his heart and rolled his eyes heavenward. "You've cut me to the quick, girl. 'Tis obvious even to me that you don't believe a word I'm sayin'."

"And that surprises you?" For heaven's sake, she wouldn't stand on her own front porch and listen to such blatant flummery.

"Of course."

"Mr. Sullivan," Mary Frances said and drew herself up to her full less-than-imposing height of five feet, two inches, tilting her head back and glaring at him. "Never have I heard such an obvious collection of falsehoods and meaningless flattery."

His mouth dropped open.

"Since you have undeniably been cursed with the Irish flair for exaggeration, I shall overlook it on this occasion." She pulled in a steadying breath and hoped it was enough to keep her voice from shaking. "However, you should know that I am not a woman to be swayed by honeyed words, moonlight, or any other such drivel that might appeal to the type of woman you are no doubt accustomed to."

"Now wait one bloody minute—"

"No, I will not." Surprising, she thought, how liberating it was to silence a man with a look. "I am well aware of my appearance. I own several mirrors, all of which afford me an excellent view of my person. Therefore, empty flattery will gain you nothing but my contempt."

On that last note, she turned and stepped across the threshold. She'd hardly taken more than a step, however, when Sean's voice stopped her again.

"And does that mirror of yours show you the green fire that spits out of your eyes when you're angry, Mary Frances?"

She swallowed heavily.

"And have you never noted the fine flush on your cheeks when your Irish is up?"

She lifted her hands to her cheeks as if she could hide that flush from him. Then she heard him take one long, single step that brought him to a stop within inches of her rigid back.

"And Mother of God, Mary Frances Donnelly." He sighed and she felt his breath on the back of her neck. "Has no one ever told you that you've a figure designed to drive us poor men into our graves with want?"

Chapter 4

❝**A**nd has no one ever told you that a quick tongue and charming manner won't work on every female you meet?"

"Find me charmin', do ya?"

Mary Frances shook her head in frustration, turned, and entered the hall. She pulled off her black cotton shawl, tossed it toward a peg on the hall tree as she passed it, and walked quickly down the hall to the front parlor.

Mary Frances felt him watching her and knew he was following her. Ridiculous, she told herself. Her reaction to the man was ridiculous. She knew empty flattery—*blarney*—when she heard it. Heaven knew, she'd been raised by the best. No one was more gifted at the art of blarney than her own father! And she'd become immune years ago to Kevin Donnelly's fancies.

But it was more than simply her father's nonsense. It wasn't Kevin alone who'd taught her so well—it was someone even her sisters didn't know about.

Why then, were Sean Sullivan's wild words having such an effect on her?

As she drew nearer to the parlor, Mary Frances heard voices and dismissed thoughts of Mr. Sullivan and his nonsense. Silently, she sent a prayer of thanks that her guests were still up and she wouldn't have to be alone with her new partner.

She stepped through the arched doorway and paused. Deliberately, she allowed her gaze to sweep the room, hoping that the familiar, soothing surroundings would work their magic on her frazzled nerves.

Soft, rose-colored velvet covered the two settees and matching twin chairs clustered around a wide brick fireplace built into the far wall. Small dainty rosewood tables were scattered about the room and the top of each was covered with a spiderweb of lace she'd crocheted herself. Lamplight fell on the well-worn Oriental carpet, giving its faded shades of blue and gray a shadowy look. Reflections of the hand-painted lamps shone on the front windows, making it seem as if there were twice as many glass-globed lamps in the room.

Mary Frances smiled to herself and let her gaze slip over her guests, still unaware of her presence.

Mr. Penny, a traveling salesman from St. Louis, had been frequenting the Four Roses for years. A timid man, he seemed to enjoy the quiet pace of her hotel. He usually stopped by two or three times a year.

Mrs. Turner, a well-to-do widow, was next. Generally, Mrs. Turner spent several weeks a year at the Roses. With no family of her own, the older woman delighted in traveling up and down the coast of California, staying at hotels familiar enough to her that they seemed like home.

Unfortunately, this year she'd arrived at the same time as Mrs. Destry.

Fiona Destry too was a widow, left with more money than family. She'd stayed at the Roses off and on through the years. And now it looked as though she had every intention of becoming a permanent resident. The older woman had sold her home in Stockton and furnished her room at the hotel with her personal belongings.

Though Frankie was fond of the old woman, on the few occasions that Fiona and Mrs. Turner had been at the hotel at the same time, the two women had been at each other's throats.

This time, it seemed to be worse than ever.

Frankie had the distinct feeling that this would be the *last* year Mrs. Turner visited the Roses.

A fire burned in the hearth, and Mr. Penny was crouched in front of it, stabbing at the glowing logs with a poker.

Mrs. Turner sat in one of the deep wing chairs, her ever-present knitting across her knees. She scowled at the old woman across from her and snapped, "There is *no* reason to be vulgar!"

Mrs. Destry's gnarled fingers gripped the edges of a book as she brought the pages close to her nose, then held them out at arm's length again in a futile attempt to read without her glasses. She seemed to be deliberately ignoring Mrs. Turner.

Mary Frances inhaled sharply and let the air slide out of her lungs in a slow sigh. *This* was where she belonged. Here, with the people who trusted her to make their stay a pleasant one.

"Oh," Mr. Penny said as he stood up and spotted her in the doorway. "How nice. You've returned."

Mary Frances smiled at the little man as he adjusted his round spectacles on the bridge of his long, sharp nose. Firelight glanced off his balding head and he lifted one hand to smooth the fringe of gray-sprinkled black hair above his left ear.

"Is everything all right?" she asked and stepped into the room.

"It *was*." Mrs. Turner mumbled and reached down to untangle the snarl of yarn at her feet. "Dinner was lovely, my dear. Simply lovely." She shot a murderous look at the older woman still toying with her book. "Despite what *some* might say."

"Gave me gas," Mrs. Destry said to no one in particular, then fidgeted with her book again.

Mary Frances smothered a smile.

"Tsk!" Mrs. Turner frowned at the white-haired woman across from her. "Really!"

"Yes, really," Mrs. Destry shot back. Turning the book slightly to catch the lamplight more fully, the old woman never took her eyes off the pages as she pointed out, "Never could stand cabbage. Comes back on a body all night long."

Mr. Penny couged delicately.

Mrs. Turner gasped and clutched her throat.

"That's why the Irish like it so much," Sean said with a laugh as he stepped into the circle of light. "You can eat the same meal twice."

Mrs. Turner sniffed and narrowed her gaze at the strange man, but Mrs. Destry chuckled. Then, as if to agree with him wholeheartedly, the old woman belched. Loudly.

"Great heavens!" Mrs. Turner muttered and gathered her knitting in her arms.

Mary Frances watched the middle-aged woman helplessly. Obviously Mrs. Turner was embarrassed both by the conversation and by her fellow guest's ill-timed eruption. Mary Frances understood exactly how the woman felt, but really, there was nothing anyone could say to keep Mrs. Destry from speaking her mind. Or, for that matter, from doing anything else.

Mrs. Turner rose unsteadily, her feet entangled in a length of yarn. Even the tightly wound braid she wore atop her head seemed to quiver with indignation. Lamplight glinted off the gold pendant watch pinned to her bosom, and her chest heaved with each righteous breath she took.

"I shall retire, if you don't mind," Mrs. Turner said. Naturally, Mrs. Destry was the first person to respond.

"Don't mind a bit, honey." Another gaseous discharge followed that statement, and Mrs. Turner shuddered violently. But Mrs. Destry wasn't finished. Finally tearing her watery blue gaze from the book she'd given up on, she looked at the prim, starchy woman and said flatly, "You got way too much steel in your stays for my taste, honey. There ain't a spot of give in you. Said so for years."

Mary Frances groaned quietly. Beside her, she felt rather than heard Sean's amusement. To his credit, he didn't add any fuel to the fires of Mrs. Turner's indignation. However, Mary Frances later thought he might have waited for a more opportune time to make himself known.

"Before you go, ma'am," he said to Mrs. Turner, "I'd like to introduce meself."

"I hardly think that's necessary, young man!" Mrs. Turner's frozen features would have quelled a lesser man.

"Ah, but there you're wrong." Sean smiled down at her, but not even his dimple could coax a return smile from the sorely tried woman. Gamely, though, he plunged ahead. "The name is Sullivan. Sean Sullivan."

"And?" Mrs. Turner's black eyebrows lifted expectantly.

Mary Frances's gaze darted from one to the other of the three interested faces staring at Sean Sullivan. She should have prepared her guests. But then again, how could she have prepared them for her new partner's arrival when she'd had no idea when he would show up?

Oh, that was a miserable excuse and she knew it. She hadn't warned anyone of a possible problem because she'd simply been pretending that it wouldn't happen. Well, now she was paying for that denial. Now she would have to spend a good bit of time assuring her guests that nothing at the Four Roses would change. That their favorite hotel would continue to be a place of quiet dignity, a retreat from the sometimes too fast and too noisy world at large.

She glanced up at Sean's smiling face and felt a small warning chill of trepidation. Bravely, she battled it down. No matter what it cost, no matter what she had to do, the Four Roses would *not* change.

"And," Sean finished with a flourish and a half bow, "I'm the new owner here."

"What?" Mrs. Turner gasped and turned to Mary Frances.

"Here now, what's this?" Mr. Penny took a half step forward and froze.

Mrs. Destry chuckled, and the noise sounded like fingernails on a chalkboard. "Well, it's high time things got shook up a bit around here," she commented when her wheezy laughter finally stopped.

"Miss Donnelly, I am appalled," Mrs. Turner said into the strained silence. Her long, patrician nose wrinkled slightly as if there were a bad smell in the air, and she took a small step back from Mary Frances. "After all the years I have spent patronizing this establishment, I find it difficult to comprehend how you can justify selling your place of business without so much as *informing* your loyal patrons."

"Mrs. Turner," Mary Frances said, sparing only a moment to glare at Sean for his ineptitude, "*I* didn't sell the hotel. My father sold his share of the business to Mr. Sullivan, who, I might add, was a bit precipitate in his introductions. He is a *half* owner."

"Still . . ." Mrs. Turner flashed a quick look at Sean's smiling face.

"Are you saying then, Miss Donnelly," Mr. Penny said quietly, "that you will still be in charge of the Four Roses?"

"Yes indeed, Mr. Penny."

"And nothing will change?"

"Of course not, Mrs. Turner."

"Nothin' *much*," Sean amended, and everyone turned to look at him.

"Amen and hallelujah!" Mrs. Destry snorted delightedly and got up to look for her spectacles.

Sean watched Mary Frances from behind as he followed her up the stairs to his new bedroom. Ordinarily he would have been intrigued by the angry twitch of her hips and the tantalizing swish of her petticoats as she walked. However, tonight he was far too concerned about the rigidity of her spine and the stiff set to her shoulders.

The woman was furious.

Hardly the way he'd hoped to start off their new partnership.

When she came to the end of the hall, she shifted the fresh linens in her arms and opened the door to his room with such a flourish, the heavy panel bounced off the wall behind it and slammed back at him as he stepped over the threshold. Instinctively he raised his hand to stop the door before it crashed into him.

Rubbing the whisker stubble on his jaw thoughtfully, Sean stepped into the room with all the care of a man walking onto a gallows. From across the room, he heard a scratching noise, then saw a tiny flicker of flame leap into life. She lifted the chimney on the closest lamp, and when the wick was lit, she turned it up, replaced the globe, and went to work.

Uneasily, Sean watched as Mary Frances stripped the quilt and sheets from the bed. Her movements were quick, practiced. The wavering light from the nearby lamp made it seem almost as if she were dancing with the shadows patterned on the wall. But her features were pulled into a tight mask of displeasure, and Sean wasn't sure quite how to get her past it. When she unfolded a fresh sheet and snapped it in the air over the mattress, it sounded like a gunshot.

Sean winced and moved closer to the bed. This couldn't go on. Better she let loose of the anger eating at her than bottle it up inside and feed on it for who knew how long. Leaning his forearms on the iron foot rail, he looked at her carefully before asking, "Are ya gonna tell me what's on your mind, lass? Or are ya just goin' to snap and snarl at me for a bit yet?"

Mary Frances lifted the corner of the mattress and tucked the sheet in. Moving quickly around the bed, she paused beside Sean long enough for him to understand that she wanted him out of her way. Dutifully he stepped aside and sighed as she continued with her work.

He reached up and yanked at the piece of leather confining his hair into a small, neat tail and raked one hand through the thick, wavy black mass.

"I can do up me own bed, y'know."

She didn't even look at him. "This is *my* hotel. It's *my* responsibility to see to my guests' comfort."

"*Our* hotel, Mary Frances," he pointed out and wished to hell she'd stand still for one bloody minute.

Instead she inhaled sharply, snapped the top sheet over the mattress, and continued with her work.

"And I'm *not* one of your bleedin' guests!"

She was moving like the devil himself was after her. Sean silently admitted that it was all his fault. All right, he might have introduced himself to her guests in a bit more subtle way, but as Calhoun always used to say, "Never whisper when you can shout."

Even as that thought entered his mind, though, Sean had to acknowledge that Seamus Calhoun had never been known for his tact.

Mary Frances finished with the sheets and topped her work with a blanket, followed by the colorful quilt. Then she started in on the feather pillows. Yanking them from their slips, she pounded and punched at them until Sean was expecting a snowfall of goosefeathers to shoot out of the fabric. He didn't have a bit of trouble figuring out just whom she wished she was punching.

"Mary Frances, I'm sorry for how I muddled up things with those people."

"*Those* people," she said through clenched teeth, "are my customers. They've each been coming to the Four Roses for years." She snatched a fresh pillow slip and began to stuff the poor bedraggled pillow inside it. "They each think of this hotel as their home away from home."

"So?" he asked and hesitantly took a step closer. "I've done nothin' to change that."

"Haven't you?" She threw the pillow to the head of the bed, grabbed the next one, and began to jam it into the embroidered linen case. "How *dare* you walk into my parlor and announce yourself as the new owner?"

"Well—"

She glared him into silence, and Sean couldn't help but think how deceptive those mild green eyes of hers were. And that pale, rose-gold colored hair was just as distracting. Looking at her, a man would think that the legendary temper of redheads was watered down in Mary Frances Donnelly. Staring into her eyes lulled a man into a false sense of security.

Mary Frances looked the picture of sweet, docile womanhood—when, in fact, there was an Irish warrior buried deep in her soul.

"If you had the slightest amount of decency," that warrior now told him, waving one finger at his astonished features, "you would have waited and given me a chance to speak to my guests privately."

"I only wanted to—"

But she didn't want to hear any more from

him. Mary Frances cut him off with a wave of her hand.

"Instead," she went on, after tossing the second pillow atop the first, "you barged in where you had no right and upset everything!" Shaking her head, Mary Frances muttered, "Poor Mrs. Turner may never get over it."

"Mother of God, woman!"

Sean's whispered shout was strained with the effort to contain his own temper. For God's sake, she was acting as though he'd tossed everybody out on their ears! All he'd done was tell them the truth she was still trying to deny.

"I didn't show up on your doorstep today out of the blue, ya know," he said, looming over her. "I know for a fact that your da sent you a telegram two weeks ago, tellin' you to expect me."

Her lips clamped down into a straight, prim line, but the deep, rapid breaths wracking her small frame told him that her fire was far from out.

When she spoke, it was clear she was fighting for control.

"That's true enough, Mr. Sullivan."

"Sean."

"But, you must understand that I had no way of knowing when or *if* you would arrive."

"But the telegram . . ."

Mary Frances drew a long, steadying breath into her lungs. "My father, Mr. Sullivan, has been known to . . . *exaggerate* the truth from time to time."

"Ya mean you thought he was lyin'."

She folded her arms across her bosom, and her fingers began to tap against her upper arms. "Not . . . *lying*, exactly. It's simply that you can never be sure that my father's told you everything."

Well now, he thought, that was certainly true enough. Kevin hadn't mentioned the fact that Mary Frances didn't want a partner. Nor had he bothered to mention what a fine-looking woman his daughter was. But all that was beside the point.

"I still don't understand why you're upset that I told those people about me bein' the new owner."

"Half owner."

"All right, then. *Half* owner."

Mary Frances tilted her head back and stared up into his eyes. A flash of admiration shot through Sean as he realized that his size didn't intimidate her in the slightest. "Because, Mr. Sullivan, I was hoping to have a chance to talk to you about your share of the hotel before any announcements were made."

Somehow he didn't like the sound of that.

"Talk to me about what?"

She licked her lips nervously, and Sean's gaze was drawn to the tip of her tongue. Suddenly he didn't much care what she had on her mind. All he really wanted to do was pull her into his arms and kiss her until neither of them could draw a breath without tasting the other.

She seemed to know what he was thinking, though he admitted silently that it couldn't have been very difficult. He watched her eyes close briefly before she started talking again.

"Perhaps it would be best if this conversation waited until the morning." She stepped quickly to one side as if intending to walk around him, but Sean's hand on her arm stopped her.

"Now, Mary Frances," he said, his voice hushed and gravelly. "We're finally beginnin' to talk here. What's the use of waitin'?"

Mary Frances looked down at his hand, his long, strong fingers curled around her upper arm. She felt the warmth of his touch clear down to her bones and knew she was in trouble.

She'd seen the look in his eyes a moment ago. And she was fairly certain that *talking* wasn't what he had in mind. A shiver rocketed through her, sending a curl of anticipation spiraling through her bloodstream.

Anticipation?

Good heavens, what was she thinking?

His thumb moved against her arm, drawing idle patterns on the sleeve of her gown, yet Mary Frances felt his touch brand those patterns into her flesh.

"Don't go," he whispered. "Not yet."

"This is highly improper, Mr. Sullivan," she said and tried to make herself move toward the door. Toward safety.

"I won't tell if you don't," he answered, and she heard the smile in his voice. She didn't dare look up at him and see that dimple.

"Mr. Sullivan."

"Sean."

Mary Frances breathed deeply, hoping for

control, but it didn't work. His hand on her arm moved slightly and his knuckles brushed against the side of her breast. She jumped, startled at the fiery intimacy.

"Say it, Mary Frances," he said and bent down until his breath brushed her ear. "Say *Sean.*"

She swallowed and wished with all her might that she could run from the room. But she couldn't. Even if he let go of her she wouldn't be able to move. Her knees were shaking too badly for that. And somewhere in the back of her mind, a guilty little voice admitted that she didn't *really* want to leave. Not yet, anyway.

"Ah, Frannie girl, say me name. It's not so hard, ya know."

Her gaze snapped to his. As she had feared, that dimple of his was a deep crease in his cheek and his crooked smile made his eyes light up with devilment.

"What did you call me?" she asked when she found her voice.

"Frannie," he said and lifted one hand to brush a stray curl from her forehead. "I heard your sister callin' you Frankie . . ."

She nodded.

"But that's no proper name for a woman like you, Frannie."

"No?" She'd never questioned it before. She'd been called Frankie by her family since she was a little girl. No one had ever thought it improper.

"No." He shook his head slowly, letting his gaze move over her features like a touch.

"There's nothin' boyish about you, lass. You're every inch a woman. And a fine, lovely one at that."

His voice was mesmerizing. She felt the deep tones rumble along her spine, and every word he spoke seemed to echo in her soul. His eyes shone with something she didn't want to recognize and his lips were only a breath away from hers.

"So if it's all right with you, I'll be callin' you Frannie." His fingertips traced the line of her jaw and slid down the length of her throat. "Do ya mind, lass?"

She tried to speak but couldn't. Finally she shook her head.

"Ah," he said, his smile growing wider, "that's grand." He moved closer to her, and Mary Frances felt as if his very size would swallow her up. "Now, Frannie girl, there's one more thing I've been wantin' for most of this day."

She swallowed heavily and tilted her head to avoid looking into those eyes of his any longer. His fingers caught her chin and turned her face to his.

"And I think you've been wantin' it too," he said just before he lowered his mouth to hers.

Chapter 5

Their lips met, his breath caressed her cheek, and for a heartbeat, Mary Frances leaned into him, enthralled by his touch. Then his tongue smoothed across her lips and she gasped. One good shove against his chest helped her leap out of his reach.

Eyes wide, hand at her mouth, she stared at him.

"What do you think you're doing?" Mary Frances managed to say, outrage defining every word.

"Well now," he said and took a half step toward her, "I thought I was kissin' you."

Mary Frances scuttled further away from him. "I'm not talking about the kiss," she said. Then she pointed her finger at him accusingly. "I'm talking about...the other thing you did."

His brow furrowed, Sean stopped and stared at her. "The other?"

Still too embarrassed to actually say it aloud, Mary Frances licked her lips nervously and hedged, "You, uh...when your... *you* know."

Realization dawned on his features, but to Mary Frances's surprise, he didn't look the least bit apologetic. Instead he appeared a bit confused.

"That was merely part of the kiss, lass."

"Hmmph! I've been kissed before, Mr. Sullivan. I'm not so foolish as that. What I meant to say was, you have no right to be taking such liberties with me."

"Well now." He grinned and crossed his arms over his massive chest. "I was thinkin' that it was both of us doin' the takin'."

Hmmm. She could hardly argue that point with him.

"So then. You're tellin' me that there's been another man sippin' at my bowl of nectar?"

"I *beg* your pardon!" As if an iron pole had suddenly been stabbed down the back of her dress, she stiffened. Nectar indeed. Sean Sullivan didn't even have the decency to know that he'd behaved improperly.

And what's more, she asked herself hotly, what gave him the right to think of her as *his*?

"It's all for the best, Frannie girl," he said quietly. "Now when we kiss, you'll know me for the better man. I can teach ya the proper way of it."

"I hardly think you're the person to be teaching anyone what is proper or not."

"Perhaps me manners are a bit on the rough side . . ."

"Perhaps?"

"But no one's ever complained about me kissin'."

"Until now."

He grinned. "That's right. Until now." Letting his arms fall to his sides, Sean took a step toward her. "So, if you don't mind, I'd like another crack at it. I've me reputation to think of."

Good heavens! Mary Frances took a deep breath, ducked under his outstretched arms, and scurried to the still open door. On the threshold, she paused and gave him a glare that had been known to freeze a man in his tracks.

Sean smiled.

"Mr. Sullivan," she said, trying to keep her voice from shaking. "While you are here at the Four Roses, there will be no more kissing. Do you understand?"

"Uh-huh."

"We are business partners."

"Uh-huh."

"Nothing more."

"Of course, lass."

She nodded abruptly. That should set him straight. For now. At least, she told herself, until she could gather her resources together and make him an offer for his half of the hotel.

The last few minutes had made it abundantly clear to Mary Frances that having Sean Sullivan in the hotel on a permanent basis was simply not possible. Surely he would be able to see that as well.

He was a businessman. She would appeal to that side of his nature. She would offer him far more than his share of the hotel was worth—and he would take it. Of course he would. Then he would be gone and she'd never have to face him again.

A three-year-old memory leaped to life in her mind. Conor James. A silver-tongued man who had whispered of love while stealing kisses in the moonlight. Then one day he had slipped out of town without as much as a backward glance.

Frankie pushed the memory away and told herself that it wouldn't happen again. This time a man's easy manner wouldn't bruise her heart. This time she would be strong. She would keep her distance. And when Sean finally left—

Her life could return to normal.

It would all work out just fine.

It had to.

"I'll say good night, then, Mr. Sullivan," she said and grasped the doorknob.

He took the few steps separating them and covered her hand with his own.

A brief burst of warmth shot up the length of her arm and Mary Frances's heartbeat quickened in response. Staring into his deep blue eyes, she felt danger swirl around her. Not a danger to her person . . . heaven knew she had no reason to suspect that the man meant her any harm—though his very size would dwarf taller women than herself. Frankie hadn't noticed anything about his behavior to suggest a mean or bullying personality.

But there was danger nonetheless. A danger to the safe, quiet, uncomplicated world she'd built for herself.

His thumb caressed the back of her wrist,

and she stared down at their joined hands. Her flesh tingled and burned as if from a dozen tiny flames. The feeling was startling in its intensity, but not altogether unpleasant.

And the fact that she found his touch ... pleasurable, was absolutely terrifying. Quickly she snatched her hand away.

He only smiled at her action. That slow, deep smile she was coming to know all too well.

"Good night, Frannie girl," he said softly. "Sleep well."

Then he quietly shut the door and she was left alone in the darkened hall.

"It's only been three days, Frankie," Maggie said and reached for her cup of coffee. "Still a bit early to get frantic, don't you think?"

"No, I don't." Mary Frances glanced around the empty saloon and gave silent thanks that her sister's husband was off somewhere. Heaven knew, as fond as she was of Cutter, she didn't need another male around at the moment.

Three days. *Only* three days, Maggie had said. Easy enough for her to talk, Mary Frances told herself. Maggie wasn't the one having to stand idly by while a stranger made havoc of her business!

"You might try giving this a chance to work out."

Frankie's gaze snapped to her older sister's. Just a short time ago, Maggie had been tearing her hair out, looking for a way to get rid of her own new partner. Now, simply because she'd ended up marrying Cutter instead of buying him out, she had the nerve to preach patience?

"I seem to remember you feeling a bit differently when Cutter first turned up owning half of your saloon," Frankie pointed out.

Maggie chuckled. "True." A soft smile touched her lovely features, then disappeared again. "But things change."

"Not always." Ignoring the memory of Sean's lips on hers, Frankie silently assured herself that there would be no more such goings-on. Therefore, she and Sean were hardly going to end up married like Maggie and Cutter.

After all, her sister and Cutter had not been strangers when their partnership began. Cutter had known the Donnellys for years.

And the fact that Frankie kept experiencing a peculiar sense of . . . familiarity whenever Sean was near had nothing to do with anything.

"All I'm sayin'," Maggie went on, leaning her forearms on the gleaming surface of the walnut card table, "is that you might want to think about this a bit before acting."

Oh no, Frankie thought. Her only hope lay in acting quickly. *Before* she could think too much about it. For the first time in years, she didn't trust herself to react rationally. Somehow, every time Sean Sullivan entered a room, practicality flew out a window.

"Why?" She nearly shouted in her frustration. Her palms flat on the tabletop, Frankie glared at her sister. "Why should I?"

"Because *you've* always been the patient one, for God's sake!"

Mary Frances bit down hard on her bottom lip. Maggie was right. She had spent most of her life fighting to conquer the Irish temper that was such a part of the Donnelly family. And until recently, she would have been willing to swear on a stack of Bibles that she'd succeeded.

One more black mark against the interloper.

"There's something else besides," Maggie added quietly.

"What?" Frankie asked, trying desperately to ignore the swell of foreboding beginning to creep through her.

"You have to remember. Cutter wouldn't be bought off. What makes you think Sean will be any different?"

A vision of Sean Sullivan rose up in Frankie's mind, and she almost groaned at the image. Strong, determined, hardheaded. She didn't need to know him long to know that he possessed each of those qualities in abundance.

All right, maybe he wouldn't be bought off. But it was certainly worth a try, wasn't it? Yes, she nodded firmly to herself. Aloud she said with more confidence than she felt, "I'm sure I can talk him into it."

Maggie didn't look convinced.

"We'll offer him more than he paid for his share." Yes, she thought, that would do it. No man would turn down such a healthy profit. All it would take was money and she would be free again. Her life would be her own and she could stop worrying and thinking about the man who slept two floors above her. Too loudly, she said suddenly. "Two or three times what he paid! He'll take it. I *know* he will."

Maggie's brows drew together and her fingers began to tap on the tabletop.

"If the family won't back me in this," Frankie said stiffly in response to her sister's expression, "I'll go to the bank and see about a loan."

"Oh, Frankie, stop it." Maggie leaned back in her chair and frowned outright at her sister. "Of course the family will come up with the money. That's not a problem. I simply don't think it will work."

"Why would a man turn down that much money to retain half ownership in a tiny hotel?"

"I don't know." Maggie shrugged slightly. "I just think he will."

"Do you know something I don't?"

"Sean's been to see Cutter."

"About what?" The words were choked from her throat and breathing suddenly became more difficult.

"He was asking where he could hire good workmen."

"Workmen?" Frankie's jaw dropped. "Why? And why didn't he ask me? What is he trying to hide?"

"I don't know." Maggie shook her head. "All he told Cutter was he wanted some work done around the hotel."

"What kind of work?" Immediately visions of strange men, hammers and saws clenched in their meaty fists, rose up in Frankie's imagination. In her mind's eye, she watched them crawling all over her beloved hotel, tearing at the polished floors, ripping down the tasteful, flowered wallpaper. She saw her guests streaming out of the building, never to come back.

"Maybe he wants to expand," Maggie suggested.

"Expand?" Frankie jumped up from her chair and began to pace nervously. Her shoe heels clicked impatiently on the pine floor and her fingers plucked at her skirt. "*I* don't want to expand! If I'd wanted to expand, I'd have done it years ago! Besides, why would he fire Molly and Dolores if he wanted to expand?"

"Fired? He fired them without even talking to you?"

"Well," Frankie admitted, turning around to look at her sister, "I suppose he didn't actually fire them. But he might as well have. It's because of him they're gone."

"What'd he do?"

"He came to San Francisco!" Frankie snapped, then quickly drew in a deep breath and reminded herself that she was the calm Donnelly. The quiet Donnelly. More slowly this time, she said, "Dolores was tongue-tied around him." Frankie's lips twisted into a frown. "Every time the man walked into a room, Dolores stood mute as a stump, staring at him with big puppy eyes."

Maggie tried to stifle a chuckle but didn't succeed. Frankie glared at her.

"It isn't funny. Dolores was always such a

good worker, and all at once she was no more help than—than—*I* would be dealing faro here at the saloon."

Maggie bit her bottom lip and shook her head.

With a sigh, Frankie added more quietly, "Last night Dolores simply left. I woke up this morning and she was gone." To give Sean his due, she added silently, he was as surprised at Dolores's departure as Frankie had been.

"What happened to Molly?" Maggie asked expectantly.

Frankie's eyes slid shut as she remembered the incident. "Two days ago, Molly's mother dropped by to see her and she ran into Sean."

A choked laugh shot from Maggie's throat before she prodded, "And?"

"*And.*" Frankie sighed heavily. "Mrs. Muldoon declared Sean to be 'a walkin' occasion to sin.'" Her mimicry of Mrs. Muldoon's thick Irish brogue was so exact, Maggie burst into laughter. Shaking her head, Frankie finished, "Then she told me that Molly Muldoon would not be stayin' at the hotel to be tempted into giving away her most precious possession to a good-lookin' Irishman who was probably no better than he had to be."

Wiping her eyes, Maggie stood up and walked to her sister's side. "You can hardly blame Sean for those two leaving."

"I suppose not," Frankie agreed, though Lord knew she hated to. "Still though, now it will be just Treasure and me. And of course, Sean Sullivan."

"God in heaven, the man's only been in town four days!"

"Exactly!" Frankie threw up her hands in frustration. "Who knows what will happen if we give him more time?"

"All right, you've made your point, Mary Frances," Maggie admitted. "Go ahead and make whatever offer you want to. The family will stand behind it."

"Thanks, Maggie."

Frankie hurried back to the table where they'd been sitting and snatched her black purse. As she walked past her sister toward the front doors, Maggie reached out and grabbed her arm.

"One thing. You haven't said how your guests are taking all of this."

Frankie frowned again and noted silently that frowning was getting to be a habit.

"Not well. Mrs. Turner left early. Of course, she never stays long if Fiona Destry happens to be there. But I think it was Sean who chased her away this time. I don't believe she cares overmuch for men." Shaking her head, Frankie went on, "Mr. Penny's stay was up anyway. And Fiona has announced that she's tired of making the trek in from her home in Stockton all the time and is going to move into the Four Roses permanently."

"That's good, isn't it?"

"Yes..." She flicked a worried glance at Maggie. "But Fiona Destry spends far too much time with Sean. Sometimes I think they're up to something."

* * *

This wasn't going well at all, Sean told himself as he reached for another log from the nearby woodpile. Four days with Mary Frances and it seemed all he was doing was driving her further away.

Grumbling under his breath, he set the log down on the chopping block, took a firm grip on the axe handle, and swung it over his head in a wide arc. The razor-sharp blade slammed down on the short, squat log and, in one blow, split it neatly in half.

Grunting in satisfaction, he set one of the halves on its end and split it again.

The hard work felt good. Working with his hands assured him that he could still accomplish a task he set for himself. Because, for the love of St. Patrick, he'd done little else since arriving in the cold, windy city.

With his shirt off and the flighty San Francisco sun beating down on his sweat-streaked back, Sean actually felt better than he had in days. For a man used to working hard for his living, inactivity was a hardship. These past few days of being cooped up inside the small hotel, inspecting it from roof to bedrock, had been a sore test of his already limited patience.

The one bright spot in all of it, though, was Mary Frances.

Sean bent down, set another log on the block, and once more began the task of splintering firewood for the kitchen stove and the hotel fireplaces. With his hands and body busy, his mind could wander.

Naturally his thoughts turned to Frannie. Frannie. Yes, he told himself, a much more suitable name for her than the boyish Frankie.

Even better, it was something shared by just the two of them. That made him smile. He didn't want to call her what everyone else in her life called her. He didn't want to be just one of the dozens of people in this town who could claim they were acquaintances of Mary Frances Donnelly. Sean wanted more of her than that. He wanted them to talk together. To laugh together. To live and love together.

"And you're doin' a helluva job makin' *that* come about, boyo," he said aloud.

He gave the axe another mighty swing, and the blade slammed into the chopping block harder than before. Tremors rocketed up the axe handle into his palms, setting his flesh to tingling. He released the smooth ashwood and clenched his fists repeatedly until the sensation passed.

But then he remembered touching Frannie's fair, smooth skin and the feeling returned, stronger than before. Tilting his head back on his neck, he turned his face toward the sun. The warmth burned into his flesh, and in the bright light shining through his closed eyes, he saw Mary Frances's features clearly.

Something in his chest tightened and a faint stirring in his groin reinforced the notion of having her for his own. He'd never felt this way about anyone or anything in his life.

And it was a bit worrisome.

Sean groaned quietly. There'd been plenty of women who'd passed through his life in the last several years. A few he'd cared for, most he had not, beyond the most casual of affections.

But never had he been struck with the simple, agonizing need for a woman that he'd felt the moment he'd looked into Frannie's eyes. Now, days later, Sean could still feel the immediate kinship that had shot through him. The knowing. The surety that they'd known each other . . . loved each other before.

"Fancies," he told himself aloud and reached for another log. He'd be better served to keep his mind on the hotel and what it would mean to his family. They'd all hoped for years to have one place to call home. Now that they'd finally been tossed a chance at it, Sean didn't have the right to go mucking it up by scaring Frannie off.

If he had the slightest sense at all, he'd spend a bit of time cozying up to her. Letting her see that he wasn't near the curse she seemed to think he was. Perhaps her father had done her a disservice by selling out his share of the hotel. But dammit all, the deed was done now, and if she'd only open her eyes and *look* . . . really look, she would see that things weren't all that bad.

For God's sake, why the bloody hell couldn't *Frannie* look at him the way Dolores had? he asked himself as he straightened up to frown at the back door of the hotel.

As if he'd conjured her up, Mary Frances opened the door and stepped onto the wide plank porch. She inhaled sharply as if for strength, then turned and hurried down the steps to the yard.

A sharp, chill wind blew in off the bay just then and swirled around him. Even with the sunlight beating down on him, Sean shivered slightly. If he was a man who put blind trust in omens, he might have been worried. But as much as Sean appreciated signs and portents of things to come, he was also stubborn enough to believe he could bend the future to his will.

With that thought firmly in mind, he planted his hands on his hips and watched Frannie cross the yard.

When she was no more than a few steps away, she stopped. Her gaze slipped over his broad chest, and he watched her eyes widen appreciatively. Sean kept his features determinedly blank, despite the sharp spurt of pleasure he felt. Though Mary Frances Donnelly might not be struck dumb in admiration as Dolores had been, at least she wasn't completely uninterested.

"Mornin', Frannie darlin'," he said before he could stop himself.

She blinked, snapped her jaw shut, and lifted her gaze to his. After clearing her throat, she said, "Good morning . . . *Sean*."

His eyebrows arched. Something was definitely different, he told himself worriedly. She was calling him by his first name and looking entirely too friendly all of a sudden.

"It's pleased I am that you've decided to use me name, lass."

She took another deep breath, and Sean tried valiantly to keep his gaze from straying to her bosom. "There is something I'd like to talk to you about," she began, and then noticed the scattered pile of wood around him. "You don't have to chop the wood, you know. I usually hire a boy from the neighborhood to do that."

"There's no need for that now, though, is there?" he said gently. "Now that I'm here?"

Nodding, she said, "I suppose you're right."

You're in big trouble, Sean, he told himself silently. *She's being far too nice and agreeable for your good. Keep your wits about you, boyo, or you're likely to come out on the short end of the pier here.*

"What was it you wanted, Frannie?"

"I wish you wouldn't—"

She stopped and clamped her lips together.

"Wouldn't what?"

"Nothing." A bright, false smile curved her lips, but it went nowhere near her eyes. "Sean, I've just left my sister Maggie, and we were discussing the situation here at the hotel."

"Were ya now?"

"Yes," she went on quickly, "and we think we've come up with an idea that will suit us all perfectly."

"And what might that be?" he asked with a forced calm in his tone which he didn't feel.

Straightening to her full, small stature, she lifted her chin slightly and looked him dead in the eye. "The Donnelly sisters are prepared to offer you twice what you paid our father for his share of the hotel."

"Ah . . ." *Here it is then*, he thought. He'd figured she would try to buy him off and chase him out. And even though he'd expected such a maneuver, it saddened him to know how badly she wanted to be rid of him. Still, as Calhoun used to say, "How can you win the war if ya don't know what you're fightin'?" Sean pulled in a deep breath, forced a smile, and said, "That's a lot of money, Frannie."

"Yes, it would indeed be quite a tidy profit for you."

"That it would."

"And you must also agree that you're really not very happy with the situation as it now exists."

"Oh, I wouldn't say that, no."

"No?"

Sean gave her a wicked smile and a wink, then took a step closer to her. "What makes ya think I'm not happy, Frannie girl?"

"Uh . . ."

"The hotel's a fine one and me room is comfortable . . . if a bit lonely."

She gasped and Sean wanted to kick himself. She already wanted him gone. There was no sense at all in adding fuel to her fire. But even when he knew better, he couldn't seem to keep his mouth from running away with him. It would do him no good at all to frighten her. Yet it was a hard thing, wanting a woman as badly as he wanted her and trying to keep his feelings to himself.

"Three times," she blurted out.

"Three times what?"

"Three times what you paid," she said and backed up a pace. "We're prepared to pay you as much as three times what you gave my father."

"No."

"You can't expect more than that." Her eyes filled with tears that she blinked frantically to keep at bay. "It's a very generous offer."

"Indeed it is," Sean said and closed the space between them with two quick, long strides, "but I've no wish to sell."

"Why not?"

A flush filled her cheeks, and he knew it was frustration, pure and simple. The ocean-scented breeze plucked long, soft strands of her hair free of its knot and set them dancing about her face. Her teeth worried her lower lip, and her generous bosom rose and fell with each short, rapid breath she drew.

"Why are you so determined to own a hotel?" she finally asked, her tone plaintive.

Sean lifted one hand and cupped her cheek. Startled, she tried to turn her face from him, but he held firm.

"It's not just a hotel, Frannie," he said and knew that he had to tell her at least *part* of the reason he'd bought his way into her life. "It's a home for me . . . and for my family."

"Family?"

Her voice was hardly more than a whisper. In fact, if he hadn't seen her lips move, he might not have noticed she'd spoken at all.

"Aye," Sean said softly, "they'll be along anytime now."

"They." She nodded to herself. "You're married, then?"

Sean chuckled and shook his head. He hoped that was disappointment he'd heard in her tone. "Not yet, lass. Not yet."

"Then who . . ."

Bending down, he brushed a kiss across her lips, then grinned. No sense in telling her too much all at once, he thought. Let her get used to the idea of family coming before she had to learn just what *kind* of family Sean Sullivan called his own.

"All in good time, Frannie darlin'. All in good time."

Chapter 6

Mary Frances popped the cookie tray into the fiery hot oven, slammed the steel door closed with a towel-covered hand, then turned back to her worktable. Tossing the clean towel over her left shoulder, she dipped her right hand into the nearby flour bag and drew out a bit. She carefully sprinkled the flour over a small area, then reached for the bowl of piecrust dough beside her.

After tipping the dough onto the flour, she kneaded it a few times, then grabbed her rolling pin and went to work.

The smooth, round wood bit into the ball of dough and flattened it. Lifting, turning, rolling, Frankie hardly had to think as her hands went about the familiar task. But think she did, and as usual her thoughts returned to Sean Sullivan.

Two days, she told herself. Two days since she'd left Sean standing in the backyard with a self-satisfied smile on his face. All in good time, indeed.

And who could blame him? she asked herself. Hadn't she stood still as a statue, staring at his naked chest as if he were a winged messenger from God? Just recalling how she'd behaved made Frankie groan, and she redoubled her efforts with the rolling pin. She stared at the rectangle of dough and paid no attention at all as it became longer and wider and thinner.

Instead she was seeing *him*. Again. Awake, asleep, it seemed all her traitorous mind could do was raise up image after image of Sean Sullivan. Lord, how could she have *stared* at him so?

Heaven only knew what he'd thought of her reaction. But was it really her fault? Frankie had never really seen a man's naked ... nude ... bare ... Oh, good heavens! She'd never seen a man without his shirt on before, and so she'd been caught unprepared for the sight of so much sun-bronzed muscle. The rolling pin stilled and she stared blankly, remembering.

And she remembered everything. How the wind lifted his hair up from his neck. How trickles of perspiration rolled down his chest and were caught by the slight dusting of curly black hair adorning his flesh. How the incredible muscles in his arms and shoulders shifted and rolled with his every movement. How every single inch of his flesh was tanned from long, obviously shirtless, hours spent outdoors.

Her eyes closed and her fingers tightened around the rolling pin.

The memory of his lips, soft against her forehead, slipped through her brain.

She squeezed her eyes shut and tried to

steady her breathing. This was all wrong. She shouldn't be having these ridiculous feelings for a man who was nothing more than a tiresome business partner she couldn't rid herself of.

But then if she shouldn't be feeling this way . . . why was she? Oh, nothing made any sense at all.

She'd spent the last two days cleaning her hotel from top to bottom and doing absolutely everything in her power to keep from bumping into Sean. And still her mind betrayed her. Thoughts of him intruded almost constantly. Even reading was no longer the pleasure it once was, because in her imagination all the fictional heroes took on Sean's features.

"Nonsense," she said aloud and forced her thoughts back to business. "All of this is nonsense." And none of it would be happening if Sean Sullivan would have the good manners to take her money and go away.

But no. Not only was he not going away, he was bringing his family to stay at the hotel. *Family.* Frankie recalled that awful moment when she'd felt sure that he was about to tell her that he was a husband and the father of ten children.

She'd actually been so relieved to hear that he wasn't married—and she was not ready yet to ask herself *why*—she'd allowed him to avoid telling her more about this family of his. Even *she* wasn't sure why she hadn't pounced on the man for more information. Maybe it was simply that she had quite a bit to worry about already. Maybe she didn't want to know any more about him than she absolutely *had* to at the moment. But that hadn't stopped her curiosity. Ever since he'd mentioned them, she'd been wondering.

Who was coming? His parents? Brothers? Sisters? Cousins? How many of them?

Good heavens, didn't he realize that if he encamped a number of his relatives on the premises, they would have that many fewer rooms to let? What kind of hotel would the Four Roses become if there were never any vacancies? The answer was simple.

It wouldn't be a hotel anymore. It would be an oversized house for the extended Sullivan relations. And how were they supposed to make the hotel pay if they were giving away the rooms? Lord, the hotel wasn't making much as it was!

A temper she was becoming much too familiar with of late began to build deep inside her. Deliberately she tamped the anger and frowned at her piecrust. It was too thin and pieces of it were clinging to her rolling pin. Ruined. Yet another black mark against Sean Sullivan, she told herself as her fingers scraped the dough from the wooden counter.

"Mary Frances?"

Oh no, Frankie thought dismally. Not Mrs. Destry. Not now.

"Mary Frances, where are you?"

"In the kitchen," she called out, not because she particularly wanted to, but because she wasn't in any position to offend her last remaining guest.

"Thought as much," the old woman yelled

back. "You always *do* tend to bake up a storm when you're aggravated."

Frankie frowned and thought about arguing. Then she glanced around the kitchen. Three cakes, four pies, six loaves of bread, and five dozen cookies stood in silent confirmation of Mrs. Destry's statement.

She sighed heavily. It appeared that once again, the Four Golden Roses Saloon would be offering desserts for sale at the meal counter. With only her, Sean, Treasure, and Fiona in the hotel at the moment, they could never consume so much food. Thankfully, most of Maggie's customers had a sweet tooth. And happily, they were willing to pay for Frankie's baked goods. At least there would be some extra money for a while.

Shaking her head, Frankie walked across the room, pushed open the swinging door, and started down the long hall to the front parlor.

"What did you want, Mrs. Destry?" she said as she rounded the corner. "Some tea, perhaps?"

"Hello, Mary Frances," a male voice said quietly, with just a hint of disapproval.

Herbert!

Frankie jumped and instinctively lifted her hands to smooth the sides of her hair back from her face. It wasn't until she'd finished that she remembered the dough on her fingers.

Stifling a groan, she took another step into the parlor and looked at the tall, thin man in the corner. Watery blue eyes stared at her through the round lenses of his glasses. Herbert held his bowler hat in his left hand and a small bunch of roses in his right. His sedate black suit coat and pants were freshly brushed and his shoes were shined to a glossy finish. From a middle part, his wispy blond hair was slicked down on either side of his pink scalp, and even from a distance, Frankie could see his Adam's apple bobbing up and down frantically.

"Have I interrupted you at your work?" he finally said after looking her up and down distastefully.

A flush of embarrassment filled her cheeks and Frankie glanced down at herself with dismay. Her once pristine white apron was stained with who knew what from the morning's baking. Below the apron, splotches of flour dotted the hem of her faded gray work dress, and the cuffs of her gown were covered with bits of dough. Her fingers curled in on themselves in a futile attempt to hide the piecrust dough clinging to her skin. And when a stray lock of hair suddenly fell down across her forehead, Frankie blew it out of her way.

"Hello, Herbert," she said quietly. "Forgive my appearance, I wasn't expecting company."

"Then I am interrupting."

" 'Course you interrupted her," Mrs. Destry snapped from the safety of her chair, across the room. "A blind man could see that."

Herbert's lips tightened, but he nodded at the old woman civilly. "Quite right, madam." He glanced back at Frankie, his pale brows arched high on his forehead. "Am I right in assuming that you have changed your mind about accompanying me on a carriage ride this afternoon?"

This afternoon? For one wild, brief moment, Frankie's mind went blank. Then realization dawned and she almost groaned aloud. Was it Saturday already?

She wouldn't have thought it possible that a week had already passed. Yet there stood Herbert. And Herbert Featherstone would *never* make such a mistake. Prompt and dependable, Herbert was always where he said he would be. And if she was honest, Frankie would have to admit that in the year she'd been seeing him, this was the first time she'd forgotten about their weekly carriage ride.

"Oh dear. I am sorry. I don't know how this could have happened."

Mrs. Destry snorted and Frankie made a concerted effort not to glance her way.

"No harm done," Herbert said, though his features belied his words. He appeared to be extremely disappointed in her and Frankie couldn't blame him. Ignoring Mrs. Destry's presence entirely, he walked stiffly toward Mary Frances and held out the flowers to her. "If you'll excuse me, I'll be on my way and you may return to whatever it was you were doing."

Frankie clutched the bouquet tightly and preceded him into the hall. Stopping at the door, she looked up at him and forced a smile.

"I'm very sorry, Herbert. I can't think how I came to forget our engagement for today."

"These things happen," he said, and now

his voice was every bit as stiff as his spine. "Think no more about it."

Sunlight slipped in through the shining panes of one of the long narrow windows on either side of the front door and splashed across Herbert's narrow face. The light glinted off his spectacles and made him wince. Ducking his head slightly to avoid the light, he said, "I have been concerned about you this last week, Mary Frances."

She gazed up at him and absently noted how the sunlight seemed to sparkle on his shiny scalp. Strange she'd never noticed just how thin his hair was until now. Then she shook her head and asked, "I beg your pardon?"

He sighed and frowned his displeasure at her inattention. "I *said* I have been concerned for you this past week."

"Why is that, Herbert?"

"At our last meeting, you had expressed a worry over the business decision your father had made." When she didn't speak, he added, "The partner he was sending you?"

Odd, Frankie thought. She'd also never noticed that Herbert tended to lisp a bit when he pronounced an "s."

She pushed that thought aside though and answered him. "Yes, yes I was."

He nodded firmly, cocked his head to one side, and waited.

Frankie blinked uncertainly.

"If you would prefer that I not involve myself in your professional affairs," Herbert sniffed after a few long moments. "I will, of course, keep my concerns to myself."

"Oh no, Herbert," she said quickly, anxious to soothe him. For heaven's sake, she *must* pay closer attention to what he was saying. Frankie simply couldn't understand where her ability to concentrate had gone. Reaching out, she laid one hand on his forearm and smiled. "You're very kind to be concerned for me, Herbert. I appreciate it, truly."

He patted her hand briefly and straightened, wincing only slightly when the sun once again stabbed his eyes. "Not at all. And I do want to reiterate what I said last week, my dear."

"Yes?"

"I am quite sure your father has done what he thinks best and you should learn to put your trust in that."

"I'm sure you're right, Herbert," Frankie said, her attention already wandering to the fact that the man's Adam's apple seemed to be constantly on the move.

"You know, my dear," Herbert went on, warming to his subject, "a man has a duty to see to the welfare of the women in his family. I'm confident that your father's decision is one that we will all come to agree with."

"I suppose," she said and jumped when the front door opened suddenly, pushing Herbert at her and sending her staggering backward.

"See here!" Herbert's voice broke as he struggled to regain his footing and see that he didn't knock Mary Frances to the floor at the same time.

Sean walked in, took in the scene at a glance, and grinned at the other man. "Sorry.

I didn't think there would be anyone hangin' about behind the door there.''

"You might have knocked, sir," Herbert told him, and Frankie couldn't help but hear the quavering note in Herbert's voice as he took in the size of the other man.

Reluctantly, Frankie silently admitted that Sean was indeed a sight to behold.

His plain white shirt was open to the waist, the sleeves were rolled up past his elbows, and the soft material clung to his sweat-soaked skin. Black pants hugged his muscular thighs, and even Sean's grin seemed larger than life.

Stretching out his hand to Herbert, he said, "Sean Sullivan."

Herbert glanced at the outstretched hand warily for a long moment before shaking it. He winced at Sean's grip, and when his hand was released, Herbert reached into his breast pocket, pulled out a starched white handkerchief, and wiped Sean's sweat from his palm.

Frankie's gaze slipped from the tall thin man beside her to her new partner. Helplessly she found herself comparing the two men and was instantly angry with herself. Herbert Featherstone was a fine man. A respectable man with a good job at one of the biggest banks in the city. He was thoughtful, dependable, and honest, and he enjoyed the same simple, quiet pleasures that she did.

Did it really matter if just the sight of him had never turned her knees to water?

No.

Inhaling sharply, she reminded herself that excitement was the one thing in her life she'd had too much of. She'd been swayed by a charmer once already, and once was more than enough. No, Frankie told herself. She'd vowed to live the rest of her life in peace. And if nothing else, Herbert was certainly that.

Quiet, unexciting, *peaceful*.

"Are you a"—Herbert looked Sean up and down thoroughly before finishing—"*guest* in this hotel, my good man?"

Sean laughed, and the booming sound rose up in the stillness and settled down over them. "Lord no, man!" Waving his hands in front of him to indicate his sweaty, dirty clothing, he asked wryly, "Do ya think Frannie there would be rentin' a room to a man this dirty?"

Frankie glanced up at Herbert and watched his pale blond eyebrows arch high over his eyes. Apparently he hadn't missed Sean calling her Frannie.

"Then you'll pardon me for asking," Herbert went on. "If you are not residing at this place, what is your business here?"

One black eyebrow lifted. "Oh, I *reside* here all right—if by that ya mean am I livin' here."

"Naturally." Herbert shot Frankie a quick, questioning look. "That was my meaning. But didn't you say you are *not* a guest at the hotel?" Shaking his head slightly, he added, "I appear to be at a disadvantage here."

"Didn't Frannie tell ya?" Sean looked at her and shook his head in mock annoyance. "I'm her new partner."

Herbert's eyes widened and his long, narrow jaw dropped.

"And if ya don't mind *my* askin'," Sean

winked at Frankie, then turned his gaze back to the stupefied man in front of him, "who might *you* be?"

"This is Herbert Featherstone," Frankie answered for the man who appeared to be incapable of speech at the moment.

When she patted Herbert's forearm sympathetically, Sean noticed and frowned.

"Herbert, eh?" Crossing his arms over his broad chest, Sean asked, "Is he your intended, then?"

"Yes," she said, pouncing on the notion that that just might dissuade Sean Sullivan from kissing her again.

It might have worked if Herbert hadn't answered at the same time.

"No."

Sean looked from one to the other of them.

Herbert, eyes even wider, glanced down at Frankie.

"No," Frankie admitted.

"Yes," Herbert squeaked, obviously realizing too late what she wanted him to say.

Sean laughed delightedly and Frankie wanted to scream.

Herbert straightened, and even his rounded shoulders squared as much as they were able.

"If you'll excuse me," Herbert said over Sean's laughter. "I really should be going." He walked a wide circle around the other man, blotting tiny beads of sweat from his forehead as he went.

"I'll see you out," Frankie snapped and tossed one last glare at Sean before following her caller outside.

Alone in the hall, Sean stared at the closed door and frowned. All right, perhaps he shouldn't have laughed. But really, the idea of Mary Frances Donnelly being betrothed to a man like *that*! Why, the notion was ridiculous! A fine, strong woman like her needed a man to match her strength.

She needed him. Sean Sullivan.

His only problem seemed to lie in convincing her of that.

For just an instant, Sean allowed himself to recall the expression on old Herbert's face as the man looked Sean up and down.

Dismissal. He'd seen it too often to not recognize it.

And in his younger days, Sean had tried to combat that look in folks' eyes. He had dressed like one of them, had tried to talk like them, had even left his family once in a futile attempt to live a more "normal" life. But all he'd succeeded in doing was losing himself.

Those people who judged him without knowing him weren't fooled by the changes he'd made. If anything, there was even more disapproval in their attitudes toward him. As if they thought less of him for trying so desperately to be what he clearly wasn't. On that point, Sean shared their disgust and quickly returned to the life and family that defined him.

He'd never looked back.

He snorted a laugh at the memories of his past foolishness and pushed one hand through his sweat-dampened hair. Who would have guessed that a woman would bring him to the same battle once again? The battle between who he was and who he could never be. Ah, but Frannie Donnelly wasn't just *any* woman . . . was she?

Over the last few years, *he* had usually been the one running away from some woman with wedding ring dreams. He'd never really thought he was the type of man who'd do well in a double harness. Still and all, though, he'd never expected to find a woman like Mary Frances, either.

And wouldn't you bloody well know it, he told himself. *Now that I've found the one woman I could build a life around . . . she isn't interested.*

For just a moment, he allowed his imagination free rein. Dimly he could see himself and Frannie together. Riding in a fine, silver-trimmed carriage, he in a splendid black suit and she dressed all in sunshine-yellow, with diamonds at her throat. How grand it would be, he thought with a smile. And just for good measure, he imagined two or three children, all well-behaved, of course, and dressed as befit the fine life surrounding them.

He blinked suddenly and the dream image dissolved like sugar in tea.

Stepping back a bit, Sean looked through the long, narrow window at the couple outside. Sunshine fell across Frannie's flour-speckled hair and set it to glowing like a candle flame. Even in her dirty apron and shapeless dress, she was enough to stir his body into eager awareness.

Sean lifted one hand and grasped the window frame. He watched silently as Herbert

Featherstone bent down stiffly and placed a chaste kiss on Frannie's forehead. Sean's insides trembled and his fingers tightened on the wood beneath his hand.

Apparently Featherstone felt comfortable enough to give Frannie a kiss—no matter how bad a one it was—in public. Well, Sean thought grimly as he turned away and started for the backyard, old Herbert didn't know it yet, but he'd just kissed Frannie for the last time.

Mary Frances found him outside, solemnly pacing off the empty lot that lay alongside the hotel. His long legs striding through the patch of wildflowers, his gaze locked on the ground. Sean was concentrating so intently that he didn't notice her until she was standing right in front of him.

He grinned at her, and Frankie felt an answering curl of pleasure deep inside. That dimple of his truly was a dangerous thing. Taking a deep, steadying breath, she told herself to ignore his practiced charm. For men like Sean Sullivan, her father, and Conor, charm was nothing more than a means to an end.

"Ya look lovely today, Frannie."

Still covered in flour, she knew very well what she looked like—a mess. But the fact that he complimented her anyway was simply more proof to her that his flattery was as meaningless as she'd thought it to be.

Ignoring his statement, Frankie lifted her chin slightly and said, "I wanted to speak to you about Mr. Featherstone."

"Ah . . . your intended, ya mean?"

She flushed and gritted her teeth.

"We aren't formally betrothed," she admitted, then added, "Yet. I simply wanted to say that I was sorry if he made you feel uncomfortable."

His ever-present smile faded a bit before he answered her quietly. "I'm long past carin' what folks like him think of me, Frannie."

Maybe he was, but Frankie had found herself in the odd position of wanting to defend him to Herbert. She'd seen the disdain in Herbert's eyes as he'd wiped his palm after shaking hands with Sean. She'd heard the unmistakable tone of superiority in Herbert's voice when he'd spoken to Sean.

And, angry as she was with Sean, she'd been even more furious with Herbert.

"Nevertheless," she said softly, "I apologize."

"It's not your place to apologize for him."

Their gazes locked, and she felt as though he was staring into her soul. Briefly she wondered what he saw. Then something inside her quaked at the thought, and she tore her gaze from his.

Searching for something to say that would send them back on the path to casualness, Frankie blurted, "What are you doing out here?"

He seemed to sense what she was trying to do, and after a long moment, he must have decided to play along. Glancing over his shoulder at the grassy lot, he answered her question with a question. "This land belongs to us, doesn't it?"

Us. She inhaled sharply and said, "Yes. Why?"

"Just wanted to make sure."

"Lovely, isn't it?" Her gaze swept over the neatly cropped grass and the small patches of wildflowers dotting the green expanse. Sitting as it did in the midst of a city block, the wide patch of grass and flowers looked like an oasis of color. In the corner of the lot stood an ancient apple tree, heavy with small white blossoms that filled the air with a delicate scent. Without even thinking about it, Frankie began to walk toward the old tree. Sean followed quietly.

Looking straight up into the tangle of branches and the small bits of sky she could see between the leaves, Frankie spoke more to herself than to Sean. "I keep meaning to hang a small swing from one of the thicker limbs. How lovely it would be to sit here on a summer night and watch the stars."

Sean said nothing, but he reached up, plucked a cluster of blossoms from a low-hanging branch, and held it out to her.

Frankie took it, lifted it to her nose, and sniffed, drawing the fragrance deep inside her lungs.

"There's a hotelier in Monterey who's been trying to buy my hotel and this land for years." She pushed a wind-blown lock of hair out of her eyes and glanced at Sean. "He wants to tear down the Four Roses and use both lots to build a big hotel. One to rival the Occidental.''

"Hmmph." Sean grinned at her. "I can imagine what you told him to do with that idea."

Frankie smiled back at him and ran the tip of one finger over a dainty flower. "I just told him I wasn't interested in selling. I like my"— she looked at Sean—"*our* hotel just the way it is."

"Quiet?" he asked. "Old?"

"Tranquil," she corrected with a slight frown. "Refined."

"Uninteresting."

Sighing, she turned her back on the tree and leaned against the weathered, peeling bark. She felt the gnarled bits of wood bite into her flesh as she stared up at him.

"If you think so little of the Four Roses, why are you determined to keep your share of it?"

He propped the flat of one hand against the tree trunk just above her head and leaned down. "Because with a few changes, it'll be perfect."

Frankie scowled at him. "No changes."

"Now, now, Frannie girl." He shook his head. "I'm a partner, remember?"

She inched further away from his arm, lifted the cluster of blossoms to her nose, and hid behind their beauty. "What kind of changes?"

"Ah, off the top of me head, I'd say—an elevator . . ."

"Elevator?" Eyes wide, she argued, "They're dangerous, from what I hear. Imagine people trusting their lives to the strength of a few wires and cables." She shook her head firmly. "No. Besides, I don't think there *is* an elevator this side of St. Louis."

"We'll be the first, then." He ignored her sputtering refusals and simply went on, "And a few more private baths, I'm thinkin'."

"Whatever for?"

"To bring the hotel out of the past, lass. It'll change the whole feel of the place." He rubbed his jaw thoughtfully. "And folks'll appreciate the privacy, I'm sure. No one likes the idea of shavin' and bathin' with strangers."

"Changes cost money, Mr. Sullivan."

"Ah now, Frannie," he crooned and bent closer to her. "We're not back to *that*, are we? And have I told ya that I do so love the sound of me name slippin' across those sweet lips of yours?"

Infuriating man! Frankie couldn't remember a time when she'd lost her temper more than she had in the last week. Why, even her father hadn't pushed her to distraction with such regularity.

"These changes of yours would cost a good deal of money, Mr. . . . Sean."

He grinned. "I'll earn it."

"And how do you propose to do that, may I ask?" She waved her free hand at his shirt, still open to the waist, and deliberately kept herself from looking at that expanse of muscle again. "By showing off your . . . person?"

Sean's smile widened and he set his other palm against the tree trunk and successfully caught her between his outstretched arms. Then he leaned in so close to her, Frankie felt the warmth of his breath brush her cheek. "So ya think I look good enough to earn a few dollars, do ya?"

Good heavens. That wasn't what she'd meant at all. Was it?

"And would you be willin' to pay to have a gander at me, Frannie?"

Fighting back her own embarrassment, she snapped, "Why should I have to pay, sir, when you seem insistent on parading before me free of charge?"

"Oooh . . ." He shivered theatrically. "That tongue of yours can be razor-sharp sometimes, Frannie love."

He stared down at her for a heartbeat longer before turning to look out over the lot. "As to earnin' the money, well. I've a few ideas."

"I am not selling this land, Sean Sullivan." She ducked beneath one of his arms and took a few quick steps away from him. "The children in the neighborhood play here. It's a lovely spot for my guests to come and take the sun."

"Don't get your hump over the wagon, Frannie," Sean told her, ignoring her outraged features. "I don't want to sell it. I want to use it."

"How?" Her gaze narrowed, she stared at him. But he wasn't looking at her. He was looking at the empty lot, and his eyes held a definite gleam. When he finally turned to her, though, he didn't answer her question.

All he said was, "You'll see soon enough."

Chapter 7

"**P**apa, please . . . you promised."

"Now, Mary Frances, it isn't so bad." Kevin Donnelly bent down and tugged gently on one of his daughter's long red-gold braids. "You'll like our new house. It's a grand place."

"I like this house, Papa." Mary Frances rubbed her small fists against her eyes and tried very hard not to cry. Her papa hated it when his girls cried. "You promised this time we could stay here forever and ever," she reminded him.

The little girl watched her father's smile slip away and thought she saw a tear at the corner of his eye. But that couldn't be so. Everyone knew that mamas and papas didn't cry. As if he knew what she was thinking, Kevin's lips curved in another of his wide grins and he reached for her. Hugging her tightly, he whispered in her ear, "I know what I said, Mary Frances, and it's sorry I am that I can't keep that promise."

She burrowed her head against his shoulder and inhaled the comforting scents of tobacco and licorice. Her papa had a fondness for licorice.

"But I'll make you a new promise this very minute, all right?"

Sniffling, Mary Frances nodded and wrapped her small arms around her father's neck. She rubbed her cheek against his and took comfort in the familiar scratch of his whiskers.

He patted her back softly and said, "I promise that you and your sisters will each have your own room in our new house." Pulling back slightly, he looked her in the eye, wiped away a single tear that hovered on her lower lid, and asked, "Would ya like that?"

"Yes, Papa," she lied because she knew it was no use telling him that she didn't want her own room. She wanted to stay where she was. In their house. With the trees in the yard and her very best friend right next door. It wasn't so bad sharing a bed with Maggie and Alice.

She would do it forever if only it meant that the Donnellys could stay in the home Kevin had promised would be theirs forever.

But Mama had already packed up her grandma's china cups. And boxes of clothing sat by the door. There was nothing Frankie could do. They were moving again.

And even as she felt her papa's arms slide around her and lift her off the floor in a warm hug, little Mary Frances knew that he probably wouldn't keep this promise either.

Sitting straight up in bed, Frankie blinked at the surrounding darkness, and for a moment she didn't even know where she was. Then she remembered the dream.

Moving day. The last one. The move that had taken them all to the Four Golden Roses Saloon. At least her papa had kept his promise that time. The saloon was their last house. And she and her sisters had gotten their own rooms.

But there were no trees to swing from and no best friends living right next door, and Frankie had never really felt that the saloon was home. In fact, she thought, she hadn't really loved a place until she'd moved into her lovely room on the ground floor of the hotel four years ago.

Then she'd begun to build the home she'd always dreamed of. A quiet, comfortable place where she would always belong. Where nothing would ever change.

She swung her feet off the bed, leaned over, and picked up a match from the small brass vase on her bedside table. Quickly she struck the match and held the tiny flame to the wick in an oil lamp beside her bed. Once the wavering flame had steadied a bit, Frankie set the glass globe in place and turned to look around her room.

The familiar sights chased away the remnants of uneasiness left behind by her dream, and she found herself smiling at the cozy nest she'd created for herself.

Starched white curtains fluttered at the windows, looking a bit like visiting spirits in the dim light. The walls were a soft summer-blue, and a local artist had painted a border of violets and ivy which seemed to cling to the ceiling. An oval frame hanging on the far wall held a portrait of her parents, and on the wall opposite, a group of ten small frames were clustered. Within each frame was a tiny, detailed painting created by the same talented artist. There were ones of the hotel, the saloon, the mine, and the family ranch. There were portraits of her and each of her sisters, but the last two renderings were pure fancy.

Using her father's vivid descriptions as a guide, Frankie had instructed the artist to paint the Donnelly home in Ireland. The small, thatched-roof cottage surrounded by green fields and flowering bushes was, to hear Kevin tell it, an exact reproduction of the home he remembered.

The last painting, though, had been born from Frankie's own imagination. Her childish dreams and fancies had been brought to life in the guise of a three-story home with a wide front porch, two giant oak trees—complete with swings—in the yard, and six children running and playing with one another and an assortment of pets.

Even from across the room, Frankie could see that last painting vividly in her mind's eye. It had been her dream for so long, she didn't really need the painting at all. But somehow, having her fondest wish committed to canvas had made it seem more real. More possible.

She smiled and turned her gaze to the two overstuffed chairs drawn up close to the now-empty hearth. Each of the forest-green chairs was big enough to accommodate two people easily. On cold, stormy days, there was nothing Frankie liked better than to curl up in one of those chairs beside a roaring fire and imagine the face of the man who would one day sit across from her.

She slid off the bed and walked barefoot

across the braided rug covering the pine-planked floor to the chairs. Running her fingers over the soft, plush fabric, Frankie glanced at the other empty chair and envisioned Herbert sitting there.

She frowned slightly as even her image of the tall, thin man seemed dwarfed by the chair. In her mind's eye, she watched him twitch and fidget, looking for a comfortable position. His spine rigid, he tried to prop his bony elbows on the arms of the chairs, only to discover that they were too wide apart to accommodate him. She imagined Herbert frowning at that.

And then all at once, the image wavered, shifted, and Sean was there.

Frankie blinked and dug her fingers into the chair back.

Now the vision of Sean was clear, distinct. The big man settled into the green chair as though it had been made for him. His big, muscled form looked completely at home. Strong forearms braced on the chair arms, Sean leaned his head back against the overstuffed fabric and stretched out his long legs toward the fire.

Frankie sucked in a deep breath and stared as her imagination took one more step.

She could see the vision of Sean glancing to his right and grinning as an imaginary Frankie hurried to him and plopped herself down on his lap. The two people held each other tightly, and when their lips met in a hungry kiss, Mary Frances said aloud, "Enough!"

Instantly the images faded, and she was left

alone in her room. Her insides quaking, Frankie stared at the empty chair as if she'd never seen it before. What on earth was she thinking? What perverse corner of her brain had conjured up such a ridiculous image?

She and Sean? Together in her room? Why, the very idea was laughable!

A sudden chill swamped her and Frankie rubbed her hands up and down her arms in an attempt to ward it off. But the chill went deeper than that, and she knew it. She'd felt it before, though never quite as starkly.

It was the disquieting chill of loneliness. A cold that bit into a person's soul and threatened never to leave.

And somehow, she thought, knowing that her vision of her and Sean together could never actually happen made the ache all the more painful.

A long moment passed before she deliberately turned her gaze away. She got up and strode across the room to the foot of her bed, snatched her dressing gown, and pulled it on over her plain white cotton nightdress.

Just slipping into the silky violet-colored fabric made her feel a bit better. She'd purchased it the year before in a wild concession to vanity. At the time, she'd told herself that no one else would ever see her wearing it and so she'd nothing to lose by indulging herself. No one ever need know that proper, plain, sparrowlike Mary Frances Donnelly secretly adored the feel of expensive silk against her flesh.

She tied the belt at her waist, pushed her loose, waist-length hair back from her face, and walked to the door. Turning for one last quick look at the chairs by the fire, she shook her head.

The problems she'd seen in her imagination could be easily solved. She'd simply get Herbert a different chair. One that would suit him.

A small voice in the back of her mind suggested a straight-backed wooden chair with a cane seat—but she ignored it.

All she needed was a cup of tea. To help her calm down and sleep.

The hotel was silent, dark. But it was a comforting silence, born of familiarity. Many times over the past four years, Frankie had risen for a late-night cup of tea. She'd always found the solitude soothing.

Her feet cold against the bare wood floor, Frankie hurried toward the kitchen where the banked fire would offer at least a bit of warmth. Spring nights in San Francisco could be cold and damp, and Frankie was grateful that summer was almost upon them.

Humming softly under her breath, she pushed against the swinging door, stepped into the kitchen, and screamed.

Sean fell backward at the same time she leaped out of his way. Clutching his heart, he bellowed, "Holy Mother of God, woman! You near scared ten years out of me life!"

Sucking in a deep breath, Frankie hung her head forward and tried to calm her racing heart. After a moment she looked up at him and shook her head. "I could say the same to you!"

"Aye, I guess ya could at that," he allowed

and gave her a sheepish smile. "Lordy, but you move quiet, Frannie. I never heard ya comin'."

She didn't bother to tell him that if she'd heard *him*, she never would have entered the kitchen at all. She'd have turned around and raced back to the safety and solitude of her room. But it was too late for that. If she left now, he would know that she was leery of being alone with him.

Besides, she thought finally, it was *her* hotel, wasn't it? *Her* kitchen? Was she going to allow her own fanciful imagination to frighten her so badly that she had to cower in her room for fear that Sean Sullivan would seduce her? Hmmph! Frankie sidestepped him neatly and walked to the stove. After grabbing the kettle, she went to the sink, cranked the iron pump until the pot was half full of water, then carried it back to the stove.

Glancing at him, she said firmly, "I'm sorry if I startled you. But I often come in here for a cup of tea late at night."

"Have ya got enough water in there for two, d'ya think?"

In the light of a single lamp Sean had obviously lit before her arrival, Frankie studied him. Her gaze moved over his sleep- rumpled hair, the half-buttoned shirt hanging outside his trousers, and his bare feet. Instantly she recalled her dream image of him, stretched out comfortably in her room. Heavens, this was suddenly all too real. Too . . . disconcerting.

But at the same time, Frankie knew she had to accustom herself to being around the man.

After all, unless a miracle occurred, he'd made it perfectly clear that he had no intention of leaving.

Tugging the edges of her dressing gown tighter, she disregarded the fact that it was the middle of the night. As for their improper dress . . . well, no one had to know, did they? Apparently he had as much trouble sleeping as she did. Perhaps this was an opportunity for them to become friends. Or at the very least . . . less adversarial.

"There should be enough for two, I think," she finally said and caught her breath at the smile he gave her.

"That's grand. Thanks." He moved off toward the pantry, saying, "To show my appreciation, I'll even brew the tea meself."

She tilted her head and looked at him. "Are you insinuating that my tea isn't quite what it should be?"

He pulled his head back far enough to see past the pantry door and gave her another quick smile. "Now, Frannie, not all of us are blessed with the knowledge of how to brew the best tea."

"Hmmm . . . it sounds as though Rose has been talking to you."

He laughed quietly. "I take it mine is not the first complaint you've heard, then?"

"Hardly."

Since he was fully prepared to make the tea, Frankie seated herself at the scrubbed white pine table. Idly she toyed with the edges of the crocheted runner lying across the middle of the table.

With quick, efficient movements, Sean set the canister of tea and the teapot on the table, then turned to stoke the fire in the stove. As warmth radiated from the cast iron, Frankie sighed and drew her legs beneath her on the chair.

Absently she rubbed her near-frozen toes as Sean began to talk again.

"To tell ya the truth," he said as he scooped tea leaves into the waiting pot, "I was lookin' for one of those cakes I saw in here earlier."

"Oh. I sent most of them over to the saloon. Maggie's always delighted to have desserts for her customers."

"Ya didn't send *all* of them, did ya?"

She half chuckled at the disappointment in his voice. "No." Pointing to a far cabinet, she said, "I kept one of the cakes for the hotel."

"Ah." He slapped his palms together and rubbed them briskly with anticipation. He crossed to the cabinet, opened it, and sighed. "Lovely! The chocolate one!"

In seconds, it seemed, he'd brought the cake to the table, cut them both generous slices, then poured the now-boiling water into the teapot. Covering the flower-sprigged pot with a clean towel, he announced, "Now in another few minutes or so, that tea'll be ready."

Frankie nodded and lifted her fork with her right hand.

"Are your feet cold, Frannie?"

"Hmmm?"

"Your feet," he said, pointing to where her left hand was still rubbing her toes, "are they cold?"

"Not so much anymore."

Sean pulled out the chair next to her, sat down, and slapped his thighs with the palms of his hands. "Put them here."

"I beg your pardon?"

"Your feet. Put them here. In me lap."

"I'll do no such thing." Frankie straightened up, pulled the hem of her robe over her feet, and tucked it beneath them.

"Ah, for God's sake, Frannie." Sean leaned toward her. "I only want to rub your feet so's ya don't catch cold."

"It wouldn't be proper."

One corner of his mouth lifted in a sardonic grin, and his dimple deepened.

"And is it proper for you to be sittin' here with me—in the middle of the night—wearin' only that delicious-lookin' silky thing?" He shook his head gently. "Ah, Frannie love. You're a sore temptation to this poor Irish lad."

Guiltily, Frankie glanced at her dressing gown. True, it was a lovely thing, but it was also very concealing. Not a trace of her nightgown could be seen, and besides, she thought wryly, her short, slightly plump body could hardly be termed alluring. If he was indeed being tempted, the temptation was in his own mind. But Frankie strongly suspected that his statement was more proof of his inability to talk without using Irish exaggeration.

"I'm quite decently covered, thank you."

"True enough," he commented, "but the delightful wrappings you're wearin' only make a man wonder what it is you're coverin'."

"*That*, Mr. Sullivan you will never discover."

"Ah, Frannie girl." He sighed heavily. "Ya must never say never, ya know. In this life, anything is possible."

"Not always."

"But often enough to keep life interestin'."

"*Mr.* Sullivan," she said, "there is no reason for you to continually pretend an interest in me that we both know goes no further than my hotel."

"Our hotel."

"Fine. *Our* hotel." Sighing, she closed her eyes briefly and tried to gather her composure. In a softer, more reasonable tone, she said "Sean, I am not accustomed to being showered with flattery—no matter how false—so I would appreciate it very much if you would refrain from insisting that I am some sort of legendary siren."

"Siren?" His eyes narrowed slightly and he cocked his head to study her. After a long moment, he commented, "Now, I wouldn't call ya a siren, exactly. Those luscious females spent their days callin' men to their deaths."

Frannie blinked, surprised that he would know about such things. Her expression must have revealed what she was thinking because he smiled at her.

"Ah, I've caught ya off your guard, haven't I, Frannie?" He shook his head and forced his amiable features into a mock frown. "That'll teach ya to be makin' judgments about folks with nothin' to base them on."

"You're absolutely right," she conceded with a nod. "My apologies."

"Nicely said, lass. Apology accepted." Inhaling sharply, he went on, "Now, as for the other . . . I think I would call you more of a fairy than a siren."

"A fairy?"

"Aye. Or perhaps a wood sprite."

"Oh, for heaven's sake."

"Now, now, let's not be belittlin' the fairies, Frannie." He glanced over his shoulder as if looking for the imaginary creatures. "They don't take to bein' made fun of, ya know."

"Sean . . ."

"As for what ya said about false flattery." Sean turned his gaze on her, and Frankie was caught by the gleam shining in their clear blue depths. "My blarney's as good as the next man's, I reckon," he admitted. Then, in a hushed whisper, he added, "But when I look at you, girl . . . I'm lucky I can talk and breathe at the same time—never mind tryin' to make up meaningless compliments."

He looked serious, she thought. But how in the world was she supposed to believe him? No man had *ever* called her beautiful. Even her own father never went further than to say that Mary Frances was blessed with a fine Irish face.

Hardly a song to her loveliness.

"No, Mary Frances Donnelly," Sean said, leaning toward her just a bit. "When I look at you, the only words that come out of me mouth are the God's truth."

Seconds passed into minutes and still she

sat there quietly, captured by the warmth in his eyes and the earnestness on his features. Her heartbeat quickened and she couldn't deny that everything he'd said had soaked into her soul like rain into dry earth.

But she couldn't afford to believe him. She couldn't allow herself to take that chance. Frankie had been raised around his kind of man. She knew all too well that what they said usually had very little to do with what they did. And though Sean's intentions might be honorable enough, his very nature would work against him.

Sooner or later, the Irish rover in him would spring to life and he would be gone. Following the next dream. Chasing tomorrow's promise and turning his back on today.

Instinctively she stiffened as if donning protective armor. "Sean," Frankie said, and silently congratulated herself on the even tone her voice carried. "I think it would be best for both of us if you would stop making improper comments about my person. Otherwise I will have to retire to my room."

"Now, Frannie," he said softly, "must ya get your Irish up tonight? Can we not sit here and talk together? It's been quite a while since I've had the opportunity to sit and chat with a lovely—"

She frowned slightly.

"Excuse me—*lady*. I promise you I'll keep me thoughts to meself." He raised his right hand and swore earnestly, "I only want to share a cup of tea with you and . . ."

She looked at him warily.

"Warm your feet," he added with an innocent shrug.

Her feet *were* cold. And if the truth be told,
it had been a long time since she'd enjoyed a
late-night chat with anyone other than one of
the maids. Besides, she thought, this might be
a good chance for her to find out a bit more
about her new partner. So far, all she'd learned
was that he was big, loved to talk, and apparently had a family on the way to take up residence in her hotel.

Chewing on her bottom lip, Frankie looked
from his uplifted palm to his sober features.
Too, maybe this was a chance to find out just
how good his word was. If he didn't keep his
promise, and went back to spouting meaningless flattery, she could simply go to her room.
At the very least, she would have her suspi-
cions confirmed that he was like every other
Irishman, and she could cease wavering. She
would know once and for all that Sean Sullivan was no different than Conor, her father,
or any of her father's cronies.

Slowly she uncurled her legs and hesitantly
set her right foot on Sean's thigh.

"That's grand. The other one too, Frannie."

Frankie glanced guiltily over her shoulder
as if expecting someone to materialize from
the shadows and scold her for her improper
behavior. When it didn't happen, she did as
he asked.

Sean's big hands curled around her toes and
the shock of his warmth rocketed up the
length of her legs to spread throughout her
body. It was more than just the heat of his

hands, too. There was something else. Something that sent lightning bolts of awareness skittering over her. She'd noticed the feeling before. It seemed to happen whenever he touched her, however casually. In some corner of her soul, it felt as though a small part of her recognized his touch.

Gently he began to rub her cold feet, and tingles raced along her spine and sent her heartbeat into a ragged rhythm.

Frankie's fingers gripped the edge of her chair seat and she held on for dear life.

"So, Frannie," he whispered, "why can't you sleep?"

She only looked at him.

"Bad dreams?" he asked.

The deep rumble of his voice, added to the warmth of his hands and the care in his tone, almost made Frankie wish that things could have been different between them. There was something about Sean Sullivan that called to her. And it looked as though it would take every ounce of her self-control to keep from feeling too much for him.

His big, strong hands moved carefully on her feet as if she were made of the finest crystal. She lifted her gaze and noticed the dark shadow of whisker stubble on his jaws and wondered what it would feel like to rub her cheek against his.

"Me?" Sean spoke again as if Frankie had asked him a question. "I had a terrible dream."

"I'm sorry," she said softly, shaking her head and forcing herself to pay attention to what he was saying, not just the timbre of his voice.

"Oh aye," he went on and held both her feet in his lap with one big hand while the other reached across the table to pour milk into the waiting teacups.

"I don't take milk in my tea," she protested halfheartedly.

"Just tonight then," he coaxed. "Hot, sweet, and milky tea makes for a good night's sleep." Then he dropped two teaspoons of sugar into each cup.

She quieted again, content suddenly with the feel of his hand on her ankles.

When he'd poured the tea and stirred both cups, Sean slid the first one to her and drew the other one close. Frankie lifted her cup and took a small sip. Hot and sweet, as he'd promised, the liquid warmed her insides as effectively as Sean was warming her outside.

His thumb moved gently over her flesh, and after he'd taken a drink of his tea, he set the cup down and moved both hands over her feet and ankles. Idly, he went on talking.

"This nightmare I had . . ."

"Yes?"

"A terrible thing." His palms cupped her heels and his fingers brushed over her ankles. "I was lost and alone, starvin' to death, and I couldn't talk to tell anyone."

A small smile curved Frankie's lips. "Strange," she said quietly, "somehow I can't quite imagine you silent."

"Thankfully, it's only happened in a

dream," he said. "But at least you're smilin' again."

Frankie set her cup down on its matching saucer and almost sighed when she felt his hands slide over the soles of her feet.

"Frannie," he asked quietly, "will you answer something for me?

"Hmmm...?" The tea and his touch had combined to make her feel warm and lazy.

"Will ya tell me what is it about me that bothers you so?"

Chapter 8

The glimmering shine in his blue eyes could have been anything, but to Frankie, it looked like disappointment. A small stab of guilt twisted inside her. She studied him silently for a long moment. His sun-bronzed skin seemed to glow like burnished copper in the lamplight. His wavy black hair was tumbled across his forehead, and his well-shaped mouth was curved in a tiny, almost sad smile.

For such a big man, he suddenly seemed ... defenseless.

"It's not you, Sean ..."

His smile widened just a bit, though disbelief was etched into his features.

"Really," Frankie added and gasped when his fingers curled over her bare toes. She sighed, then went on slowly, "It's more the *kind* of man you are."

"And what kind is that?"

"Irish."

He snorted a short laugh. "You're Irish too, Frannie girl."

"Yes, so I know what I'm talking about."

"What *are* you talkin' about?" He did want to know what she was thinking and why she always seemed to be on the verge of flight whenever he was near. But, Lord help him, keeping his mind on what she was saying was almighty difficult when she kept scooting about and moving her legs against his lap.

He'd known from the first moment he'd seen her that it would be magic to touch her. Whether she knew it or not, Mary Frances Donnelly was a sensual creature. A woman made to touch and be touched. A woman born to be caressed and loved.

Swallowing heavily, Sean forced his hands to stray no higher than her ankles. He'd promised to be good—and dammit, so he would— if it killed him.

But every stroke he made brought a new, throbbing ache to his body. His groin tightened uncomfortably against his pants, and it was all he could do to stifle the groan building in his chest.

Still, he had to go slow. Move carefully. He must show her that she enjoyed his touch. He must convince her that she wanted and needed him as much as he did her.

"I'm talking about dreamers," she said in a whisper, and the word hovered in the air between them. "And Irish dreamers in particular, since they're the kind I know best."

"There's nothin' wrong with dreamin', lass," he said as his hands caressed her now warm feet. At the moment, he conceded silently, he had quite a few dreams of his own. And she was in every one of them.

"True." She sighed and straightened a bit as if afraid of relaxing too deeply in his presence. "Their dreams are fine. It's the day-to-day living that gives them, and those around them, trouble."

"What kind of trouble?"

She stared at him for a long moment, and Sean could see that she was trying to decide whether to answer him.

And then she started talking.

"Once before," she started, "about three years ago, I listened to a smooth talker—much like you, with his charm and his flattery. But I found out that what a man says isn't always what he means."

"What did he do to ya?" Sean wanted to know. He also wanted to know who the bastard was so he could go give the man a few sound thumps about the head and shoulders.

"It doesn't really matter anymore."

"Aye, it does."

Frankie inhaled sharply, then blew the air out again. "He flattered me, told me he loved me—and then one night that summer, he simply left town. Without a word."

Sean cursed the man wherever he was and said, "So, because of one fool, all men are to be tarred with the same brush?" She opened her mouth, and he held up one hand to cut her off. "Never mind. I don't think I want an answer to that just yet."

She nodded and gave him a small smile. He didn't see any pain in her eyes. It was a sure bet, he thought, that the man no longer mattered to her. All that remained was the bitter lesson she'd learned.

Strange, they had been talking about dreams a moment before. And as Sean studied her, he thought that she herself looked like a dream.

Frankie shook her head and Sean watched her hair spill over her shoulders. Lamplight played on the pale, fiery strands, giving them a life of their own. His gaze shifted to her face and the exquisite curve of her throat.

The edges of her silk dressing gown had slipped apart, making the white cotton nightgown visible. Her lush, full breasts pressed against the fabric when she moved, and Sean could see the small, rigid buds of her nipples.

He licked his suddenly dry lips and bit down on the inside of his cheek. Somehow, he managed to keep his hands moving, gently stroking her flesh. If he gave in to his urge to sweep her into his arms, he knew the spell would break and his time with her would end.

Determinedly he gathered up enough strength to meet her gaze squarely, and it was only then that he noticed the faraway look in her eyes.

"Have ya never had a dream come true?" he whispered, and his hands stilled.

"Only one," she said quietly, and her gaze began to move about the homey, welcoming kitchen.

"This hotel?"

"Yes."

Then she began to talk and Sean felt as though she'd forgotten all about him and was talking as much to herself as to anyone else.

"I'd wanted a place of my own for so long, you see." She breathed slowly, deeply, and folded her hands neatly in her lap. "It was everything to me. A place to belong. A place I'd never have to leave if I didn't want to. A place that was mine."

"Ah." He nodded in understanding. "And then I come along, is that it?"

She darted a quick look at him. "It wasn't *you*, Sean. It was the fact that my father would do this to me. Sell my home. The one thing I'd wanted all my life."

"But maybe," he said quietly, aware of the building anger in her voice, "maybe Kevin wasn't so much doin' something *to* you as something *for* me."

"What?"

"Well, my family and me, we've been lookin' for a place for quite a while. You're not the only one who had a dream of a home, ya know."

"I suppose not," she conceded. "But for how long? You're a rover by nature, Sean."

The barb hit home. He'd been on the move most of his life, and truth to tell, he'd enjoyed the constant travel. Every morning looking out on a new world. Every day different from the day before. New faces, new towns, new adventures.

It was how he'd lived his life. And it had been a good one. He'd never before imagined that the day would come when he'd be interested in planting his big feet in one spot. Until now. One look at Mary Frances had been enough to convince him he didn't want to take another step unless she was with him.

And maybe that notion wasn't half bad. She could travel with him, couldn't she? Of course she could. The question was, *would* she?

Would she be able to uproot herself? For that matter, could he really be content in one place?

He didn't know, God help him.

All he knew for certain was that he wanted Frannie in his life.

How he was going to make that happen, he had no idea.

Naturally, though, with the luck of the Irish at work, the woman he wanted couldn't see him for dust.

"I'll grant you that I've spent most of me life wanderin' about. But a man can change, Frannie."

"And a leopard can change his spots?" Sadly she shook her head.

"I'm a man, not a bloody cat."

"And you're a rover, not a stayer."

"You're wrong, lass."

"No, I'm not." Straightening up, she pulled her feet from his lap, tugged the edges of her dressing gown tight together, and lifted her chin. "Maybe a part of me wishes I was . . . but I'm not wrong."

"Frannie . . ."

She held up one hand to silence him. "Oh, I know that right now, for some reason, you've convinced yourself that you're happy here. That you want to stay."

"*You're* the reason!" Frustration was beginning to mount despite his best efforts. "If you'll let me talk . . ."

"But sooner or later, Sean Sullivan, your wandering blood will ring true—and you'll be off." She stood up, shivering just a bit when her bare feet touched the cold plank floor. Then she looked down at him, and Sean ground his teeth together at the stamp of sad resignation on her face. "You wouldn't set out to hurt me or anyone else. I *do* believe that. But it would happen all the same." She lifted one hand and reached toward him, and he held his breath, sure she was going to touch him. He could almost feel her hand cupped against his cheek. But then her hand dropped to her side as suddenly as a puppet's whose strings have been cut.

Taking a deep breath, she exhaled slowly and said, "When that day comes, Sean—when you finally take it into your head to go—I won't be the sad, lonely woman you leave behind. I refuse to let that happen to me again."

In the sudden silence, he tried to talk, but for the life of him, he couldn't think of a bloody thing to say. How could he argue with a woman who had already made up her mind about him? And if he *could* argue . . . What could he say? How could he prove to her he wasn't going to leave?

When he wasn't even sure of that himself.

"As partners in the hotel," she said, and Sean blinked, forcing himself to concentrate, "there is no reason why we can't be friendly. I'm sure that if we both make every effort, we'll be able to work together companionably—for however long you're here."

Friendly. Companionably.

For however long he's there.

Sean grumbled under his breath, but somehow managed to keep his thoughts to himself.

"All I ask," she added, as she walked to the hallway door, "is that when you're ready to leave, you sell your share of the hotel to me. I'd not like to have to worry about a stranger coming in here again."

Bloody hell.

The woman had a head as hard as the stony ground of Ireland.

"Sean?"

"What?"

"Will you?"

"Will I what?"

"Will you promise to sell your share of the hotel to me when you're ready to leave?"

"Oh." He couldn't help the sarcasm coloring his voice. "*This* you're willin' to take me word on, eh?"

She flushed, but much to Sean's disgust, the color in her cheeks only made her more lovely.

"Yes, I will."

"But you won't take my word for it that I'm not leavin'?"

Slowly she shook her head.

"Fine, then." He pushed himself to his feet and stood to face her solemnly. "I give you me word. If I should decide to leave town, I'll sign over my share of the hotel to you."

"Thank you."

She pushed against the swinging door and

had almost stepped through it into the hall when his voice stopped her.

"But Mary Frances."

Half turning, she stared at him through sorrowful green eyes. "Yes?"

"I'm makin' another promise here and now."

"Please don't."

"Listen to me well, Frannie girl," he said. He took a step toward her. "On my oath, I am not goin' to leave this hotel, San Francisco, or *you*." Sean's gut tightened and a small thread of unease wound through him. Here, now, he meant the promise he'd just made. He could only hope that he was a better man than she took him for.

"Sean—"

"I know you don't believe me," he cut her off quickly, "but you'll see it for gospel soon enough. Time will tell."

One corner of her mouth lifted, then fell again. "Yes, Sean. Time *will* tell."

"Have you lost your wits, child?"

Frankie smothered a sigh and kept her gaze locked on the mirror above the hall tree. Carefully she smoothed the sides of her hair back and up into the coronet of braids encircling her head. Then she picked up her plain, dark blue bonnet, tugged it on over the braids, and tied the ribbons under her chin.

"Well?" Mrs. Destry demanded, staring into the reflected image of Frankie's eyes. "Do I get an answer, young woman? What do you have to say for yourself?"

Really, Frankie thought, it was a good thing she was heading out the door to Mass. If ever a person needed some quiet time for prayer, it was Frankie Donnelly. Years of restraint, years of training herself to be calm, in control, were dissolving away daily.

Not only did Sean Sullivan push her beyond the limits of her patience, but Mrs. Destry, her one remaining customer, was beginning to do the same.

Of course, all Frankie really had to do was remind the old lady that she was a guest at the Four Roses. That Mary Frances Donnelly was a grown woman with a mind of her own and no need of a nanny.

But Frankie just couldn't bring herself to hurt the old woman so. Instead, she told herself, she would light an extra candle at the statue of St. Timothy and ask him to give her strength.

"Mary Frances." Mrs. Destry tugged on Frankie's arm until she turned around to face her. "I've been comin' to this hotel since before you owned the place."

"I know and I appreciate the fact that you've remained so loyal," Frankie said quickly and snatched up her small black bag. If she kept walking, Mrs. Destry would have no choice but to give up the chase. Frankie simply couldn't imagine the old lady, cane in hand, racing down the street trying to keep up with her.

"That's not what I'm talkin' about, young lady."

Good heavens, Frankie thought with an inward sigh. Did *everyone* have an opinion on how she should live her life?

"I'm talkin' about that Sean. Are you listenin' to me, girl?"

"Hmmm?" Frankie started, blinked, and turned to look at the old woman behind her. "Yes, of course I am, Mrs. Destry," she said. "It's only that Mass begins in a few minutes and I wouldn't want to be late . . ."

"He's a fine figure of a man, Mary Frances, and one whose like I haven't seen darkenin' the doors around *here* before."

"Mrs. Destry," Frankie said patiently, "Sean Sullivan is my partner. Nothing more."

"Not for lack of tryin' from what I hear."

"What have you heard?" Frankie spun about quickly. Good Lord. Had the old woman somehow gotten wind of the conversation she and Sean had had in the kitchen the night before? No. Impossible. How could she have?

"Don't get your drawers in a twist," Mrs. Destry muttered and leaned both hands on the head of her carved walnut walking stick. The eagle's head on the cane knob had always reminded Frankie of the old woman herself. Now more so than ever.

The old lady's chin jutted forward, her snow-white was hair scraped back along her narrow head, and her long, straight nose fairly twitched with indignation.

"I ain't sayin' there's been talk—"

"I should hope not!"

"But a body'd have to be blind in both eyes

not to see that the man has set his cap for you."

Slipping the strings of her bag over her wrist, Frankie abruptly turned around and walked to the door. Grasping the knob firmly, she said over her shoulder, "Nonsense, Mrs. Destry." She hoped she sounded more confident than she felt. "Now, if you'll excuse me, I should return in about an hour or so."

"Fine, fine," the old woman said and hobbled toward the door. "You do what you must, but you mind what I say, too."

"Yes?" Frankie couldn't hide her sigh, and this time didn't even attempt to.

"Sean Sullivan is a man who could show you how to live your life, girl. I do believe he's just the man for you, Frankie." The older woman smiled at her. "Why, if you'd just give him a chance, he could put a real gallop in your get-along."

Frankie drew herself up straight and fought down the blush creeping up her neck. "Perhaps, Mrs. Destry, I prefer a canter to a gallop."

"Perhaps, Miss Donnelly," the old woman mimicked, "you shouldn't oughta downcry what you know nothin' about."

Enough! Frankie told herself silently and yanked the door open. Pulling it closed behind her, she congratulated herself on her restraint. A resounding slam would have felt wonderful.

She hurried down the front steps, turned to the right at the end of the walk, and started

on her three-block trip to St. Timothy's
Church.

Mass had already begun when Sean arrived.
The mingled scents of incense and candle
wax wrapped themselves around him and he
was blanketed by memories. Instantly, flashes
of times long past raced through his mind.

Sunday mornings with his mother, sitting in
a crowded church, squeezed in among several
hundred Irish worshippers. The odors of stale
sweat, hair pomade, and camphor rising up
from seldom-worn suits would combine to
make young Sean's stomach turn in protest.
Almost every Sunday, he'd left Mass with a
sour stomach that wouldn't right itself until
Monday morning.

But it wasn't only Sundays. There were Lent
services, Easter Sunday, Stations of the Cross,
Ash Wednesday, Holy Days of Obligation,
and midnight Mass on Christmas Eve. And
that wasn't even counting the times Sean's
mother had dragged him off to daily Mass to
pray for something special.

A frown touched his lips briefly. Strange, all
that praying hadn't done his mother a bit of
good. She'd died anyway, much too young.
She'd worked herself to death in the Irish side
of St. Louis known as Kerry Patch.

He swallowed heavily past the knot in his
throat. Sean hadn't been to Mass in years.
Since his mother's death, actually, when he'd
first begun living and traveling with Calhoun.

Calhoun had been of the opinion that since
the priests taught that God was everywhere,

there was no sense ruining a perfectly good Sunday morning by going inside a building and listening to some priest rattle on forever. Better, he'd said, to simply sit in the open glory of God's creation and say a simple "Thank you."

And Calhoun, Sean had noticed early on, had always seemed a happier man than those who arranged their lives according to services at the local church.

Now, with the hushed movements of the crowd ringing in his ears and the fluid, familiar yet strange sounds of the priest's Latin rumblings, Sean wished with all his heart he could turn and run outside.

But he'd come for a purpose. He'd come to be with Frannie in her church. And do it he would.

Grimacing slightly, he reached up and ran one finger around the inside collar of his shirt. If she knew him better, she would appreciate just what this was costing him. Why, simply wearing a tie made him feel as if he were about to be strangled. And with the black suit-coat he hadn't worn in years, clinging to his arms and shoulders, Sean was so hot and uncomfortable, it was as if he were facing hell's gate.

He quickly glanced at the altar, saw the priest kneel, heard the altar boy's bells ring, and knew the reading of the Gospel was to begin. His frantic gaze searched the crowd for Frannie. Maybe he was wasting his time tiptoeing down the center aisle, staring into the faces of strangers.

If he knew her, he told himself, she'd have a seat close to the front and right on the end of the pew, where she could see the service clearly. He felt the people's eyes on him, staring into his back. It was always the same. For however brief a time, those who'd made it to church on time could feel themselves more pious than those who stole in late.

Beads of sweat began to trickle down his forehead, and he reached up to brush them away. Maybe, he thought dismally, Mrs. Destry was wrong. Maybe Frannie had gone to a different church altogether.

Then he saw her. Just as he'd thought, she was very nearly at the front of the church. Her plain blue bonnet covered most of her glorious hair, but as she knelt, head bowed in prayer, Sean's gaze swept over the curve of her neck and the few golden strands of hair that had escaped their confines.

Stepping quickly, he moved to her side, tapped her gently on the shoulder, and waited for her to move.

She turned to him with a slight frown, but when she recognized him, her jaw dropped and her eyes widened in shock.

"Will ya let me in, lass?" he whispered as she scooted further into the pew on her knees, Sean slipped in just as the priest stepped up to the pulpit.

The congregation took their seats and cocked their heads as one to listen to the priest.

Sean felt her gaze on him and turned to look

at her. Smiling gently, he whispered, "I'm sorry I'm late."

After Mass, Sean and Mary Frances joined the stream of people stopping to greet the priest, who stood waiting outside the front door.

When it was their turn, Frankie could hardly find her voice. Surprise still gripped her. All through the last half of the Mass, she'd alternately stood and knelt beside Sean, feeling his warmth and enjoying his companionship.

Though she'd never really admitted it to herself before, Frankie had often wished that Herbert was Catholic. Oh, not that she believed in any old-fashioned ideas of only marrying within your own faith, but she'd always been a little envious of the other women in church accompanied by their husbands and children.

It wasn't that she minded so much attending church services alone ... it was simply that she would have liked the amiability of sharing this part of her life with someone she cared for. But the one time she had suggested that Herbert accompany her to church, he'd reacted as though she'd suggested he walk through fire.

Strange, she told herself now as she glanced covertly at Sean's smiling face, she hadn't once considered the fact that Sean, being Irish, was most likely Catholic. Nor, she thought, had it occurred to her to invite him to Mass.

It would have been the neighborly, kind thing to do, she told herself and was slightly ashamed that she'd left him to make his way alone. Still, she assured herself silently as they neared the priest, she could make it up to him now by introducing him to Father Gallagher.

The older priest, in his black cassock and red vestments, looked the very image of warmth. The lines on his face were deeply etched from years of laughter, and his pale blue eyes glittered with an inward happiness that showed in everything he did. He had a head full of thick, wavy black hair, lightly sprinkled with strands of silver. His deep, booming voice carried only a hint of the Irish brogue he'd begun life with.

Father G, as everyone called him, turned his beaming smile on Mary Frances before welcoming Sean.

"And who is this big fellow who can creep down the center aisle with hardly a sound made to ruin the Mass?"

Sean grasped the man's outstretched hand, and his eyebrows lifted slightly at the strength of the priest's grip.

"Sean Sullivan, Father."

"And how do you know our Mary Frances, Sean?"

"He's my new partner in the hotel, Father," Frankie said before Sean could react.

"Ah." Father Gallagher nodded slowly and looked the younger man up and down. "So you're the one Kevin sent, then."

Sean straightened under the priest's scrutiny.

"I hope we'll be seeing a lot of you, Sean."

"Aye, Father." Sean glanced down at Frankie and caught her eye as he went on, "That you will."

"I see . . ." Father Gallagher said thoughtfully, then looked away from Sean to the young woman beside him. "And you, Mary Frances," he said, "will you be coming by the church this afternoon as usual?"

"Of course," she said and ignored Sean's questioning gaze. "I'll be back in an hour or so. Will that be all right?"

"Fine, fine," the priest told her. Then he gave her a little nudge to get them moving again. "Go have your dinner. We'll be here."

As the two of them began to move away, Father Gallagher spoke again, this time in a soft undertone that was clearly meant for Sean.

"God's watching you, son. And so am I."

Chapter 9

⌒◯◯⌒

Frankie stepped to the dining room window. As she passed a small lampstand, she reflexively centered a tiny, hand-painted china clock until it was square in the middle of an Irish lace doily. Satisfied, she went to the window, pulled the edge of the dining room drapes aside, and peered through the half-inch-wide space. It was the best spot in the hotel from which to observe the lot next door.

Her gaze shot directly to Sean, standing amid a pile of fresh lumber that had been delivered while they were in church. She shook her head in reluctant admiration. How Sean had convinced the mill to work on a Sunday was beyond her. But then, she told herself as she watched him lean down to listen to Mrs. Destry, he *did* have a way with him.

He'd certainly become a favorite with Mrs. Destry quickly enough. Frankie couldn't remember the last time the old woman had taken the sun—yet there she was now, happily perched on a chair Sean had dragged outside for her.

Frankie studied Mrs. Destry closely and

frowned as the old woman said something to Sean that brought a smile to his face. If only, Frankie thought dismally, she could read lips. What she wouldn't give to know what those two were talking about.

A quick movement to one side of the lot caught Frankie's eye, and she flicked a glance in that direction. Three or four of the local boys were hovering nearby, seemingly as fascinated with Sean and what he was up to as she was.

Just then Sean laughed, and the deep, rolling sound carried through the tightly shut windows to her. Her heartbeat staggered a bit, and she turned her gaze toward him in time to see Sean toss his head back and give himself over to the laughter still shaking through him.

Unwillingly, Frankie's gaze slipped over his naked chest in admiration. He was a finely built man. And it was no wonder at all why he was so deeply tanned. It seemed as though the man spent a good deal of his time disrobing.

Something inside her turned over at that thought, and she swallowed heavily with a tremendous effort to regain her composure. In fact, it was difficult to tear her gaze away from what seemed *acres* of bronzed, muscled flesh. But she did, giving herself a mental pat of congratulation on her self-control. Still, she wished she could open the window a bit without drawing his and Mrs. Destry's attention.

It was becoming decidedly warm in the dining room.

Sean bent down, lifted a huge stack of lumber into his arms, and moved the raw, unfinished planks further back on the lot. She followed him with her eyes and couldn't help but remember their walk home from church.

She'd so enjoyed having someone to walk with. And talk with.

A slight frown tugged at her lips as her conscience taunted her. It wasn't just *anyone's* company she'd enjoyed. It was Sean Sullivan himself that had made the walk so pleasant. Reluctantly, she admitted that she'd relished the fact that the other ladies at St. Timothy's hadn't been able to take their eyes off Sean.

He was so tall and rakishly handsome. And, she told herself, he looked *wonderful* in a suit coat and tie—even if he'd tugged that tie off almost the moment they were out of sight of the church.

If only, she mused, he weren't so . . . *wild*. So . . . undisciplined, so . . . unrestrained. Maybe they could have—no. Never mind, she told herself sternly. It served no purpose at all to even entertain such notions.

Sean was what he was. And though she was beginning to actually enjoy his company, he certainly was *not* the kind of man she should be building fantasies about.

As she watched, he picked up another load of lumber and stacked it neatly with the first batch. Frowning, she wondered, not for the first time, exactly why he was building a fence around the lot. All he'd been willing to say about it was that the fence wasn't for the purpose of keeping the neighborhood children off the grass.

An image of Sean grinning down at her flashed into her brain. Immediately she recalled the teasing note in his voice when he'd said, "Ah, Frannie lass, you've a real soft spot for those kids, haven't ya?"

"Yes, I do," she'd answered.

She hadn't been able to deny it. But then, why *should* she? She did enjoy the children. Frankie liked the sounds of their laughter. She liked listening to them play and shout to one another. She liked knowing that the kids had a safe place to play without having to worry about being run over by a dray wagon or a carriage.

Sean had stepped closer to her, and she could smell the clean fresh scent of soap clinging to him.

"You should have children of your own, Frannie. At least five or six of them."

"That's a difficult thing for a maiden lady to accomplish, Sean," she reminded him as a blush stole up her cheeks.

He touched her cheek gently as if feeling the heat of her embarrassment. "Maiden lady be damned, Frannie love. You were made for more than that."

"I'm twenty-four years old, Sean," she told him, stiffening deliberately. She simply couldn't afford to allow herself to be swayed by the gentleness in his tone. "I'm a spinster."

"Ah, that's just a word, lass." He grinned at her again and her gaze flew to the dimple in his cheek. "And an ugly word at that. It has nothin' a'tall to do with who you are."

"It has everything to do with the fact that I don't have children of my own."

"Nothin's forever, Frannie. Things change."

"Not if you're careful."

The recollection faded and Frankie was left alone with her thoughts. Twenty-four and a spinster. She blinked. How had the years slipped past her so quickly? She'd always planned to have one or two babies by the age of twenty-four and to be well on her way to a third.

She sighed, realizing one couldn't plan on *anything*. The fact that she was no longer the sole owner of her own hotel was evidence of that.

The tiny china clock beside her began to chime delicately. It stopped at five bells, and Frankie dropped the drape back into place. That late already? she thought. She'd have to hurry if she was to be on time at St. Timothy's.

Determinedly she turned her back on Sean and left the room to change clothes.

"Ah, Fiona," Sean said on a laugh as he turned to Mrs. Destry. "If you were a few years younger..."

The old woman barked out a laugh that sounded as though it had scraped against her rib cage on its way out. "If I was forty years younger, boy, I'd chase you till you dropped."

Sean looked beneath the woman's lined, hawklike features and bent-over form. He stared deeply into her faded blue eyes and briefly saw the woman as she must have been in her youth.

He gave her a slow wink and said, "If it was you doin' the chasin', I wouldn't have been runnin'."

Again, that dry, rasping laugh shook her until she finally drew in a deep breath and waved one gnarled hand at him. "Enough of this now," she said, a smile still curving her lips. "We were talkin' about Mary Frances, weren't we?"

Sean sighed, bent down, and picked up the rest of the lumber. Shifting it in his grip, he walked the dozen or so steps to the stack he'd made in the center of the lot and set the planks down carefully. As he stood up, he brushed his big hands against his thighs.

Mary Frances Donnelly. She was all he thought about. All he dreamed about. And now, thanks to Fiona Destry and her well-meant advice, all he talked about as well.

"I tell you, boy," the woman said firmly, "if you want her, you're gonna have to grab her right up like you would a stack of flapjacks."

Sean shook his head and shivered a bit as a blast of cold ocean air slapped him. Crossing the lot until he was once again beside Mrs. Destry, he said, "That's no way to treat a lady, Fiona."

The old woman snorted inelegantly, and Sean smiled.

"This particular lady is durn well stuck in her ways—you'll need two mules to pull her out! Bein' gentle and easy ain't gonna do it."

Sean snatched his shirt from the grass and shrugged into it. "I've been doin' fine," he told her.

She snorted again to show him what she thought of his progress. "A kiss or two?" Fiona Destry shook her head sharply, and two long strands of hair slipped from her center part to lie on either side of her face. "I warn you," she went on, waving one finger at him. "If you don't get a move on soon, that tall, skinny milksop'll win her over."

Sean frowned at the thought of Herbert Featherstone. Though the man hadn't come around today, the threat of him was never far from Sean's mind. After all, Featherstone had been courting Frannie for a year or more. Sean had only had a week or so with her.

"You'd better worry," Fiona said, pleased with his silent frown. "*He's* what she thinks she wants."

"If that was so, she'd have married him by now," he shot back, worry lacing his voice. That particular argument didn't convince even him.

"Faddle!" Fiona grimaced in distaste. "That ol' beanpole doesn't have the brass to ask her!"

"Then there's nothin' to worry about, is there?" He squinted into the low-hanging sun and winked at one of the boys who was sidling ever closer to the lot.

Fiona was lost in thought for a moment, and when she spoke, it wasn't what Sean wanted to hear.

"I think you've got *him* worried. Who knows? He just might take a stiff drink of hot cocoa and dredge up enough spine to do the deed!"

Sean frowned again at that possibility. Then he saw the first boy move in closer. Instinctively he gave the lad a half smile.

"She needs a man like you!" Fiona slammed her cane tip into the ground, then had to tug it free of the dirt. "Someone to put some fire in her life! She's too damned young to act so old."

"Fire, eh?" Sean asked and squatted down on his haunches to look Fiona dead in the eye. "And what would a calm, quiet soul like yourself know about fire?"

"Think I was born old?" She snorted again and her age-spotted hands began to caress the eagle-headed knob of her cane. "My man, Bill, Lord rest him, was a fire-breathin' forty-niner, son." She lifted her narrow chin. "Made and lost two fortunes before you was even born. Then he made a third just for the hell of it!"

A soft smile touched Sean's face. He'd heard the wistful pride in her tone. He could see the shine of old memories in her eyes. "Sounds like quite a man," he said quietly.

"Worth a dozen of any others I've met since," she allowed. "Only reason I ever had to cuss him was for dyin' and leavin' me to spend all that money alone." Her voice broke disconsolately. Abruptly, though, Fiona sniffed, rubbed her beaklike nose with the back of one hand, and glared at Sean. "Anyhow, I know your kind of man—and I say you're just what she needs."

Sean grinned at her. "If only she was as easy to convince as you."

"Hmmph! If it was easy, it wouldn't be worth the bother."

Just then they heard the front door open and close quickly. Sean and Fiona turned to watch Frankie hurry down the steps and along the walk. As she passed the small knot of children, she smiled and said, "Hello, boys."

All three of them bobbed their heads, and the boy closest to Sean muttered, "Afternoon, Miss Frankie."

She kept walking and then paused in front of the grassy expanse.

Sean looked at her with all the eagerness of a blind man with his sight just returned to him. Her simple black gown was plain and unadorned. On her head she wore a short-brimmed gray bonnet that barely covered her coronet of red-gold braids. She carried a snowy white apron over one arm, and as she spoke, she threw a heavy black shawl about her shoulders.

"I'm off now, Mrs. Destry," Frankie said. "I shouldn't be more than an hour or two."

She only glanced at Sean, then spoke to Fiona again. "There's a cold ham in the kitchen and fresh bread in the pantry. I've also left a stew simmering on the stove."

"That's fine, girl," Fiona returned. "We can make do."

Frankie nodded. "I'll see you when I return, then."

And she was gone. Moving quickly down the still-crowded street, she never looked back and indeed seemed to be hurrying faster with every step.

Sean stood up and watched her go. Frowning, hands at his hips, he asked, "Where's she goin' at this time of day?"

"To clean the church."

"Ah, that's right."

"The Ladies' Guild. Sunday afternoons they gather at St. Timothy's and clean the place for the coming week."

"Well now . . ." Sean rubbed his jaw thoughtfully and stared into the distance. Already he could hardly make out Frannie from among the bustling crowd. "She really shouldn't be walkin' alone, now should she?"

"No," Fiona agreed, satisfaction ringing in her voice. "Now that you mention it, she surely shouldn't. And you know, it'll be dark before she's through."

"Oh, aye." Sean began to stuff the tail of his shirt into his waistband. "Can't have her walkin' in the dark unescorted now, can we?"

Fiona snorted again. Sean was coming to think of that habit of hers as part of her charm.

"You don't have to convince *me*, boy. Only her." She pushed herself up from her chair and leaned heavily on her cane. Slowly she started for the front door.

"Here now," Sean said and took her arm. "Wait just a minute." Turning to the closest of the three boys, he called out, "You there!"

The boy shifted, looked over his shoulder, then turned back and pointed one finger at his own narrow chest.

"Me?"

"Yes, you. What's your name?"

"Tommy."

"Well, young Tommy, come here."

The boy hurried over and only spared one brief glance at his friends waiting on the walk.

Sean looked down at the child carefully. In an instant, he took in the patches on the boy's knickers, the gaping hole in the toe of his left shoe, and the obviously outgrown stockings he was wearing. Tommy's dirty blond hair hung down into wary brown eyes, and as Sean watched, the child pushed that hair out of his way.

There was a stiff, defiant look about the boy that reminded Sean of himself at that age. Poor, undoubtedly hungry, and too proud to let anyone see it. Well, he thought quickly, maybe there was something he could do about that.

"Will you do me the favor of seein' my friend here safely inside?"

"I don't need no help," Fiona barked and slapped at Sean's hand, still clamped gently around her elbow.

Tommy grinned, "Sure, mister. Say," he added and looked past Sean at the pile of lumber, "what're you buildin'?"

"A fence, boyo," Sean told him.

"To keep us out?" Tommy cocked his head and stared up at the huge man in front of him.

No doubt the children were used to being chased off. All of them had the hard, capable look about them that proclaimed to the world they'd been looking after themselves for far too long. It wasn't difficult for Sean to imagine the local storekeepers wanting to keep the children from hanging about. It couldn't be good for business, seeing hungry children looking hangdog at groceries they couldn't buy. It was enough to upset the "quality" customers.

Yes, he thought, the world was a hard enough place when you belonged somewhere. A child on his own had the hardest row to hoe.

His own memories were enough proof of that.

Staring down into Tommy's sharp gaze, though, Sean smiled. These children had one thing more than he'd had when he was first on his own.

Mary Frances Donnelly.

Not only did she allow them to play on soft, green grass, he was willing to bet she fed them from time to time too. He'd seen the looks those kids gave Frannie when she stepped out of the house. Admiration, respect, and even love were easy enough for a body to spot.

"Well?" Tommy prodded. "You tryin' to keep us out or not?"

"Nah . . ." Sean's eyebrows rose and wiggled wickedly. "I'm tryin' to keep somethin' *in*."

"What?"

Even if he'd been trying, the boy couldn't hide his curiosity.

"That I'll tell ya tomorrow," Sean began, then jerked his head toward the other boys straining desperately to hear what was being said. "*If*, that is, you and your chums there would be interested in helpin' me build the bloody thing."

"For cash money?" Tommy's dark brown eyes gleamed in anticipation.

"Of course for cash money," Sean slapped the boy on the back and bit off an oath at the boy's slight weight. "When a man works, he expects to be paid, doesn't he?"

Tommy's shoulders stiffened and his meager chest puffed out with pride. "Right, mister, we're interested all right."

"Good!" Sean released Fiona into Tommy's care and told the boy, "I'll expect you all at eight, then. In the morning. On time."

"On time." Tommy nodded.

"And if you know of one or two others . . . you might bring them along as well."

"Yes sir!" Tommy grinned excitedly at his friends.

Sean glanced down at the boy and gave him a long, warning stare. "You take good care of my friend Fiona here, though. I'll have no man workin' for me who don't know how to treat a lady."

"I'll treat her like she was my own granny." Tommy lifted one dirty hand as if taking an oath.

"Granny, indeed." Fiona snorted.

"St. Timothy's, you say?" Sean asked her as he started walking.

"That's right. And remember what I told you!" she called out after him. "No wastin' around, now!"

Sean waved one hand high over his head in a signal that he'd heard, but he didn't stop or look back.

Fiona Destry shook her head as she stared

after him. A long moment passed before she looked down at the boy tugging on her arm.

"Don't pull so, child! I ain't a piece of taffy, you know!"

Tommy grinned at her.

"And what's so all-fired funny, I want to know?"

"You even talk like my granny."

Fiona sniffed and smiled gently at the little ragamuffin. "Fond of her, are ya?"

"Hell no!" Tommy laughed and winked at her. "Meanest old biddy you ever did see right up till the day she died!"

"Why you little . . ." She swung her cane at him halfheartedly, but Tommy ducked in time, just as she'd planned.

"C'mon, lady, I got to get you inside like the mister said."

"Hmmph! I ain't no package to be delivered, you know."

As Fiona and Tommy passed the other boys, she snapped, "You all might as well come along too. Got some stew on the stove and some fresh bread."

The scruffy boys looked at each other and then at Tommy.

He shrugged and kept walking.

Fiona stopped dead and glared at the children. "Are you comin' or ain't ya? I purely do hate to eat alone!"

Tommy looked up at her and saw one corner of her mouth twitch in a tiny smile. Slowly he turned to his friends and grinned. "Come on. Granny here is all right. Just a little cranky."

"Cranky, is it?" Fiona started walking again and Tommy had to hurry to keep up. As she moved, she went right on talking. "Why, you kids got no idea what cranky is! I remember a time when . . ."

The motley little crew disappeared inside the Four Roses, and when the last boy in closed the door behind them, Fiona's voice was still rattling on.

Sean pushed the heavy swinging door open just an inch and sent up a silent prayer of thanks when the panel didn't squeal a protest. Peeking into the church, he saw a group of four ladies clustered around Father Gallagher.

The priest's voice echoed in the stillness.

"If you'll take care of the confessionals, Mary Frances, the other ladies will do the sacristy and the altar today."

"Of course, Father."

Sean heard Frannie's soft voice and saw her move off to the left. Then the door he was hiding behind blocked his view. Gritting his teeth, he waited impatiently in the vestibule of St. Timothy's until Father Gallagher and the other three ladies had made their way down the center aisle and disappeared through a door beside the altar.

Only then did he slip through the wide, oak-paneled door at the rear of the church. Quickly Sean glanced about him, looking for the confessionals.

A slow smile settled on his features when his gaze came to rest on three free-standing, intricately carved booths, their doors hanging wide open. The tallest cubicle, the one in the center, held a small cushioned chair designed to keep the priest comfortable during long, interesting confessions he was forced to listen to. The booths on either side of that one were narrow and unpleasant-looking, with unpadded wood-plank kneelers.

Perfect for the penitents, Sean told himself wryly. Immediately, though, he shook his head free of such thoughts. He wasn't here to compare the lives of priests and penitents. He was here for one thing. To see Mary Frances. To talk to her.

He watched as she stepped out from behind the three confessionals and walked into the priest's booth, dustrag in hand. His body tightened, and even he was surprised at the strength of his response to her presence. Good God, he thought, what he wouldn't give to be able to—

He brought that thought to an abrupt halt. His eyes rolled heavenward as if expecting to see a jagged lightning bolt pierce the roof and stab his chest as punishment for having lustful thoughts in the House of God.

When nothing happened, Sean told himself that the Lord probably understood exactly what he was going through. Didn't He create Mary Frances? After all, Sean was only appreciating a job well done.

After a quick look over his shoulder, to ensure that they were still alone in the church, Sean followed her.

He moved soundlessly over the stone floor, stepped into the confessional Frannie had walked into, and closed the door behind him. He heard the latch catch with a solid click.

Mary Frances gasped and spun about. She couldn't see a thing in the inky blackness. Fear came and went quickly. She didn't know what was going on, but she knew somehow that she wasn't in any real danger. Besides, all she had to do was shout for help and Father Gallagher and the others would come running.

Still, though, it was an odd sensation. In the narrow confines of the confessional, she was all but leaning against the faceless stranger before her. There was no room to move. Together they were wrapped in a warm, dark silence.

She could hear breathing. In fact, she felt that breath ruffle a stray curl lying on her forehead.

Tall, her mind whispered. Someone tall and big. She inhaled deeply. Tall, big, and smelling of soap and pine.

The stranger drew a long, deep breath and whispered, "Bloody hell, it's dark in here with the door shut, isn't it?"

Chapter 10

"Sean?"

"Surprise, Frannie love."

"Sean, what are you doing here?"

He chuckled softly in the darkness, then Frankie felt his hand brush against her breast. She gasped and tried to jump back. But there was nowhere to go, and she fell against him again.

"Sorry, lass," he whispered. "I didn't mean to, uh . . . I was just tryin' to reach up and get me hair outa my eyes."

"Shake your head," she said quietly through gritted teeth.

"Aye," he whispered again, and she couldn't help but think that for a man who was able to move silently, his whisper sounded near to a shout.

"Why are you here?" she demanded, squinting into the blackness, trying desperately to see him. It was no use though, not a pinprick of light disturbed the darkness.

"I only came to see ya. Talk to ya."

"We could talk at the hotel," she reminded him huffily.

"Aye, but we don't."

"Sean," Frankie said, trying to force a patience she didn't feel into her voice. "You shouldn't be here. If anyone were to see us . . . shut up in here together like this . . ." Lord, she shuddered at the thought of it.

"No one knows," he told her. She felt his breath brush her face. "The others are in the sacristy."

"Then please go before they come back." Urgency strained her voice despite her best efforts. But she couldn't bear the idea of Father Gallagher and the other ladies happening upon her and Sean. Whatever would they think?

She knew very well what they'd think. And what they'd say. Even the best of people couldn't resist spreading a juicy bit of gossip.

And what better fodder for the gossip mills than two people shut away together in a tiny confessional? In the dark? Alone?

Especially if one of those people was Mary Frances Donnelly. Lord, she could almost hear the talk now. "It was only a matter of time," they'd say. "What more could a body expect of a woman practically raised in a saloon? Didn't her own sister own a saloon? And what about that other Donnelly girl? Alice . . . *Al*? The one who wears trousers and curses like a man?" Frannie'd heard the gossips throughout the years as she was growing up. And she had long ago decided to never be the brunt of sharp tongues again.

Oh Lord, Frannie thought, she'd worked so hard for so long to make people forget her origins. Instantly, visions of her shattered reputation leaped into her mind. As if in a nightmare, she saw the good parishioners of St. Timothy's turning their backs when she approached. She saw them drumming her out of the Ladies' Guild. She saw the look of disappointment on Father Gallagher's dear features.

Oh, good heavens.

"Saints above." He sighed and she sensed rather than saw him move his head around, exploring their surroundings. "It's as black as the inside of the devil's own heart in here, isn't it? Hell, no wonder folks don't linger in confession. I'd spit it out quick too . . . just to get outa this tiny, dark space."

"For heaven's sake, don't curse in church," she snapped.

"Suppose you're right there," he admitted, but Frankie thought she detected a smile in his voice. Whatever could he find in this to laugh at? There wasn't the slightest thing laughable about any of this!

"Please, Sean," she said, attempting again to sound calmer than she felt. "Please just go. Quickly." Silently she added, *while there's still time to save my reputation*.

"On one condition."

"What?"

"You let me walk ya home."

"Yes," she agreed instantly. It was getting hot inside that small booth. Frankie stretched her neck a bit and smacked her forehead against his chest. She tried to draw a deep breath, but her throat closed momentarily as though there weren't enough air. Swallowing heavily, she thought she could hear her own heartbeat and frantically started counting the ragged beats. She *had* to get out of that confessional. "Yes," she repeated quickly. "You may walk me home—anything—just please open that door and go."

"Anything?"

She didn't need a light to know what expression was etched onto his features. Frankie heard the half-teasing, half-serious tone of his voice. She heard his breath catch and felt him exhale in a long rush.

"Sean . . ."

"One small kiss, then."

"A kiss? In *church*?"

"In the confessional. Not church." He chuckled softly. "Well, not *exactly* church."

"Absolutely not." She shook her head and once more ended up smacking her face into the hard, solid warmth of his chest. "A confessional is *not* the place for such things."

"It's the perfect place," he said, and it sounded as though his harsh, rough whisper was booming out around them. "My, it *is* close in here, eh?" he added and took her hand in his. "As long as we're in the confessional," Sean said softly, "I'll confess my 'sin' right after you kiss me if you like."

"To whom?" she shot back. "We're in the priest's cubicle."

"To you, if you care to hear it."

"There's no need to be sacrilegious."

"I'm not, lass," he insisted while stroking his thumb across the back of her hand. Frannie could have sworn the temperature suddenly jumped ten degrees higher. "It's only fair I confess to you since my greatest sin is *because* of you."

"I beg your pardon? Me?"

"Oh, aye," he breathed. "The lustful thoughts of you are drivin' me mad. And they must be sinful," he added, "because I enjoy 'em far too much."

"Good heavens."

"Aye." Sean chuckled again, and this time she felt his chest shake with the sound. "Heaven too comes to mind when I'm near you—though it's more like hell, not touchin' you."

"Sean, you mustn't—"

"Mustn't what? Love you?"

"Yes."

"I do, you know."

"No!"

"Ah, yes."

Frankie couldn't breathe. She couldn't speak. She felt his presence more distinctly than she ever had before. Every nerve in her body tingled. Her mouth was dry, and there was a strange curl of excitement spiraling through her.

He loved her?

Lord, she wished she could see his face. How awful it was to have a man say something like that and not be able to read the expression on his face. In his eyes.

On the other hand, though, perhaps the inky blackness was a blessing. She didn't have to look at him when she told him—what? Not to love her?

One couldn't very well tell another person how to feel. Could one? No, of course not. Oh, good heavens, the moment she most needed her wits was the moment they chose to be silent.

"Sean, we can't talk about this now," she finally said for lack of anything better. "Please. You must go. Quickly."

"After me kiss."

"Oh, very well." If he wouldn't leave without a kiss, she had no choice really, had she? Frankie tipped her head back as far as she was able and waited.

A heartbeat later, his mouth came down on hers.

It was an incredible sensation. In fact, that's *all* it was. Sensation. She couldn't see him. She couldn't lift her arms to hold him even if she'd wanted to, which of course she didn't—she could only stand perfectly still and allow his mouth to kiss hers.

As if taking advantage of the fact that she couldn't dart away from him, Sean coaxed her lips apart with his tongue. After a brief instant of shock and surprise, Frankie had to admit, at least to herself, that it wasn't nearly as bad as she'd thought it would be. If she'd only been a bit more patient when he'd tried this before, she might have experienced this exciting yet languorous feeling days ago. Then she sighed into his mouth and allowed herself to enjoy the luscious feel of him inside her mouth.

He groaned quietly, and surprisingly Frankie heard a similar sound issue from her own throat. Her lungs screamed for air, but it felt as though she'd forgotten how to breathe. She leaned into him for support. Unusually bold in the darkness, Frankie hesitantly touched the tip of her tongue to his. His breath caught, and she felt a shudder ripple through him.

Somehow she'd never imagined that a man could be as affected by a kiss as a woman.

Almost before that thought was completed, Sean broke away from her, lifted his head, and gasped for air like a drowning man breaking the surface of the water.

Licking her lips, Frankie laid her head against his chest and listened to the racing beat of his heart. Her legs felt limp, and if there'd been room, she knew she would have fallen to the floor.

"Great God in heaven," Sean muttered thickly.

"Amen," Frankie put in and didn't feel the least bit sacrilegious.

He laughed shortly and bent down awkwardly to kiss the top of her head.

"Frannie, me love," Sean said, sounding as breathless as if he'd just run a foot race. "I'd best get that door open now, while I still have the strength to appreciate the fact that we're in a church."

"Yes," she whispered and tried to give him enough room to turn around in.

"That's it," he said, then grunted when she stepped on his foot. "It's all right, just move a bit further and I'll reach around here for the knob."

A long minute passed. Time enough for

Frankie to recall her startling response to Sean's kiss and for her to begin a short set of prayers as penance.

"For the love of—" His disgusted voice broke off abruptly.

"What is it?"

"Ah, the bloody door's jammed."

"Oh no . . ."

"Now, let's not give up that easy, shall we?" he muttered and shoved at the door again.

Frankie heard him straining to open the door, and when nothing happened, she had to force herself to ask, "Are we trapped in here?"

The dread in her voice reached him and Sean gritted his teeth. No, by damn, they weren't going to be trapped. He wouldn't do that to her. If they were forced to call for help, the priest and those women would never look at Frannie in the same light again.

She'd be compromised good and proper, and it would all be his fault.

"No," he said, more harshly than he'd planned. "I'll get us out if I have to break the damned lock."

"Oh my . . ."

"Now, it's probably just stuck is all." He hoped fervently that he sounded more confident than he felt. The bloody doorknob hadn't budged a bloody inch for all his turning. Turning his head to peer through the darkness in her direction, Sean told her, "Scootch yourself back as far as you're able."

"I have."

"I need a bit more room, though," he said

thoughtfully. "I know. Climb up on the chair, love."

"What?"

"If you're up on the chair, I can have another inch or so to get a good hearty shove goin'."

She sighed and he heard the rustle of her petticoats as she stepped up onto Father Gallagher's chair.

"All set now?"

"All set."

"Hold on to your hat then."

Turning sideways toward the stubborn door, Sean backed up a pace and slammed his shoulder into the unmoving panel. His huge body crashed against the wood and the resulting noise boomed into the silence. But otherwise, nothing happened.

"Blasted, good-for-nothin' . . ."

"Are you all right?"

"I'm fine," he said wryly. "And you'll be happy to know that the door is still doin' nicely as well."

"Oh dear . . ."

"Not to worry," he said, then added, "try to hold on to somethin', Frannie lass."

Again he slammed his powerful body into the doorway, and this time, though the door didn't budge, the entire confessional seemed to rock precariously.

"Sean, maybe we should just call for help."

"No, by heaven, we won't," Sean told her and glared at the black space in front of him. He'd be double damned if he'd let a bloody damned door beat him! "This is the one that'll do it now, lass. Hang on!"

He inched back to the chair's edge, felt Frannie's dress brush against his cheek, then, growling under his breath. Sean threw himself at the portal.

The confessional groaned, rocked for a long moment, then slowly began to tip over. Immediately Sean tried to throw himself back toward Frannie, hoping to even out the bloody box. But it was too late. As the cubicle continued on its slide downward, Frannie fell off the chair and Sean caught her to him instinctively.

Her low moan of distress accompanied them on their short fall.

With a crash that sounded like a clap of thunder in a closet, the confessional slammed onto the stone floor of the church.

Seconds passed.

Flat on his back, Sean winced, then groaned quietly. The back of his head felt as though someone had hit him with a sledge hammer. Bloody stone floors.

Frankie's breath brushed his cheek, and his arms tightened around her slightly. As she straddled him, her full breasts pushed into his chest and her legs lay on either side of his hips. Another time, another place, he would have been a happy man.

"Are you all right?" he whispered.

"I think so." Her voice was muffled against his chest. "Are you?" she asked, moving slightly.

"Aye. Hit me head a bit, and your elbow's in me throat."

"Sorry." Frankie moved her arm, and Sean swallowed gratefully. "Do you think anyone heard?"

Sean rolled his eyes. She had to know that folks down the street had probably heard that bloody damned box fall over. But, he told himself, if she wanted to have some small spark of hope until the very last minute, it was all right with him.

"Maybe not," he said.

"Good. Can we get out now?"

Hmmm. How to tell her that the infuriating cubicle had fallen flat on its door? They were stuck even faster than they'd been before.

Frankie shifted position slightly, and Sean swallowed back a groan. Church or no, if she didn't stop wiggling atop him, there was going to be trouble.

As he glanced down at her, Sean noticed for the first time that he could actually make out her features. A spurt of optimism streaked through him and he tilted his head back, following the small ray of brightness. What he saw brought a smile to his face.

In the fall, the roof of the little booth had been knocked loose. The tiniest crack of light peeped at him, and Sean thought for a moment that perhaps all was not lost. All it should take was one more good push against that piece of wood and the two of them could climb to freedom.

"Here now, Frannie," he whispered as he began to tug his arms out from underneath her.

"What is it?"

"Look there," he said. "At the ceiling."

"Oh my."

"I'll have that out in a shake, lass." Once his arms were free, Sean reached up and gave that panel a mighty punch. The square of wood jolted free and clattered on the stone floor.

"All right then, lass," Sean told her. "Climb over me and scoot on out." Obediently, Frankie started moving. Her right knee drew up dangerously close to Sean's groin, and he sucked in a gulp of air. "Go careful now," he muttered thickly.

Frannie's hat was lying against her back, the black ribbons still tied beneath her chin in a bedraggled bow. One of her braids had been knocked loose in the fall and was now dipping in front of her right eye.

Still, she smiled to herself as she scrambled toward the patch of light. As if moving through a black tunnel toward the promise of heaven, she ignored Sean's grunts and groans as she crawled across his hard, muscled body.

She stared at a spot just beyond the confessional. A rectangular slash of colored sunshine fell from one of St. Timothy's stained glass windows, and Frankie thought it was the most beautiful thing she'd ever seen. Odd, how everything looked brighter, cleaner, prettier, when you hadn't seen *anything* for a while.

Freedom.

After what seemed like hours trapped in that tiny booth with a man who created all sorts of confusing feelings inside her, Frankie was almost free again.

Her palms met the cold, rough stone floor and she grinned.

Then a slight, quick tapping sound penetrated her brain, and Frankie, head still bent low, glanced to her right. Only inches from her, one gleaming, polished black shoe was tapping furiously against the floor.

Frankie's eyes squeezed shut. She actually *felt* her heart drop from her chest. Biting down hard on her bottom lip, she frantically tried to think of something to say. But how on earth was she going to explain.

No matter *what* she said, the facts remained the same. She'd been locked inside a confessional with a man. Anything could have happened. And still she groped for the words she so desperately needed.

Her dilemma came to an abrupt end when Sean's muffled voice floated up from the confessional.

"Don't stop now, love. With me face buried in your petticoats I can hardly breathe!"

Someone close by gasped.

Frankie groaned, swiveled her head, and let her gaze travel slowly up from the still tapping black shoe. From her position on the floor, it seemed to take forever before she met Father Gallagher's glowering steely-blue eyes.

The three women from the Ladies' Guild formed a half circle right behind him. Each woman's features were a study in surprise and disapproval. Eyes wide, lips pursed, and one of them was holding one hand to her chest as if physically keeping her heart from leaping out of her body.

"Frannie girl," Sean called out again. "If you want to get this straightened up before the good father and the others happen upon us, you'd best let me out of here."

"By all means, Mary Frances," Father Gallagher said quietly. "Allow your young man to join us. There's much to discuss."

Sean's bellowing whisper broke into the strained silence. "Was that himself?" he asked. "Father Gallagher?"

"Yes." Frankie sighed.

"Jesus, Mary, and Joseph," Sean whispered.

"Indeed," Father Gallagher agreed.

They were married by candlelight an hour later.

After bending down and giving his reluctant new bride a chaste, quick kiss, Sean straightened up and looked at the handful of people gathered nearby.

Once they'd made it out of that bloody confessional, Father Gallagher had proven himself to be a fair but hard man. There was no backing down from what he considered Sean's duty to Mary Frances.

Oh, not that the priest had really believed anything untoward had gone on in that little booth. In fact, the priest had made it quite clear that he knew very well Mary Frances would never do such a thing. But, he had said as he had looked Sean square in the eye, not everyone else would have shared his opinion.

As it was, the three ladies on the cleaning committee, once recovered from their shock, had scuttled out of the church to spread the word.

Sean shook his head and remembered the disgusted look on the priest's face.

"It never seems to matter to them that gossiping is a sin."

"Well now," Sean said with a smile he wasn't feeling. "If you stopped all sinnin', you'd be out of a job, wouldn't ya?"

Father Gallagher's eyes narrowed thoughtfully. "Speaking of sinning, do you not feel a shred of guilt for your behavior in the House of God?"

Sean glanced at Frannie and saw a red flush of embarrassment steal up her already rosy cheeks. "Nothin' happened, Father. I swear it."

"*Nothing?*" The priest's eyes shot to Frannie, who crumbled under the man's direct stare.

"We kissed, Father."

"Ah . . ."

"One kiss," Sean told him. "If a sin at all, it's merely venial . . . hardly a mortal one."

"And you're to be the judge of that?"

Sean glanced at Frannie again and saw that all this talking was only making her feel worse. Immediately he vowed silently to do all he could to hurry the good priest along. If he'd just dish out the penance, Sean and Mary Frances could be on their way to putting this all behind them.

"Well, Mary Frances," Father Gallagher said softly, and Sean heard the concern in the man's voice. "There's really only one thing to do, isn't there?"

Her eyes widened slightly as she stared at the priest, but after a long moment, she ducked her head. "Yes, Father."

The priest nodded, satisfied, and turned to Sean. Sean felt the man's gaze spear through him like a sharpened blade. He shifted uncomfortably in his chair.

"We'll have the ceremony in front of the altar."

"Ceremony?" Sean whispered and waited for an explanation, though he had a fairly good inkling of what was coming next.

"The wedding."

"Weddin'?" He looked at Frannie and found no comfort in her tear-laden eyes.

"Of course." Father Gallagher stood up and leaned both palms flat on his desktop. Jutting his chin forward, he glared at the younger man. "It's the only way to salvage Mary Frances's good name."

"But nothin' happened . . ." Sean complained and couldn't understand the rush of panic that was flooding him. Why was he fighting the notion of marrying Frannie? Why did the very idea of being yoked to a lovely woman who turned his insides to water and his body to solid rock, have him wishing he was on a fast horse riding a straight road to *anywhere*?

Hadn't he admitted to her only a short while ago that he loved her?

Hadn't he been entertaining thoughts of his own along these very lines for the past few days?

Yet a rebellious voice from the back of his

mind shouted that thinking about being bound and gagged and actually *doing* it were two very different things!

Him?

Married?

His throat closed up tight at the thought. What if he didn't like it? What if he was no good at it? What if he made her so bloody miserable that they were both unhappy?

Jesus! The possibilities for disaster were astounding!

What was he supposed to tell his family when they arrived? He could just imagine what their reaction would be to *that* news.

Especially Honora. A reluctant smile touched his features, then vanished. Honora wouldn't take the news of his marriage well at all. He knew bloody well she'd had her heart set on Sean marrying Sophia one day. To keep the family intact and protected. Poor Dennis would have his hands full trying to keep Honora from flying into a fury at the ruination of her plans.

And Ryan. That one would be all too pleased with Sean's marriage. He'd had his eye on Sean's position in the family for the past two years. This was all the ammunition he'd need to step in and try to take over.

Sean shoved one hand through his hair and tried to think.

Leaving the others aside for a moment, he'd wondered what was he supposed to tell Frannie when it was time for him and the family to leave again. The summer season was almost upon them. By the time the others finally reached San Francisco, it would be only a couple of weeks before it was time to be on the road again.

Holy Mother of God, how had he ever gotten into something like this?

His huge fists clenched and unclenched at his sides. His teeth ground together with the effort to keep his mouth shut and his panicked questions to himself.

Glancing quickly at Frannie, he saw the very same misery he was experiencing flash across her face. She looked so small, so vulnerable . . . so bloody disheartened, he wanted to comfort her. It was all he could do to keep from reaching out and grasping her hand in a comradely squeeze.

But it was those very same soft feelings that had brought him to this spot, and so he did nothing.

Instead, his mind raced on. What possible good would be served by forcing a wedding on two people who weren't ready for any such thing?

Another voice came to him then, low and soft as if drifting up from his heart to his thick head. It reminded him that the purpose served was to save Mary Frances from wagging tongues more prone to viciousness than any wild animal. When all was said and done, there was really no choice at all.

A moment later, with a sigh he was unable to disguise, Sean had looked up at the priest and nodded shortly. "A wedding it is, Father."

Sean blinked and came back to the present. He shook away the last of his recollections and looked down at the little woman in front of him. Mrs. Destry was smiling as if she'd won the sweepstakes. Dutifully he bent down, and she kissed him lightly on his cheek. Then, giving that same cheek a gentle pat, she whispered, "Don't look so grim, boy. Things have a way of working out."

Sean nodded and turned slightly to face the man striding up to him. His new brother-in-law thrust his hand out, and Sean grasped it in a tight squeeze.

"You've picked the best of the bunch, Sean," Cutter told him, and his wife Maggie jabbed him in his side. "After Maggie, of course," the gambler added belatedly.

Maggie stepped up to him and tugged at his lapels until Sean bent down slightly. She planted a quick, hard kiss on his mouth and grinned up at him. "Welcome to the family, Sean."

"Thanks," he said stiffly, but he wasn't looking at Maggie.

Instead, his gaze was locked on an unsmiling woman in black.

His bride.

Chapter 11

Frankie pulled her dressing gown tighter around her, curled her legs up under her, and snuggled deeper into the cushions of her chair. Folding her arms across her chest, she stared at the blazing fire in the hearth and didn't even see the flames.

The cup of tea on the table beside her was untouched and she hadn't been able to take a bite of supper. In fact, she hadn't even spoken since leaving St. Timothy's.

She couldn't.

She was still too stunned to take it all in.

Shaking her head, she glanced at the matching chair on her left. Not too long ago, she'd imagined Sean sitting comfortably in that chair. Now it was no longer her imagination she was dealing with . . . he had every right to come into her bedroom and plop himself down.

He had the right to more than just her chair, she thought suddenly. A quiet groan choked out of her throat and Frankie cupped her face in her hands.

Sean Sullivan.

Her husband.

Hesitantly, she turned her head and peeked through her fingers at the bed behind her. The quilt was neatly folded back, revealing fresh white sheets. Her eye was drawn instantly to the embroidered border edging the sheets and pillowslips.

A delicate daisy chain with an occasional butterfly on the wing had been worked painstakingly in pale shades of rose and yellow. Frankie knew every stitch. Every thread. She'd been doing fine needlework most of her life and had embroidered dozens of sheets and pillowslips for her hope chest.

They'd been carefully packed away for years, awaiting her marriage.

Well, she told herself as her hands dropped to her lap, that marriage was finally here. The wedding night she'd once thought would never come, was upon her at last. And her own bridal linen was proof of it.

No doubt, she thought glumly, it had been Mrs. Destry who'd told Treasure to delve into Frankie's hope chest when it came time to make up the bed. A couple of years ago, Frankie had made the mistake of showing Fiona Destry the cache of fine things she'd been hoarding most of her life.

But Mrs. Destry and the maid shouldn't have done it. They shouldn't have wasted Frankie's efforts on what was no more than a farce of a marriage.

It simply wasn't right.

No one should be forced into a marriage to serve convention.

But haven't you been striving for conventionality your whole life? the voice in her head asked. *Haven't you longed for rules and order? Haven't you done everything in your power over the last several years to build the very kind of life that had made this . . . marriage a necessity?*

If she hadn't married Sean, there wouldn't have been a tongue in all of San Francisco that didn't delight in telling the tale of Mary Frances Donnelly's interlude in the confessional. As it was, the story was probably being told right now with accompanying gasps of disbelief and outrage. The only thing that would take the sting out of the retelling of it would be the fact that she and Sean had married almost instantly.

Of course, the marriage wouldn't quiet the gossips right away. No doubt there would be talk for weeks yet—but eventually they would move on to other topics. And Frankie's *reputation* would be salvaged.

After all, where was the excitement in gossiping about a married couple having a tryst?

But how was she supposed to act toward her husband now? Was she supposed to pretend that they'd married for love? Was she supposed to welcome Sean into her bed and hope that whatever attraction existed between them would be enough to build a life on?

Frankie uncurled her legs and pushed herself to her feet. Deliberately keeping her gaze from falling on the bed again, she walked across the room and stopped beside one of the wide double-framed windows. Pulling the draperies aside, she looked into the darkness, but instead saw only her own reflection in the shining glass.

Unable to meet her own worried gaze, Frankie dropped the drapes back into place and spun about, her gaze shifting unerringly to the bed.

Soon, she knew, Sean would be at her door, expecting her to welcome him into her room. But good heavens, how was she supposed to conduct herself? Certainly *this* situation was entirely different from a normal marriage.

It didn't matter *what* Father Gallagher had said.

Immediately after the wedding, Father G had taken Frankie off for a private chat. Huddled in the back of the church, the priest had spoken in a hushed tone that seemed to echo in the vast vestibule.

"Now I know this isn't the kind of wedding you always imagined, Mary Frances."

Only in nightmares, she had thought furiously. It was only the fact that she'd been raised to respect members of the clergy that made Frankie willing to talk to the man at all. As it was, she had to bite down on her tongue to keep from shouting at him.

This isn't fair!

This isn't right!

The past couple of hours had passed in such a blur, she'd hardly known what was happening. Father Gallagher had sent word to the Four Golden Roses Saloon, so that Maggie, Cutter, and Rose Ryan could be present at her wedding. And for some reason, Sean had asked that someone go to the hotel and bring

Fiona Destry for the service as well.

And so the wedding she'd dreamed of her entire life had consisted of a few short sentences and an audience of four, if one didn't count the snickering altar boys—and Frankie didn't.

For the life of her, she couldn't remember the ceremony. She'd stood mute at the altar, stunned into silence. In fact, everyone was silent. Except of course for Maggie. At least twice, Frankie had heard the unmistakable sounds of Maggie chuckling.

Her own sister. The traitor.

"But however it's come," Father Gallagher was saying, "the deed is done now and it's left for you to make the best of it."

The best of it. How in heaven could she make the best of it? Sean Sullivan was the very type of man that she'd always sworn to avoid. Wild, noisy, unconventional—he would never be happy leading the kind of quiet life that most appealed to Frankie.

It was as if the priest could read her mind.

"I think Sean is a good man," Father Gallagher went on to say. "A bit rough around the edges, perhaps, but a good man nonetheless."

Rough? she couldn't help thinking. *Jagged* was closer to the truth.

"Mary Frances," the priest continued, "none of that matters now. All that matters is that you and Sean are man and wife. Joined together in the eyes of God. And in the eyes of the church. As you know, marriage is forever."

Forever. The word seemed to echo on and on in her brain.

"This union can be one of joy or misery," he said firmly, his sharp blue eyes staring into hers. "Depending on how *you* treat it."

"Me?" she couldn't help arguing. "Hasn't Sean any responsibility in this at all?"

"Of course he has, child." A patient, long-suffering sigh escaped the man as he continued. "But as we all know, a woman is the heart of any marriage. If she has a happy, giving heart, it will be enough to ensure joy for the both of them. If she's a harpy, though," he warned, narrowing his gaze, "unforgiving and accusing, no one but Satan himself will take joy in the union."

Frankie frowned at the memory and put Father Gallagher out of her mind. It still irritated her no end that her old friend had placed the survival of her marriage entirely on her shoulders. But at least one thing he'd said struck home.

According to the Catholic Church, marriage was indeed forever. And if she was going to have any kind of happiness in her life, she would simply have to make the best of the situation as it was. Sean Sullivan was her husband now, like it or not. Although, she reminded herself, *acceptance* of her marriage was a far cry from *delight*. She wrapped her arms about her waist and hugged herself tightly. Sean had successfully claimed her hand in marriage—he hadn't claimed her heart.

But, as Father Gallagher had said, the deed was done. There was no turning back.

Lifting her chin slightly, she straightened her shoulders, dragged a deep breath into her lungs, and marched across her bedroom to the dressing table. She sat down on the cane-backed chair, and stared at her reflection for a long moment before picking up her hairbrush. Her thumb caressed the back of the cherry-wood brush, then she began to pull the bristles through her hair. Over and over, she brushed until the long, wavy, red-gold tresses crackled and flew about her head like an oversized halo.

When she was finished, she leaned toward the mirror and pinched both cheeks to bring color to her too pale flesh.

Smiling grimly at her efforts, Frankie reached for a cobalt-blue bottle and carefully pulled out the crystal stopper. The faint, sweet scent of violets drifted to her. She touched the cool glass to either side of her throat and then, daringly, to the cleft between her breasts. Then she replaced the stopper and set the fragile bottle down in its rightful place.

Pasting a false, confident smile on her face, Frankie told herself that when her groom arrived—she would be ready.

He had to go downstairs and face her.

Sean swallowed one last swig of whiskey and tossed the half-empty bottle carelessly beside him on the bed. He had to talk to her. To tell her ... what? That he was sorry? A fine thing for a groom to be saying on his wedding night!

"Bloody hell!" he grumbled aloud. What the

hell kind of wedding night was *this*? he wanted to know. And a second later, he answered his own question. "The only kind you deserve."

Suddenly he leaped up out of bed, slammed his forehead into the low-hanging beam, and, moaning, fell back onto the mattress.

Once the lightning bolt of pain slicing through him faded into a maliciously throbbing ache, he chanced sitting up. Slowly. With one hand on the rapidly forming knot in the center of his forehead, Sean eyed the deadly beam, then sent a malevolent glare toward heaven. " 'Tis no more than I deserve, I grant ya . . . but wasn't I in enough pain already?"

He scooted off the edge of the bed, wincing at the hard, unyielding pressure in his groin. The pain in his head erupted when he stood up, momentarily taking his mind off the fact that he was hard and ready for Frannie—but couldn't claim her.

Cursing under his breath, Sean stomped across the floor to the door. His fingers curled around the knob, and as he gave it a twist and yanked the door open, he told himself it would be best to get his mission done with.

He stood in the silent, darkened hall, his brain racing. What he really wanted to do was take himself off to the saloon and drown his misery in three or four bottles of good Irish whiskey. In the next instant, though, he acknowledged that he couldn't do that to Frannie. He'd already done more than enough damage to her.

If he left her—on their wedding night—in

favor of a saloon, well, what the gossips would have to say didn't bear thinking about. He wouldn't put his wife through that.

He took a step and stopped again.

Wife.

Married. Jesus, what had he done to her? This was all his fault. If he hadn't acted like a farmboy in the city for the first time, everything would be as it had been. But no, Sean Sullivan was not a man to do anything by halves!

No. When he saw the woman he'd been waiting for his whole miserable life, he went after her with no thought to her feelings at all. Until what he finally ended up doing was embarrassing her in front of her priest and her friends and shaming her into a marriage she didn't want.

"Oh aye," he said to himself, "you're a fine fella, you are."

As he stomped down the stairs, Sean's head pounded with each step. He grimly accepted the pain as penance for being an ass. But as if the pain wasn't enough, his memories began attacking him. In his mind's eye, he again saw Frannie's face when she'd said, "I do."

Never had a set of features more plainly screamed out, "I don't" than hers. Yet she'd gone through with it. He'd almost hoped that she wouldn't. For one brief moment, Sean had hoped that she would tell them all—particularly him—to go to hell. And for the life of him, he couldn't understand why.

He'd told her only hours ago that he loved her. And he did. That was one solid truth in all this mess. His groin began to ache again, and he cursed under his breath. Aye, he did love her—he loved her enough to wish her a better husband than the one she'd gotten today.

Where, he wondered, had the stark terror come from? Almost from the moment Father Gallagher had said the word *marriage* . . . Sean hadn't been able to breathe.

Maybe it was the word itself.

Marriage.

Married.

He shuddered.

Sounded too bloody much like *buried*.

Ah, Lord have mercy! he thought and rubbed his eyes with his fingertips. The chill in his soul had iced his blood, and he felt as though he might never be warm again. He'd hurt Frannie. He'd done her a terrible disservice. Through his own lust, he'd sentenced her to being married to him.

Well, there was only one answer. The same one that had occurred to him earlier. The very reason that he was on his way to talk to her, instead of lying down beside her, gathering her into his arms and easing the pain of wanting her.

He would keep his distance. Now, when it was too late, he would keep his distance. The irony of *that* wasn't lost on him, despite the amount of liquor he'd consumed.

"Blast and bloody damnation," he muttered and started across the second-story landing toward the last flight of steps to the ground floor.

It was a hard test he'd set himself.

But one that would be in the best interests of Mary Frances herself. At least *this* he could do for her. If he kept his distance, maybe she could get the marriage annulled in a few months. Then she would be able to *choose* a husband. Not have one thrust upon her.

A tiny voice in the back of his cowardly brain called him a liar. It wasn't all for Frannie that he was making this grand sacrifice. It was for himself as well.

No matter the wanting. No matter the times he'd told himself that he loved her and wanted to be with her always.

The fact of the matter was, he thought, sighing, Sean Michael Sullivan was worried.

Hell, he'd been a rambler most of his life. Even Frannie herself had said that. *And you,* he reminded himself silently, *told her that people can change.*

"Bloody hell," he whispered and shook his head slowly. "Ah God, Frannie love ... I'm sorry."

When he reached the bottom of the stairs, Sean kept walking and didn't stop until he was standing outside Frannie's bedroom. He lifted one hand and gently knocked on the door.

The door opened almost immediately and Sean had to stifle the groan choking him.

She stood in front of him, her hair wild and soft about her head and shoulders. The soft, sweet scent of her reached out to him even as her pale green eyes told him she was no happier about the situation than he was.

"Can I talk to ya for a minute, Frannie?"

Surprise flitted across her features, then was abruptly gone. But she pulled the door open wider and stepped aside for him.

She smelled the whiskey on him as he passed her.

He walked across the room to the fireplace and there he stopped, staring down into the flames.

Frankie crossed to one of the overstuffed chairs, stood behind it, and curled her fingers into its soft, cushiony back. She wasn't sure what he was about to say, but from the look of him, she wasn't going to like it.

Long moments passed, and the only sound in the room was the crackle and spit of the flames devouring neatly stacked logs.

Finally, though, Sean swiveled his head to look at her.

"Ah God, Frannie. I'm sorry about what I've brought us to."

"You're . . . *sorry*?" Her fingers clutched at the fabric beneath her hands. He'd turned her world upside down, created a scandal in her church, forced her to be married on an hour's notice . . . and he was *sorry*?

"Aye, I am an' all." He shoved one hand through his hair and Frankie waited. Sean swayed slightly on his feet, and she began to wonder how much liquor he'd consumed before coming to her. Had he needed to be *drunk* to face her?

"I want ya to know," he went on, his voice sounding slow, uneven, "that I'll take care of . . . everything."

"You'll take care of what?" A slow-burning anger began to swell in the pit of her stomach. Somehow she managed to keep her voice even as she said, "*It's* already taken care of. We're married, Sean. Remember?"

He squinted at her, winced, and raised one hand to cup his forehead. For the first time, Frankie noticed a growing knot on his head and wondered how he'd come by it.

"I remember." He nodded abruptly and moaned quietly.

Frankie's lips quirked, then straightened again. She should be sorry the man was in pain, she supposed, but somehow she couldn't quite manage any sympathy for him.

"I've thought it out," Sean continued, obviously determined to say what he'd come to say. "About the weddin'—about us—and I've come to a desh . . . des . . ." He licked his lips, then tried again. "I've *decided* to stay away from ya."

"Stay away," she echoed through gritted teeth.

"Aye." He inhaled sharply and swayed just a bit. "It's for the best, lass."

"Is it?" Her fingernails dug into the chair's fabric.

"It is." He glanced at her, gave her a half smile, and finished lamely, "If we don't . . ." He jerked a thumb at the bed behind them. "Well, if we don't, you can get yourself an . . ."—he paused and framed the word carefully—"*annulment*."

"Annulment?"

"Aye. Itsh . . . It's only fair."

"Fair."

Deliberately, Frankie released her grip on her favorite chair. If she didn't let go soon, she knew she'd rip the material to shreds. Slowly, quietly, she rounded on him, taking each step with the care of a man stepping through a pen full of hungry lions.

She should have been pleased when Sean started to back up from her advance. But truthfully, she was simply too angry to care. Unthinkingly, she snatched a small rose-colored pillow from the chair seat and began to slap it against one palm.

"Annulment? *You've* decided, have you?"

He nodded.

"And when shall I arrange for that, do you think?"

"Whenever you want, lass."

"Ah, then *that* you'll let me decide?"

"Frannie love—" he started, but she cut him off quickly.

"Don't call me that."

"If you'll let me tell ya—"

The pillow slapped against her palm again.

"No." Amazing, she thought wildly as a rush of anger filled her. It was . . . exhilarating, surrendering to fury. All those years of practicing control, of learning to tamp the Donnelly temper, dissolved as she looked at the man who was and *wasn't* her husband. "I've heard enough for one night."

She'd walked him across the room and not even noticed until he was poised directly in the door frame. His hair stood out around his head and, unbelievably, he raised his arms to reach for her.

"Frannie . . ."

"Oooooh!" She threw the pillow into his face and had the satisfaction of seeing his head snap back on his neck just before she slammed the door closed and turned the brass key in the lock.

"You look like hell, boy," Fiona said as she poked him with the tip of her cane.

"Good," he grumbled as he opened his eyes and stared up at her. "I'd hate to feel as bad as this and no one be able to tell."

"I've seen plenty of folks the mornin' after a weddin' night and I got to say, you don't exactly look the image of a happy bridegroom."

Sean squinted up at her. The morning sun was pouring in through the windows bordering the front door, and it was almost more than he could bear.

Every square inch of his body hurt. The hard wood floor beneath him felt like a bed of nails and the pounding behind his eyes was hideous.

"Care to tell me," Fiona said, leaning both hands on the eagle's head knob of her cane and bending over him, "why the groom spent his wedding night on the floor outside the bride's bedroom?"

"No." He smacked his lips together and frowned. His mouth tasted like a muddy field.

The old woman sighed in disappointment. "I didn't think so. Don't guess you want to tell me who hit ya either?" she asked, staring pointedly at the lump on his forehead.

"Walked into a wall," he muttered, and carefully rolled onto his knees before staggering to his feet.

"Uh-huh."

Stifling the groan building in his chest, Sean swallowed, forced his eyes open wider, and asked, "Have ya seen Frannie yet today?"

"Nope."

Good, he thought. Maybe she was still abed. If he was quick, he'd have time to get a cup of coffee before facing her again.

He started walking toward the kitchen and pretended he didn't hear Fiona when she said, "Odd way to start off a marriage, I must say."

When he slipped into the kitchen, the swinging door had barely shut behind him when he came to a sudden stop. There opposite him, looking as though she'd gotten no more sleep than he had, was Frannie.

"Good morning," she said, and the stiffness in her voice matched the rigidity in her spine.

"Good morning, Frannie."

"Sleep well?" she asked, one eyebrow lifting slightly.

"No," he admitted and glanced at the coffeepot longingly. "Not very."

"Neither did I," she said and snatched a thick, white mug from the counter. Pointedly keeping her eyes averted from him, she stepped to the stove, grabbed a towel, and picked up the coffeepot. As she poured the coffee, she said, "But, during the course of a long, sleepless night, I did at least have time to think."

Sean took the cup from her and winced when she slammed the coffeepot back down on the stove. His ears were ringing in time with the clamorous pounding in his head. He pitched his voice loud enough to carry over both those noises.

"Aye, well, I did some thinkin' an' all . . ."

Frannie blinked, startled at his shout.

"And I think that you an' me should talk some more, Frannie lass," he added, lowering his voice just a notch.

"Oh, do you?"

She'd spoken so softly, he wasn't really certain of what she'd said. But the look on her face was plain enough. She was in no mood for a civil conversation.

Hastily he took a gulp of coffee and felt the boiled, bitter brew burn its way down his throat. Well, they were *going* to talk. Civil or not.

"What I said last night," he began, "about the annulment?"

She turned her back and began to knead the bread dough on the sideboard.

Sean went on. "It's best for ya, lass. With an annulment, you can find yourself the kind of man you deserve."

"So," Frankie said softly, "what you're saying is that you have no interest in bedding me."

"That's not what I said."

"You never *did* want me, did you, Sean?"

"What? Are ya *mad*, woman?"

Frankie slapped the bread dough, then lifted her fist and punched it solidly.

Sean took an unsteady step backward. Just in case.

"I don't think so."

"You're wrong, Frannie . . . I want you—"

Frankie studied him thoughtfully for a long moment. From his red-streaked eyes to his whisker-stubbled cheeks to the dark circles beneath his eyes, he showed all the signs of a man who'd spent the night more awake than asleep.

He swallowed more coffee, then stood silently, waiting.

"It occurred to me last night"—after she'd discovered that her new husband was already looking for a way out of their marriage, she added silently. Frankie swallowed back the anger beginning to bubble again inside her. Though the release of her temper the night before had felt liberating, she needed a clear head to deal with the man in front of her.

"The truth is, Sean Sullivan, that you pursued me for one reason and one reason only."

"Frannie . . ."

"Despite your protestations of love and admiration, there was only one thing on your mind while you were chasing after me."

"That's true enough, lass," he said and set his coffee cup down with a thud. "I pursued you because I wanted you more than anything or anyone in my life."

For one brief, heart-stopping minute, she almost wished she could have believed him. Then she pushed that little fantasy aside.

"*That* is only part of the truth." She slapped the bread dough into a loaf, laid it in its pan, and smoothed the top with one shaky hand.

"Huh?"

"Oh, you wanted something all right. Wanted it badly. You wanted my hotel, Sean."

"What?"

"You can't deny it, though I wish you would try."

"Give me a bleedin' minute and I sure as hell will!"

"From the moment you bought my father's share of the Four Roses, it was your plan to have it all."

"Good God, woman!"

"And to get it, all you had to do was compromise me."

His features were tight, pinched. A muscle in his jaw was ticking spasmodically. His full, usually smiling lips were nothing more than a grim line.

She turned her back on him, picked up the bread pan, opened the stove door, and shoved the pan inside. Hot air rushed out of the stove and blasted her in the face. She gave the heavy steel door a strong, quick push and it slammed home with a clang. Then she turned back to glare at him.

"Well, you got what you wanted, Sean. You're my husband. You have complete *legal* control of the hotel."

"Frannie . . ."

She shook her head firmly and continued. "But you have *no* rights to me."

"Dammit, woman!"

"And if you ever come to my room again," Frankie warned him, "I'll throw something a lot heavier than a pillow."

Chapter 12

"L ike this, Sean?"
Sean raised his head and looked in the direction of the reedy voice. George, one of little Tommy's pals, was looking at Sean with a hopeful gleam in his eyes. Still holding his hammer, the boy pointed to the newly finished section of fence.

"Aye, George." He managed a small smile for the kid. "That's a grand job."

George grinned, grabbed another plank, and started hammering again.

Sean groaned and stretched out on the sun-warmed grass. He tried to blot out the sound of five young boys, each armed with a hammer and each trying to shout over their combined noise. But it was no use.

And a part of him realized that the resulting pain was no more than he deserved. With a sigh, he closed his eyes tightly against the bright morning sunshine.

Sean couldn't even remember the last time he'd drunk as much as he had the night before. He'd learned long ago that the momentary pleasure to be found inside a whiskey bottle was never worth the pain of the morning after.

But today—although the inside of his mouth felt as thought a herd of filthy cattle had wandered through it and his head was still pounding—this hangover was nothing compared to the tongue-lashing Frannie had given him.

He'd left her in the kitchen more than two hours ago and still he could hear her hurt, angry tones echoing in his head.

Not that he blamed her any. She'd had more than enough reason to be angry. And hurt. But if he hadn't felt so near to death, he might have given her more of a fight.

And was he really wrong? he asked himself. Was it wrong to be cautious? To recognize a mistake for what it was and try to correct it?

A mistake.

He opened his eyes and the sun sliced into his brain. As if doing penance, he kept his eyes wide open and accepted the pain.

His marriage to Frannie *was* a mistake. Wasn't it? Hell, it had happened so fast, even *he* didn't know for sure. All he was certain of was that he still loved Frannie. He still wanted her more than anything in this life.

And the thought of being tied down in one place still terrified him.

"Got a snootful, did ya?"

Sean's gaze shifted to one side and he looked up into Tommy's dark brown eyes. The boy was shaking his head, his dirty blond hair falling across his forehead. Tommy pushed it back with one grimy hand, then plopped down alongside Sean. "Betcha your head is fair to bustin'," he commented.

"I'll live."

"Guess so."

Sean watched the boy idly tug one patch of grass after another out of the ground and toss it aside. Obviously there was something on his mind.

"Do ya want a shovel?" Sean asked quietly. "It'd be a sight quicker than the way you're doin' it now."

Immediately the boy stopped what he was doing. He propped his elbows on his knees and cupped his face in his hands. Tommy stared at the man, watched him for a long moment, before speaking.

"Hear you and Miss Frankie got hitched yesterday."

Sean's eyebrows lifted. Word did indeed travel fast.

"Where'd you hear about that?"

The boy shrugged. "Around. Did ya?"

"Aye, we did."

"Hmmm."

"What is it?"

"Well, I was wonderin'," the boy said, "What're we s'posed to call Miss Frankie now? *Mrs.* Frankie?"

In spite of his miserable mood, Sean smiled. "No need to change. Miss'll do fine."

Tommy nodded and glanced around him to make sure his friends were all occupied and not listening to his conversation. Then he turned back to Sean and said quietly, "I'm glad you married her."

"Why?"

The boy shrugged his narrow shoulders and scrunched his face up in distaste. "The other fella don't like us much."

"Other fella?" Sean repeated, fascinated but still a bit confused, thanks to the lingering effects of the liquor.

"Yeah. That tall, skinny one that comes sniffin' around her all the time."

Herbert. Even through the fog in his brain, Sean didn't have any trouble at all dredging up the image of Frannie's former suitor.

Funny though, he thought idly, he hadn't given the man a thought until Tommy mentioned him. And he was willing to bet Frannie hadn't either.

Then the boy started talking again and Sean returned his attention to him and listened.

"He's forever tellin' Miss Frankie that she shouldn't oughta let us hang around here." Tommy scowled and started picking at the grass again. "Says we're hooligans."

Sean frowned. Herbert Featherstone should learn to keep his mouth shut around children.

"He ain't no kind of man for her," Tommy said quietly and glanced at Sean.

"An expert on marriage, are ya?" Sean tried for a teasing note, but the boy wouldn't be swayed.

"I seen my share."

"I'll wager you have at that," Sean said solemnly. Instantly an image of the kinds of marriages the boy had probably seen flashed into his brain. Sean had plenty of memories of his own to dredge up. Not of his own parents'—

Sean's father had died when Sean was just a boy. And his mother hadn't lived much longer after that.

But he could recall plenty of what he'd seen growing up in Kerry Patch. Instantly the years fell away. He could almost smell the corned beef boiling. He could remember the chill of cold winter nights huddled in shacks with more spaces between the boards than nails. He remembered it all much too clearly.

Memories of husbands and wives screaming at each other. Of men raising their fists as well as their voices against the very women they'd once promised to honor and cherish. The haunted, shadowed eyes of wives long since resigned to losing the men they'd married to despair and drink.

Ah, poverty was an ugly thing, he told himself. When people have nothing, he thought, they tended for some reason to turn on the one person they should have been clinging to.

And it was the children who ended up paying the price.

Sean looked at the boy's too thin, dirty face and tried to guess his age. From the size of him, he couldn't have been more than nine or ten. And already his eyes were as old as the hills.

For the first time in hours, Sean's mind turned away from his own problems.

"What about your own folks?" he asked.

Tommy shrugged, looked away from the man, and squinted into the distance. "Don't got any."

"What happened, boyo?" Sean whispered.

"Ma died a while back," the boy said, half chewing at his bottom lip. "Never had no pa."

"Where d'ya live?"

"I get by," he said confidently, and immediately some of his swagger was back. "Most nights one of the boys lets me sleep on the floor at his house and when it's warm I stay on the beach."

"Uh-huh."

Tommy shot Sean a quick, hard look. "I don't need nobody feeling sorry for me, mister. I do just fine."

" 'Course ya do, boy," Sean agreed quickly. "No one's sayin' any different."

"All right, then." Tommy turned to watch one of his friends pound nails into fence planks and missed the thoughtful glance Sean sent him.

A moment later, a young redheaded boy ran up the front walk and stopped beside Sean.

"Your name Sullivan?"

"Aye. Who're you?"

"Telegram," the boy answered and dug into his shirt pocket. Pulling out a wrinkled, yellow sheet of paper, he handed it to Sean and raced back out of the yard the way he'd come.

A curl of foreboding settled into the pit of Sean's stomach. Lifting the paper carefully, as if expecting it to explode, he slowly unfolded it and smoothed out the wrinkles.

He read the short message once. Then again. It hadn't changed.

"Ah Lord . . ." Sean tossed one arm across his eyes and crumpled the paper in his other fist.

"What's wrong?" Tommy asked.

"What's right, ya mean," Sean shot back.

Behind closed lids, he saw the printed words as clearly as if he was reading them again.

LEAVING TODAY FOR SAN FRANCISCO STOP SHOULD BE THERE IN DAY OR TWO STOP HOPE YOU'RE READY STOP SAMPSON MISSES YOU STOP.

Judging by the date on the wire, the family would be arriving any day. Hell, for all Sean knew, they were just blocks away that very minute.

Well, that's perfect, he thought grimly.

The fence wasn't finished . . . he had a new bride who couldn't stand the sight of him . . . and soon eight more people would be arriving.

And he still hadn't told Frannie anything about the family that would soon be there.

Just bloody perfect.

"Well," he said with a groan as he pushed himself to a sitting position. "We'd best finish this fence in a hurry. We'll be needin' it in no time."

Tommy jumped up grinning and hurried to help.

Frankie slipped into the saloon and stopped. She let her gaze move over the lunchtime mob of people and couldn't help but wish she was anywhere but there. Ordinarily she tried to steer clear of the Four Golden Roses Saloon.

Every time she set foot in the place, memories of her childhood leaped up in her mind to torment her. Oh, not that she'd had a miserable childhood by any means. She'd had two parents who'd loved her—at least until their mother died giving birth to Teresa. And she'd had her sisters.

But still, the saloon reminded her of the inconstancy of her young life. Of the frequent moves and the disruptions they'd all had to live with. Disruptions she'd thought she was finished with until the night before.

Now, she thought, it looked as though her own church had sentenced her to a lifetime of disruptions.

Grimly, Frankie clamped her lips tight together and swept her gaze over the crowd. If she was there at all, her sister Maggie would be easy to spot. A tall, beautiful woman with a head full of bright red hair was not easily missed.

"Frankie!" a familiar voice called, and she turned toward the sound.

Maggie Donnelly Cutter was halfway down the wide staircase separating the saloon from the living quarters. She wore a skin-tight emerald-green silk gown with a bodice so low it was barely there at all. Grudgingly, Frankie admitted that the gown looked wonderful on Maggie. As did most things.

Frankie lifted the hem of her own serviceable gray gown and hurried to meet her sister.

"What are you doin' in here?" Maggie asked and set both hands on her hips. "Shouldn't the blushing bride be at home in the strong arms of her handsome new husband?''

Frankie felt a flush steal up her cheeks, but before she could say a word, Maggie was shouting across the room to the bartender.

''Jake! A bottle of champagne for me and my sister. We're going to do some celebrating!''

''Comin' up, boss,'' the man behind the elegant bar called back.

''And while you're at it,'' Maggie yelled over the crowd, ''give everyone a free drink. In honor of Frankie's marriage.''

A healthy cheer rose up from the crowd, and a few of the well-dressed men shouted good wishes to Frankie.

She inhaled sharply and started climbing the stairs. Pausing briefly beside her sister, she muttered, ''May I speak to you? In private?''

Maggie blinked, and the smile on her face dissolved. ''Sure thing, Frankie. Go on up to the office. I'll be right there.''

Ten minutes later, Frankie was still pacing, waiting for Maggie. She paid no attention to her elegant surroundings. The paintings and fine china vases stuffed with fresh flowers meant nothing to her. She had no interest in staring out the office window at the view of the city.

All she wanted to do was talk to her older sister. If she ever showed up!

A knock on the door startled Frankie and she jumped.

''Who is it?''

''Who do you think?'' Maggie answered.

"Open the damned door, Frankie."

Mumbling to herself about Maggie's unfortunate habit of cursing as fluently as any sailor, Frankie hurried to do as she was told.

Maggie stepped into the room, balancing a silver tray. On the tray was an elegantly wrought silver ice bucket in which a huge bottle of champagne rested regally. Alongside that were two tall, delicate crystal glasses, designed to look like the fragile petals of tulips.

"You looked like you could use the champagne," Maggie pointed out as she carried the tray to her desk and set it down.

"I don't drink," Frankie reminded her.

"Maybe you should."

"It wouldn't help."

"Couldn't hurt."

There was no pop, so Frankie assumed her sister had opened the bottle downstairs. In seconds, Maggie was handing her one of the glasses, brimful of pale amber bubbling liquid.

"Now," Maggie said, pouring a glass for herself, "take a sip, then tell me what's brought you to the saloon."

Frankie stared at her glass for a long minute, then tentatively took a sip. The small swallow seemed to sparkle all the way down her throat. Her lips twisted at the taste, but she *was* thirsty after her long walk to the Coast.

She took another swallow and looked up at Maggie.

"Rose won't be coming in here, will she?"

"No. She left to do the marketing." Maggie perched on the edge of her desk and crossed her feet at the ankles. Swinging them gently to and fro, she sipped her champagne, then asked, "What's wrong, Frankie?"

At least Rose wasn't there, Frankie told herself. If there was one thing she didn't need at the moment, it was Rose Ryan's delight. The older woman had taken a liking to Sean the moment she'd met him. And at the wedding the day before, her satisfaction had been clear to everyone.

Having to talk to Maggie would be humiliating enough. She wanted as few people as possible to know that she'd been a fool.

"Frankie?" Maggie's feet stopped swinging and she set her glass on the desktop. Frowning slightly, she asked, "Did Sean . . . *hurt* you last night?"

Yes, he did, Frankie bemoaned silently. *But not the way you mean.* She looked at her older sister and started talking. In short, clipped sentences, Frankie told Maggie everything. She finally stopped after describing the morning's encounter with her new husband.

"Hmmm . . . the virgin bride," Maggie whispered more to herself than to Frankie.

Lord, Frankie thought and tipped the glass up until the rest of the bubbly liquor slid down her throat in a burst of fizz and sparkle.

Then she asked quietly, "What do I do?"

"Go home," Maggie said simply.

"Why should I? It's his hotel now. It's all he really wanted."

Maggie shook her head gently. "I don't think so, Frankie. I've seen the way he looks at you."

"Hmmph," Frankie shot back. "You mean

the way the Raffertys would look at the Mother Lode? If they ever found it, that is."

Maggie chuckled.

But Frankie looked over her shoulder uneasily as if simply saying their names out loud would cause the Rafferty brothers to magically appear. Just the thought of those three elderly prospectors was enough to make her blood run cold.

As old friends of her father's, the three brothers had been a part of her life for as long as Frankie could remember. They were also unkempt, uncouth, and completely unpredictable. Sean, she thought wryly, would get along with them famously.

"Oh, Frankie." Maggie said and slipped down from the desk. "The way Sean looks at you has nothin' to do with money *or* the hotel."

Frankie was not convinced.

Maggie took her sister's hands in hers and squeezed them.

"Even that very first night," Maggie told her, "at dinner here at the saloon, he looked as though he could gobble you up."

Frankie shivered. For some strange reason, she wasn't sure if she wanted to believe Maggie or not. True, she was married to the man ... and love between her and her husband would have been wonderful.

And yet ...

"I think the big lummox loves you," Maggie said quietly.

"Hah!" Frankie pulled her hands free and wrapped her arms about her waist. Pain stabbed at her. No matter what Maggie said, Sean had made it perfectly clear how he felt. If he'd loved her, he would have consummated the marriage that he'd practically forced on her. It was surprising to discover how much it hurt to know that he didn't really love her. And at the same time, she was furious with herself for caring. She shouldn't care. Should she?

No. Of course she shouldn't. What did it matter to her? It wasn't as if she loved him.

Frankie shook her head slowly and said, "No, he doesn't love me. He only said that to get the hotel."

"Said it, did he?"

"Yes, he said it. But what does that matter? Only a short while after declaring his love for me, he was trying to back out of a marriage forced on us both by his actions."

"He tried to back out?"

Frankie glared at her sister. "Weren't you listening to me at all?"

Maggie shrugged and smiled at her.

Sighing, Frankie said, "Yes, he tried to back out. Not in so many words," she admitted, "but he certainly didn't run to the altar."

"Seems a bit unusual, doesn't it, if he was trying to marry you to get the hotel?"

Hmmm. She hadn't thought of that. Her brows drew together, and she tapped one finger against her chin thoughtfully. It was true. If he'd really wanted control of the Four Roses, he should have been overjoyed at the prospect of a hurried marriage.

"But if he does care," Frankie argued, "why

did he hold me at arm's length the moment he had a legal claim to the Roses?"

"Arm's length?"

"Yes."

"Ah," Maggie said slowly, "then the two of you *really* didn't . . ."

Frankie stiffened. She thought she'd made that point clear when she'd explained the whole situation earlier. It had been humiliating enough to admit the first time. Swallowing down the small remaining bits of her pride, she answered softly, "No, we didn't."

"Well now, that's interesting."

"I'm delighted you're intrigued."

Maggie shook her head and didn't bother to hide the smile on her face. "Honestly, Frankie," she said, giving her younger sister a quick shake. "Don't you see?"

"See *what*, for heaven's sake?"

"He's scared!"

"Scared? Sean Sullivan . . . scared?" Frankie shook her head. No, it was hard to imagine that big, burly man with the confident air and the easy manner as being afraid of anything.

"Terrified," Maggie said, the smile on her face evidence of how much she was enjoying all this. "That big Irishman is afraid of *you*, Frankie."

"Don't be ridiculous."

"Think about this for a minute, Mary Frances."

She sighed, drained her champagne glass, and waited. Frankie didn't believe a word of any of this and was beginning to wish she'd never come to Maggie for advice in the first place.

"You say he spent a lot of time followin' you about, payin' you compliments and such."

"All the time."

"And he stole a kiss or two?"

Frankie cleared her throat. "Yes. One or two."

"And he even came flat out and admitted that he loved you?"

"Yes. When we were trapped in the confessional. Just before Father Gallagher found us."

"Then I'm right. I know I am." Maggie turned and walked back to her desk. After pouring herself another glass of champagne, she walked back to Frankie's side and refilled her glass as well.

"Lord, it took me *weeks* to get Cutter to admit he loved me. But Sean already has. He *does* love you, Frankie. That's what has him so scared."

"Why would he love *me*, of all people?" Her fingers curled around the delicate stem of the glass, and she stared blankly into the champagne.

"Because, dear sister," Maggie said firmly and lifted Frankie's chin with the tip of one finger, "It's obvious he's a man of rare taste and distinction. He can see past your disguise to the treasure within."

"Disguise?"

"Uh-huh." Maggie stepped back and looked her sister up and down thoroughly. "Why, if you'd only let *me* pick out your clothes, there's no tellin' *what* the man might do." Shaking her head gently, Maggie added, "What you see in these frumpy . . . dresses is beyond me."

Frankie looked from Maggie's flamboyant gown to her own plain gray day dress. Briefly, she wondered just what it might feel like to wear silk and lace out in public. But just as quickly, she let the thought go. No matter how she tried, Frankie would never be the silk and lace kind. Excepting her dressing gown, of course. Firmly she told her sister, "No thank you, Maggie. I'll stay as I am."

Maggie shrugged but looked disappointed. "All right, it's up to you." She took a long drink of champagne, then said pointedly, "But if you should change your mind and suddenly decide that you want to bring that husband of yours to his knees, let me know. I've a deep yellow gown that would suit you beautifully. One look at you and Sean Sullivan will be feeling like he's been hit by a train."

Frankie giggled, then clamped her hand over her mouth. From behind her hand, she said, "All he's feeling now is a hangover."

"It's good for him," Maggie told her. "A little suffering . . . a little guilt . . . many a man's been brought to heel by less."

Chapter 13

⌒⌒◯◯⌒⌒

Sean pushed through the door, stepped into the kitchen, and gasped. The big, homey room was as hot as the halls of hell itself. Sweat immediately beaded on his forehead, and he felt as though he couldn't have drawn a breath if his very life depended on it.

His only thought as he crossed the room was to reach the back door as quickly as possible. He didn't even hear Frankie yell, "Don't," as he threw the door wide and let the ocean breezes whip through the room.

"Blast it!" she said and Sean turned in time to see her throw a dish towel to the counter in disgust.

"Lord, woman," he asked, wiping his forehead with the back of his hand. "Are ya tryin' to roast us all alive?"

"No," she snapped and stared down at the pan in front of her.

He stepped closer to the counter and looked into the pan holding her attention. His eyebrows lifted as he studied the mess in the pan, golden-brown and no more than an inch or so thick. He'd never seen anything like it.

"What is it?" he asked.

"What *was* it, you mean." She threw one disgusted glance at him, then picked up her discarded towel. Using the cloth to protect her hands, she picked up the still-hot pan and set it, along with its mysterious contents, into the sink. "It *was* a soufflé," Frankie said and shook her head.

"What happened to it?" Not that he cared, Sean told himself. Nor did he know what a soufflé was supposed to look like. But talking about that was better than discussing what he'd come to say.

"You opened that door, the cool breeze hit it, and it fell."

"Oh. Sorry."

She spun around and Sean stared at her. That plain gray dress of hers clung to her generous bosom and there was a long streak of flour across her cheek. Her face was flushed from the heat of the room, and the few strands of hair lying on her forehead had dampened and curled. The sleeves of her dress were rolled back, displaying creamy forearms peppered with a golden burst of freckles. There were stains on her apron and she looked tired enough to fall asleep on her feet.

Sean wanted her so badly he thought he might die of it. His groin tightened and he felt as though a giant fist was wrapped around his heart, slowly strangling it. His every instinct cried out for him to grab her and hold her tightly. To bury himself inside her until her warmth became such a part of him that he would never be cold again.

But to do that would be to accept the marriage, and he didn't know if he could. God, how he wanted to. He'd never wanted anything as he wanted to be Frannie's husband. But what if he was no good at it? What if he made her and himself miserable? Wasn't it better to avoid the risk at all than to endure the hurt of a failure?

"Did you want something, Sean?"

"Huh?" He shook his head and told himself that he would be better served if he tried not to think about bedding Frannie. Of course, since the moment he'd seen her, that had been *all* he'd thought about. Trying to stop at this late date just might be impossible.

"Sean?"

"Oh, sorry, lass," he said finally. "Me mind's wanderin' a bit."

"Maybe it's the drink."

He frowned. The alcoholic fog was long gone, but he didn't think she'd believe him if he told her it was her own sweet self that was muddling up what was left of his brain.

"I'm fine," he said. "Thank you for askin'."

"I am your wife," Frankie said a bit too sweetly. "Your health is my concern."

Hmmm. He rubbed his jaw with one hand and studied her. She didn't look any different than she had that morning. Except of course for the obvious results of her cooking frenzy.

Sean gave the room a quick glance. He couldn't even count all the baked goods lined up on every available inch of space. Cakes and pies and cookies were stacked next to loaves of bread. A pan of what looked to be baked apples sat at the back of the stove, still simmering in their cinnamon-flavored juices. Biscuits and cornbread were piled high on the far end of the counter, and beside them sat row after row of gingerbread men. Sean was oddly pleased that none of the tasty-looking little men was missing any appendages. It was . . . reassuring, somehow.

So, he asked himself, if nothing had changed except her baking habits, why was she suddenly being so nice to him?

But, as Calhoun would say, "Don't question a gift—just grab it and say thanks."

In that spirit, Sean was grateful that she'd decided to be a bit more congenial toward him. Heaven knew, when he told her about his family, he would need all the help he could get.

"Is there something you wanted, Sean? I'm in the middle of baking, as you can see."

His eyebrows rose nearly into his hairline. "Lord above, what is there left to bake? As it is, it looks as though you've used up a good ten pounds of flour."

Sean didn't even realize he'd spoken aloud until he saw her stiffen and lift that chin of hers defiantly. "Maggie's customers buy my baked goods. It's a good bit of extra money that we . . . that is, the hotel, can use."

"Ah well, that's good."

Her lips lifted in a half smile. "I'm happy you're pleased." Then a moment later, she asked, "Was there something you wanted?"

Besides yourself? he wanted to ask. But no, it made no sense to delve into that again. And yet nothing had made sense since the moment he'd walked into the hotel and found her lying in a dead faint.

In fact, his entire life had been shattered from that moment—he just hadn't realized it until now. He had spent the last several years enjoying the life he'd made for himself very much. But he'd never counted on a pair of soft green eyes and a mass of strawberry-gold hair. He'd never planned on wanting a woman as much as he wanted her. And God help him, he'd never thought beyond the want to the rest of it.

Not for a single blasted moment had he thought past the idea of bedding her. If he had, he might have been able to control himself enough that they wouldn't have been forced into marriage.

A marriage it was clear she didn't want any more than he did.

But it was well past time to be thinking on what-might-have-beens. Dragging a deep breath past the knot in his chest, he said, "Can we let go of the rest for a minute, love?"

She winced at the endearment, and something inside him twisted.

"I've somethin' I need to tell ya, Frannie."

"What?"

"I got a wire today. From the family." He paused a moment to let his words sink in. "They'll be here anytime."

"Yes?"

"Well," he said, surprised that she asked no questions, "I thought you should know, so you could be ready for them."

"Ready how?"

How indeed? he thought. Maybe he should have explained about the family before. But at the time, he'd thought it would be more fun to surprise her with them. After all, the explanation could only fall far short of the reality. But that wasn't the whole truth either. Actually, he'd hoped that she would be fond enough of him by the time the others arrived that she would accept his family more easily.

Now, though, Sean was beginning to think that it might have been better if she'd known what to expect.

"I think I understand," she said slowly.

"Huh? Understand?"

"Yes. You're trying to tell me that you'd like for your family to think this is a *real* marriage."

"No, that's not—"

"Well, Sean," she went right on, sailing past his attempt to interrupt her. "This *is* a real marriage. Consummated or not, we are married. So don't worry." Frankie walked over to the counter and stopped when she was just a step or two away from him. "I'm no more anxious than you for people to suspect the truth."

He stared down into her green eyes and wanted to lose himself in them.

"It's bad enough that *I* know you only married me for my property." She drew in a breath and added, "It's hardly something I want others to know."

"Frannie," he ground out.

"Please call me Frankie," she whispered.

"That other name only reminds me of the lies."

"I wasn't lyin'," Sean said and reached out to grab her. His hands closed around her upper arms and dragged her to him. Then his right hand moved, slipping up over her shoulder to cup the back of her head. His fingers threaded through the mass of hair and he heard hairpins dropping and scattering on the kitchen floor.

Startled, Frankie could only stare up into his hard, tight features.

She read the want, the need in his eyes, and her certainty about his reasons for marrying her wavered. Maybe Maggie had been right. Maybe he *did* care for her. Maybe it wasn't simply the hotel he was interested in.

His gaze moved over her features slowly and she felt each glance like a touch. Her heartbeat quickened and her mouth felt suddenly dry. Here was the magic he'd worked on her from almost the first day they'd met. Here was the reason she'd wound up being compromised into this marriage.

"Frannie darlin'," he whispered. "I know I've hurt ya, but believe me it wasn't my intention."

She nodded, willing to believe at least that much.

"You're beautiful, lass," he went on, smoothing her hair with his fingertips. "So beautiful . . ."

His hands on her arms sent warmth spiraling through her body, and she stopped thinking. She didn't want to think now. She only wanted to feel. Heaven help her, she loved the feelings that swept her when he touched her. She loved the excitement that sparkled in her blood whenever he kissed her.

Here then was something she hadn't admitted to Maggie. Something she hadn't admitted even to herself until that very moment.

She couldn't do as he asked, though. That undeniable need building in her body urged her on, and once more she moved against him. That hard, strong part of him dug into her flesh again, and she arched into him instinctively.

"Frannie love." Sean dipped his head and dropped a quick kiss at the corner of her parted lips. "You're killin' me."

Only that morning she'd warned him to stay away from her. And now, with his body pressed against her, she only wanted him closer. For now, for this moment, Frankie let go of the anger and the questions and the doubts. For however briefly, she wanted to experience what only he could make her feel.

She licked her lips and concentrated on the warm, tingly sensation between her legs. It was so...unusual...so thrilling. Sean ducked his head and kissed the length of her throat. Frankie tipped her head to one side, giving him access to her flesh. Her breath came in short gasps and her heartbeat thundered in her ears.

Why was it that Sean Sullivan could stir such incredibly different emotions in her?

"Saints in heaven," he muttered thickly and

raised up before letting his forehead rest against hers.

"It feels . . . wonderful," she breathed, and inhaled the sharp, clean scent of him, drawing it deep into her lungs. She felt his own ragged breath brush her cheeks, and her lips parted, as if to capture his breath and make it her own.

"Aye, I know," he finally whispered.

"You do?"

"Oh, aye." He swallowed, lifted his head a bit, and looked down at her. Frankie stared up into his gaze and was a bit surprised to realize that she wasn't embarrassed in the slightest. Heaven knew how she could be . . . discussing such things with him as if she were talking about nothing more intimate than the price of coffee.

"What is it?" she asked again. All she wanted to do now was concentrate on the feel of his big hand cupping her behind. It was such a deliciously sinful feeling. Frankie wiggled her bottom and felt his fingers press into her flesh. Her eyes squeezed shut. A soft moan escaped her lips.

"Jesus, Mary, and Joseph," Sean whispered as if for strength before telling her, "it's the wanting, love. It's your body cryin' out for mine to become a part of it."

Her eyes flew open again.

That feeling between her legs tripled in strength and she felt an incredible damp warmth rush to that aching spot. Swallowing heavily, she forced herself to ask, "Do you feel it too?"

"Lord love ya." He gave her a crooked smile and his cheek dimpled. "Do ya not feel this?" he asked and arched his hips against her.

That rigid knot of flesh dug at her and she nodded slowly.

"That, me love, is my body's answer to your body's call."

Her breath caught in her chest. Was that strength meant for her? Was his tense body poised in waiting for hers?

Frankie's hands moved to his shoulders and her fingers dug into his muscular back. If she didn't hold on tightly, she would certainly fall into a heap. There was no feeling at all left in her legs beyond an incredible tingling weakness.

Once she felt steady enough, she rocked her hips against his to feel his body's desire again.

He sucked air in through clenched teeth, and Frankie stopped moving abruptly.

"Do ya understand now, Frannie? A man's body doesn't ache with wanting a blasted hotel. I want *you*. I have since the moment I met ya." He sighed heavily and added, "And I'll probably *still* want ya when I'm too old to remember *why* I want ya."

She blinked at his bald, simple statement. Had he really been living with such an aching need for more than a week? Frankie licked her lips and saw his gaze lock onto her tongue's darting movement. Dear Lord, she didn't know how he'd managed to hide the torment he must have suffered.

"How do you stand it?" she asked aloud.

"By bein' near you," he murmured, his gaze

caressing her features. "By touchin' you and listenin' to your voice. By indulgin' myself in your quick tongue and even quicker mind."

"Doesn't that make it worse?" she asked innocently. "The wanting, I mean?"

"Worse and better all at once," he assured her.

She shook her head.

"Ah, Frannie, there's more to wantin' than just the beddin'." He inhaled sharply and said, "If I couldn't have the one, I wanted the other. It was enough to kiss you." He dipped his head and claimed her lips in a too brief kiss. "To touch you." His hand on her behind stroked her through the fabric of her gown. "To smell the scent of violets when you were near." He buried his face in the crook of her neck and nibbled her flesh at the base of her throat.

Frankie's head fell back, to allow him easier access. His lips and teeth worked at her skin and gooseflesh rippled along her spine.

Everything she'd felt since the humiliation on her wedding night faded away. Every thought splintered. Every concern dissolved.

All that mattered at that instant was Sean's body leaning over hers.

No matter what he'd said, Frankie knew that if her body were to burn every day as it did now, the fire would kill her. She needed the answer to her question. She needed to know how to survive the onslaught of such powerful sensations.

No, she told herself firmly, she needed to know how to make them stop.

Pushing that thought to the back of her mind, Frankie ignored the rational, sensible part of her brain for the first time in years. She didn't want it to stop. Just for now, she wanted to feel. To experience the blossoming fire in her body. To feel it burn through her.

As Sean's mouth moved over her throat, his left hand shifted from her bottom and reached up to undo the top buttons of her dress. Her eyes closed, and she shivered as each button slipped free and his lips moved down her chest.

Eagerness like she'd never known before rushed through her. The fire in her blood quickened, and breathing became difficult. Her brain once again began to race with notions, one wilder than the next.

She had to know more. She had to feel the burning claim her. And the only man who could possibly teach her about that fire was holding her in his arms. Her husband.

He was the only man who'd ever created such sensations in her. His was the only touch that left a stinging warmth branded onto her flesh long after he'd released her. And most importantly, *he* was the only man with the right to touch her.

Who better to teach her about this fascinating blend of desire and throbbing pain than her husband?

And if the marriage wasn't all she'd once hoped for, at the very least, this . . . *need* would be answered and she could go on as she had before.

Surely he could help her end this terrible,

wonderful longing. Once he'd quenched the fire in her blood, they could go on without each other. Surely *one* night wasn't too much to ask in exchange for throwing her life into turmoil.

Frankie smiled softly, leaned into the hard, broad wall of his chest, and wrapped her arms about his neck. Rising onto her toes, she touched her lips to his briefly.

"Ah, Frannie," he said, "don't go startin' somethin' we might both regret."

"Ah, Sean," she retorted, "let's not think about regrets right now. Let's not think at all."

Before he could say anything more, Frankie took his mouth. Gently at first, her lips moved over his. Then she felt his breath come out in a soft sigh and she became emboldened. Her teeth tugged at his lower lip and she ran the tip of her tongue along the curve of his mouth.

His strong arms tightened around her and Frankie gasped when her feet left the floor entirely.

Holding her easily against him, Sean smiled grimly. He grabbed a handful of her hair, pulled her head back, and stared into her eyes.

"Ya don't know what you're askin', Frannie."

"Then teach me . . . *husband*."

He studied her for a long, silent moment, and Frankie held her breath.

"If I be damned for it . . . then so be it," he muttered.

He dipped his head to hers and she gave herself up to the astonishing sensations coursing through her. Fire leaped to life in her bloodstream. She felt as though she were burning up from the inside.

Burrowing in closer to him, Frankie held on tight and opened her mouth to his questing tongue. Damp, wild caresses swept the inside of her mouth, and her tongue met his every touch and returned it.

A groan shuddered through him and he turned sharply, pressing her back against the wall. Holding her in place with one hand, he let his free hand wander over her. Frankie tore her mouth from his and gasped for air. Her hands braced on his shoulders, she leaned into his touch, and when his right hand cupped her breast, her body arched against him.

The open vee of material at her chest seemed to call to him and he buried his face in the valley between her breasts. She felt his tongue trace over her heated skin. Every caress was like a brand. She wanted to move against him, feel him pressed close to her, but she couldn't move.

Feet high off the floor, she hung suspended against the wall, supported only by his immense strength.

"Sean," she whispered plaintively and heard the soft moaning tone in her voice.

He let her slide slowly to the floor, and when her feet were on the ground again, he didn't give her time to think. With both hands free now, Sean moved rapidly. His fingers flew to the apron, still pinned to her dress. Quickly he opened the pins and shoved the white bibbed apron down around her waist.

Drawing in deep, ragged breaths, he met

her gaze briefly, then turned to look at the row of buttons marching down the front of her dress.

He paused, waiting for a reaction, and Frankie answered his unspoken question by lifting one of his hands and placing it firmly against the pearl buttons. She watched a small smile curve his mouth, then she closed her eyes and tipped her head back against the wall.

One by one, the rest of her buttons were freed. She felt the cool ocean breeze as it slipped past her through the open back door. There was still enough rational thought left in her brain to be grateful that her small backyard was entirely enclosed by a high fence. With Fiona napping and Treasure gone for the day, they had the house to themselves. No one would burst in on them unexpectedly.

Then all thought fled. Her insides twisted as Sean pulled the thin fabric of her chemise open to expose her breasts. Never had her generous bosom felt heavier, fuller. The cool air swept in, and her already rigid nipples tightened expectantly.

She squeezed her eyes shut more tightly and her hands curled into fists at her sides. What would he think of her? What was he going to do?

And, dear God, *when* was he going to do it?

She heard him sigh and hoped it was a sigh of pleasure.

"Frannie love," he whispered and she felt him trace the tip of one finger around the circle of her nipple.

"What?" she ground out.

"Open your eyes, love."

"No." She shook her head firmly and felt the plank wall scrape against her scalp. She couldn't look at him *now*.

He chuckled softly and smoothed his thumb across the tip of her nipple.

Frankie gasped and her back arched.

"Frannie me darlin'." he said again. "I'll do no more until you open those beautiful green eyes of yours."

Oh God, she didn't want him to stop. Frankie had had no idea that she possessed such an affinity for sin. She wanted more. She wanted . . . Oh, she wasn't even sure *what* she wanted. All she was certain of was that she hadn't had enough. Not yet.

She slowly opened her eyes and stared at the ceiling.

"Look at me, love," he prodded gently.

She licked her lips, took a deep breath, and glanced down briefly. Then she gasped and flicked her gaze back to the ceiling.

It didn't help though. As much as she stared at the whitewashed pine planks, all she saw was Sean Sullivan, kneeling in front of her, his mouth only a breath away from her distended nipple.

That warm dampness between her legs spread and Frankie had to grit her teeth against the throbbing ache that had settled there.

"Frannie, look at me," Sean said once more.

"I . . . can't," she whispered.

"Do ya not enjoy my touch?"

"Yes," she admitted quickly. "Yes, I do . . .

but I can't—*watch* you as you touch me."

He leaned in close and pressed a brief kiss on her nipple.

"Oh God . . ."

"It's all right, love," he finally told her and lifted the hem of her skirt with one hand. "I'm sorry I asked it of ya. Look where ya please. As will I."

But she hardly heard him. His hand was on her leg and moving slowly over her calf. Frankie shuddered slightly and stared sightlessly at a knothole in a ceiling plank.

She felt his hand creep up her leg an inch at a time as if he was afraid of frightening her. Through the sheer fabric of her pantaloons, his touch was like a flame. Instinctively she widened her stance just a bit and slapped her palms flat against the wall for support.

A moment later, she was glad of whatever support she could find. Sean's mouth closed over her nipple and his tongue began to stroke the hardened bud until Frankie thought she would go mad.

A soft whimper left her throat, and Frankie was helpless to stop it. Sean must have heard it too, because he began to lavish even more attention on her breasts. Moving his head from one to the other of them, he took each nipple into his mouth in turn and gently scraped the edges of his teeth against the tender flesh.

Frankie swallowed heavily and felt her leg collapse when his hand cupped the back of her knee. She lifted her hands to his shoulders then and held on tightly, determined to experience everything she'd always wondered about.

And then he began to suckle her and her fingers dug into his shoulders. "Sean!" she cried, and her voice was no more than a strangled gasp.

He seemed to know she didn't want him to stop. Again and again, his talented mouth tugged at her flesh. Gently, persistently, Sean suckled her, and the sensations rocketing through her pushed Frankie beyond what she'd thought she could bear.

The incredible feeling of his mouth on her, drawing her into him, shattered her defenses. Feeling bold and daring, she lowered her gaze and watched him at her breast. Tears of pleasure leaped into her eyes, and she blinked them back, suddenly needing to see everything.

His black hair tumbled across his forehead and lay against her own cream-colored flesh. His eyes were closed and on his features was a look of such . . . adoration, Frankie's breath caught in her chest.

She lifted her hands to cup his head, and when she pushed his hair back from his eyes, he released her nipple and tilted his face up to hers.

"Are ya all right, Frannie?" he asked, turning his face far enough to place a kiss on her palm.

She nodded, her throat too tight to speak.

"Do ya want me to stop?"

A long moment passed before she smiled softly and shook her head.

"Good," he told her gently. "Because I'm not near finished yet."

Then his hand slid up her thigh and Frankie jumped.

Leaning close to her breasts again, Sean's tongue darted out and flicked a swollen nipple. Her fingers tightened in his hair.

"You're lovely, lass," he said gently. "And ya taste like heaven itself."

A sheen of tears filled her eyes again, and she lifted one hand to rub them away. All of her life she'd thought of herself as the short, plump sister.

Plain Frankie.

She'd never had the beaux that her sisters had. In fact, except for the brief experience with Conor James, the only man to come courting at all had been Herbert Featherstone. And the closest he'd ever come to complimenting her was to comment on her "fine mind."

It had never bothered her though . . . at least she hadn't thought she'd minded being plain Frankie. Until now. Until this man had looked at her too plump body and declared her lovely.

A smile hovered at the edge of her lips as she realized that she was feeling so good, she even heard music.

She watched Sean lean in close and take her nipple into his mouth again. Frankie held his face in her hands and let the imaginary music she heard accompany the wild desire building in her.

Sean's hand moved higher up her leg, and

the juncture of her thighs tightened in anticipation. So close, her mind whispered. One
more moment and the ache would be eased.

One touch and she would be at peace again.

The music in her head grew louder and
louder. Sean's lips and teeth moved on her
flesh with abandon. She twisted in his grasp,
somehow keeping time with the music.

And then he stopped.

But the music went on.

Letting his hand slip from beneath her
dress, Sean pulled back from her and sat on
his haunches, listening.

"Do you hear it too?" she asked, trying to
ignore the fact that he had stopped too soon.

"Huh?" he asked, cocking his head as if to
listen more closely.

"The music," Frankie said softly, reaching
out to ruffle his hair. "I thought my mind had
created it, but it's getting louder."

"Yes," Sean said and stood up slowly, like
an old man.

"What is it, do you think?" she asked.

"Sounds like a band." Sean spoke quietly,
stiffly. Before Frankie could protest, he'd
drawn the edges of her chemise together and
had neatly done up half the buttons on her
dress.

"Sean?" she said and tried to hide the note
of disappointment in her voice when the last
button was securely fastened.

"Frannie, this is why I came in here to talk
to you."

A screechingly loud trumpet blast shattered
the rhythm of the music.

"What do you mean?"

He jerked his head toward the front of the hotel, where the noise now sounded as if it were coming from the front parlor.

"That. I wanted you to know—"

"Miss Frankie!"

She jerked away from Sean and looked at the kitchen door and the hallway beyond.

Sean cursed under his breath at the interruption.

Running footsteps clattered on the wood floor and got louder as someone neared the kitchen.

Instinctively Frankie's hand flew to the bodice of her dress, checking to be sure that she was decently covered.

"Miss Frankie!"

She recognized the voice now.

Tommy.

The moment his name leaped into her mind, the boy burst through the swinging door into the kitchen. Glancing quickly from Sean to her, he cried out, "Hurry, Miss Frankie! You gotta come see! It's wonderful!"

Frankie stared at the boy for a long moment. His small face was lit from within and his happy grin was magical. Eyes wide, he was practically dancing from foot to foot. He tossed a quick glance back over his shoulder, then turned around to look at her again. Frankie had never seen the usually stoic boy so excited. A smile curved her lips and she glanced at Sean to share her pleasure.

But his features were shuttered and there was a shine of regret in his eyes.

Frankie's smile faded a bit as a seed of worry began to take root in the pit of her stomach.

But Tommy wouldn't be ignored. He raced forward, grabbed her hand, and began to tug her toward the hall.

Chapter 14

Tommy ran down the length of the hall, pulling Frankie along. Behind them, Frankie heard Sean following and noticed that for the first time, his footsteps sounded loud and heavy.

The front door was standing wide open and the music, ear-stabbingly loud now, rushed into the hotel. Horns, drums, and a wheezing organ came together in an exuberant if off-key rendition of "Dixie."

Another blast of an out-of-tune trumpet joined the noise, and Frankie winced.

She began slowing her steps as she neared the door. That seed of worry in the pit of her stomach had taken root and was even now blossoming into a huge tree of anxiety.

Tommy finally gave up on hurrying her and dropped her hand so he could run ahead.

Sean came up beside her and she stopped in her tracks. He lifted one huge hand as if to touch her, then let it fall to his side again.

"I wanted to tell ya," he started, his voice pitched loud enough to carry over the music still blasting from the yard.

"Tell me now," she said.

And then the music stopped. In the sudden profound silence, Frankie stared at Sean, waiting. A long minute passed before they both heard a voice from outside calling, "Sean! Seaneen, boy! Where are ya?"

A lilting Irish brogue colored the otherwise harsh voice, and Frankie's eyebrows lifted slightly.

"Seaneen?"

He shrugged. "She's always called me that. It's the Gaelic way of sayin' little Sean."

"I know what it means," Frankie said stiffly. "What I want to know is . . . would that be your family arriving?"

He nodded.

"And do they always travel with a band to announce their arrival?"

"Ya could say that."

That wonderfully warm, wicked glow in which she'd been wrapped a few minutes ago was completely gone now. In its place was a prickly sensation of coming trouble.

"Miss Frankie," Tommy shouted from the yard, "come on out here! You gotta see the circus!"

A circus?

Frankie's gaze shifted from Sean's pained face to the doorway. Slowly she started walking toward the late-afternoon sunshine splashed across the porch. On the threshold, she stopped. Eyes wide, she stared openmouthed at the unbelievable sight on the street.

Four brightly colored wagons were strung

out along the front of the hotel. The horses pulling those wagons each wore a long, snow-white, feathery plume in its halter and even the trace chains were decorated with bells and garish beads.

On the roof of the last wagon in the bunch was an old organ. As she watched, a young man climbed down from the roof and ran around to join another man on the driver's perch.

Frankie's gaze drifted over the other wagons, each gaudier than the last. The rattle of trace chains and the tinkling sound of bells caught her attention and Frankie turned to watch the first of the wagons move through the wide gate of the still unfinished fence surrounding the grassy lot next door.

Perched on the driver's seat was a big woman with wild, wind-blown gray hair. Her red and yellow shawl was tied across her big bosom, and her boot-clad feet were braced on the kickboard in front of her. She held the reins competently enough, but the language she used to convince the horses to obey her will was turning the very air blue.

"You no-good, slab-sided sons of bitches! Get up there," she yelled, and Frankie recognized the voice. This was the woman who had called Sean *Seaneen*. "Move along you stupid bastards or I'll have your innards in a stew pot this night!"

Frankie's jaw dropped. Giving a quick glance around, she noticed for the first time that a crowd had formed on the sidewalk. On-lookers had gathered and were staring with open fascination at the foulmouthed old woman.

Traffic on the street had come to a halt and there were shouted protests from the dray wagon drivers who were trapped by the small parade.

A shrieking noise blasted into the air, and Frankie looked around quickly for the fool who insisted on blowing that blasted horn.

As if on cue, the guilty party stepped from behind one of the wagons. Frankie's eyes widened and one hand flew up to cover her mouth.

If she hadn't seen it, she wouldn't believe it.

An elephant.

Obviously still a baby, the animal trotted up to the line of boys hanging on the fence and lifted its trunk. Touching first one child, then the next, the elephant trumpeted again and the children dissolved into fits of laughter.

"Holy Mother of God," Frankie whispered and tore her gaze away from Tommy and his friends.

As she stood in stunned silence, Mrs. Destry slipped past her through the doorway. Cackling delightedly, the old lady slammed her walking stick down on the steps, then carefully made her way to the yard, obviously enjoying the commotion.

Frankie, though, was not.

She spun around and tilted her head back to stare up at Sean.

"A circus?" she said hotly. "Your *family* owns a circus?"

"No." He stiffened slightly and explained, "My family *is* the circus."

"And you didn't think it important enough to tell me that a circus would be moving into my hotel?"

"*Our* hotel."

Her jaw snapped shut.

"I tried to tell ya," he said. "That's why I came to see ya in the kitchen."

Memories of what had happened just a short time ago filled her mind and made her cheeks flush. She remembered all too well why he hadn't gotten around to telling her about this family of his. But still, he'd been in town more than a week. There'd been plenty of chances for him to talk to her. To warn her.

But would it have helped? she asked herself. No.

How could anyone prepare for a *circus*, of all things?

"We'll talk later," he promised. Then he stepped past her, jumped down the steps, and ran through the crowds and around the fence gate. He climbed up on the lead wagon, gave the woman a quick kiss on the cheek, and took the reins from her hands. Frankie watched as he snapped the leather straps in the air over the horses' backs and neatly guided them into their new home.

"Isn't this somethin'!" Tommy shouted to her from the fence, and Frankie could only nod.

Disruptions.

She snorted a short, humorless laugh. She'd thought *Sean* was going to be an interruption of her nice quiet life. Now not only was there Sean to deal with, there was an entire circus load of disruptions descending on her.

Shaking her head, she fell back against the doorjamb and watched her peaceful little world disintegrate.

Frankie's head was still spinning an hour later when everyone had gathered in the front parlor.

Strange, she thought, that though the hotel was *her* home, she was the one who felt out of place. Her gaze followed Sean as he moved around the room, shaking hands and exchanging hearty hugs. Out of the corner of her eye, she noticed young Tommy, eyes still wide, sidling soundlessly into the room. He took up position alongside a tall bookcase and quietly eased himself into the shadows where he could watch and not be seen.

"Frannie!"

She swiveled her head around to face Sean. He stepped beside her, took her hand, and threaded it through the crook of his elbow. In a loud voice to be heard above the low hum of conversation, Sean said, "I'd like to introduce you all to someone." He paused, glanced down at her, and took a deep breath. "This is Mary Frances Donnelly . . . Sullivan. My wife."

A collective gasp of surprise rose up from the cluster of people. Frankie's gaze slipped from one to the other of them quickly, hoping to judge their reactions to Sean's announcement.

"Frannie," Sean went on and pointed to a couple across the room. "This is Phoebe and Devlin O'Connor. They walk the wire for the Calhoun Circus."

Frankie smiled at the two people with the open, friendly features. Then the woman reached behind her and drew two children out into the open. Softly, Phoebe said, "And these two are Bridget and Butler."

Even without the introduction, Frankie would have known that the four people belonged together. Each of them had warm, brown hair and brown eyes. And all of them wore the stamp of inner happiness on their faces.

"The kids too are wire walkers in the fine tradition of the O'Connor family," Sean added, and Devlin gave him a half bow in thanks.

"Next, Frannie love"—Sean swung his arm to an older man with a full head of thick, black hair—"is Dennis Traherne. He handles the tickets and the money and still manages to keep the rest of us in line." Dennis was about sixty, Frankie guessed, and the deep lines on his face all appeared to have been caused by the wide smile he gave her. Obviously Dennis Traherne was a man accustomed to smiling. Barrel-chested and broad-shouldered, he was also very likely a man used to hard work.

"And my name," a deep voice close by said, "is Ryan."

Frankie looked to her left and watched a tall, auburn-haired man approach. Beneath her hand, she felt Sean tense, but she didn't look up at him. She couldn't seem to tear her gaze away from Ryan's pale, icy-blue stare.

When he reached her, Ryan lifted her free hand and brought it to his lips. The tip of his tongue slanted across her knuckles, and Frankie pulled her hand free. Sean stiffened and took a half step forward, but the other man took a small step back at the same time. One corner of Ryan's well-shaped mouth tilted and a knowing glint appeared in those strange eyes of his.

"Ryan Grady," Sean said and Frankie heard the gravel in his voice. "He's a clown."

Ryan flashed an angry gaze at Sean, then shifted his eyes back to Frankie.

"A clown true," he told her in a voice pitched so low it seemed as though he were sharing intimate secrets with her alone. "Among other things." His dark red brows lifted slightly as he inclined his head toward her. "I am a man of many gifts." Glancing at Sean one last time, he said a bit louder, "And Sean should remember that one of my specialties is knife throwing."

Frankie moved closer to Sean's side. Looking into Ryan Grady's eyes was enough to send cold chills down her spine, and she didn't much care for the look he was sending Sean either.

"I am next, I believe," a soft, silky-smooth voice announced, and a lovely woman stepped up to Frankie. Gently pushing Ryan out of the way, she held out her hand and waited for Frankie to take it. When she did, the woman smiled. "You have great strength, Mrs. Sullivan."

"Frankie, please."

"And I am Sophia."

"Sophia Cruz," Sean amended.

Sophia only smiled. "One name is surely all that I need."

"Sophia is our fortune teller," Sean said, and Frankie thankfully noticed that his tone had softened.

"I prefer . . . seer," Sophia said and nodded gently as she stepped back into the small knot of people.

Sophia's black eyes glittered with the knowledge of the centuries, but there was also a warmth in their depths that Frankie hadn't been able to find in Ryan Grady's eyes. Her thick, straight hair fell in a blue-black line to the middle of her back.

Frankie just managed to stifle a sigh. She'd always wanted hair so black it gleamed like a crow's wing.

"And then there's me."

Frankie spun to her right, responding to the angry tone instinctively.

The woman with the wild gray hair stood up from the settee where she'd been chatting with Fiona Destry, and walked to stand in front of Sean and Frankie.

"Frannie," Sean said softly, "this lovely creature is Honora Calhoun. Himself's widow and the leader of this little troupe."

Honora. Frankie thought silently. Gaelic for honor. She met the woman's cold blue gaze squarely. Unlike Ryan's gaze, there was nothing secretive about the look she directed at Frankie. There was nothing hidden in her manner.

The woman was plainly furious.

Planting her sun-browned, work-worn hands on her wide hips, Honora Calhoun looked from Sean to Frankie and back again. "Married, is it? Without tellin' us? Without waitin' on us? Do we mean so little to ya, then?"

"Of course not, Honora."

"Then why?" She turned her gaze back to Frankie, but her words were clearly meant for Sean. "What did the little minx do to get you in a snare?"

Frankie straightened her spine and met the woman glare for glare. She might have been leading a quiet life these last four years or so, but she'd been raised with three sisters. She knew well how to handle herself in a cat fight.

But Sean didn't give her the chance.

"Hold your tongue, Honora," he ground out from between clenched teeth. "Frannie's me wife and I'll expect you to be civil."

"Civil, is it?" Her gaze swept over Frankie quickly, then dismissed her. "Fine an' all. Civil I'll be. But I want to know one thing, Sean Sullivan . . ."

"What?"

"Are you stayin' with *her*"—she jerked her head at Frankie—"or comin' on the circuit with us?"

"The circuit?"

Honora scowled at her and gave her a look usually reserved for a slow-witted child.

"Aye. The circuit. Do ya think we stay in one place and make the audiences come to us?" She pushed her gray hair out of her eyes and finished, "This is a *travelin'* circus, Mrs. Sullivan. And the travelin' begins in just a few weeks."

Surprised, Frankie turned and looked up at Sean. He refused to meet her gaze though. Instead he stood silently glowering at Honora.

"Ah . . ." that woman said slowly, "ya didn't know that, did ya? Strange that your *husband* wouldn't tell ya a thing like that."

"Oh," Frankie lied. "You misunderstand. My *husband* tells me everything." Determined to stand up to Honora, she added, "I simply hadn't realized how soon the circuit would begin."

Honora eyed her thoughtfully.

Sean stared at her in open admiration.

"Well now," Dennis said abruptly, shattering the uncomfortable silence. Honora moved off then and returned to her seat beside Fiona, where she snatched up her glass of Irish whiskey. The woman took a quick, long drink as Dennis continued, "I think it's time we gave thanks to our own Sean for all he's done in preparin' for us."

The others grinned, but Sean's uncomfortable gaze shot to Frankie.

Their eyes locked as they listened to Dennis.

"It's a lovely place here and I know it'll work out fine." He lifted the glass in his hand and said, "I propose a toast!" Turning to face Frankie, he smiled broadly and offered, "To the newest member of our family, Mary

Frances Sullivan. May she be as happy as we
are for her."

Frankie looked away from Sean then and
forced a smile she didn't feel.

"Hear, hear."

"Well said."

"Good job, Dennis."

"To Mary Frances."

A movement on her right caught Frankie's
eye and she turned her head. She was in time
to see Honora Calhoun deliberately set her
glass down, refusing to drink to Sean's new
wife.

Frankie swallowed past the knot in her
throat and looked back at Sean. A tight frown
on his face told her that he too had seen Honora's actions.

As he stepped out into the night Sean
thought about how things had just become
more difficult than he had ever anticipated.
Seeing everyone again had filled him with such
confusing emotions. Oh, he was delighted to
hear their voices and listen to the stories they
had to tell. But at the same time, he didn't feel
that sense of belonging that he'd always felt in
their company. Instead of joining in the story-
telling and helping to plan the next season's
journey, he'd found himself watching Frannie
instead. He'd followed her gaze as she studied
the members of his family, and he'd wondered
what she was thinking.

He clearly recalled the look of shock on her
face when she'd first spied the show wagons.
But to give her her due, she'd hidden what-

ever she was feeling from the others. Like the
kind soul she was, she'd fed them and worked
like the very devil to make them feel at home.

Hell, she'd even been patient with Honora!

Just the thought of the woman he'd considered a second mother for the last thirteen years
made Sean furious. He'd never seen her like
that. The Honora Calhoun *he* knew would
never think of treating someone badly—least
of all in her own home.

But tonight she'd gone out of her way to
make sure Frannie felt the cold chill of disapproval.

Grumbling to himself, Sean walked out of
the yard and around the fence to the lot. At
least the crowds had finally gone home. A wry
smile touched his lips as he realized that he
should have expected people to line up in the
streets to watch the Calhoun Circus come in.
Most folks loved a parade of any kind. And
the chance to see a real live elephant didn't
come along all that often.

He shivered as a blast of ocean air swept
down the street. The wind seemed to bite at
him, driving its cold teeth right down to his
bones. Sean stuffed his hands into his pants
pockets and turned into the lot, blessing the
fact that the buildings on either side of him
blocked the wind.

He took a moment to look at the wagons
that had been such a part of his life for so long.
Rationally, he knew that the huge wooden
wagons were shabby and well-used. The paint
covering the walls of the wagons was faded
and peeling. The slogans and images that had

caught his imagination thirteen years ago now looked old and forgotten in the bright day-light.

But at night, in the pale, soft light of the moon, the old show wagons regained their magic. The moonlight disguised their flaws and lent them an air of enchantment that the harsher sunlight stole from them.

Loud snuffling and the rattle of a chain drew Sean to the far corner of the lot. There, in the center of a hastily built cage made of bales of straw, was Tiny, the baby elephant. Sean stepped into the pen with the animal and rubbed the elephant's back absently. Tiny slapped the man with his trunk and began to tug at Sean's shirt as if looking for something.

"I've no treat with me, Tiny," Sean apologized. "Tommorow, I promise, eh?"

Tiny snuffled again and turned away, clearly displeased.

Sean smiled and stepped out of the pen. Leaning on the top bale of straw, he watched the baby elephant, but his mind was far away.

How many times over the years, he wondered, had he done this same thing? Wandering about in the night, listening to the familiar sounds, breathing the scents so much a part of the circus. When he was a boy, he'd found magic in the old wagons. He'd found Calhoun and a family. A place to belong.

But was the magic still there for him? he wondered as he tugged a long piece of straw free of its bale.

A footfall behind him caught his ear and Sean turned sharply. Raking the lot with a slow, careful gaze, he stared into the night, trying to distinguish shadow from substance.

"You always were quick," a voice said, "even as a boy."

Sean relaxed his stance and watched Honora step out of the shadows and walk toward him.

A tall woman with a strong, bulky build, Honora Calhoun walked with a confidence that had been years in the making. Loyal to her friends and a terror to those who opposed her, Honora was a force to be reckoned with at any time.

But tonight, Sean felt himself more than a match for her.

The memory of her treatment of Frannie was still too fresh in his mind.

"Why'd ya do it, Seaneen?" she said as she stepped into the patch of moonlight directly in front of him.

"It's a long story, Honora."

"How bloody long could it be?" She threw her arms wide in disgust. "You've only been in this blasted city for a bit more than a week!"

He wasn't about to tell her how his marriage had come about. Hell, he'd married Frannie to keep the gossips from talking. It wasn't likely he'd go spreading the stories himself.

"You're circus, Sean," she continued in a rush. "You should've married circus."

Sean snorted. "Who? Sophia?"

"And why not Sophia?"

"Because I don't love her, for one."

"And you *do* love this . . ."

"Yeah, I do." Sean nodded abruptly and

shot Honora a black glare. "And her name is Mary Frances."

Honora ignored that last statement and took off on another tangent. "You never answered me inside, boyo. Are you goin' with us . . . or are you stayin' behind. With your new *wife*."

Sean decided to ignore the sneer in her tone. He understood what was bothering his old friend. She worried constantly that members of her little troupe would up and leave.

He felt a small bubble of amusement well up inside him. Whether Honora knew it or not, she was very much like Frannie. Neither of them adapted to change at all well.

"What's it to be?" the big woman asked sharply. "Her? Or us? your family."

"She's my family now, too," Sean said quietly and saw Honora flinch. "As for the other . . . I don't know yet. It's too soon. Too . . . unsettled."

Even as he said it, he could hardly believe it. Only the day before, it had been sure enough in his mind. He'd planned to leave and let Frannie find the proper life for herself. Now here he was telling Honora that nothing was settled yet.

Lord save him, but he was confused.

"Unsettled." She spat the word back at him. Taking a deep, shuddering breath, Honora glanced at the hotel next door, then looked back to Sean. "This hotel was only meant to be a winter quarters for us, Sean. Have ya thought about that?"

He nodded slowly and let his gaze slip to

the lighted window of Frannie's bedroom.

Honora followed his gaze and shook her head.

"How important can she be to you if you didn't even tell her about the circuit? Married people talk, Seaneen. Me and Calhoun never had a secret between us."

"I know," he said softly, never taking his eyes from the soft yellow lamplight in front of him.

"And do ya know this?" she asked quietly and reached up to cup his cheek. Turning his face toward her, Honora looked deeply into his eyes and said, "Love isn't always enough, Sean."

He knew that. Hell, he'd been telling himself that very thing for the past couple of days. Loving her wasn't enough. She needed a man who would be the kind of husband she wanted.

It was why he'd decided to keep his distance from Frannie.

Then he remembered their brief time together in the kitchen and acknowledged that it would be harder than ever to keep from touching her now.

Honora gave him a hearty slap on the back and Sean staggered slightly.

"Well, Sean, you've a couple of weeks yet to realize you don't belong here anymore than your wife belongs in one of our wagons." She nodded shortly and spun about on her heel. As she walked back to the hotel, Honora called out, "See that you use your time for thinkin', Sean . . . not feelin'."

He stared at Frannie's window and muttered, "Easier said than done."

Chapter 15

Sean slipped back into the hotel quietly and closed the door behind him. Pausing for a long moment in the foyer, he looked around the place that had become so familiar to him. A slow, thoughtful smile crossed his face as he realized how quickly the Four Roses had become such a part of his life.

And not only the Four Roses—seeing Frannie every day, hearing her voice, and on those rare occasions, kissing her, holding her, had become almost as important to him as breathing.

When had it happened? he wondered. Which day? Which hour? Or was it as he'd thought that first moment she'd looked into his eyes? Had they really known each other before? Loved each other before?

Everything inside him insisted yes. And rationally, it was the only explanation he could think of to describe the incredible strength of the bond that continued to draw him to her, even though he knew it would be better for both of them if he could find a way to sever that tie.

Sean sighed, pushed his thoughts aside, and allowed himself a long minute to enjoy the welcoming atmosphere of the hotel.

A soft glow fell from the iron-worked chandelier overhead, and he smiled to realize that Frannie had left the candles burning for him. With the long-handled brass candle snuffer, he slowly pinched out the flames.

Besides, he didn't need light to know what lay around him. The hotel had been his home for close to two weeks. And for a man used to sleeping in different hotel rooms every night, or under the bed of a wagon, the old place had quickly become home to him.

The vase of flowers on the entry table, the hall tree with the tiny crack in the mirror, even the paintings on the walls seemed to breathe a sigh of welcome to him. With the lights extinguished, he set the snuffer back in its proper resting place with a smile. Sean knew all too well that in the morning, Frannie would know at a glance if it was the slightest bit out of position.

He heard the subdued ticking from the wall clock in the front parlor, and it sounded like the hotel's heartbeat. Everyday noises of the old building settling for the night reached him in the stillness, and he smiled. The creaks and groans sounded like old friends, and he suddenly felt much warmer than the temperature in the room warranted.

Then another sound intruded, and his smile faded. Someone talking. In a hushed, deep tone.

He glanced off to his left. Frannie's room.

Frowning, he set off down the hall quietly. As he neared her door, he saw the shadow of a man standing just outside her room. A slice of light fell through her partly opened door and illuminated Ryan Grady's sharp features.

Anger erupted in his chest and Sean felt as though he might choke on it. For a moment that seemed to stretch into eternity, he studied Ryan's profile. Sean knew what the man was up to. Hadn't he been watching Ryan for years? Sean had seen the slow smiles and the guarded winks. He'd heard the man use his deep, rumbling voice to entice unsuspecting women into doing things they wouldn't normally have considered.

More than once over the last ten years, the circus had left town more hurriedly than they'd planned just to help Ryan escape some irate father or husband.

And now the bastard thought he'd try his nonsense on Sean's *wife*?

In seconds, Sean was down the hall. His gaze took in Frannie's features and he was relieved to see that she was grateful for his arrival. By the way she was hiding behind her door, it was obvious she was ready for bed. Her head poked around the edge of the door, her long, strawberry-gold hair spilling down in a lush fall of curl and light.

And it irritated the hell out of Sean that Ryan Grady had seen it.

Glaring at the other man, Sean said, "Get yourself off, Grady." He felt the fire in his chest flare up into a raging inferno.

Ryan spared Sean the briefest of glances,

then looked back at Mary Frances. A soft, wicked smile touched his face as he said casually, "I was just wishin' Frannie a good night."

"You've said it," Sean managed to say around the tight knot of rage in his throat. "Now go on."

Ryan straightened up from the wall and stuffed his hands into his pockets. The smirk on his face told Sean that Ryan Grady wasn't bothered by the implied threat in the big man's tone. Eventually he moved off down the hall toward the stairs and his own room on the third floor.

Sean pushed past Frankie and entered her bedroom.

"Thank you for appearing when you did."

Still too angry to speak, Sean merely nodded, then looked away from her quickly. There was no reason for her to suffer his bad temper. The person he wanted to shout down was Ryan. Not Frannie.

"I was glad to see you," she said quietly from behind him. "But why exactly did you come to my room?"

Needing a bit of distance between them, Sean walked across the floor to the front of the fire burning in the hearth. When he heard her shut the door, he finally said, "I heard Ryan. And I know him. I wanted to see what he was up to, botherin' you at this late hour."

"I see."

Sean frowned into the flames. Did he hear a note of disappointment in her voice? No, he told himself. It was merely his own wishful thinking.

"And now?" she asked. "Ryan is gone. Why are you still here? With me?"

He pulled in a deep breath and deliberately forced himself to keep from turning and looking at her. He didn't want to see the reaction on her face. If it wasn't what he hoped for . . .

"It's better this way. Like you said . . . no one needs to know our business."

"Are you saying that you're planning on staying in my room with me?"

One corner of his mouth lifted, but he didn't turn around. He'd heard the nervousness in her voice. And he really couldn't blame her. For a woman who preferred that nothing in her life ever changed, she'd had to put up with quite a bit lately.

But, he told himself, at least she didn't sound appalled at the notion of his staying in her room.

"Isn't that what you wanted?" he asked, still studying the dancing flames in front of him. "For my family to think of this marriage as normal? A *real* one, I think you said?"

"Yes, but . . ."

"Then this is the only thing we can do." He risked a glance at her over his shoulder and almost groaned. Her teeth were tugging nervously at her bottom lip and there was a flush of high color on her cheeks.

Wearing only her white cotton nightgown, with her hair all tumbled down around her shoulders, she looked like an angel. But angels

weren't supposed to tempt poor fools, were
they?

His groin tightened and he tried not to think
about what was under that prim nightgown of
hers. He tried desperately not to remember the
soft, pale skin of her breasts. He told himself
to forget entirely what that flesh felt like in his
hands. His brain warned him not to recall the
low throaty sounds of pleasure she made
when he took her nipples into his mouth.

And he didn't listen to any of his own warn-
ings. He couldn't. If it had meant his life, he
wouldn't have been able to push those memories from his brain.

Resolutely he looked back at the fire.

Lord, it was going to be a long night.

Frankie crossed her arms over her chest and
rubbed her upper arms slowly. Watching him
stare into the fire, she wondered what he was
thinking. Wondered what he'd thought about
finding Ryan Grady right outside her bedroom
door at that hour of the night.

Heaven knew that she herself had been appalled to find the man looming over her. She
squeezed her arms tightly when she remembered that soft knock on her door.

She had hoped to find Sean standing there,
since she had quite a few questions she
wanted answered. Most importantly, she
wanted to know why he'd never mentioned
that he would be leaving town in a few weeks.

But then she'd opened the door to find not
Sean, but Ryan Grady . . . smiling at her.

Thankfully, Sean had appeared before Ryan

had a chance to do anything more than leer at her. And she didn't even want to know what had been on Ryan Grady's mind.

Frankie pushed away thoughts of Grady. With Sean here now, there were other things to think of.

Sean bent down, picked up another log from the wood box, and laid it gently atop the flames. Sparks and ashes flew up the chimney, and the fire fed eagerly on the fresh wood.

Silhouetted against the glow of the fire, he seemed determined to keep his back to her. Frankie studied him thoughtfully and waited another long moment or two in silence. She'd hoped that he had come to talk. Apparently though, he didn't know where to start.

"Why didn't you tell me about them?" Frankie asked.

He straightened up and spread his thick, muscled legs far apart. She could almost hear him thinking, weighing each possible answer. But still he didn't turn to look at her.

"They would have been a bit hard to explain," he said at last.

"You could've tried."

"Yeah," he agreed and grabbed the poker. Jabbing at the smoldering logs, he watched the clouds of ash rise up with the wind. "Yeah, I could've."

"That's all you're going to say?"

He glanced back at her briefly. "What would ya have me say? You're right. I should've told ya about them."

"Tell me now," she demanded. By heaven, if she was going to be forced into living with a *circus*, then she at least wanted to know more about them.

"Tell ya what?" Sean asked with a shrug. "They're here now. You've seen them all. There's nothin more to tell."

"Why don't you start with how you came to be part of a circus?"

She watched him twirl the heavy poker in his hands as if looking for something to do. Silence stretched out between them and she was beginning to think that he wouldn't answer when he spoke suddenly.

"I was thirteen," he started. His tone held a far-off tinge to it, as if he was speaking to her from across the years. "Cold. Hungry." He snorted a half laugh. "The circus was performing in Kerry Patch and—"

"Kerry Patch?" she interrupted.

"Aye. Kerry Patch. The Irish quarter in St. Louis. A miserable place of poverty and hopelessness." He sighed and shook his head slowly. "And yet, for all that, the place was . . . *safe*."

"Safe?"

"I don't suppose it really was," he admitted grudgingly. "But there is a feeling of safety in things familiar. No matter the reality."

Frankie's eyebrows lifted as she glanced quickly about her room. Familiar. Safe. Yes, she knew about such things. Hadn't she built a protective shell around herself by huddling behind the safe walls of familiarity? Sameness?

"My mother had died a few months before so I was on me own."

"You were just a boy," she couldn't help saying.

"True, but I was big for me age."

Frankie smiled in spite of herself and swept her gaze over his imposing form. She could well imagine a young Sean, already bigger than most men.

"Anyhow," he went on, "I sneaked into the circus 'cause I didn't have any money. Calhoun caught me at it."

She heard the smile in his voice and found herself smiling with him.

"Instead of tossin' me out on me . . . *ear*, Calhoun took me to his wagon and Honora fed me till I thought I'd bust. They didn't have children of their own, and after hearin' about me folks bein' dead and gone, the two of them decided that I should stay with them."

"Just like that?" Frankie's opinion of Honora Calhoun inched up a notch.

"Aye." He sighed. "Just like that. And I never left. It's been me home and they me family ever since."

His story certainly explained his loyalty to the Calhouns, she told herself.

"Then," she prodded, "you bought your share of the hotel as a place for the circus to live? Is that why they're here?"

He shook his head and set the poker back down. It clanged against the other andirons, and the noise sounded like a gunshot in the strained silence.

Sean sighed. "No. Not a permanent home. Only a place to winter quarter."

"What do you mean?"

He turned around and faced her slowly. "Winter quarters is where the circus stays when the season is over."

"What season?" She moved over to the bed and plopped down on the edge of the mattress.

"The troupe follows a circuit through the spring and summer. We stop at all the small towns on the route we map out during winter quarter. We give shows, stay a day or two, then we're off again." He shrugged and stuffed his hands into his pockets. "To the next town."

"Sounds like a hard way to live." And Frankie knew she could never lead a life like it. To wander from place to place, never having one spot to call home.

"It's not a bad life."

"Where did your circus stay before you had the hotel?"

"Usually shared quarters with another troupe in Texas." Half turning, he dropped onto one of the chairs in front of the fireplace. "And then Kevin, your da, made us such a grand deal . . ." His voice trailed off and he stared again into the fire.

Kevin. Frankie dredged up an image of her father. When he finally came home from his travels, she told herself, she was going to have several words with Kevin Donnelly.

But for now, there were one or two things she still needed to know. For instance, with his family in the hotel, they hadn't any room to spare.

Staring at her husband, Frankie drew one

leg up beneath her and asked, "This winter, Sean? When you family is staying here . . ."

"Yes?" He turned to look at her and his gaze locked on her bare right leg, dangling alongside the mattress.

"How are we supposed to make enough money to run this hotel," she asked sharply, noticing where his attention had drifted, "if every room is taken by a member of your family?"

He lifted his gaze to hers.

"I've a plan."

"I've heard that before," she reminded him.

"Aye, ya have."

Idly, she began kicking her right foot back and forth. His gaze shifted again to follow the swing of her leg. After a moment or two, he blinked, shook his head, and stared back into her knowing eyes.

"The lot."

"The lot?" Frankie's leg stopped moving. Immediately her mind drew up an image of the small grassy lot now just beginning to bloom with the flowers she tended. "I told you. I'm not going to let you sell that lot."

"I don't want to sell it!" Sean snapped. "Hell, it's part of the reason we wanted this place."

"Why?" She watched him through narrowed eyes.

"We need a place to train in winter, as I told ya."

"And?"

"And we're goin' to use the bloody lot."

Frankie shook her head, confused. But, determined to get her question answered, she asked, "How will your training make any money for the hotel?"

"Simple, me love." He smiled, then just as quickly the smile faded away. "We charge the good citizens of San Francisco to come and watch the circus at work."

Frankie stared at him. "Will people actually do that? Pay to watch you practice?"

"Enough of them will."

"You're sure?"

"Frannie darlin'." He almost smiled again. "How do ya think we eat durin' the winter?"

Frankie inhaled sharply and blew it out again. If he was right, one of the biggest problems facing the hotel had just been solved. They might even have enough income to perhaps expand a bit. Maybe the Four Roses Hotel could open a restaurant as well. Her imagination took off with the possibilities. But just as suddenly, her flights of fancy came to a shuddering stop.

There was one more thing yet that Sean hadn't explained. And to her mind, it was the most important point of all. Why he'd never mentioned the fact that he would be leaving.

"Frannie, if we're goin' to keep talkin' . . ." He waved one hand at her robe, lying on the foot of her bed. "Would ya mind puttin' that thing of yours on? It'd be a sight easier to keep me mind on the conversation if you were covered a bit more."

She glanced down at the concealing nightgown she wore. Covered from the base of her throat to the tips of her toes, Frankie didn't know what on earth he was talking about. Why, she was as good as wrapped in a thick cotton blanket now.

Then a single thought occurred to her and she just managed to hide her smile.

Who would have thought that Frankie Donnelly could tempt a man even when she was draped in yards of plain, unadorned white cotton? For just a moment, she wondered how he might react if she were to wear one of Maggie's decadent gowns.

A chuckle bubbled through her. Why, the poor man would probably have a stroke!

Strange, but she rather enjoyed the fact that Sean was aching with want at the mere sight of her.

As her father might have said, she was getting a bit of her own back—for all the frustration and upsets Sean had caused her.

Frankie glanced at her robe and quickly made a decision. This situation was far too delightful to dismiss so quickly.

The robe would stay where it was.

And Sean would have to remain uncomfortable.

As Maggie would say, It would be good for him.

"I'm awfully warm, Sean," she told him and began to swing her foot back and forth again. "And since I'm decently covered, I don't think I'll bother with the robe just now."

Sean squeezed his eyes shut and swallowed heavily.

Frankie pulled the hem of her gown up just an inch or two.

"Now," she said, her voice clear and firm. "Why don't you tell me why you never mentioned that you'd be leaving?"

He stiffened a bit and sucked in a gulp of air like a drowning man going down for the third time. But he didn't answer.

"You weren't going to tell me at all, were you?" Frankie suddenly asked, sure she was right. "You were just going to disappear?" She snorted and shook her head. "So you are quite a bit like Conor after all."

"Not a bit of it," he shot back.

"What's different?" she asked heatedly. "He disappeared, and so will you."

"He did it for his own fool reasons."

"And you're different?"

"Aye, I am." Sean pushed himself out of the chair and crossed the room in several quick strides. "When I go, it'll be because it's best for *you*."

"Oh yes." Frankie rose from the bed and planted herself directly in front of him. She had to tilt her head back to look at him. "The annulment."

"That's right."

"And that's supposed to fix everything?"

"With an annulment you can get married again in the church."

"Yes." She poked him in the chest with one finger. "But I'll still be a divorced woman! And a divorced woman is not exactly looked on with favor, you know."

He rubbed the back of his neck with the palm of one hand.

"What would ya have me do, woman?"

"I don't know!" she snapped right back at him.

"Jesus, Frannie!" Sean threw his hands wide and let them fall to his sides again. "I thought you *wanted* me to disappear from your life!"

"Well, I did before," Frankie answered, jutting her chin at him. "But it's different now. We're married."

A harsh, strangled laugh choked out of his throat, and Frankie gritted her teeth at the sound.

"Married, are we?" he asked, more of himself than of her.

"In the eyes of the church—*and* California—yes."

"But nowhere else."

"That was your choice."

"*My* choice?" he echoed, slapping his own chest with one huge hand.

"You *are* the one who keeps talking about annulments."

Sean inhaled slowly and Frankie watched his broad chest expand. Several long moments passed and she heard him muttering under his breath. It sounded suspiciously like he was counting to twenty. In the silence, Frankie took the opportunity to gather her own composure. She drew it close around her like a warm, comforting shawl and waited for what he might say next.

She didn't have to wait long.

He folded his arms in front of him, looked down at her, and asked her a pointed question of his own.

"Why is it you're so willin' to have me in

your bed now, lass? It wasn't so long ago, you were doin' all ya could to keep away from me."

Frankie somehow managed to keep her gaze locked with his, though she suddenly wanted to duck her head and hide in the shadows of the dimly lit room. How could she explain something to him that she didn't completely understand herself?

All she knew was that when Sean held her in his arms, her knees turned to water. And God help her, she didn't want to go through life being the only wife in America who'd never been bedded by her husband.

But she wasn't about to tell him all of that. Instead she swallowed, took a deep breath, and simply said, "We're married, Sean. Whatever your talk of annulments . . . however the marriage came about . . . we're married now."

They stared at each other silently, each of them thinking, each of them trying to guess what the other was feeling.

The air seemed to pulsate with the raw emotions flooding the two of them. The snap and hiss of the fire sounded like an angry crowd of people deprived of a fight they'd come a long way to see.

Sean shook his head slowly and gave her a half smile.

"Holy Mother of God, Frannie," he finally muttered and reached for her. "The two of us make a fine pair, don't we?"

Tentatively, Frankie returned his small smile and stepped into his embrace. Laying her head against his chest, Frankie listened to his heartbeat and was pleased to find it throbbing with a harsh, pounding rhythm to match her own. Her left hand slid down from his shoulder along the wall of his chest, and as she smoothed her palm across his snow-white shirt, she felt a low rumble of pleasure move through him.

She raised her gaze to his face and found him watching her too. Frankie stared into his clear, deep blue eyes and knew she wanted him more than she'd ever wanted anything else in her life.

But it was more than want, she knew. The feelings swamping her went far beyond lust. She wanted more than the touch of his hand. She wanted more than to be a wife in name only. But at the same time, Frankie wanted much more than a quick tumble in the sheets and the consummation of a marriage that neither of them had sought.

She wanted Sean to love her.

As she loved him.

Frankie blinked, stunned by the abrupt turn her thoughts had taken. Looking into his familiar features, she wondered how such a thing could have happened to her and gone unnoticed.

Shouldn't there have been bells?

Lightning bolts of awareness?

Something?

God help her, she loved him.

She loved a giant.

Who lived with a circus.

Slowly he lifted one hand and cupped her cheek. With all the care of a man caressing fine, fragile crystal, his thumb moved across her cheekbone. Frankie turned her head into his hand and let the warmth of his touch invade her.

She felt him sigh and saw a flash of regret dart across his eyes before it was gone again.

"Frannie darlin'," he whispered, his gaze moving over her features as if he were a starving man staring at a banquet. "I've made a right muddle of everything, haven't I?"

"Sean . . ."

"Shhh . . ." He lowered his head and stopped her speech with a quick brush of his lips across hers. Frankie's breath caught and her heartbeat thundered in her ears. After a second's pause. Sean dipped low again and took her mouth one more time.

He tasted her breath and had to fight to control the groan welling up inside him. Softly, carefully, he caught her lips with his, and it wasn't until she leaned into him that he forced himself to pull back.

She moaned slightly and let her head rest on his chest.

Sean's arms closed around her tightly as his eyes squeezed shut. God! How was he supposed to live with the temptation of her and not surrender to it? He inhaled sharply and tried to ignore the scent of her that filled him.

It was a hard task he'd set himself. But the task must be met. Though he knew she was right—a divorced woman would not have an easy time of it—it was still better than living with a man who could only disappoint her. Hurt her.

No matter how much he wished it otherwise.

Frankie lifted her head and looked up at him.

His gaze locked with hers, his jaw clenched, Sean picked her up and slowly walked around to the other side of the bed. With her new realization still making her brain spin—and Sean's kiss playing havoc with her heart—she almost didn't notice when he set her down on the mattress and stepped back.

But as he turned and started walking toward the two overstuffed chairs in front of the fire, Frankie sat straight up and stared at him.

"What are you doing?"

"Sleepin' in these bloody damned chairs," he muttered.

"But why?"

"It's for the best, Frannie love."

"Best for *whom*?" She pushed her hair out of her eyes and stared at him. "I just told you an annulment isn't the answer!"

Sean pulled one chair close to the other. Then, as he tugged his boots off one at a time, he grumbled, "You must trust that I'm doin' this for both our sakes, love."

"Doing exactly what?" she demanded.

"Keepin' me distance."

Sean dropped into one of the chairs and propped his feet on the seat of the other. Leaning back into the softness, he deliberately closed his eyes and crossed his arms over his chest.

"You don't *want* to bed me?"

He opened one eye and looked at her. Frankie felt his piercing glare all the way across the room.

"Let's not go into that again, shall we?" he said. "What I want and what I'm goin' to do are different things, lass."

"Sean . . ."

"Me mind's made up," he interrupted, and Frankie wanted to throw something at him. "Now you'll do me the favor of goin' to sleep, love. *Please.*"

Frankie forced herself to breathe deeply, slowly. Mentally she counted to ten, then twenty, then finally fifty. And still she wanted to hurl something heavy at his thick head.

It appeared, she told herself angrily, that she was going to remain just what Maggie had called her.

The virgin bride.

Frankie dropped back against her pillows, pulled her quilt up, and leaned to one side to blow out the single burning lamp. Then she lay perfectly still in the darkness and stared at the shadows playing on the ceiling.

Hearing Sean shift uncomfortably in the chairs was no consolation at all.

Chapter 16

Three days later, Sean was moving around like a man in a trance. Something had to give soon, he thought. He simply couldn't keep going on the two or three hours of sleep he was getting each night. He rubbed the back of his neck, hoping to work out what seemed to be a permanent kink in his muscles.

It was those bloody chairs, he told himself. How was a man of his size supposed to sleep sitting straight up? But even as that thought whipped through his brain, a small voice in his head whispered that his problems had nothing to do with those chairs. No, he wasn't getting any sleep at night because he was sitting there, wide awake, listening to Frannie rustling the sheets he should have been sharing with her!

Sean rubbed his whisker-stubbled jaws viciously. He knew she couldn't be doing it on purpose, but Lord! the way that woman shifted, turned, and twisted in her bed was driving him mad. Every movement she made tore at him. Every breath that left her chest echoed in the stillness of the room. Every sigh that slipped past her throat stabbed at him.

Night after night, Sean sat in that chair he was coming to hate and imagined himself lying beside Frannie instead. He imagined her turning to him ... laying her head on his chest ... throwing her legs across his.

And he imagined other things as well.

Over and over, he recalled in torturous detail those few stolen moments they'd shared together in the kitchen. From that tender scene, he'd gone on to envision others. He saw himself in her bed, his body covering hers. He saw her looking up into his eyes as the pleasure they shared claimed her.

And every night, his body, rock-hard and unrelenting, punished him for keeping a safe distance from her.

It didn't help any to know that their deception was working. The family assumed that his and Frannie's marriage was a real one in every sense of the word. Sean had caught Ryan's envious eyes on him more than once, and even Honora was settling down a bit. Faced with what she saw as an unchangeable fact, she'd relented enough that she now spoke to Frannie with civility, if not friendliness.

Sean stood up and tossed the paintbrush in the nearby can. Sampson's wagon was finished and much improved by the new coat of red paint. He flicked a quick glance at the hotel. The fresh paint wouldn't make the slightest bit of difference to Sampson, he knew. Sam would be happy wherever Sean put him. It was his gift.

A gift that Sean had admired a time or two over the years.

Childish laughter rang out and Sean swiveled his head toward the sound. A boy of about three years old sat high atop his father's shoulders, clapping his small hands and grinning delightedly. The man and his son were only two of a small crowd of curious townspeople gathered at the fence. Already it had started, he thought. Sean smiled absently at the bunch, then turned away.

Looking around, Sean's gaze moved over the other three wagons, parked in a semicircle across the entrance to the lot. Beyond the wagons, stretched out all the way to the back fence, the training rigs had been set up.

There was a heavy wire, strung up no higher than three feet off the ground. The O'Connors could practice their craft on the low wire without having to string up the netting. In the back of the lot, away from everyone else, Ryan's boards and targets were arranged in such a way that he could use any or all of them to rehearse his knife throwing without worrying about killing anyone who happened to wander by.

Sophia had pitched her tent, a wild conglomeration of colored scarves and silks, in the opposite corner. The flap was standing wide, in invitation to anyone who might care to have his fortune read and his fate described. Sean snorted to himself. Perhaps he might be well served by a visit with Sophia himself.

Nearer the cluster of wagons, small tables were set up holding mirrors and pots of face paint—the life's-blood of clowns. All of them took a turn at being the clown at one time or another. Wigs and gaudy costumes lay nearby in a spill of color tumbling from one of the many Calhoun trunks.

And thinking of trunks, Sean noted as Tiny trumpeted his existence, he must figure a way to get the elephant out into the open for a while. It would do the little fella a world of good to be out and running for a spell.

"Well done, Tommy!"

Phoebe's musical voice caught his attention, and Sean looked over at the O'Connor setup.

Tommy, dressed in tights and leggings borrowed from Butler O'Connor, stood at one end of the wire, a proud grin on his face. Obviously he'd managed to make it all the way across the wire, this time without falling.

The boy had been spending almost every waking moment with the O'Connor family. In fact, Tommy, Butler, and Bridget had formed an inseparable threesome. Where one went, the other two were close behind. Tommy was at the lot every morning at dawn and hadn't been leaving until well after dark. And last night, the boy hadn't left at all. Instead, he'd spent the night with the O'Connor twins in their room on the second floor. The whole hotel had heard the three of them laughing and playing hours after they were supposed to have been asleep.

Phoebe and Devlin appeared to be as taken with the boy as their children were. Often Sean had seen Tommy sidling up to Phoebe for a quick stolen hug or a soft word. And when

Devlin talked about the wire walking, the man had never had a more rapt audience and student than Tommy.

Sean grinned as the boy started across the wire again, his scrawny arms stretched out on either side of him for balance.

It wasn't a one-sided situation either, with Tommy doing all the learning. Not an hour ago, Sean had watched young Tommy teaching the O'Connor twins how to jump onto the back of an ice wagon. He'd had to clamp his lips shut to keep himself from calling out a warning about the dangers of being caught under the big dray horse's hooves or the heavy wheels of the wagon.

Then, in seconds it seemed, the three children were leaping off the back of the wagon and grabbing the huge chunks of ice they'd thrown off into the street. Sean smiled, remembering their cold, reddened cheeks and lips as the three of them wandered about sucking on the ice and soaking one another with the frigid water.

He blinked at the memory and stood perfectly still, watching Tommy's performance until the boy had made it safely to the opposite end of the wire. Sean wasn't sure if it was nerve, desire, or talent driving Tommy, but the boy was good.

Turning away, Sean lifted a hand and waved to one of the neighbors watching the goings-on. Then he slowly walked through the small crowd of curious people to the unfinished fence. A bit more work, he told himself, and it'd be complete.

As he grabbed a hammer, he closed his eyes briefly and listened to the noise surrounding him. From a nearby wagon came the sounds of Honora and Fiona cackling together like a couple of old hens. Further away was Ryan, arguing hotly with Dennis. Sean heard the kids shouting and Devlin's patient voice straining to be heard.

He flicked a quick glance at the hotel. With all the bustle and noise, Sean found he rather missed the quiet he'd had when Fiona was the only guest. Hell, he missed talking to Frannie. Amazing, he thought, how cold a bedroom could seem when two people were as far apart as the two of them were.

But it was all for the best. Wasn't it? His plan was working. He hadn't bedded her—though it was killing him. When he was gone, she could get an annulment. She'd be happy. Find the right man.

Not Herbert though, he thought quickly. For God's sake, not Herbert. Sean told himself that he'd have to find a way to get rid of Featherstone before leaving. He simply couldn't bear the idea of Herbert Featherstone with Frannie. No. Tommy had been right about that. Herbert wasn't the man for Sean's Frannie.

Nodding to himself, he picked up a handful of nails and bent to the fence. It would all work out. He'd be out on the road with the family. She'd be fine. And so would he—eventually. Surely if he was away from her long enough, this feeling he had for her would fade.

Wouldn't it?

* * *

"What do ya think?" Fiona asked, peering through the frayed curtains of Honora's wagon.

At the other end of the small window, Honora pulled the curtain back and looked out at Sean. He was watching the hotel again, with a woebegone look on his face. Abruptly Honora dropped the curtain and turned to her new friend. "I think you were right."

Fiona too dropped the curtain, then slapped her palms together in satisfaction. "Told you, Honora. That boy's got it bad."

"Aye, he does." Honora reached for the bottle of Irish whiskey and poured a good portion of the amber liquid into two small crystal glasses. She handed one to Fiona and took a sip before saying, "But that's not to say it couldn't change."

Fiona choked on the whiskey and glared at her friend through streaming eyes. "It ain't goin' to change, Honora, and you'd best get used to it. I seen this kinda thing before. Not often, mind you. But enough to know it when I see it."

"What *thing*?"

"A love that springs up so fast and so sure that it's as if it was meant to be all along."

Honora snorted. She'd tried to pretend for the last few days that Sean didn't love Frankie. That it was simply a case of infatuation gone too far. That Frankie was nothing more than some sort of female devil who'd conspired to ruin the Calhoun family be stealing Sean away.

But it hadn't worked. No matter how nasty

she was to Frankie, the woman didn't return her venom. Quiet and unassuming, Frankie wasn't the harlot type at all. And her plump body and dowdy clothing didn't exactly scream out the word *temptress*. In fact, she was just what she seemed to be. A nice young woman who didn't deserve the treatment Honora was heaping on her.

"Deny it all you want, it won't alter anything."

"Dammit, Fiona, this wasn't supposed to happen."

Fiona waved one hand at the other woman and reached for the plate of crackers between them on the bench seat. "What? Are you in charge of makin' plans for every livin' thing?"

"No, but..." All her other plans had worked out. She'd trained Sean to be the perfect front man for the circus. And so he was. She'd hired Sophia mostly to draw the male crowd. And so she did. She and Calhoun had taken Sean in when he was but a boy, and he'd become the son she'd never been granted.

"Exactly," Fiona chortled, "no buts."

"Dammit all, I need him on the road."

"Buffalo turds." Fiona shook her head. She'd only known Honora a few days, but they'd found common ground almost at once. Both women had lost husbands they dearly loved. And neither of them had any children of her own.

But Fiona's love for Frankie and Honora's for Sean was as strong and true as any blood connection.

"What'd you say?"

"You heard me, Honora." Fiona leaned in closer to the other woman. "We both know you don't need Sean to keep the circus going. You just want him with you. You don't want to let him go 'cause you're afraid you'll lose him forever."

Honora glowered at her.

"You said yourself that Ryan's wanted that job for quite a spell now."

"Yes, he wants it." The other woman tossed back the rest of her whiskey and poured herself another. "But I don't know that he can do it."

"Sure he can. Hell, he ain't a bad sort." Fiona shook her head and pushed back a lone strand of silver hair that drifted down over her forehead. "You can see that in his eyes. There ain't nothin' ugly hidin' in there. Just a man with too much ambition and not enough room to grow."

"I don't know . . ."

"Hell, all the boy needs is somethin' to keep him so busy he won't have time to get himself into muddles."

Honora's lips thinned mutinously, and she glared at Fiona over the lip of her whiskey glass as she took another sip.

"It's easy for you to say," she said after swallowing the smooth liquor. "If all goes as you want it to, you'll have not only Frankie, but Sean as well."

"And you'll have a home here, every winter. Sean'll be here waitin' on ya, and just maybe, you crotchety old fart, you'll get some grandchildren outa this too!"

The other woman smiled fondly at the thought, then straightened up. "Who's callin' who crotchety?"

Fiona cackled, and her laughter sounded as if it was being squeezed out of her tiny body. "I notice ya didn't argue about the other."

Honora smirked. "Aye, well. Takes one to know another, I guess."

Fiona laughed so hard she started choking, and Honora gently slapped her on the back.

"Here now, don't you go dyin' on me, old woman, before we get this worked out."

"I ain't dyin'," Fiona slapped the other woman's hand aside. "Hell, I ain't had this much fun in a coon's age!"

As they bent their heads closer together, Honora said, "First, we need a plan."

The elephant, at least, stayed outside.

The monkey was another matter entirely.

Frankie had tried to be patient. After all, not only were the circus performers her only guests, they were also her in-laws.

She hadn't said anything when Ryan had "borrowed" her best kitchen knives so he could rehearse while his own knives were out being sharpened. She'd remained patient when Honora and Fiona had taken over her kitchen for a day-long cooking contest. And Frankie hadn't even uttered a word when the O'Connor twins and Tommy slid down the banister, flew off the end of the railing, and toppled the hall tree. Or even when Phoebe and Devlin, responding to the crash, had chastised the children by lecturing them on the importance of balance.

But, she told herself firmly, enough was enough!

She glared at Sampson.

The chimp bared his teeth in a mocking smile and chattered gleefully. Sampson had curled his long fingers of one hand around the base of a brass wall sconce and was now swinging to and fro like a gate in a slow breeze.

Frankie took two steps toward him.

Sampson shook his head and let go, landing on his broad feet. Instantly the chimpanzee ran up the stairs toward the second floor, his bowed legs pumping, his narrow shoulders dipping from side to side, and his diapered bottom wiggling with his quick movements.

"You hairy little beast!" Frankie muttered and hurried after him. She lifted the hem of her dress and started up the stairs, keeping her gaze locked on her opponent. She'd hardly covered more than two or three steps when Sampson reached the head of the stairs.

On the landing, he turned to face her. He raised his long arms high, threw his head back, and laughed. The piercing notes of his voice shot through Frankie's head as if someone had jabbed her in the ear with a needle.

Determinedly she took another two steps and stopped when Sampson suddenly climbed the railing and perched on the banister.

Frightened despite her anger, Frankie

glanced from the little ape to the wood floor far below him. Gritting her teeth, she tried to keep her voice steady and friendly.

"Get down, Sampson," she soothed and moved another step closer.

Sampson shook his head quickly and grinned at her.

As she watched helplessly, he stood up on the banister and swung his arms back and forth for a moment before launching himself toward the iron chandelier hanging over the foyer. Frankie winced and hunched her shoulders expectantly. Candles, knocked free by his big feet, fell with a clatter and broke into pieces on the floor.

"Oh, dear heavens!" Frankie sighed and watched the little chimp as he hung from the fixture. Worriedly she glanced at the metal bracket holding the chandelier in place.

She considered calling out to Sean. But tucked away in the third-floor room they'd chosen for Sampson, he probaby wouldn't even hear her call to him. No one wanted to share a room with a chimp and besides, Sampson was too spoiled to stay in a cage. Frankie sighed as she recalled that Sean was even now installing bars on the room's windows, to keep Sampson in check. She couldn't help but wish that he'd done the job yesterday, rather than finishing that fence.

Sampson shrieked, curled his legs over one of the iron spokes on the lamp, and hung upside down, chattering at Frankie. She was fairly certain that in chimp language, he was shouting something along the lines of "Can't catch me!"

Under the chimp's incessant noise came a groaning sound that drew Frankie's gaze back to the metal bracket on the ceiling. It was tearing loose! Even as she watched, one of the bolts was yanked from the wood and the chandelier dropped about half an inch.

Sampson's mouth snapped shut and he turned his head this way and that comically, looking for whoever had disrupted his fun.

"Sampson, come to me," Frankie said. She kept looking from the straining metal to the stubborn chimp and back again.

In her imagination she drew a vivid portrait of Sampson lying on the floor of the foyer, smashed under the weight of the iron chandelier. She couldn't let that happen, she told herself suddenly and reached out both hands to him.

Sampson ignored her presence entirely and continued to swing back and forth.

Frankie heard the metallic shriek again and leaned over the stair railing. If the chimp would only try, he could practically reach out and touch her hands. Sampson's weight on the old iron fixture caused it to drop another couple of inches, and this time the little chimp scrambled around until he stood, balancing himself on the iron spoke.

Frankie saw the fear and confusion on his face.

"Come to me, Sampson, come on," she urged, knowing that every time the chimp moved, the lamp came closer to falling.

The bracket groaned again, convincing Sampson to hurl himself at her. She caught him and staggered backward into the wall behind her.

Frankie's arms closed around his little body just as the last bolt pulled free and the chandelier crashed to the floor below.

Sampson's entire body trembled. Arms and legs wrapped around Frankie tightly, he buried his face in the crook of her neck and shook his head. Her anger disappeared and her heart melted as she listened to the half-garbled cooing noises rushing from his throat. Instinctively, Frankie patted his back gently.

"It's all right now, Sampson," she said calmly, quietly. "You're fine and that bad lamp is gone. Frankie won't let it hurt you ever again."

His breathing was ragged and if she hadn't known better, she would have sworn he had the hiccups. "Would you like a cookie, Sampson?" she asked and drew her head back to look at him.

He didn't lift his head but his trembling had calmed a bit. Frankie smiled to herself. She should have thought of it before. She'd learned the hard way that Sampson would do anything for a cookie.

Hadn't the little scamp climbed to the very top shelf of the pantry to reach the cookie jar? Knocking everything else off the shelves in the doing?

Frankie turned and began walking back downstairs, her arms still wrapped securely around Sampson.

Heavy footsteps echoed throughout the hotel as someone came running down all three flights of stairs. When she reached the bottom of the steps, Frankie turned and waited for Sean. It had to be him thundering around. No one else at the hotel was heavy enough to make that much noise.

He appeared at the head of the stairs and stood there like a wild man, his hair flying around his face and his chest heaving with the effort to breathe.

"What is it?" he shouted, and Sampson burrowed closer to Frankie. "Are ya all right?"

Her heart lurched in her chest and a warm, tingling feeling crept through her limbs. No matter how she tried to stop it, her body continued to respond to his presence. Despite the fact that he'd made it quite clear he had no intention of consummating their marriage.

She wondered just what Father Gallagher would have to say about this situation! Frankie had done her best to be a wife—but to accomplish that, she needed a husband!

For the love of St. Patrick, what more could she do? She'd shown him that she was willing to take her place as his wife. She'd made every effort to be accommodating to his family. She'd even stopped berating him for snatching her hotel out from under her.

But by thunder, everyone had her limits. Frankie wasn't sure just when her feelings about the big Irishman had changed, when she'd made the fateful error of falling in love with him. The only thing she was certain of was that marriage—for her at least—was for life. But a lifetime with Sean was beginning to look bleaker every day.

Not only was her former peaceful life forever shattered, but she was in serious danger of living to be an old woman bearing the title *oldest living virgin bride*.

Good Lord!

Her gaze stabbed at him and it was small consolation indeed to watch him shift position uneasily. When she finally deigned to speak to him, her voice was as cold and empty as her marriage bed.

"As you can plainly see, we are both quite well." Then she turned her back on him and started walking toward the kitchen. "However, I would appreciate it if you would carry the chandelier outside."

"What in the name of God happened?" he shouted, and she glanced up to see him leaning over the banister, staring down at the broken light fixture.

Wisely he kept his gaze averted from hers.

"Sampson had an accident, poor dear," she said quietly, her hand still patting the hairy little body clinging to her.

"Poor dear?" Sean sounded breathless, stunned.

"Yes," she answered. "And now we're getting a cookie."

"A *cookie*?"

"Yes." She smoothed her hand over the chimp's head slowly, comfortingly. Frowning up at Sean, she jerked her head toward the mess on the floor. "Would you please take the chandelier away?" she repeated stiffly. "I don't want it to frighten Sampson."

"Away?"

"Yes." Scowling at him, she demanded, "Why are you repeating everything I say, for heaven's sake?"

"Repeating?"

Frankie rolled her eyes, then began soothing Sampson again. "Don't you pay any attention to Sean, sweetheart. Auntie Frankie will take care of you."

She disappeared down the hallway, and Sean stared after her.

"Auntie Frankie?"

Chapter 17

A knock at the front door sent Frankie flying down the hall. Her skirt clutched in her hands, she held the hem up over her knees and out of her way. Glancing back over her shoulder as she ran, she laughed out loud. Sampson, chattering noisily, was hot on her heels. Using both of his fisted hands to propel himself along, he caught up with her just before she reached the door.

Frankie dropped the hem of her skirt and clapped one hand to her breast as she struggled for breath. When Sampson tugged at her dress, she looked down into his grinning features and smiled. Then she leaned down and smoothed the flat of her hand across the top of his head.

Ever since she'd saved him from the chandelier two days before, Sampson had been her constant and devoted companion. And strangely enough, she truly enjoyed his company.

Especially at night.

Frankie smiled wickedly. Now she didn't have to lie in her bed listening to Sean's disgruntled mumbling and whispered curses. Since Sampson had taken to sleeping in her bed, she listened instead to Sean telling the little monkey to stop his chattering.

She grinned and took Sampson's outstretched hand in her own. She was all in favor of anything that annoyed Sean Sullivan.

The impatient knock sounded again and she squeezed Sampson's hand before turning to answer the summons.

Throwing the door wide, she tossed her long, loose hair back over her shoulder and looked up into Herbert's horrified face.

"Herbert!" she gasped in surprise. Good heavens! She'd forgotten all about her former suitor. In fact, she hadn't given him a moment's thought in days. "I haven't seen you in ages!"

He stretched his scrawny neck against his too-high collar and said, "I've been in Sacramento visiting Mother."

"I hope she's well," Frankie said, though she knew that Mrs. Featherstone was *never* well. For a woman in the pink of health, she spent a good deal of time reclining on a couch with a bottle of smelling salts close to hand.

"As well as can be expected," he intoned, "for a woman in her condition."

Then he turned and pointed his index finger at the crowded lot. "Would you care to explain what has happened here in my absence?"

Hmmm. Where on earth should she begin? With the circus? Or with her marriage? Lord. She lifted one hand and rubbed her temple slowly. How had she forgotten to tell Herbert that she was married?

Stammering in his agitation, Herbert glanced over at the lot and said, "Show people! Sh-sh-*show* people! Right there. In o-o-open view of ev-ev-everyone!" Swiveling his head back around to stare at her, he asked, "Have you l-l-lost your mind?"

Frankie blinked. Looking up at the red stain flushing Herbert's cheeks, she felt the first glimmer of temper begin to brew inside her. As she watched him, his eyes bugged out and beads of sweat dotted his forehead.

"There are p-p-people on the sidewalk," he went on, spitting just a bit on his "p's." "Staring at the hotel! It's most unseemly, Mary Frances!" He tugged at his collar with one finger and swallowed so desperately, his Adam's apple leaped up and down in his throat. "If Mother were to find out about this . . . I think it would kill her."

Sampson tugged at Frankie's hand and hissed at Herbert.

Horrified, Herbert leaped backward and was forced to fling his arms wide in an awkward attempt to regain his balance before tumbling down the front steps.

Once he'd caught himself, Herbert stared down at the little chimpanzee and his jaw opened and closed quickly, like a fish suddenly tossed on a dock to flop and flail helplessly.

"What is *that*"

"*He*," Frankie said pointedly, "is Sampson."

"Sampson?" Herbert was now beginning to

wheeze. "Mary Frances, you cannot seriously try to tell me you are allowing wild animals the freedom to roam your hotel at will!"

Well, she thought absently, *at least he isn't stammering any longer*.

"I am appalled, Mary Frances," Herbert went on, apparently unable to tear his horrified gaze from Sampson's hissing features, "that you have allowed such proceedings in my absence."

"I beg your pardon?" she asked carefully. "What does your absence from the city have to do with my actions?"

"Apparently *everything*!" he snapped and finally managed to look at her directly. "But," he added with an obvious attempt at control, "I must take some of the blame onto my own manly shoulders."

Frankie flicked a quick glance to those narrow shoulders and managed to keep her mouth shut anyway.

"I should have known that a woman would be swayed by a pretty face and a smooth demeanor."

"What?"

Sampson chortled something and tugged on her hand. Frankie only mumbled, "Hush a moment, Sampson. Please," she added to Herbert, "*do* go on."

"The moment I met that new partner of yours," Herbert said, reaching into his breast pocket for his handkerchief, "I knew there would be trouble. But still . . ." He dabbed at the sweat on his pink-skinned forehead. "I had hoped for better from you. I had almost convinced myself that you were unlike other women."

"Oh really?" Frankie asked, fascinated in spite of her growing temper. "In what way?"

Sampson hissed again and Herbert took one more step back. "Well, for one thing, you've never been one to overconcern yourself with your appearance. You've always dressed sensibly. Modestly."

Dowdily, Frankie inserted mentally. A quick glance down at her ever-present gray dress seemed to accentuate what Herbert was saying.

"And for another," he went on, his chin lifting and his voice reaching pompous heights, "you are, in your own way, naturally, quite a bit like Mother."

Good God.

"Your tidiness is an excellent example."

Sweet talker! Frankie frowned slightly. Sean told her she was lovely. Herbert complimented her tidiness.

"You have a respect for order, quiet." He lifted one hand and pointed at the interior of the hotel. "Why, during the year we've been ... *courting*"—he blushed a deeper shade of rose—"not a single piece of furniture has ever been moved. Not once." Herbert straightened up and tugged at his lapels. "That is one of the very qualities I admire most about you, actually, *and* the one in which you are closest to Mother, if I dare say."

She stared at him, appalled.

Her mind whirling, Frankie thought back to the one time she'd actually been presented to

Mrs. Featherstone. The tall, thin woman looked astoundingly like her only child. And the couch on which she lay had been surrounded by the knickknacks and odds and ends of a lifetime's worth of collecting. Frankie still recalled quite clearly how she had actually had the temerity to lift one of the ceramic squirrels from its doily for a closer inspection.

Herbert had quickly relieved her of it and set it back down. His mother had then leaned over and readjusted the figurine until it was precisely in its original position.

Heavens above! Was she really like that? Frankie wondered. Was she really as rigid and unchanging as Mrs. Featherstone? If not for Sean's arrival, Frankie knew she would undoubtedly have eventually married Herbert.

Would she then have become Mrs. Featherstone?

She swallowed heavily. Now *there* was a sobering thought.

"And it is because of these qualities that I am willing to overlook the fact that you have apparently leased your property to those"—he shuddered delicately—"disreputable people."

Staring at him blankly, Frankie saw his gaze shift momentarily to the interior of the hotel before coming to rest on her again. Perhaps, she thought, he was afraid Sean was listening.

Frankie realized suddenly that she didn't want Sean overhearing Herbert's insults. It was one thing for *her* to voice an opinion or two on his character, it would be quite another to have Herbert making judgments!

How had she never before noticed just how

narrow Herbert's outlook on life was? Why, it was a wonder he had ever been willing to socialize with a saloonkeeper's daughter in the first place.

But that thought was neither here nor there. At the moment, all that mattered was that she get rid of Herbert.

Quickly.

Before she lost control of her temper, which was rising with every idiotic statement Herbert made.

"I am curious though," the man said, interrupting her thoughts, "why exactly did you lease the land? If you needed money that badly, my dear, you might have come to me."

Go to Herbert for help? Hmmph! The thought never would have occurred to her. How odd. Even as angry as she was at Sean most of the time, if she needed help on something, Frankie wouldn't hesitate to turn to him. But Herbert? No. If faced with a problem, she would have dealt with it alone.

Isn't it strange? she thought. She had once actually considered marrying that man.

Frankie shook her head. Was it possible that he didn't hear himself? Was it possible that he actually believed he'd been complimenting her for the last several minutes?

Then as she looked into his eyes, bland behind his spectacles, she decided that, yes, that's exactly what he thought.

But to be fair, Frankie had to admit that Herbert was behaving no differently now than he had for the past year. It wasn't *he* who'd changed so drastically.

It was Frankie.

Drawing a deep breath of the cool spring air into her lungs, she told him, "I didn't lease them the land, Herbert. As guests of the hotel, they naturally have complete use of the yard."

"Guests? *Guests!*" His already thin voice broke and he gave himself over to a brief but exhausting coughing fit. Frankie instinctively reached toward him, but he waved her concern away. When he'd finally contained himself again, he looked at her as though she'd sprouted another head. "Do you mean to say you've allowed *those* people rooms in your establishment?"

Sampson hissed again and swung his left foot at Herbert.

Herbert sidestepped the chimp nicely.

Frankie chuckled.

"Mary Frances! You're not safe, my dear. Simply not safe! A woman alone with . . ." He shuddered, and Frankie wanted to smack him. Again. "*Them.*"

The slowly building temper she'd felt simmering was now on the boil, and she gave it free rein. She'd tried to be polite. She'd tried to be understanding. But really, she had far too much work to do to stand there listening to Herbert Featherstone rant all afternoon.

She plopped her free hand on the curve of her right hip, tilted her head to one side, and said, "I'm not alone, Herbert. Though even if I was, I wouldn't be in any—"

"Not alone?" he broke in rudely. "By that I assume you mean Treasure?" Shaking his head patiently, he said, "Hardly a *proper* chaperone, my dear. No, I insist that you allow me to escort you to someplace suitable until your . . . guests depart."

Frankie snorted and Herbert blinked in surprise.

"Someplace safe? Where do you suggest? The saloon?"

"Good heavens, no. That wouldn't be any more proper than your present situation."

Had it never occurred to the man that Frankie had been *raised* in that saloon?

He tapped one long finger against his chin, and Frankie, watching him, couldn't understand what on earth she'd ever seen in the man. "I know!" he blurted happily. "You can stay with Mother! Or, even better—at my house!"

"Herbert!"

He blushed, assuming she was shocked by his suggestion.

"I shall, of course," he said quickly, "stay with Mother myself while you are encamped, as it were, in my home."

Frankie almost smiled. Almost. She'd really dragged this conversation on for much too long already. When he'd first arrived at her door, Frankie had dreaded breaking the news of her marriage to the man. Heaven knew, she'd never meant to hurt him.

But now, after listening to Herbert's insults and narrow-minded opinions about her and the female sex in general, she was rather looking forward to the expression on his face when she told him her news.

"Yes," he was saying to himself, "that will work out nicely. We shall have to arrange to be married, naturally. Mother's health couldn't bear it if there was talk."

"I don't think my husband would approve," Frankie said politely.

"I'm sure your family will come 'round when they realize how very much you need my—" He stopped suddenly and cocked his ear toward her. "What did you say?"

"I said, Herbert"—Frankie couldn't quite disguise the smile on her face—"that my husband wouldn't approve of you and me announcing our engagement."

"Husband?"

"That's right."

He inhaled sharply. "And *whom* might I ask have you married?"

Frankie lifted her chin proudly. "Sean Sullivan."

"You *married* him?" Herbert dabbed his handkerchief at his forehead again, then moved on to his upper lip. "That—that—partner of yours? How? When? *Why*?"

She looked at him carefully and knew that Herbert Featherstone would simply never understand. How on earth could she explain the powerful attraction that had drawn her and Sean together? Herbert would never have been caught in a compromising position in a confessional, of all places!

Lust was not a word that Herbert was even remotely familiar with.

Unfortunately, lately her husband seemed just as unfamiliar with the term as Herbert.

Suddenly very tired, Frankie sighed and said, "I think you should go now, Herbert."

"But—"

"You heard her, mister," a voice from behind Frankie spoke up. "Git."

Herbert jumped back, missed the top step altogether, and tumbled down the last two steps to the yard. Eyes wide, jaws agape, arms and legs flying, he looked like a scarecrow that had been torn from its post and tossed aside.

Frankie glanced to her left and saw Honora step up beside her. The older woman was glaring at Herbert with enough active dislike to set the man on fire.

Sampson began his wild chattering and tugged frantically at her in his attempt to rush at the fallen man. Frankie merely tightened her grip on the chimp's hand. Looking down at Herbert, still sprawled on the walk, she said, "Please, Herbert. Just go."

She didn't watch him get up and leave. Instead she stepped back inside, waiting for Honora to join her, then quietly closed the door.

Still bristling from the insults she'd overheard, Honora peeked through the window at the man outside and muttered, "Good riddance, I say!"

"He's a good man," Frankie felt obliged to say. Despite his narrow-mindedness, which she'd only just begun to notice, Herbert Featherstone was basically kind. He was also honest, hardworking, and loyal.

Something Honora Calhoun should appreciate, she told herself.

"Hmmph!" Honora snorted and turned to face Frankie. "A good man? Not from what *I* just saw."

"Then your vision is as lacking as his," Frankie told her quietly. She glanced down at her companion and whispered, "Come, Sampson," leaving Honora alone in the hallway.

Herbert stared at the closed door for a long moment before pushing himself to his feet. Still stunned by everything Frankie had told him, he almost didn't notice the woman who suddenly appeared at his side.

Later, he couldn't imagine *not* noticing her.

"You are not hurt?" she asked, and her voice sounded like music.

"No," he blurted, and for the life of him couldn't think of anything else to add. All he could do was stare into her dark eyes. Eyes that seemed to capture the world in their depths.

"I am glad," she said with a shy smile.

Herbert swallowed and let his gaze drift over her. Long night-black hair fell in a straight line down her back, and her simple yet elegant rose-colored dress made her golden skin glow like burnished bronze.

Then she took his hand in hers and clasped it between both her palms. Closing her eyes briefly, she looked at him again and sighed. "You are the one for whom I have waited."

"Me?" He couldn't help asking. "You've waited for *me*?" As far as Herbert knew, the only person who had ever waited for him was his mother. Even Mary Frances, the moment his back was turned, had married someone else. And yet this lovely woman had said she waited for *him*.

She turned his palm over and pointed to one long line down the center of his hand. Following it with the tip of her nail, she whispered, "This is you and this"—she stopped and pointed at another smaller line bisecting the original one—"is me." She shrugged, smiled up at him, and said, "The line after our meeting is thicker. Stronger."

"By heaven," Herbert said, drawing his palm closer to his eyes, "it *is*."

"Come with me, and I will tell you about the future." Sophia linked her arm through his and smiled up at him. "*Our* future."

Herbert swallowed nervously as he glanced down at her small hand tucked so trustingly into the crook of his elbow. Her smooth, golden skin looked lovely. Hesitantly, he covered that hand with one of his own. Her flesh was warm, soft to the touch.

"I am Sophia," she said and turned her magical eyes on him again.

"Herbert," he managed to croak.

"Herbert." She said his name, and it sounded like a song.

They began to walk slowly out of the yard and around the fence. "Tell me about your mother, Herbert," Sophia went on as she drew him across the lot toward the privacy of her tent, "and I shall tell you how I will make her well."

"Who?" he asked.

* * *

"All right," Honora conceded grudgingly. "The girl's got spunk. I give her that."

"Told ya she did." Fiona's laugh wheezed into the crowded atmosphere of Honora's wagon, the one place the two women could talk together without being overheard or interrupted. "All she ever needed was somebody to bring out the life in her. I knew it would be Sean the minute I set eyes on him."

Early-afternoon sunshine slipped in through the holes in Honora's curtains. It lay in spotted patches across the tiny area already littered with clothing tossed haphazardly over the furniture and floor, and the half-finished costumes poking out of partly opened drawers. At least two dozen hats hung from widely scattered pegs on the walls, and a huge, stuffed calico cat named, of all things, Coriander, perched on a high shelf. The cat's blank, glassy stare annoyed Fiona and she deliberately kept her gaze from straying anywhere near him.

"I still don't like the idea of leaving Sean behind when we start the circuit."

"I thought we had this settled. Untie them apron strings, Honora! Else you'll hang yourself with 'em." Fiona shook her head and caressed the eagle-head knob of her cane. "A man like him don't take to strangleholds from nobody. Least of all his ma."

Honora smiled softly. "I do think of him as my son."

"Hell, 'course ya do. And why wouldn't ya?" She reached out and patted her friend's hand gently. "Thing you got to do is to get your mind set to think on Frankie as a daughter."

"Hmmm . . ." Honora nodded thoughtfully. "She surely did stand up to that skinny fella that was tearin' into us so."

"That's my Mary Frances!" Fiona grinned. "Why, under all that hush and nonsense, she's got a fire in her that won't be stopped."

"And it burns for my Sean?"

"It surely does."

Honora scratched her head and looked at Fiona out of the corner of her eye. "Then why haven't they . . . I mean, you said you think they haven't, um . . . well."

"I do." Fiona leaned against the chair back and shook her head. "You can tell if ya watch 'em together. There's none of those long looks and soft touches goin' on. If they was bouncin' the springs together, there'd be a helluva lot more cooin' than shoutin' goin' on.

"Sean's walkin' around here like a bear with a sore paw and Frankie ain't been much better. Hell, the only one she's even polite to anymore is that blasted ape!"

"I suppose you're right." Honora sighed. "But how can we fix whatever's ailing them? It's not likely either of them would thank us for buttin' into their bedroom."

"True." Fiona smiled and wiggled both eyebrows. "Howsomever, I been doin' some thinkin' here lately and I believe I come up with a plan . . ."

Honora leaned forward and listened. Then a slow, satisfied smile curved her lips.

Chapter 18

S ean placed the flat of his palm against the swinging door and slowly, carefully, pushed.

He smiled to himself as the door swung open without a sound. Amazing what a touch of grease could do for a stubborn hinge.

He poked his head around the edge of the door and gazed around the interior of the kitchen. He wanted ... no, *needed* to talk to Frankie, and he didn't want a bloody audience when he did it.

It was painfully hard to find her alone these days. And the nights were no better. She was usually asleep by the time he went to their room. Either that or she was feigning sleep— which, he wasn't sure. During the day, every time he tried to talk to her, some member of his family interrupted. For reasons of his own, Ryan had steered clear of Frankie, and Sean was grateful. Though he knew Ryan meant her no harm, he'd rather the charmer didn't spend much time with her. But even with Ryan out of the way, that still left quite a few people making demands on her time.

She was either cooking to keep everyone fed, or ironing and sewing costumes, or helping with the children, or talking with Dennis, or listening to Sophia's sage advice . . . Hell! There was always something!

But tonight he would have his say, if he had to toss someone out of the room to have privacy! He smiled again as he noted that but for Sampson, Frankie was alone in the room.

Perhaps the gods had finally decided to favor Sean Sullivan.

Busy washing dishes at the sink, Frankie had her back to him and didn't see him enter the room. Sampson, though, did.

Seated at the kitchen table, for all the world like a bloody king, Sampson threw his head back and screeched a warning.

Frankie spun about, hands dripping water all over the floor, and Sampson picked up a nearby spoon and began to pound the tabletop.

"Sean!"

Sean frowned at Sampson. "Traitorous little ball of fur!"

Frankie snatched a clean towel and dried her hands as she walked to stand beside the chimp. Sean's gaze never left the chimp.

Scowling, he remembered that until Frankie had come along, Sampson had been *his* special pet. Now, though, the bloody ape was just as likely to sink his teeth into Sean's hand as look at him.

Just the night before, when Frankie had finally drifted off to sleep, Sean had crept up close to the bed. All he'd wanted to do was indulge his need to look his fill of her. Sampson had watched him instead. And when Sean had given in to the urge to touch Frankie's hair, the damned ape had actually *hissed* at him!

Rather than take the chance of waking Frankie with the noise involved in killing her pet, Sean had gone back to the bloody chairs he hated even more than he was beginning to detest Sampson.

It was a hell of a note to be jealous of a damned chimp, he told himself. But he couldn't help it. Every time he saw Sampson cuddled in the bed with Frankie, Sean wanted to lift the little beggar by the ears and boot him upstairs.

Sampson seemed to know just what Sean was thinking. He bared his teeth in a mocking grin and actually *laughed* in time with the maniacal beat of his spoon against the table.

"What do you want?" Frankie shouted over the noise.

Sean glared at the chimp, but the racket didn't stop, so he shouted back. "Herbert was here."

"Yes?"

"Why didn't ya call me?"

She stared at him as if he was speaking Gaelic.

For God's sake. Didn't she know how he'd felt when Honora had told him about Featherstone's appearance? Didn't she understand that he would've wanted to be by her side when she faced down her former suitor?

No, he thought grimly. Judging from her expression, she did not.

"I didn't need you," she said over Sampson's enthusiastic pounding.

"Dammit," Sean countered hotly, "I'm your husband!"

Her eyebrows lifted into high arches above her astonished eyes. Slowly she raked him with her gaze and finally met his angry stare with one of her own.

"Husband, are you?" Deftly Frankie slipped the spoon from Sampson's grasp. She grabbed a cookie from the plate in the center of the table and handed it to him.

The sudden silence in the room made Sean feel like an unwanted guest at a wake. He shifted uncomfortably but didn't look away from her.

"Yes, your husband."

"Only when it suits your purpose," she countered quickly.

Sean glanced down at her hand, resting protectively on Sampson's shoulder. Jealousy rose up in him again, and he frowned at the ape.

Sampson grinned at him.

Sean took a couple of slow, deep breaths before speaking again. Then he kept his voice low, patient. "I've tried to tell ya—"

"Yes, yes," she interrupted, waving her towel at him dismissively. "I know. You and your annulment."

"Aye."

"Fine."

"Nothin's *fine*, dammit!" he shouted, then caught himself. He didn't want to fight with her! Bloody hell, she had a hard head, though! Abruptly he reached across the table for her hand.

Sampson hissed at him.

Sean pulled his hand back quickly.

Frankie slipped the chimp another cookie.

"You miserable little turncoat, you," Sean muttered thickly and stared at Sampson as the chimpanzee munched happily on his treat. "Turn your back on your friends for a sweet!"

Sampson grinned again.

Forgetting about the blasted animal, Sean looked at his wife. Enough of this, he told himself. It was time she knew exactly what he was thinking. He was bloody tired of feeling guilty for doing the decent thing!

Why couldn't she see what this was costing him? Why couldn't she show him some of the same compassion she gave that damned ape!

"Don't you see," he started.

"It's late, Sean," she said, and turning her back on him, she walked to the sink. "And I'm tired."

Her steps were quiet and he glanced down to see she was in her bare feet. A smile flashed across his face and was gone again when he realized that she also wasn't wearing any stockings. Or, by the droopy looks of her skirt, petticoats either.

He swallowed, sucked in a gulp of air, and noticed for the first time that her glorious hair was hanging free down the length of her back. The red-gold curls danced just above her waist and shimmered with her every movement. His fingers, itching to thread themselves through the soft, silky mass, curled into fists at his sides.

How could he not have noticed that she'd forsaken that blasted crown of braids she always wore? Because, he told himself, he'd avoided her company in the past couple of days, mistakenly thinking that his need for her would disappear if he didn't see her.

"You're wearin' your hair different," he whispered before he could stop himself.

She stiffened slightly, then snatched her dishcloth and began to scrub the pan in the sink.

"I didn't have time to do it up."

"It looks grand."

"Thank you."

Not much of a conversation, he conceded. But at least they were talking.

"Frannie love."

She straightened her spine until he thought it might snap.

"I want ya to understand . . ."

She didn't stir. The rag in her hand stilled and she stared blankly at the wall in front of her.

Hardly encouragement, he thought. And yet, what more could he expect?

He inhaled, sighed, and began haltingly. "When the good father, uh . . . found us in church and insisted we marry—"

"You tried to get out of it."

"Aye. Aye, I did." He took a step toward her, then stopped. "But not for the reasons you might think."

"Hmmph!" She wadded up the dishcloth

and tossed it into the pan of water, sloshing warm liquid down the front of her dress. Gripping the edge of the sink tightly, she said, "Oh, then you *did* care for me, eh? It wasn't just lust that had you chasing after me? You didn't want to bed me?"

"Well of course I did!" he snapped. "What man wouldn't?"

She didn't say a word.

"But marriage?" He took another slow step, waiting for her to turn and hurry away from him. She didn't. "Ah now, lass, that's the thing. That priest said *wedding* and I wanted to run until I dropped."

"Thank you very much."

"Bloody hell! This isn't comin' out like I want it."

Frankie dropped her hands into the soapy pan and grabbed her cloth, wrung it out, then plunged it back into the water.

Looking for something to do, he thought. Trying to keep her hands busy. Sean could understand that. Hell, didn't he have blisters all over the palms of his hands from the work he'd done in the past few days?

"Ah Frannie," he said slowly, "it's not that I didn't want to marry *you*. It's that I'm a poor bet for a husband. You should have better."

"Oh, I should?"

"Aye, love."

"Like Herbert, for instance?"

"Hell no! *I'm* better than Herbert!"

"Are you really?" She spun around to face him, the dripping wet dishcloth still in her grip. "Herbert didn't *trick* his way into my life by buying my hotel out from under me. Herbert didn't whisper sweet words, make unseemly advances, and then try to squirm out of his obligations."

He scowled at her. "Herbert wouldn't know sweet words if they jumped up and bit him on the—"

Her eyebrows lifted.

"As for squirmin' out . . . I'm here, aren't I? We're married, aren't we?"

"You're leaving," she pointed out quietly. "Aren't you?"

"Dammit, lass!" Sean threw his hands wide. "A bloody couple of weeks ago, you were doin' everything you could think of to chase me off! Ya even tried to *buy* me out!"

"This is different."

"Why?"

"I . . . don't know."

A brief spurt of hope shot up in his chest, then quickly dissipated.

"Look, Frannie. I know you think an annulment is a bad idea . . ."

She watched him. Waiting.

Sean reached up, rubbed his chin briskly, then faced her. "But it's not. I've thought it all out. You didn't want to marry me, Frannie. And even if ya *had* married me for love, I'm not the man you should have by your side." He shook his head and shrugged helplessly. "Hell, ya said it yourself. I'm a rambler. I don't even know if I *could* stay in one place."

She shook her head slowly. "When you were busy chasing after me with your blarney and promises, you didn't seem to think you'd have a hard time staying."

And if truth be told, he thought, he'd like nothing better than to give it a try. But it wouldn't be fair to Frannie. What if he failed? What if he made her more miserable staying than he would have by going?

"No matter what I say, you still think an annulment will solve everything?"

"That's right." He shoved his hands in his pockets so she wouldn't see them shake. Just the thought of leaving her to another man made Sean want to go out and stand in front of Ryan's targets. At least a knife would be quick.

This dying day by day was a miserable thing.

She stepped forward. "So, I can get another husband . . . and what do you get?"

What did he get?

He got the road. Miles of empty road and years of even emptier days.

"I know," Frankie said and took another step, swinging that wet cloth as she walked. Droplets of water flew in high arcs all over the room. "You get to do whatever you want to do. *And* you get to come back *here*. To the Four Roses every winter."

He hadn't thought of that. But naturally, he would stay somewhere else. Wouldn't he?

"And what do you think I should do with this new husband of mine while you're in town?"

The gleam in her eye had him worried.

"Well, no doubt you'll have it all thought out for me by next winter."

"Frannie love."

"But first maybe you should choose this new husband for me."

"What?"

Hell, he didn't even want to think about her with another man. He bloody well would not go and pick one out for her.

"Well, you seem intent on doing my thinking for me—why not choose a mate for me as well?"

"Frannie, you don't under—"

"*I* don't understand?" she interrupted, and he nodded and backed up a pace. "I understand everything, *Seaneen*."

Sean winced.

"I understand that my father betrayed me. My husband didn't want to marry me. Then that same husband lied to me about his family." Her voice was climbing with every sentence. There was a high flush of color on both her cheeks that made her pale green eyes look like a storm at sea. "And *then* that very husband leaves me to be called virgin bride by my sister, because he wants to be sure I can get an annulment when he leaves me!"

Lord, help me, Sean prayed silently.

"Even *Herbert* simply informed me that we would announce our engagement!"

Engagement? Why that skinny-assed, presumptuous—

"Even *he* did my thinking for me!"

"Now Frannie, I think you're—"

She threw the soaking wet dishcloth at him.

It smacked against his face and clung to him. He reached up slowly and peeled it off.

Marching up to him, Frankie stopped within an inch of him and jabbed his broad chest with one finger.

"Now *you* listen to *me*, Mr. Sean Sullivan!"

He looked down at the tiny woman who stood no taller than his breastbone and didn't even consider arguing with her.

"You and the other men in my life are through doing my thinking for me." Her index finger curled into her fist and she pounded on his chest stubbornly. "Maybe I'll get an annulment and maybe I won't. *I* will decide. But I'll tell you one thing for sure, Sean."

"Yes ma'am?"

"If you ever try to touch me again, I'll . . ." She held her breath and shook as she tried to think of something dastardly enough to do to him. Finally she settled for lifting both hands and shoving him into the wall. Screeching her fury, she stomped through the swinging door and set it flying hard enough to smack into his surprised face.

Rubbing his forehead, Sean looked after her, speechless.

The only sound in the room was that damned chimp laughing at him.

Only mid-afternoon and the crowd was still growing.

In the relative quiet of her front yard, Frankie watched the mob of people on the lot next door. Every day there seemed to be more and more people gathered to watch the Calhoun Circus performers rehearse acts.

Generally, the people were well-behaved and they'd had no real trouble. Even Frankie's neighbors were happy for the most part. The shopkeepers didn't mind the crowds because their business had nearly tripled since the Calhouns had arrived in town. It was inevitable that the crowds would wander in and out of the shops on the street. And the restaurant across the road from the Four Roses usually had people lining up outside waiting for a table.

But Tiny was a problem. Oh, he attracted crowds, certainly. Mostly it was the children who loved visiting with the baby elephant. But people were beginning to complain about the loud, blaring trumpeting sound he made. Especially since it seemed that Tiny preferred performing at night.

Still, as problems went, it was a small one.

The Four Roses was making quite a bit of extra money these days too. Frankie had taken Sophia's advice and set up a small table in the lot to sell refreshments. It was really amazing just how much people were willing to pay for a snack!

Not to mention, Frankie told herself, all the money they'd taken in from the people willing to pay to watch the circus performers. Sean had certainly been right about *this* much at least, she thought. And the rest of the troupe assured her they'd make even more money come winter. Then they would have the time to set everything up properly and give scheduled performances.

Frankie's gaze slipped to where Treasure sat behind the table laden with lemonade, coffee, cookies, and cakes. She shook her head as she watched the young maid make change and simper ridiculously at every male passing by.

With arms crossed over her chest, Frankie let her gaze sweep over the milling crowd until she located Sean. With a group of children, her husband was smiling and patiently explaining the fine art of juggling. As he stood up, braced his feet wide apart, and began to toss five brightly colored balls in the air, Frankie frowned.

Just looking at him sent spirals of need curling through her body. Something deep within her stirred to life and her breath came in short, ragged gasps. It seemed she had very little control over her reaction to him. Even knowing that her dear husband planned to have their marriage annulled did nothing to quell her desire for him.

Angry, happy, sad, or furious . . . Frankie wanted him.

Dammit.

"Frankie? You all right?"

She turned abruptly at the voice calling her name and forced a smile to lips that felt frozen and stiff.

Her older sister had visited several times since the Calhouns had arrived. It seemed that even Maggie Donnelly Cutter was not immune to the lure of the circus.

"Hello, Maggie," she said. "Yes, I'm fine."

"You don't look fine."

It was pointless to argue with that. She knew she must look like death on a bad day—but there was nothing to be done about it.

She raked a quick glance over Maggie and stifled a sigh. Even away from the saloon, Maggie insisted on wearing her outrageous gowns. She called it good advertising for the Four Golden Roses Saloon. And Frankie was a bit surprised to find that her sister's apparel didn't bother her nearly as much as it used to.

Maggie's sapphire-blue silk gown was trimmed in black lace at the sleeves and bodice. Naturally, in comparison, Frankie felt like a washerwoman.

"How're you getting on these days with that husband of yours?"

"About the same."

"Mary Frances Donnelly!" Maggie set her hands at her narrow waist and frowned at her. "Do you mean to tell me that you still haven't—"

"Maggie!" Frankie looked around hastily, then frowned at her sister. "For the love of heaven, will you keep your voice down?"

"You haven't, have you?" Shaking her beautifully coiffed head, Maggie said slowly, "Well, I must admit. I thought you were made of sterner stuff, little sister."

"I can't do it alone, you know."

Maggie laughed. "No, but you could start it alone." She leaned in close and winked. "Believe me, he'll rush to catch up."

"Not Sean." Frankie turned her head away and looked at him. "He's decided that the best thing for me is to have an annulment."

"What?"

She nodded and smiled as Sean dropped one of the balls he'd been juggling and it bounced off the top of his head.

"Do *you* want your marriage annulled?"

Did she? She'd been so furious when Sean had first laid out his plan that she might have said yes at the time. But now . . . now she was beyond anger and beyond the hurt.

Frankie wanted to shake him. She wanted to bounce something *heavy* off his hard head. But did she want an annulment?

"No."

"Then do something about it before it's too late."

"Like what, Maggie?" Frankie asked. "Shall I overpower him, render him helpless, and then have my way with him?"

Maggie tilted her head to one side and stared at Frankie as if she'd never seen her before.

"My goodness, this *is* a new Frankie!" She grinned conspiratorially. "I like her."

Frankie gave her a wan smile.

"There's more than one way to overpower someone, sister. And as for having your way with him . . . why not?"

"Maggie . . ."

"It's up to you, Mary Frances. If you want him, it sounds to me like you're going to have to get him." She winked again and pointed across the lot at her own husband. "It worked with Cutter."

Frankie studied her sister thoughtfully. She

remembered very well how Maggie had brazenly admitted to tempting and tormenting Cutter until the man finally surrendered to the inevitable.

"How exactly did you do it?"

Maggie cocked her head, stared at her for a minute, then gave her a slow grin. "Little sister," she started, "it's easier than you might think. As for Cutter, he proved to be most susceptible to low-cut gowns and black silk stockings."

Frankie's eyebrows lifted.

"But it doesn't matter much what you're wearing," Maggie assured her. "Just so long as you know when to take it off."

"Maggie . . ."

"Actually," her sister went on, tapping her index finger against her chin, "you might want to try undressing in front of him."

"Oh Lord." She'd have to do it in the dark, she told herself, so Sean couldn't see the blush that would no doubt stain her face bright red. Unfortunately, if it was dark, there wouldn't be much point in undressing for his benefit, would there?

Maggie reached out, squeezed Frankie's shoulders briefly, and reassured her. "Don't worry. Just do everything *very* slowly. Believe me . . . you won't have to finish for yourself." Smiling gently, Maggie added, "You don't *have* to do anything, Frankie. It's up to you."

Up to her, Frankie repeated silently. Well, wasn't that what she wanted? To be able to think and do for herself? Maybe Maggie was right. Maybe it was time Mary Frances Donnelly stood up for herself and told Sean what *she* wanted.

"All right," she vowed quietly, "I'll do it."

"Good girl!" Maggie crowed, then changed the subject. "Say, do you think Ryan Grady might be willing to come to the saloon one night and perform? Our customers would love it!" She waved toward the knife thrower and his captivated audience. "Just look at Cutter over there! He's been watching Ryan for the last hour already."

"I'm sure he'd be delighted," Frankie said, and knew that it would only take one look at the women who worked at the Four Golden Roses Saloon to convince Ryan to perform.

"Hey you two!" another voice shouted, and both women turned toward the street.

Mary Alice Donnelly had already climbed down from her lathered horse and was tying the reins around one of the pickets in Frankie's fence.

"Al," Maggie shouted back. "What are you doing here?"

The third Donnelly sister marched up to them, slapping her palms against her thighs. Dust flew up from her buckskin trousers and she pulled her hat off to wave it away. One long, thick auburn braid tumbled free of the hat and fell down past her hips.

"What the hell is goin' on here?" she asked, staring around her at the circus acts and the crowd.

"Later." Maggie waved the question aside and voiced her own again. "What are you doing here?"

"I went by the saloon to see you, and Rose told me you and Cutter were here . . ." Alice's voice trailed off as she shook her head in amazement. "A *circus*," she whispered, awed. Then a heartbeat later, she grinned at Frankie and said, "I got Maggie's wire about you marryin' the new partner. Which one is he?" She jerked her head at the crowd. "Whoever he is, he's bound to be more interesting than Herbert."

"I don't know," Maggie said thoughtfully. "You haven't seen Herbert lately."

True, Frankie thought. Her former suitor was a changed man. Of course, spending hours at a time with Sophia might have something to do with that. Herbert Featherstone and a gypsy fortune teller . . . who would have guessed?

"You can meet Sean later," Frankie told her younger sister. "For now, tell us why you rode all the way in from the mine."

Mary Alice plunked her hat back down on her head and tugged the brim low. "There's big trouble brewing at the mine. We've got to wire Da. Get him to send help."

Chapter 19

~~~◯◯~~~

"Sure I could hire local men," Mary Alice said sharply. "But this fella who's coming in from Denver is just too damned powerful. He could buy up the locals and get them to cause me all kinds of trouble." Glancing over at Maggie, she asked, "Do you know where Da is now?"

Maggie spoke up. "Sean's the last one to have seen him. Did he tell you where he was headed?"

"Kansas City," Sean answered, then leaned back in his chair and studied the faces around him. He hadn't really expected to be included in the emergency meeting of the Donnelly family. But when he would have stayed away, the others nearly dragged him inside. Cutter, in fact, made a point of saying how much he was looking forward to having another man in the group.

"Kansas City ... let's see ..." Maggie thought for a minute, then asked, "What's his favorite hotel in Kansas City? Anyone remember?"

As much as he enjoyed traveling and seeing

331

new things, Kevin Donnelly was a creature of habit as well. He had certain hotels in almost every big city across the country that he favored with his presence whenever he was in town.

After a long moment, Al shouted triumphantly, "Noble House!"

"That's it," Maggie agreed with a grin.

Sean shook his head and took another sip of whiskey. Family. They knew each other so well. And were so willing to have him join them. Here was a family who accepted him. Needed him. It felt good to be looked to for an opinion. To be asked advice about more than where to pitch the main tent or which towns to visit on the circuit. To have his thoughts listened to.

Although it could have been better, if Frannie had seemed the least bit pleased about having him at the meeting.

He glanced at her, sitting in the corner of the settee, watching her sisters and brother-in-law argue about Mary Alice's problems. Frannie hadn't looked at him once since they'd entered the parlor. And when Alice had offered a belated toast to their marriage, Frannie had pointedly set her glass down on the nearest table, refusing to drink.

Sean drained his glass and stood up. He supposed he deserved her anger. Yet at the same time, a voice inside him shouted at the injustice of bearing her anger simply because he was trying to look out for her. He went to the sideboard, picked up the whiskey decanter, and walked around the room, refilling glasses. Maggie, Al, and Cutter, like Sean, were all having whiskey. Frannie was the only dissenter, preferring her glass of sherry.

And that about spells things out, he told himself. Frannie. Different from everyone. Different from every woman he'd ever known.

When he'd finished playing host, he returned the crystal decanter to its place, and as his fingers rested on the bottle, his mind settled on that word again. Host. He wasn't playing a part. Sean Sullivan *was* the host. It was his parlor. His and Frannie's. His home. His and Frannie's.

For as long as he stayed.

The tips of his fingers slid down the crystal bottle and caressed the fine wood of the sideboard. Familiar objects. Familiar faces.

Frannie.

How could he give them up? Walk away? Pretend he'd never belonged? But even as he thought about staying, he worried about the circus. How could he simply leave them without a front man? He'd done the task for years. If not him, then who would ride ahead to the towns on the circuit? Who would talk the farmers into hanging posters on the sides of their barns? Who would do all the hundreds of tiny tasks that together kept the circus moving?

Sean sighed and turned around to face the others. His gaze settled on the back of Frannie's head and he stared at her blankly until Cutter's voice shook him out of his reverie.

"I think Sean and I should ride to the mine with you, Al." Cutter threw him a quick, silent glance, and Sean nodded in agreement.

"Thanks, but no."

"It shouldn't take more than a day or two," Cutter said, ignoring Al's protest.

"That's fine," Sean told him.

"Cutter," Al broke in sharply. "You're not listening to me."

"That's what he does best," Maggie teased.

Cutter frowned at her.

"I don't need you and Sean right now," Al went on. "If you two go back with me, it might just make things worse. And I'd rather hear back from Da before we do that."

"I don't know—" Cutter started.

"Trust me," Al interrupted, then added, "I don't need you right now. But in a month or so, that may change."

Cutter shook his head, clearly unhappy with the situation. But finally he agreed. "All right. But you send for us in a month. You hear?"

"Deal." Al lifted her glass and took a healthy swig of the strong Irish whiskey.

Sean wasn't paying attention at all anymore. Frannie had turned to stare at him the moment Al had said that she'd need him and Cutter in a month. Her features masked, Frannie's eyes said everything she was thinking. And Sean had no trouble at all reading the message she was sending him.

A month. Al might need his help in a month. But he wouldn't be there. He'd be out on the road somewhere. Alone. Riding from town to town ahead of the circus.

Clenching his jaw tightly, Sean sipped the whiskey and felt its warmth spread through his limbs. He only wished the fire were hotter. Brighter. Because there was a cold deep inside him that the whiskey wasn't touching.

"I still don't understand why you want to bring Da into this," Maggie said. "If you don't want to hire locals, go down to Los Angeles. There are men down there ready and willing to fight for a dollar."

"Yeah, I know," Al said. "And I thought about it. But we all know Da's going to be sending me a partner anyway." She snorted a laugh and waved one hand at Maggie and Frankie. "Why should he stop with you two? There's still me and Terry Ann to torment."

"Thank you very much," Cutter said softly and raised his glass to her.

"No offense, Cutter. But you know Da. Any day now, I'm expecting to get a wire telling me about *my* new partner." Al shrugged. "So I figured I'd wire him first. That way he can at least send me somebody useful. And send him now. When I need him."

"She has a point," Maggie conceded.

"All right then, it's settled. The wire goes off to Kevin tonight," Cutter said. "Anything else from anyone?"

"One thing," Frankie spoke up and everyone turned to look at her. "Al, on your way back to the mine, can you stop at the ranch?"

"Sure." Al shrugged again. "But why?"

"I'd like you to take Tiny to the family ranch."

"Tiny who?"

Maggie laughed.

"Tiny the elephant," Frankie told her. "The

neighbors are starting to complain about his noise. Besides, it might be good for him to be somewhere where he can stretch his legs a bit."

Sean's eyebrows lifted. He had to admit, it was a good idea. But Al wouldn't be able to handle the elephant on her own and he was about to say so when Alice cut him off.

She whistled, low and long. "How the hell do I get an elephant to do what I want it to do?"

Again Sean tried to speak, but this time his own wife was ahead of him. It seemed, he told himself, that Frannie had been doing some thinking about this.

"Ryan Grady," she said. "It'll only be a day or two. Ryan can go with you and help with Tiny."

"Wait a minute," Sean broke in. "I don't think Alice should be travelin' with Ryan alone."

Al bristled slightly. "Why not?"

"Well, he's . . ." Sean rubbed his jaw and paused, trying for the right words. "A bit . . ."

"Forward," Frannie finished for him.

Mary Alice Donnelly laughed and stood up. "Don't worry about it, Sean. This Ryan of yours can take care of the elephant. *I'll* take care of *him*." Snatching her hat from the table in front of her, she chuckled gently. "Terry Ann's not going to like this, though."

"What?" Maggie asked.

"Any of it. The elephant *or* bein' left out of this meeting."

"Can't be helped," Cutter said quietly and

stood up as well. "Maggie and I have to get back to the saloon. You watch yourself, Al. And send for me and Sean when you're ready."

"I will, I will," she repeated tiredly.

Frankie leaped to her feet and started for the door. "I'll go send that wire to Da so you can be on your way, Al."

"I'll leave after I get something to eat."

Sean crossed the room hurriedly and grabbed Frankie's forearm. "I'll go with ya," he told her.

"That's not necessary."

"It's near dark," he said. "I don't want you walkin' the streets alone."

"I've done it before," she informed him, then added pointedly, "and no doubt I'll be doing it again."

Ah Lord, the woman had a knack for knowing just how to drive the knife home.

"We'll send Ryan in on our way out," Maggie said.

"Good," Al replied, already on her way to the kitchen. "Tell him to hurry it up. I want to be back on the road in twenty minutes or so."

"Shouldn't you wait for sunup?" Sean asked, still holding on to Frankie so she couldn't escape.

"No need," Al called over her shoulder. "I've been traveling the road to the ranch my whole life. I could do it blindfolded."

Before he could answer, Frankie yanked her arm free, spun around, and left the room. Every other thought fled. It was all he could do to keep up with her.

* * *

Though she walked right beside her husband, Frankie thought, she might as well have been on the other side of the country. Except for the few minutes of conversation required at the telegraph office, neither of them had said a word.

He shouldn't have bothered to come, she told herself, although a quick glance at his features assured her that he probably was a deterrent to anyone with mischief on his minds. One look at Sean's glowering face and even the most stouthearted villain would no doubt run for the hills.

Frankie sighed, pulled her black crocheted shawl more tightly around her shoulders, and bent into the strong, cold sea wind. The rushing air lifted her hair from her neck and sent prickles of gooseflesh down her spine. Sea salt stung her cheeks, and every indrawn breath carried the scent of fish from the docks.

So familiar, she thought, and yet so different.

Everything about her home and her city seemed different to her since Sean had come into her life. Would she ever be able to walk down these streets without remembering the sound of his footsteps beside her? Would she ever look up at the moon and not remember how his black hair shone in the moonlight? Would she ever be able to hear an Irish brogue without remembering what her name sounded like when it rolled off his tongue?

"Cold?" he asked suddenly, and his voice startled her.

Though she was freezing, Frankie defiantly answered, "No."

"The lie would come easier if your teeth weren't chatterin'," he said softly.

"We're almost home—I mean," she corrected herself quickly, "the hotel is just around the corner. I'll be fine."

She didn't miss the quick flash of sadness in his eyes, but Frankie wasn't moved. If he wanted the hotel to be home, she demanded silently, why was he leaving?

"Come here," Sean said and reached for her.

"I said I'm fine."

"Humor me."

His right arm shot out, dropped around her shoulders, and pulled her against him. Nestled into his side, Frankie felt his warmth soak through her, and for some idiotic reason, she wanted to cry.

As they rounded the corner, they saw Honora standing in the dark, alongside her wagon.

When they were close enough, Sean asked, "Something wrong?"

"No," the older woman said as her gaze swept over the two of them. "But I do need a little help."

"I'll go inside then and leave you to it," Frankie whispered and pulled away. Reluctantly, it seemed, Sean released her.

"No, no, no," Honora reacted quickly and grabbed Frankie's right hand. "I need both of you."

"Honora . . ."

"It'll only take a minute, I swear."

Sean caught Frankie's eye and shrugged. After a long, thoughtful pause, she nodded.

"That's grand," Honora grinned and tugged Frankie closer to the wagon. "Now you go on in," she said.

"Well, what's the problem?" Sean asked as he was hustled into the wagon right behind his wife.

"I'll show you when we're all in there," Honora shot back and gave him a shove.

Frankie moved to the front of the wagon and turned to watch Sean enter. The old wooden wagon lurched when he stepped inside and swayed a bit with the extra weight. There was no more than a foot or two of space separating them, and Frankie's heart began to pound erratically. Somehow, the close confines of the wagon lent a sort of intimacy between them that hadn't existed on their walk.

Just beyond Sean, Frankie saw Honora's wild mane of gray hair lift and twist in the brisk wind. Moonlight fell on her timeworn features and gave her sudden grin a wicked look.

Then the door slammed shut, plunging the two of them into blackness. Before either of them could react, they heard the sound of a key turning in the lock.

"Honora!" Sean bellowed, and Frankie thought she heard china rattle in response.

"Calm down, Seaneen," the woman called through the door.

"Open this bloody door, woman!" he shouted and pounded on the solid panel of wood.

"No."

Sean paused in his tirade, stunned by the quiet, simple word. As Frankie's vision grew accustomed to the darkness, she thought she saw him turn and stare at her.

Her hands stretched out in front of her, Frankie walked the two or three steps to the door. Her hands slapped into Sean's back and she pulled them away as if she'd been burned.

"Honora," she said patiently, "whatever it is you're doing, we want you to stop."

"Nope."

"Goddammit, Honora."

"Seaneen," the woman said over his shout, "Fiona and me think it's time the two of you worked out whatever's botherin' ya."

"Fiona?" Frankie breathed. She couldn't believe it. Mrs. Destry and Honora had schemed together to do this?

"What's between us is between us, Honora," Sean tried again. "You've no right to go lockin' us in here. We're both adults, we'll do things the way we see fit."

"If you're both adults, maybe you should try actin' like it." Honora's response was lightning-quick. Obviously she'd been prepared for a battle. "Now," she went on thoughtfully, "maybe I'll come and let the two of you out in the morning."

"The morning?" Frankie echoed.

"Maybe?" Sean asked.

"Or not," Honora said.

"I'll get us out," Sean promised through gritted teeth.

"I don't doubt you'll try," Honora called, and her voice sounded farther away this time.

"But you'd damned well better not break my door down in the doin'."

Sean sucked in a gulp of air but Frankie spoke up quickly. "That's something to think about, Sean. Remember what happened the last time you tried to break down a door?"

Visions of the tipped-over confessional rose up between them.

While Sean growled and grumbled at the woman who had obviously already left, Frankie looked at her surroundings. At second glance, she noticed that it wasn't a complete darkness surrounding her. There were a few tiny splotches of moonlight sneaking through the holes in Honora's curtains.

And even as she made a mental note to buy enough fabric to make new curtains, Frankie spotted a box of matches. Quickly she grabbed them, pulled one free, and struck it. In the tiny, quivering flame, she saw a lamp standing ready nearby. When the wick caught and held, Frankie slipped the chimney back in place and turned the wick up a bit. In the soft glow of lamplight, she noticed that her surroundings were clean and tidy. There was a small glass of water holding a tiny bouquet of wildflowers. And beside it on the table was a plate of fried chicken and an open bottle of wine.

A soft, slow smile curved her lips. Frankie tossed a quick glance at her husband's broad back as he studied the door frame, looking for a weak spot. In flashes of memory, Frankie recalled her earlier conversation with Maggie. Something about rendering Sean helpless and having her way with him?

On her right was a narrow trundle bed, freshly made up and topped with the quilt from her own bed. Chewing at her bottom lip, Frankie turned and looked back at the wine, then at Sean. Annulment, eh? she thought. Well, maybe not.

After sending a quick, heartfelt prayer of thanks to the two older women who'd planned all this, Frankie dismissed them from her mind and set to business.

"It's no use," Sean muttered heavily. "That door's as thick as iron. I know. I cut it and hung it meself, two years ago."

Frankie poured two glasses of wine and handed him one as he backed up until he could sit on the edge of Honora's bed.

"Well then," she said quietly, "it seems there's nothing we can do until morning."

"Aye, I'm sorry about this, Frannie." He took a sip of the wine and let it slide down his throat. Breathing was difficult in the close atmosphere.

"Oh," was all she said. Then she picked up a piece of chicken. "Don't apologize. I know you had nothing to do with this." She sunk her teeth slowly into crisply fried chicken breast. As she chewed, she added, "You've made it perfectly clear that you have no interest in bedding me."

No interest, he thought with an inward groan. He shifted his hips uncomfortably on the thin mattress. His body tight and hard, Sean tried desperately to keep his mind and his gaze off her. But with her standing no more than an arm's reach away, it was impossible.

He drank some more wine and prayed for oblivion.

It was his only hope.

"This chicken is wonderful," she said and turned to him. "Would you like some?"

"No," he ground out.

"Are you sure?" She set her chicken down on the plate and looked at him through wide, innocent eyes. "Perhaps a breast?"

Dear God.

"Or would you rather have a thigh?"

He was going to die.

When he didn't say anything, Frankie shrugged delicately, then began to lick chicken grease off her fingers. One by one, she stuck her fingers in her mouth and sucked at them.

Sean couldn't look away. He couldn't breathe. He stared at her mouth as her lips and tongue moved on her own flesh. His groin stiffened until he thought his manhood would burst through the confines of his trouser flap. Minutes crawled by, and if he hadn't known better, Sean would have thought that she was doing all this purposely. To torture him.

But Frannie, he told himself, was not the kind of woman to do a thing like that to a man.

Then she set her wineglass down and stretched her arms high over her head. Bending first one way, then the other, she groaned softly with each movement. Sean's gaze was riveted to her bosom. In the soft glow of lamplight, he watched the buttons of her shirt strain and pull in their efforts to slip free. He licked his suddenly dry lips and hoped for just a glimpse of the chemise that was hiding her breasts from him.

Then she stopped as suddenly as she'd begun and turned to look at him.

"If you don't mind, Sean," she said softly, "I'd like to lie down and get some sleep."

"Oh!" He leaped up from the bed and blessed the heavens that Honora had left them only the one lamp. If the light had been any brighter in that wagon, Frannie would surely have seen his hard, aching body outlined against his pants. Taking one step to his right, he allowed her to pass by. He tried to back up out of her way, but it seemed he hadn't gone far enough.

As she passed him, her breasts brushed against his chest and he felt the hard, pebbly tips of her nipples. He closed his eyes and tightened his hands into helpless fists.

Once past him, she turned her back on him and quickly undid her buttons.

"What are you doin'?" he managed to say.

"I'm only taking my shirt off," Frankie answered. "It would be far too uncomfortable to sleep in. Why? Will it bother you?"

"No!" All he'd have to do was wear a blindfold all night, he thought. That shouldn't be too much trouble.

"Good. You are my husband, after all," she said. "For now."

He frowned slightly and forgot to look away. When she began to slip out of her skirt, he stammered, "Don't you think you should, uh . . . keep your clothes on?"

"For heaven's sake, why?"

She turned around to face him and Sean groaned, his hands curling into fists.

In her chemise and petticoats, she was everything he'd been thinking and dreaming of for days. All he had to do was tug on one little pink ribbon, and her breasts would be bared to him. As they'd been on that one glorious night when he'd finally discovered the taste of her. The feel of her. The scent of her.

Sitting on the edge of the mattress, Frankie held out her right leg toward him. "Would you mind untying my shoes for me?"

Shoes. They should be safe enough. And at the very least, he could take his mind off the swell of her breasts.

He cupped her small foot in his hands and deftly undid the laces of her shiny black boots. When he'd slipped it free, she held up her left foot.

"And the stocking?" Frankie asked and lay back on the mattress.

He didn't speak and Frankie shut her eyes. But she felt his hands on her calves. She felt him reach up and pull the stocking free of her pantaloon and then roll it down her leg. When she lifted her right leg for him to do the same again, she was astounded at how much effort the movement took. Her whole body felt . . . heavy . . . full.

She could hardly believe she was behaving like this. And yet, from the moment she'd started teasing him, a flush of excitement had blossomed between her legs. A damp, warm heat engulfed her, and every time he looked at her, it burned brighter.

Maggie was right. If she had to start it alone, she would.

He pulled her right stocking off but didn't release her foot. Instead his thumbs were moving over her ankle and the sole of her foot. Frankie shivered and sighed gently. Slowly his hand slid up her calf, caressing, smoothing her flesh with his palm.

She twisted gently in his grasp and tried to let him know without words that she enjoyed his touch. When she felt his hand creep beneath the hem of her pantaloons, her body jerked in response.

"Ah Frannie," he said, and his voice was low, tight. "A man can only stand so much, ya know." Sean leaned in closer, grasped her chemise ribbon, and tugged it.

She held her breath and concentrated on the feel of his big, work-roughened hands gently pulling the edges of the fabric apart. Frankie watched his face as he looked at her, and the hunger in his eyes was unmistakable.

His right hand began to stroke her breast and when his fingers smoothed over her rigid nipple, Frankie gasped.

"God help us both, Frannie love," he whispered and went down on one knee in front of her. "But I can't take another moment without the feel of you in me hands." He dipped his head, took her nipple into his mouth, and stroked her with his tongue.

Her body was on fire. Tremors of excitement

rippled through her. A pulsing, throbbing kind of ache was centered in the damp heat of her core and Frankie knew that if he didn't touch her, she would die of want.

She threaded her fingers through his hair and sat up straighter, pushing her breasts toward him. He seemed to know what she was asking for and immediately shifted his attentions to her other breast. Stroke after stroke, touch after touch, he fed the inferno raging inside her.

One of his hands slipped down to the inside of her thigh, and Frankie wanted to shout at him to touch her. To ease the ache throbbing uncontrollably. Instead she wiggled her hips until she was closer to him.

As he knelt between her thighs, Sean's hands began to roam over her body. Through the thin fabric of her pantaloons, Frankie felt the warmth of him soaking into her bones.

He rose up on his knees and claimed her mouth in a kiss that told her his need was as great as her own. Then, abruptly, he tore himself away and bent to take one of her hard nipples into his mouth again. Rolling his tongue around the sensitive flesh, he began to suckle her, and Frannie groaned helplessly.

His right hand swept up the inside of her thigh and cupped the throbbing, aching core of her. Frannie jumped at first contact, then as a soft moan escaped her throat, she arched into his hand.

"Sean," she breathed and moved again. "It . . . hurts."

"Pain?" he asked, lifting his head from her breast. "Or need?"

"Oh God." Frankie moaned and lifted her hips again. "*Need*, Sean. Need."

"Aye, lass," he said softly, pressing a gentle kiss into the hollow of her throat "I, too, feel that pain. And now, even if I'm damned for it tomorrow, we'll ease the pain together."

"Yes," she answered and gasped when she felt his hands move quickly to the waistband of her petticoat. In seconds, it seemed, she was naked from the waist down, her petticoat and pantaloons lying in heaps on the floor of the wagon. Frankie felt the cool spring air on her flesh and moved against the sheets, delighting in the sinful scrape of cotton against her skin.

Then Sean's hand dipped to the warm, aching juncture of her thighs and she gasped, arching high off the bed into his arms.

"Ah, Frannie love," he whispered, "just relax now and feel me with you."

She went limp in his grasp and gave herself over to him.

Sean held his breath and looked at the treasure he'd waited so desperately to see. Soft, red-gold curls lay protectively over the secrets she'd guarded her whole life. Tenderly, Sean brushed the tips of his fingers over her mound, and Frankie gasped again, her luscious thighs parting even further for him.

He could hardly breathe. Sean didn't dare think about what the morning would bring. For the moment, all he wanted, all he needed, was this time with Frannie.

He pulled away from her only long enough

to tug his own clothing off. Tossing it to the floor, Sean saw her watching him as he leaned into her again. Her gaze dipped to his hardened manhood, and he saw a brief flash of fear dart across her eyes.

"It'll be all right," he soothed and immediately began to stroke her flesh until she was twisting and tossing with a need so great she wasn't thinking about anything else.

Immediately he slid his palm down the inside of her thigh until he reached what he'd waited so long for. Sean's fingertips stroked the hard bud of her sex and he felt her quiver.

"Sean?" she said, her voice breathless with surprise and wonder.

"It's all right, love," he whispered. Then he touched that warm, hard spot again, smoothing his fingers over the dampness until her hips began to move in time with his caresses. "Just close your eyes, Frannie girl. I won't hurt you."

"It . . . doesn't . . . hurt," she said between gasps of air.

"That's grand, darlin'," Sean told her quietly and moved his left hand up and down her thighs while the fingers of his right hand explored the inner secrets of her body.

When he dipped one finger inside her, Frannie jumped slightly. But quickly his thumb began the stroking caress that soothed and excited her.

He watched her full breasts heave in her quest for air and he felt her hips rock against his hand. Sean's thickened manhood pressed against her hip and when, in her excitement, she reached down and touched him, he nearly shattered.

Frannie's inexperienced, hesitant touch spiraled through him more intensely than he'd ever felt before. Her fingertips explored his hardness until he thought he might explode. Finally he took her hand away and held it. Afraid he might end this glorious joining far too soon.

Her fingers curled around his and squeezed tightly. Her head tossed from side to side on the nearly flattened pillow. Her eyes were closed, every emotion she felt was stamped on her features, and Sean's heart almost burst as he looked at her.

Then his gaze slipped down the length of her plump, perfect body. He took in every curve, every inch of desirable, creamy flesh. His eyes dropped to the delicate pink folds beneath his hand. His own heartbeat staggered slightly and when he began to move his fingers in and out of her warmth, Sean couldn't look away.

Her body rocked against his hand and every arch of her hips made him ache to plunge himself inside her. Her red-gold curls brushed against his tanned fingers and the colors swirled together in his brain until he could hardly tell where he left off and she began.

Inching backward down the mattress, his fingers still moving in and out of her body, Sean knelt between her legs. His need to kiss her damp flesh, to taste her, was too strong to be denied. And, almost as if she knew what he was going to do, her thighs fell open as if parting in invitation. Her hips rocked wildly with the plunging touch of his fingers, and when he pulled his hand free, she groaned aloud.

Blindly reaching for a handhold in her whirling universe, Frankie's hand came down on his shoulder. He looked up at her through desire-glazed eyes, and what he saw in her green gaze told him that she wouldn't stop him now. She'd come too far down the path of want to turn back. She needed his touch every bit as much as he needed to give it to her.

"Sean," she said, and her voice broke on a sigh. "Help me. I don't know what to do."

He turned his head slightly, kissed the hand that lay on his shoulder, and whispered huskily, "That's all right, love. *I* know." And as she watched him, he dipped his head and took her sensitive flesh into his mouth.

"Sean!"

Frankie's fingers bit into his shoulder but he didn't notice the pain.

His hands cupped her bottom and his tongue stroked over her damp, hot flesh until she was trembling and writhing in his grasp. Frankie's hips moved in a wild rhythm and Sean fed her frenzied need for release. As his tongue tormented the bud of her sex, he slipped one finger inside her. He felt her muscles bunch around him, felt her body go taut with expectation. Knowing she was nearing the end, Sean lifted his head, lowered himself over her, and entered her body with a rush.

Frankie gasped, stiffened, then slowly re-

laxed into the feel of his hard strength inside
her. Inch by inch, he pushed his way into her
tight flesh. Inch by inch, he felt her body welcome him, surround him with warmth. And
when he met the barrier that was the last thing
standing between him and joining with her
completely, Sean shattered it with a swift,
hard thrust.

Frankie grabbed at him and dug her head
back into the pillow. Sean waited tensely for
her to adjust to his presence at her center.
Every instinct in him screamed for him to
move. To plunge in and out of her. To take
them both to the heights awaiting them.

And still, he waited.

Finally Frankie's hips moved and she drew
her legs up, clasping his hips with the inside
of her knees. Only then did Sean begin the
dance again.

She moved her hips with him, taking him
deeper inside her with every thrust. Frankie
pulled at his shoulders, then raked her nails
down his back, silently demanding everything
he had to give.

And when he couldn't draw out the pleasure any longer, Sean slipped one hand between their bodies and caressed her sex until
she shuddered violently in his arms. With one
final thrust home, Sean's world exploded in a
rush of exquisite release and a sense of right-
ness. Together, they rode the crest of pleasure
until they lay spent and trembling in each other's arms.

Chapter 20

"Well? What do ya think?"

Honora rubbed her chin and stared at the locked wagon. Bright morning sunlight played on the old wood and almost made the faded blue paint look new again. After a long minute, Honora turned to look at the old woman standing next to her.

Huh! *Old?* Hell, Fiona was just a year or two older than she was. Jesus, where did all the years go? It seemed that only yesterday, Sean had been a skinny, hungry, lonely little boy. And now he was locked in a wagon with his wife.

Studying Fiona, Honora told herself silently that the woman was quite a surprise. She looked the image of a quiet little old lady. But it had been *her* idea to trap Sean and Frankie inside the wagon.

Honora had really enjoyed this time with Fiona. It was good to be able to sit and talk to another woman near her own age.

It had been too long since she'd had a close, woman friend. And even longer since she'd had a friend who wasn't circus.

But Fiona Destry had been worth the wait. Who else would have come up with such an outrageous plan? Imagine locking up two people, who'd done little but snarl at each other, in a wagon too small to breathe in without bumping into each other.

She turned her head and stared at the wagon in the lot next door. It was almighty quiet. *Too* quiet, she thought. Had they killed each other? No. More than likely, they were still sleeping off the loving.

Sean had finally found someone. And as much as it pained her to admit it, Honora grudgingly allowed that Frankie Donnelly was a good match for him. Better than Sophia would have been.

Honora had been wrong about Sophia. She'd been wrong about Frankie. Maybe she was just getting old. Hell, another season or two and maybe she'd think about staying put at the Four Roses. Just think what deviltry she and Fiona could get up to if they only had enough time!

"So?" Honora said, more to herself than Fiona. "Do I unlock the door now?"

Fiona nudged her and laughed shortly. "Leave 'em be till after breakfast. No hurry to let them out, is there?"

Honora shook her head. "Not to me. The minute I open that damned door, I'm gonna get an earful from himself, I'm thinkin'. And I'd rather listen to him on a full stomach."

She turned around, opened the front door, and waved Fiona inside. "After you."

* * *

Sean's palm smoothed across Frankie's arm and shoulder. He felt her breath, warm on his chest, and thanked the stars that circus wagons were so small, the trundle beds were especially narrow. The only way for the two of them to get *any* sleep at all had been to entwine themselves together.

Which, naturally, had led to very little sleep.

He opened his eyes and stared at the tiny splotches of daylight poking through the holes in the curtains. The night was over. That magical time when everyone but the woman in his arms had disappeared had come to an end.

Now it was time to think of the consequences of his actions.

There would be no annulment.

A wry smile tipped up one corner of his mouth. God help him, if they'd consummated the marriage just one more time, it might've killed him. But then, there were worse ways to leave the earth than by being loved by Frannie Sullivan.

He never would have guessed, not even in his wildest imaginings, that Frannie would turn out to be so passionate. So . . . inventive. She snuggled in closer to him, mumbled something in her sleep, and snaked her arm across his chest. Sean ground his teeth together in an attempt to keep from squeezing her. Dear God, he wanted her again. And again. And again.

One night would never be enough. A thousand nights wouldn't be enough.

Just lying beside her, hearing her gentle laughter in the darkness, feeling her soft, smooth hands explore his body, had been more than he'd ever dreamed. More than he deserved.

His wife.

He lifted her left hand carefully and stared at the thin band of gold on her ring finger. He had bought it for her during the hour the priest had given them to get ready for their wedding ceremony. It was a simple piece of jewelry that could reshape his life. Bringing her hand close, he kissed the ring, then placed another kiss in the center of her palm.

She stirred against him, and he willed her to go back to sleep. To sleep until he'd thought of a way out for the two of them. Until he'd come to some sort of decision that would point the way toward what he should do.

Frankie shifted, stretched, then tipped her face up to his. "Good morning."

"Good morning, love."

Frankie's smile wavered a bit, but she managed to hold on to it. Even cuddled against his warmth, with his huge arm draped across her back, she felt a chill steal through her. She studied his familiar features in the growing light and saw the guilt—the indecision on his face.

Memories of their night together rose in her mind. In brief, intense flashes, she remembered everything they'd said and done together. Frankie scooted closer to him and felt the ache in her strained muscles. He'd warned her that a virgin shouldn't be so greedy on her first night of love.

But she hadn't been able to stop herself.

After that first joining, it was as though something inside her had ripped open. Need, want, and desire she'd never imagined had spilled from her in a river of emotion that demanded attention. She hadn't been able to touch him enough. To feel enough of his hard, strong body pulsing inside hers. She loved the feel of him, lying atop her. She loved the soft rush of his breath against her cheek.

And she loved holding him inside her. Frankie squeezed her eyes shut and remembered locking her legs around his waist. She remembered digging her nails into his buttocks, pulling him ever deeper inside her until she knew that she felt him touch her soul.

Frankie dipped her head and kissed his chest. Never again would she doubt his love, either. Whatever happened next, she *knew* he loved her. She felt it pour from him as easily as his seed spilled into her womb.

But at the same time, Frankie knew that the loyalty and love he felt for Honora and the others was tugging at him too. She opened her eyes again and looked up into his. His shining blue gaze shimmered with regret and the shadow of goodbye.

Frankie bit down hard on her bottom lip. She wanted him to stay with her. To run the Four Roses with her. She couldn't even imagine going back to the quiet, uneventful life she'd treasured such a short time ago.

But she only wanted him to stay if it's what *he* wanted as well. Frankie inhaled sharply and told herself it would be better to live without him than to live beside him knowing he was only there because he thought it was his duty. Because he thought he owed it to her. Rather than live like that, she would wave goodbye with a forced smile on her face.

"Frannie, me love," he said, as if instinctively speaking before she could say anything. "Thank you."

"What?"

"I said thank you." His hand smoothed up and down her back gently. "For givin' me more tenderness and showin' me more love in one night than I've ever known."

Her breath caught in her throat, Frankie had to take several breaths before she could speak past the knot of emotion welling up inside her.

"Thank you, Sean," she whispered finally, blinking back an unexpected sheen of moisture in her eyes.

"Thank *me*? For what?"

A blush stole up her cheeks even as she thought how ridiculous it was to blush over a conversation—when she hadn't blushed at all during their lovemaking the night before.

"Thank you for making sure that I don't die the virgin bride."

His arm around her shoulders tightened. "Ah, Frannie, maybe that would've been—"

"Don't," she interrupted, reaching up to lay her fingertips against his lips. "Don't apologize. *Please.*"

"I can't."

Surprise caught at her. She'd thought sure he would be full of regrets and recriminations.

"God help me." He sighed and lifted one hand to comb his fingers through the tangled mat of her hair. "I'm not a bit sorry."

At least, she told herself, she had that. At least he didn't regret what they'd shared. Snuggling closer to him, Frankie traced her fingertips across his chest and whispered, "I'll miss you."

She felt him stiffen. When he spoke his voice was dry, hard.

"What d'ya mean?"

"When you leave," she said, "I'll miss you."

"About that . . ."

She shot up from his side, pushing against the wall of his chest. Here it comes, she thought. Now he'd offer to stay with her. Not because he couldn't bear the thought of leaving her. But because Sean Sullivan couldn't do less. It was clear in his tone. The resignation. He was prepared to meet his duties. He was prepared to take his medicine.

He was offering himself up on a sacrificial altar.

Well, Frankie Donnelly Sullivan would be no man's medicine. She refused to become the altar on which he sacrificed his life. If she allowed that to happen, they'd never be happy together. His sacrifice would always stand between them.

Taking the sheet with her, Frankie quickly scooted off the edge of the bed, climbing over him with no more care than she would have used scaling a fence.

He grunted as her knee took him in the abdomen.

"Frannie love," he said hoarsely, "we have to talk."

"There's nothing more to say," she muttered as she bent down and began the hunt for her clothing.

"After last night?"

She swiveled her head around to stare at him briefly. "Last night doesn't change anything."

"It changes *everything*!" he countered.

Frankie shook her head, dropped to her knees, and reached far under the table for her pantaloons. Idly she wondered how they'd managed to get kicked so far out of reach. Then a smile tugged at her as the memory came to her. Ah yes, she thought. The table.

Still smiling, she snatched up the garment and continued with her search.

"Are you listening to me?"

"Of course. You said last night changes everything. Like what?"

"For one thing," he said, his voice getting louder, "you might be carrying a child at this very moment."

She stopped, rose up on her knees, and hugged her sheet to her. Keeping her gaze averted from him, Frankie grinned. A baby? Oh heavens, how exciting! And she'd so feared that she'd never be a mother. Just the thought of her abdomen swelling with Sean's child had her reaching for her belly. Lying the flat of one hand protectively over what could be her child, she kept her voice even as she asked, "And if I am?"

"Well . . ." he started, swinging his legs off the bed.

"I'm a married woman," Frankie said and

spotted her petticoat hanging from a peg underneath one of Honora's hats. Hmmm ... Shaking her head, she added, "There's nothing wrong with a married woman being with child."

"But if I leave, you'd be alone!"

Frankie snorted. Glancing at him, she said, "Hardly alone. I would have Maggie, Cutter, Rose, Alice, Teresa, Fiona ..."

"And what about me?"

She shrugged and tried to sound matter-of-fact. "I'll still be here when the circus returns next winter."

"Next winter?"

"Yes." Frankie stopped, hugged the sheet close, and quickly counted on her fingers. "Why, if there *is* a baby, you'll probably be here when it's born."

"Probably?"

"*Very* probably."

Sean frowned and Frankie hid a smile.

"Besides," she went on, "it was only the one night. There probably won't be a baby."

"One night, yes," he countered, "but *three* times."

"Well, yes. But still. I'm probably not pregnant."

"Probably?"

"*Very* probably."

Frankie could almost hear his brain spinning as she slowly got dressed. Good. She'd made her stand perfectly clear. Now, whatever he decided, he would decide for himself. Not because of what he thought he owed her. A slow grin curved her lips, but she kept it hidden from the man behind her.

Two days later, Sean was lying beneath one of the wagons, greasing the axle, when Ryan Grady walked up. The other man squatted down on his haunches and waited for Sean to say something.

Sean snorted a laugh and slid out from under the wagon. "That's quite a black eye you've got there, Ryan. Run into some trouble, did ya?"

Both men stood up and Ryan ducked his head to avoid looking at Sean. He shrugged, winced, and answered, "A bit."

"This trouble wouldn't go by the name of Mary Alice Donnelly, would she?"

Ryan slanted a wry glance at him. "It was a lovely night. Full moon. Soft wind. Campfire." He shook his head and sighed. "Ah, she looked grand in the moonlight. When I told her so, she smiled at me."

Sean bit his bottom lip, folded his arms across his chest, and waited. He'd never seen Ryan so humbled, and he found he was enjoying the experience.

"So," Ryan was saying, "I put my arm around her and stole a kiss."

Sean's eyebrows lifted.

"One little kiss," Ryan repeated, raising one hand as if taking a vow. "I swear it."

"And she hit you?"

Smirking, Ryan shook his head at the memory. "Curled up her dainty little fist and knocked me on my ass."

Sean's laughter shot into the stillness. After a moment, Ryan joined in.

Ruefully he admitted, "That's a hell of a woman—but painful!"

"Aye, well, maybe you've learned a lesson, then."

Ryan smiled and glanced up at Sean. "Yeah. I learned that you're a braver man than I am—marrying into that family."

As Ryan turned and walked back to his own wagon, Sean glanced at the hotel. His gaze locked on Frannie's window, he stared as though he could see through the glass and curtains to the woman inside.

Family.

Frannie.

They hadn't been together since the night in the wagon. As if they'd both realized without saying so that making love again would only make the pain of parting harder to bear. In fact, Frannie was doing all she could to distance herself from him already. She kept Sampson with her constantly, and at night she made sure to keep herself discreetly covered at all times.

But it did no good. Nothing did. Not keeping himself busy. Not Frannie's avoiding him. Nothing could keep his mind from turning again and again to that night in her arms.

He remembered every moment.

Every touch.

He passed her in the hall, and she smiled.

He sat across the supper table from her, and she smiled.

The others talked about getting on the road, and she smiled.

It was as if for her, he'd already gone.

"I get to go with 'em," Tommy said and jumped from foot to foot in his excitement.

"That's wonderful, Tommy," Frankie said and caught him as he hurled himself at her for a hug.

"Phoebe and Devlin say I'm nearly as good on the wire as Bridget and Butler already!"

"I've seen you," she said, fighting back the sting of tears in her eyes. "You're very talented."

"Phoebe's makin' me my own costume and she says I can be an O'Connor if I want to."

"I'm so happy for you, Tommy," Frankie said and ran her hand over his clean, shining hair. He'd changed so much from the tough little street child. A couple of weeks of steady meals and love and affection from the O'Connors, and Tommy was confident, happy, and eager for the future.

She *was* happy for him. But oh, she would miss him, too.

"You'll take care of Sean for me then, won't you?" she asked, and Tommy pulled his head back to stare up at her.

"You mean he ain't stayin' with you?"

"No."

The boy shook his head and spoke softly, under his breath. "I don't understand. Honora said—"

"Don't you worry about a thing, Tommy. You just have a wonderful time and remember everything so you can tell me all about it next year. All right?"

He nodded and stepped back. After a long look at her, Tommy turned and ran out the back door, leaving her alone in the kitchen.

Frankie's empty hands curled into the fabric of her skirt. The silence of the room beat down on her. Tommy. Sean. Sampson. Even Honora and the rest of them—she would miss them all. All too soon, the Four Roses would once again be the quiet, dignified hotel it once was.

It was what she had wanted so desperately.

And she'd gotten her wish.

Why then did she feel like crying?

The wagons were loaded. The goodbyes had been said. The horses were in their traces, stamping their hooves in their eagerness to be off.

Frankie shivered in the predawn air and hugged her shawl tighter about her shoulders. As she stood on the front porch beside Fiona, her gaze drifted from one wagon to the next. Honora was already perched on the driver's seat, unfurling the small whip she used to make noise over the horses' heads. Sampson sat on the woman's lap, chattering.

Dennis, atop the wagon he shared with Ryan, was still half asleep, but slapping his own cheeks in an effort to wake up. Ryan sat astride a bay mare that stood alongside the wagon.

The O'Connors sat close together, with all three children peeking out from their wagon's high front window.

And most surprising of all, Sophia was seated next to, of all people, Herbert Featherstone. Frankie shook her head and smiled. To be with Sophia, Herbert had left his job and his mother behind. And Frankie would have dearly loved to have seen Mrs. Featherstone's reaction to the news that her only son was running off to join the circus.

But at least, Frankie thought, Herbert looked happy. In fact, he looked more easy and at peace than she'd ever seen him.

Lastly, her gaze shot to the big man on the huge black horse.

Sean.

Her heart broke and she felt the jagged pieces tear at her soul. He was leaving. It would be months before she saw him again. Day after day, week after week, month after month, the calendar stretched out ahead of her, and all Frankie could see in her future was darkness.

"For God's sake, you ain't really gonna let him go, are ya?"

Frankie didn't even glance at Fiona. She felt that if she moved, her control would splinter and she would fling herself off the porch and beg him not to leave her.

"I can't stop him."

"Sure ya could, if ya tried."

"He has to *want* to stay, Fiona. I won't beg him."

"Damned fools."

Silently Frankie agreed. They were both fools. Fools to love each other. And fools to turn away from it.

Then she felt Sean's gaze on her and she looked at him.

Even from across the yard, Frankie felt the fire in his eyes. It warmed her through down to her toes, and she wondered idly if she would ever feel that warmth again.

He'd tried to talk to her. He'd tried to say goodbye, but she wouldn't let him. She hadn't been able to bear the thought of looking at him and hearing him say that he was leaving. Even the night before—his last night in town—Frankie had pretended to be asleep when he'd come to her room.

She'd heard Sampson chortle a greeting. She'd felt Sean's presence in the room. And even though her eyes were closed, she knew when he stepped next to her bed and reached down to touch her hair lightly. Behind her closed eyes, tears had welled up and she'd had to roll onto her stomach to keep him from seeing them spill down her cheeks.

"There they go." Fiona sighed heavily.

Frankie watched Honora lead off down the street. Sampson was jumping up and down on the seat, screaming out his goodbyes, and the sound was almost swallowed by the rustle and clank of the trace chains.

Their first stop, Frankie knew, would be the Four Roses Ranch, where they would pick up Tiny. Then the Calhoun Circus would be off on their months-long circuit.

Frankie shivered slightly. Sean held her gaze for a moment longer, then resolutely tugged at his horse's reins and started the animal down the street. She watched his form until he disappeared in the early-morning mist. Then slowly she followed Fiona inside.

Sean waited for the flood of eagerness to fill him. He rode his horse at the head of the line of wagons and listened to the familiar sounds and voices behind him. Soon, he kept telling himself, soon that rush of expectation ... of excitement would sweep down on him, and all would be as it always was.

But nothing happened. The hours crawled by and the scenery slowly shifted from city to country. And still he was caught in the grip of a black shadow that threatened to suffocate him.

It was, he knew, the shadow of what he'd left behind him.

Frannie.

His love.

His wife.

And maybe his one chance at the kind of happiness he'd always thought was out of his reach.

What did it matter if he was tied down in one spot? He frowned at the open country around him. Here he was, on the road, traveling off to adventure—and all he could think of was the Four Roses Hotel. Where Frannie lived.

Where *he* lived.

In a burst of thunder and fury, the truth rattled his soul until he thought he might fall from his horse.

His life was back in San Francisco.

With Frannie.

Nothing else mattered. Not adventure. Not travel. Not even, God help him, Honora and the others. Without Frannie, he had nothing.

With her, he had everything.

And he'd been fool enough to run from her!

He yanked on the reins of his horse and drew the animal to an abrupt halt. Turning it quickly, Sean raced back to Honora's wagon.

"Whoa," she called, tugging at the reins. When the team had stopped, she cocked her head and stared at Sean. "So? You've come to your senses, then?"

He laughed and felt good for the first time in days.

"Aye, Honora. I have."

"High time."

"I'm a stubborn man."

"Aren't they all?"

He grinned at her, then sobered. "I have to go back."

" 'Course ya do, boy."

"I hate to leave ya with no front man . . ."

"Ryan's chompin' at the bit to have a go at your job."

"Do ya think he can do it?"

Honora nodded slowly and gave him a patient smile. "I do. And if I have any trouble with him," she added wickedly, "I'll just send for that sister-in-law of yours. She ought to put the fear of God in him."

Sean inhaled deeply and let his gaze move over the four wagons. Then, slowly, he looked back at Honora. The woman who'd been his mother for most of his life.

He opened his mouth to speak, but for the

life of him, couldn't think of a thing he could say.

Honora saved him. Again. By making it easy for him to leave.

"Get goin', Seaneen. You're holdin' us up!" She tightened her grip on the reins, patted Sampson, and added, "You have our rooms ready come winter . . . ya hear?"

"I hear, Honora. We'll be waitin'."

She jerked him a nod and cracked the reins sharply, and the wagon lurched forward.

Sean sat on his horse and let the others roll past him. He accepted their waves and well wishes and told himself he was a lucky man. Not many had two families to call their own.

When Ryan drew to a stop beside him, Sean stuck out his hand. Ryan grabbed it and shook it firmly.

"You're goin' back, then."

"Yeah."

"I'll do a good job, Sean," he said, and Sean saw the promise in the younger man's eyes.

"See that ya do," he told him as he released Ryan's hand. "Else I'll send Mary Alice after ya!"

Ryan grinned, touched his now healed eye, and shuddered. "See ya come winter," he said and spurred his horse into a trot.

Sean stared after them for a long moment, then turned his horse toward the hotel. Toward Frannie.

Toward home.

She'd baked two cakes and three dozen cookies already and the day wasn't half over yet.

Sighing, Frankie wiped her hands on her apron and walked out of the kitchen. Her heels clicked on the wooden floorboards and the tiny sounds seemed to scream into the silence. All morning she'd found herself waiting for the sounds of Sampson's feet padding after her. For the children's laughter. For Honora's and Fiona's spirited arguments. She even missed Dennis's snores drifting up from the easy chair he'd claimed for his own.

How would she ever live until next winter?

How would she survive the empty days and the lonely nights?

She laid the flat of her hand against her belly and prayed again that she might be pregnant. If only Sean had left her with that much a part of him, she wouldn't feel so alone.

Sunlight streamed in through the front windows and lay in delicate patterns on the gleaming floorboards. Frankie stared at the lights and wondered if she should go upstairs and check on Fiona. But no, she told herself. The old woman was worn out and had insisted on a nap.

Besides, the two of them had plenty of time to talk together. Since Fiona had decided to make the Four Roses her permanent home, Frankie had begun planning to give her own downstairs room to the older woman so Fiona wouldn't have to negotiate the stairs every day.

And, too, that room was filled with memories. She would never be able to sleep in the room again. Sean's image was too clearly there.

Frankie turned and stepped into the front parlor.

Her gaze swept over the familiar furnishings until it came to rest on the Beleek votive that had been her mother's.

She walked across the room and carefully picked up the fragile piece.

Staring down at the creamy china with its soft peach-colored flowers, she whispered, "Ah, Mother. Did I do the right thing? Should I have begged him to stay? Should I have told him how much I love him? And how lonely I'm going to be without him?"

"Ya might've tried," a deep voice behind her said gently.

Frankie's heart stopped.

She set the votive back down on the table and turned around slowly.

Scan stood framed in the doorway. In his loose white shirt, skin-tight black pants, and knee-high boots, he looked just as he had the first time she'd seen him.

"You came back," Frankie said and knew she sounded foolish.

"I had to," he answered and stepped into the room.

"Why?"

"You know why."

"Tell me."

"Because I love you. Because I can't live without you." He crossed the small space between them and pulled her into the circle of his arms. Wrapping his fingers in her hair, he pulled her head back and stared down into her eyes. "Because bein' tied down with you *is* the adventure. Because you are everything to me and more." His gaze moved over her face, and Frankie felt the sting of tears in her eyes. This time she let them fall.

"Because, Frannie love, without you . . . there's nothing in this wide world for me." He lifted one hand and smoothed his index finger over her cheeks, rubbing away her tears. "Ah, God save me, lass, I love you so much my heart hurts with it."

Frankie's arms encircled his neck, and she smiled up at him. "Welcome home, Sean darlin'."

Epilogue

❦

Four Golden Roses Saloon — two weeks later

"**W**here is she?" Maggie demanded and started pacing again.

"Sit down, Maggie," Cutter said sharply. "You're making us all crazy with this frantic walking back and forth."

She frowned at her husband, then turned to her sisters.

"Where do you think she is?"

Frankie sighed. "You've asked us that twice already, Maggie. We don't know. No one's heard from her since she went back to the mine."

"Cutter and me can be out there in a day or two," Sean offered, his fingers curling around Frankie's.

"Maybe you should go, Cutter," Maggie said and looked at her husband.

"Why is everyone so upset?" Teresa demanded and leaned her elbows on the dining room table. She looked around the room at her sisters and brothers-in-law each in turn before continuing. "This isn't the first time Al has been late for a meeting."

"No," Maggie shot back, "but this is the first time she's been late while there's big trouble at the mine."

"I still think she decided to run for cover before Da can send her a partner." Teresa glared at Cutter, then Sean. "You two are all right, but *I'm* not going to be married off to someone I never met just because Da sends him to me!"

"He hasn't sent *you* anyone yet," Maggie reminded her a bit too sharply. When Teresa frowned, her older sister mumbled, "I'm sorry, Teresa. It's just that I'm worried about—"

The door swung open suddenly, and they all turned to look at Mary Alice. She was covered in dust and grime from her ride, and sweat made small, clean streaks across her forehead and cheeks. Her long auburn braid was studded with bits of grass and a few leaves, and there was a freshly torn hole in her buckskin pants. Shadows filled her eyes, and the dark circles beneath them screamed out the fact that she needed sleep desperately.

"Jesus, Mary, and Joseph!" Maggie muttered. "What happened to you?"

"It's a long story." Al sighed and used the last of her strength to walk across the floor and drop into a chair.

When she stretched out her long legs in front of her, Maggie noticed a smear of blood on her sister's right thigh.

"You're bleeding, Al."

"Yeah, I know." She let her head fall back

to rest on the high back of her chair. "Did ya hear from Da yet?"

"Yes. The telegram came yesterday." Cutter pulled it from his inside pocket and slid it across the table to Al.

She sat up straighter, picked up the yellow paper, and slowly unfolded it. Tiredly, she read it aloud.

MARY ALICE STOP DON'T WORRY STOP REIN-
FORCEMENTS ON THE WAY STOP NEW PART-
NER BE THERE SOON STOP LOVE DA

Mary Alice snorted, then dropped the wire to the tabletop. Leaning on the shining surface, she rested her forehead on her crossed arms.

Just before she fell asleep, she said quietly, "I hope he can shoot."

Avon Romantic Treasures

*Unforgettable, enthralling love stories,
sparkling with passion and adventure
from Romance's bestselling authors*

LADY OF SUMMER *by Emma Merritt*
77984-6/$5.50 US/$7.50 Can

TIMESWEPT BRIDE *by Eugenia Riley*
77157-8/$5.50 US/$7.50 Can

A KISS IN THE NIGHT *by Jennifer Horsman*
77597-2/$5.50 US/$7.50 Can

SHAWNEE MOON *by Judith E. French*
77705-3/$5.50 US/$7.50 Can

PROMISE ME *by Kathleen Harrington*
77833-5/ $5.50 US/ $7.50 Can

COMANCHE RAIN *by Genell Dellin*
77525-5/ $4.99 US/ $5.99 Can

MY LORD CONQUEROR *by Samantha James*
77548-4/ $4.99 US/ $5.99 Can

ONCE UPON A KISS *by Tanya Anne Crosby*
77680-4/$4.99 US/$5.99 Can